The Mercenary's Blade

Eleanor Swift-H

© Eleanor Swift-Hook 2022.

Eleanor Swift-Hook has asserted her rights under the Copyright, Design and Patents Act, 1988, to be identified as the author of this work.

First published in 2022 by Sharpe Books.

Table of Contents

County Durham, September 1642
Chapter One
Chapter Two
Chapter Three
Chapter Four
Chapter Five
Chapter Six
Chapter Seven
Chapter Eight
Chapter Nine
Chapter Ten
Chapter Eleven
Chapter Twelve
Chapter Thirteen
Chapter Fourteen
Chapter Fifteen
Chapter Sixteen
Chapter Seventeen
Chapter Eighteen
Chapter Nineteen
Chapter Twenty
County Durham, September 1642
Author's Note

THE MERCENARY'S BLADE

County Durham, September 1642

The dead eyes of the ginger cat stared back at Dutch from its severed head.

"You know for sure, Reverend Fanthorpe? There's no mistake?"

"This is witchcraft. No mistake."

Dutch looked from the cat's head to his dead sheep and sighed. They were high on the dales above his house.

"So we feared, though we prayed it wasn't so. To think in Pethridge, such a thing."

"There will be more than one witch," Fanthorpe said, sounding like the puritan preacher he had been before this career as a hunter of witches. "All the signs are plain."

Privately, Dutch thought Fanthorpe looked like an overgrown crow. Clad in black from head to knee, his sharply angled face gaunt beneath close-cropped grey hair and a tall-crowned black hat. He seemed the kind who would enjoy pecking at dead things.

"More than one?" Dutch echoed doubtfully.

"Of course. But fear not Mr Sawyer, the Lord watches over us and has us in his keeping. Let us pray for deliverance from this evil."

Dutch bowed his head as the sonorous drone of Fanthorpe's prayer washed over him, while his mind drifted entirely elsewhere.

King Charles, like a rebel in his own realm, had raised his standard in late August, summoning the lords and their retinues to help subdue his unruly parliament. The winds of war now blew with increasing ferocity over the landscape. The rich and powerful picked sides, raising men from their lands and urging their neighbours to do likewise. Soldiers, tested in the fire of endless German wars, were creeping back to find fresh green fields for their bloody harvest.

Against the huge canvas of such events, Dutch felt insignificant, but there was no avoiding their impact. In the meantime, the immediate problems besetting him at home loomed larger in his life than any clash of mighty powers.

The loss of the sheep was another blow to his ailing Weardale farm. Times were hard but Dutch had managed to find a way to turn things around for a while. The sturdy rebuilding of the house and the growth of the flock through careful purchase had been his work. But his source of gold had run dry before the changes were complete. With the disruption of the wool trade first from the Scottish invasion and occupation two years before, and now from this new quarrel, it was becoming a daily struggle to make ends meet and keep food on the table.

Those thoughts ran through his mind like water along a river, familiar and steady. But serious as the state of the world and the loss of any livestock might be, a more troubling matter still dominated his thoughts. How was he going to explain to his eldest lass, Pippa, that her favourite ginger tom, the one she had raised from an orphaned kitten, had met its end?

THE MERCENARY'S BLADE

Chapter One

The moment he entered the alehouse Gideon Lennox knew he had made a mistake.

The air was thick with smoke as the hearth had a poorly set chimney. Mingled into the smoke was the flat malt scent of cheap ale, the reek of crude tobacco and rancid mutton from the spluttering rushlights. Beneath it all was the human taint of sweat, vomit and piss.

Chatter and laughter faded as he opened the door. By the time he took a pace within, every head turned in his direction. He became acutely aware of how his lawyer's clothing must make him appear in a place like this.

If things had gone as planned, he would have been here in daylight, but his mare had a loose shoe and he had wasted a couple of hours finding a farrier to restore it. If he hadn't been running out of time to fulfil his commission, he might have chosen the wiser course of seeking a respectable inn overnight, rather than chancing his fortune here after dark.

Patches of light punctuated the gloom but showed no one who matched the description of his quarry: *It is a simple task. You will know him when you find him. He is distinctive. White hair, hook nose and eyes that the ladies would pluck to set into rings if they could.*

The room was silent. Cheerful conversation replaced by hostile coldness. These were unsettled times and the rule of law was far from secure—especially here where the sons and grandsons of border reivers had never fully neglected their violent heritage.

Gideon pretended not to notice. He continued forward, trying to draw reassurance from the length of steel he wore on his hip and trying not to recall the scathing comments of his fencing master regarding his ability to wield it. It was too late to regret allowing the man provided by his employer for his protection to wait outside.

A middle-aged woman emerged from the shadows with a jug of ale and a nearly toothless smile.

"How may I be of service, good sir?"

At least Gideon hoped that was what she said. The mix of dialect and missing teeth made for an accent so thick she could have been cursing him for all he knew. He mustered a return smile for her benefit and pitched his voice to carry to the whole room.

"I am making some enquiries, which will be both to my profit and that of your guests—so a drink for all here, if you please. Then if you have a private room, I will have my ale there and be glad to reward any man who may wish to bring me news of one called Philip Lord."

He had expected the promise of free drink would take a little of the chill from the atmosphere. It usually did. But the woman stared at him and shook her head. Benches scraped as a number of the men stood up. Glancing around, Gideon realised belatedly it was a long way back to the door.

A man blocked his retreat. His muscles would have made a blacksmith weep, although no one would ever envy his face. 'Homely' was probably how his mother described him, but Gideon doubted the rest of the world would be that kind. At least not behind his back.

THE MERCENARY'S BLADE

"Philip Lord?" echoed the gargoyle. "Not a name we've heard before in these parts. So you can be on your way."

"Then you have done me a favour indeed," Gideon said lightly, although his heart was thudding hard. "I can take my leave without wasting the time of any here. Thank you for that."

He took an experimental step towards the door and its human barricade. The gargoyle showed no sign of moving. Instead, his facial expression shifted into something that might, on any normal face, have been a smile.

"But maybe your—uh—*friend* comes by one day. If you tell us your name, we could let him know you're looking for him."

"You're too kind," said Gideon, his mouth dry. It seemed foolish to think a London lawyer would get any consideration from such people. "You can say Sir Bartholomew Coupland wishes to speak with him."

A hand with a grip like a manacle seized his wrist from behind and before he could react beyond a gasp, his sword vanished from its scabbard, and he was spun around. Off-balance, he staggered back into a solid wall of muscle, losing his hat in the process. A powerful forearm wedged under his chin. The gargoyle's other huge hand gripped both Gideon's wrists together behind his back.

The hostess picked up a rushlight. By the yellow flickering glow Gideon stared into a face framed by hair so pale it looked white. The face had gemstone-clear aquamarine eyes that held no trace of emotion as they studied Gideon from behind a finely shaped patrician nose.

Yes. This face was certainly distinctive. Distinctive in a manner that would have women turning to look twice and men wishing they could have a similar distinction. A moment later the face was transformed by a predatory smile of even, white teeth.

He was taller than Gideon himself. His body was well proportioned, and he carried himself as a man with full confidence in his own ability. Gideon placed him somewhere in his early to mid-thirties.

His clothing, by which so much about a man could generally be judged, was extravagant in cut, typical of the new breed of military man, returned from Europe at the first whiff of powder smoke. A pistol was stuck negligently into a broad crimson sash. On his left hip was a long-bladed sword, basket hilted, with a pommel that was curved on the top and had two small triangular points. It looked well used and cared for, the tool of a craftsman. Gideon's own sword, though it had cost him a deep purse, was like a lady's embroidery needle next to it.

Gideon needed no introduction to tell him that he had found Philip Lord. The realisation froze the blood in his veins.

"I would know your secret, Sir Bartholomew. It will make me more gold than the alchemists' stone."

His accent was northern English but subdued beneath educated southern tones, with traces from across Europe and the Mediterranean. As exotic as the immaculately groomed appearance of its owner.

"My s-secret?"

"The secret of regaining lost youth. Although I think most would prefer to keep their original face rather than find a stranger staring back at them from the mirror." The chilling gaze flicked to the man holding Gideon. "But there might be those who would welcome the chance to be recast as someone new and start afresh. Eh, Thomson?"

Which earned some laughter. But Gideon stayed silent, his mind spinning with fear, trying to seek firm ground.

"Coupland sent you to find me," Lord made it a statement, not a question.

"Yes."

"What are you worth to him in one piece?"

"I—I don't—"

"Just answer the question," said the gargoyle. The arm muscle at Gideon's throat tightened, making it harder for him to breathe.

"Thomson," Lord said, his tone one of amused tolerance. "Your enthusiasm is appreciated, but let the man get some air beneath his ribs so he may speak."

The pressure at his throat eased and Gideon gasped. The thick, alehouse atmosphere invading his lungs was as welcome as a spring breeze. Philip Lord moved closer, any trace of humour gone, his eyes as merciless as the North Sea in winter.

"Since you are clearly not Sir Bartholomew, who are you?"

"Gid—Gideon Lennox. I am a lawyer."

At the slightest nod from Lord, Gideon found himself suddenly free and nearly collapsed to his knees at the abrupt release. A strong hand gripped his arm and steadied him, brief and impersonal.

"Thompson, tell Shiraz to deal with the man who was with him."

A draught of clean air marked the opening of the door as the gargoyle left.

"Gentlemen," Philip Lord made an elaborate gesture to include all within the room. "We have rehearsed the steps of this dance. Make ready."

There was a swirl of purposeful movement as Gideon was steered towards the rear of the alehouse.

A few steps further into the gloom revealed a door opening to a private chamber so small there was room for no more than a table with one bench pushed back hard to the wall. A shuttered window graced the plain walls, which were no cleaner than the common room. Lord pushed him into the room and pointed.

"Sit."

Gideon took the seat indicated on the bench behind the table. Lord closed the door and leaned against the wall beside it. He looked down at Gideon, much as a butcher might assess livestock.

"You came to find me, and you have. What now?"

"The man who was with me, is he...?"

"Unharmed as yet."

Gideon chased rapidly through the few facts he knew about Lord for one which could serve him. To make them both step outside the immediate moment to a place where differences were not resolved with violence and bloodshed.

"You were at Oxford," he said. "I was too for a short time."

The other man nodded. "So we were both there. And I am in no doubt we also share some tastes in literature and preferences in food. But right now, my interest lies more in what—or rather who—has brought us to share this moment in this place. Sir Bartholomew Coupland. What exactly did he charge you with, regarding me?"

Gideon swallowed.

"Well, he mentioned you were reading theology, had an interest in mathematics and—"

Something shifted in Lord's expression that in another man Gideon might have thought was quickly hidden amusement.

"Did he also tell you of the rumours that I have personally killed a thousand men? That I am wanted for treason? Made a career as a mercenary captain in the empire? Was a slaver—or a slave, depending on the account you prefer—in Livorno? The pampered lover of the French Queen? A Barbary pirate?" The cold eyes shifted their gaze. "I have a busy life and that is an interesting ring you wear. May I see it?"

Taken completely off guard, Gideon glanced at the heavy gold ring on his hand. It was an old, swivel ring, made for his great-grandfather and the only item he possessed from his mother's family. The well-worn signet was hidden within, leaving the ring appearing plain. He instinctively closed his hand and drew it closer to his body.

"Please," Lord added pleasantly. "I would prefer to have the ring and not take the finger also."

There was no menace, simply a statement of fact.

Removing the ring, Gideon set it on the table between them, despising himself as he did so. Lord scooped it up in an elegant, long-fingered hand. Then, straightening, slipped it into the pocket in his breeches without so much as glancing at it.

"I wasn't told you were a common thief." The loss of

the ring smarted more than all the other indignities and threats Gideon had received and he already regretted simply handing it over.

"Not common, I assure you," Lord said, resuming his place by the door. "I suppose you were also not told why such prominent and upstanding gentlemen as Sir Bartholomew and his esteemed Tempest associates have an interest in so nefarious an individual as myself?"

"About the rumours, yes, I was told. And that some were even true. But I wasn't told why Sir Bartholomew had any interest in your affairs. It seemed a private matter of which he was reluctant to speak."

"Not even so far as a message you were to deliver to me?"

Gideon spread his hand on the table and rubbed his finger where the ring had sat. He contemplated denial. He contemplated creating an outright lie. He jumped as the blade of an eating knife landed between his splayed fingers. Its point embedded in the pocked wood of the tabletop, firmly enough that it didn't move until Lord stepped away from the wall and retrieved it.

"There was a message," Gideon admitted. "I was charged to deliver it to your ears alone and in private."

"Of course, in private."

Lord looked around the tiny room with exaggerated care, turned swiftly to the door and pushed it open, revealing that there was no one crouching outside ear to the wood. Then he closed the door and looked down at Gideon

"We are alone, my brave Hermes, in such privacy as none in the world may hear what passes between us. Our walls are not stout, *and this the cranny is, right and sinister.* So from your lips to my ears, what did your employer send you to tell me?"

Gideon felt the colour rising in his face. His anger at being ridiculed masked the knot of fear in his chest, lending him the courage to meet Lord's tercel stare.

"I'm not sure it is appropriate under these circumstances," he said. "I will deliver the message when we are elsewhere. Somewhere—"

"Safer?" Lord suggested, his voice gentle. Then he shook his head and sighed. "Alas, the giddiness of poor Gideon! How old are you? Twenty-three? Twenty-four? What did you do to upset your patron so young? Seduce his only girl-child? Lose him money in a venture? Mess up a lawsuit?"

Gideon kept his face schooled to stillness but on the last sally, the turquoise eyes glittered.

"Oh, my Giddy One! So that was it. And you were offered this chance to redeem yourself and return covered in prodigal glory to a feast of fatted calf. Only now do you realise you have been sent to place your neck in the lion's jaws."

The voice had lost its playful tone and hardened into steel. Lord's hand moved so his fingers rested on the complex weave of his sword's hilt. Gideon tried not to be intimidated. He tried to imagine that instead of posing a lethal threat, this man was simply another clever adversary in some legal debate.

"I believe it would be prudent for both of us to wait for a more auspicious opportunity," he said. "Emotions can run high and consequences under such circumstances can be unfortunate." The words sounded pompous, even to his own ears.

"Ah, I see it now," Lord said. "My reputation precedes me. A cold-blooded killer, quick to anger and seldom in full control of my wits. There! Your face betrays the truth of it. But that charge, my Giddy One, is not entirely true. I am always in full control of my wits. *I know, sir, what it is to kill a man; it works remorse of conscience in me. I take no pleasure to be murderous, nor care for blood when wine will quench my thirst.* Besides, why should you fear for your safety with me? I have no reason to harm so much as a single red moustache hair on your rose-cheeked face. However, I do need to hear the message. That is not something about which I can allow you any choice."

Gideon realised, belatedly and with more than a passing stab of anger at his stupidity, that he had been doomed from the moment he had stepped into the alehouse. But, with care, he could perhaps walk from defeat. He drew a deep breath.

"Very well. I am to require you to submit yourself freely to the king's justice, by surrendering your person to Sir Bartholomew at a time and place of your own choosing. I am to inform you that your case, though desperate, is far from hopeless and that Sir Bartholomew has powerful allies willing to speak for you." Gideon hesitated, weighing up how to finish the appeal. "I am to emphasise his consideration for you and he wished me to assure you that he feels there is a certainty of clemency."

Although he nodded, Lord appeared neither surprised nor reassured. He remained attentive as if expecting there to be more.

"That is what I was asked to say to you," Gideon insisted.

THE MERCENARY'S BLADE

Lord sighed with exaggerated exasperation.

"Did no one tell you that lying is only for lawyers, physicians and whores? 'No this will not cost much', 'Yes, you will feel better soon' and 'Oh my! I have never seen one *that* big before!'." His body shifted with each speech, taking on a complete portrayal of each character by stance, voice and gesture, as skilled as any professional player on a stage. Then he was himself again. "But wait, I forget, you *are* a lawyer. And you, my Giddy One, are telling me fibs so warts will grow on your tongue. Now. Give me the part of the message that—being not entirely devoid of intelligence—you have realised you do not want me to hear."

Gideon had seen the expression on the faces of men condemned to hang. He had seen some stand, still as rock, and receive the news as if they were deaf. He had seen some dragged away sobbing or lash out in fury. One, a boy of twelve, had simply stood there as if unable to grasp the inevitability of it and asked 'Why?' over and over as they took him away. Which was exactly how Gideon felt at that moment.

But, being far from unintelligent, he also knew that saying the words made no difference now. He cleared his throat and tried to speak with as much confidence as he could.

"I was to say that I am here in his place to charge you as Sir Bartholomew would in person if he could but find you himself. That he only awaits confirmation that you are indeed back in England before putting in motion all the necessities for your case."

Lord's face fell with an exaggerated expression of regret. Shadows caught his profile, painting the aquiline nose and strong jawline in elongated caricature on the wall beside him, like some Punchinello puppet.

"Oh poor Giddy One, here all alone, with no one the wiser as to where exactly you might be, the only one who can confirm for certain that I am indeed even in the country." He shook his head and sighed. "And you an honest lawyer too, such a rare breed."

Pushing himself away from the wall Lord drew the basket-hilted sword in a single smooth action as if it were a living extension of the hand that held it. Gideon stared numbly at it. The blade gleamed in the weak light with its double-edged sleekness and sheen of deadly beauty.

"But you said—" he protested, trying to rise from the bench even as a strong hand pushed him back down. The ice-water eyes viewed him dispassionately, as no more or less of an object than the bench he sat on.

"I say many things, Giddy One, not all of them are true. But if it means anything at all to you I am truly sorry that I have to do this." He sounded as if he meant it.

In all Gideon's imaginings of the ways death might eventually visit him, one in which it came in the backroom of a cheap alehouse at the hands of a man to whom he was nothing more than an inconvenience, had somehow been missed out. Gideon closed his eyes, ashamed of his own cowardice and waiting for the pain to come. He wanted to pray but couldn't get past 'Oh God!'.

Instead, against his will, his mind spiralled back, as if seeking a way things could have been different. It was a galling irony that his reputation for being astute had been what led him to this.

He had always been good at noticing how events and

THE MERCENARY'S BLADE

facts fitted together, asking the right questions and collecting information which could win a dispute for a client. He had taken pride in and nourished the ability. That reputation led to his being offered work in Newcastle, where the incredibly wealthy families who made up the Hostman coal cartel had been clutching at straws for any possible legal redress for their financial losses during the recent Scottish occupation. It had also been the reason he had wound up being reprimanded for looking too closely at their affairs and highlighting some possibly illegal irregularities in their dealings—irregularities which would have made the redress they were seeking hard to justify.

And it had been the same reputation, he had been assured, that had led to his recent employment by Sir Bartholomew Coupland. The offer of well-paid work on the very eve of his intended return to London seemed a godsend. At the time, with little to show for his northern expedition except empty pockets and disgruntled clients, the offer of a princely sum simply to find a man and deliver a message was more than welcome.

Except now Gideon knew he had been about as unastute as it was possible to be. The clues had been there all along, he had simply been too blind to see them, and he was going to pay the ultimate price for his mistake…

It was then he realised he had been sitting, body tensed, with eyes squeezed shut in anticipation, for an uncomfortably long time. At that same moment, the sound of the door slamming shut was simultaneously drowned out by a loud grunt from beyond it. It was the kind of sound an ox might make when pole-axed, as was the heavy thud that came a moment later. Then a scream that was feminine and hysterical. It stopped abruptly and pandemonium broke loose. Gideon could hear benches and tables being overturned, men shouting and feet running.

Opening his eyes, Gideon found himself, against all expectation, alone in the small room.

Even more unexpected, he was alive.

For the length of a drawn out-breath, nothing else seemed to matter except that incredible fact and the relief that came with it. Then he noticed liquid, dark as treacle in the rushlight, was seeping under the door. It looked beautiful—richly red, like liquid ruby on the packed mud floor. He realised what it must be, but his limbs refused to respond to the desperate need to move. The trickle of blood flowed over the floor, pooling here and there on the uneven surface, towards the fine leather of his boot. It was the horror of it touching him that broke the spell.

Struggling to his feet, Gideon lunged at the shutters. With fingers made too clumsy by panic, he grabbed the bolt that held them closed and jerked it down. It jammed and he had to waste precious time working it free, cursing the delay with each movement. Then the shutters opened and the cool of the night beckoned him through the window. He had no idea where he would go—but he knew he had to escape that place of violence and death before it engulfed him too.

The window was just big enough for him to push through headfirst, arms outstretched in front. A shutter ripped a broad strip of wool from his breeches and grazed the skin beneath. He rolled forward, tucking his head down as the walls finally released him.

The roll wasn't exactly a tidy manoeuvre and he fetched

up hard against a tree. As he recovered, the sound of footsteps nearby alerted him to the fact that he was not alone. Crouching against the rough bark, Gideon held his breath.

The steps came closer to the tree and then a familiar lightly melodic voice called to him, from the dark. Philip Lord.

"Your enterprise has saved me a task. Come, Giddy One, we must flee, save our lives and be like the heath in the wilderness."

Heart pounding, Gideon cursed inwardly and stayed still. The voice spoke again, close by now, sounding amused.

"You have nothing to gain by trying to conceal yourself. I saw you come through that window like a fox from a coop with the farmer in hot pursuit." Lord paused, then added speculatively, "or was it practice gained escaping your cuckolds?"

Something in Gideon snapped and he launched himself towards the taunting voice, wanting only to silence it. His fists met flesh and then they were wrestling on the ground. He had only boyhood scraps to call on for experience, and the overwhelming desire to throttle the life out of the man who was the cause of this fear, anger and humiliation. But for some reason he couldn't seem to get a grip on his foe. Every time he grasped a limb or tried to pound a fist into flesh, the grip was broken or the flesh was gone. Slowly he became aware that the other man was shaking.

Good if he were afraid. Gideon had swallowed enough fear that evening to last him a lifetime. He seized one wrist, then the other, and knew that he was winning, that he had Lord where he wanted him. Then he heard the choked burst of sound and realised that the reason his opponent was shaking was from laughter.

A moment of movement and the world turned upside down. Gideon found himself flat on his face, arms pinned at his sides by immovable knees, legs trapped by the weight of his victorious foe.

"A pox on you, whoreson," he snarled.

"Oh God who looks over innocents and fools, why have you delivered this one to me?" Lord said, mockingly reflective. "And which is it anyway? Innocent—or fool?"

"At least I'm not a thief or a murderer!" Gideon spat.

"Well, there is that to be thankful for," Lord said. "But the time for games has passed. Your presence here when the ambushing force you did not invite along arrives is as inadvisable for your future health as for mine. Now, I can either tie you like a Michaelmas hog and you travel broadside, or you can start to behave like a rational adult in a dangerous situation and ride pillion in the regular way. You may choose."

In response, Gideon struggled, fiercely.

"You killed a man."

"Two men," Lord corrected, "and I ordered the deaths of three more. And I could make it a fourth, by the simple expedient of leaving you here to greet good Sergeant Hoyle, whichever Tempest child rides with him, and all their worthies. But you are young, Giddy One, undoubtedly foolish and most probably innocent. So that would surely be a crime in the eyes of the Lord."

The last words were accompanied by a blow to his jaw which dazed him. He was unable to resist as his wrists and ankles were bound and a piece of muslin cloth that tasted as though it had recently been wrapped around mouldy cheese was pushed into his mouth.

His captor gave a low call, sounding for all the world like a young owl, and a figure emerged from the night mounted and leading another horse. Gideon was hefted unceremoniously as a sack, onto the withers with the new arrival mounting behind him. The rider set off at a brisk trot along the road, leaving Lord and the other horse behind.

They hadn't gone far from the village when somewhere behind them a huge orange flower blossomed noisily in the darkness. Something large was on fire. Soon after, heralded by the sound of hooves on soft ground, they were joined by Lord, who led Gideon's own mare. He spoke quickly to the other man in a language Gideon did not know. Then the two men pushed the horses forward at a ground-covering pace.

It was the most uncomfortable and undignified experience Gideon had known and plummeted the misery of the night to a new nadir. It seemed to last for eternity, and at times he wondered if he had in truth died in that backroom and this was hell. His face chafed against the saddle, his wrists and ankles chafed in their bonds and his body ached all over. His torment was completed by the sensation that he might at any time choke on the gag.

At one point they stopped and moved him to be tied over the saddle of his own mount, but the change merely marked a slight difference in the precise points of pain and discomfort. Even if he had been of a mind to try and work out the direction or look for landmarks, the darkness made that impossible.

It wasn't yet dawn when they finally stopped.

Beyond exhaustion, his limbs cramped from their constraint, back twisted, face sore from rubbing on cloth, leather and buckles, Gideon knew only relief. He was taken from the horse, carried into a building and upstairs. When he was dropped onto a straw pallet, blissfully soft and still, he scarcely even noticed his bonds being released as sleep was already reaching out with irresistible arms to claim him. The voice he had already learned to hate followed him down into blessed oblivion.

"You may not think so now, Giddy One but you will thank the Lord for this."

THE MERCENARY'S BLADE

Chapter Two

Nick Tempest, recently created Captain Nicholas Tempest of Colonel Sir Bartholomew Coupland's Regiment of Horse, poked at the ashes of the burned-out alehouse with the toe of his boot and listened to the soldier's report.

"Three men, sir, maybe four. Hard to be sure yet."

Nick nodded but didn't turn around. Instead, he tipped the brim of his hat to shade his eyes from the autumnal sunlight and looked around. A huddle of cottages attempted to impersonate a village. The church nearby was the only solid-looking structure in sight. By good fortune, the alehouse stood alone so the fire had not spread.

Some village children had come to stare at the ruined building and two of them were throwing stones to scare the ducks on the pond beside it. Under a tree, a dog sniffed at a figure slumped in sleep. Sergeant Hoyle had already dragged the drunkard to his feet when they first arrived, an old soldier injured in the foot and the mind by Dutch service. If he hadn't had more important matters to deal with, Nick would gladly have had him taken to the house of correction. There were too many such vermin around. One less was always a blessing.

Picking his way back across the burned ruin, past the men he had set to search through the charred remains, Nick headed to where another of the troop waited with a nervous-looking villager. The man seemed unable to stop talking. As if the more he spoke the more he would be believed.

"I saw the flames, but there was nothing we could do. We all ran out. Dod wanted to get water from the pond, but what could we do? Was all ablaze. You couldn't get close. Was like the pit of hellfire. What could we do? We saw the fire and ran out—"

"What happened to the owner? Margret Armstrong, you say she is called?" Nick demanded, cutting into the flow of words.

"She was in a state. Nothing would do except she went straight off to her sister in Hexham. Middle of the night or not. My wife told her she could stay with us, which was Christian kindness, but she'd have none of it. So she told her—"

"You know where this sister lives in Hexham? Her name?"

"Not rightly, no. Maggie never spoke much of her. Come to that I don't know I'd ever heard of a sister before. She'd a brother, hung for sheep stealing years ago, but I never remember her saying about a sister. Not until last night when nothing else would do except that she left right away."

"She was on foot?"

"No. She had that old bay gelding Widow Baker sold her two years ago. Nice enough horse, but not worth the half of what—"

"A woman travelling alone by night? And no one thought it odd?"

"Oh she weren't alone, there were her boys with her."
"Her boys?"
"Oh yes, five sons and the nephews too. They had been

visiting the week. They said they were all going to Newcastle, word being there was recruiting there by the earl. I told them I thought they were a bit slow to get there for those so keen to fight but—"

"How many sons and nephews?" Tempest snapped out the words, his patience fraying. The villager seemed not to notice.

"There were five sons and then another four or five nephews. Maggie'd never spoken of being a widow before. But then if those lads had left her on her own in the world so long as they did, I can't say I am surprised. You'd be ashamed to have family like that, wouldn't you? I think—"

Nick lifted a hand to silence the man and addressed the soldier instead.

"Find out what these men looked like. If any had white hair or not." Not waiting for a response, he walked away eager to remove himself from earshot as quickly as possible. He crossed to where his uncle was waiting.

"He was here." Sir Bartholomew Coupland brushed at a few flakes of ash the breeze had deposited on his deep lace collar. There was more on the wide brimmed hat, beneath which the baronet's brow was creased into a frown. Nick had long since decided he would rather stare into the muzzle of enemy artillery than have to endure the steel of his uncle's accusing gaze.

"He was here. And we nearly had him."

"So what went wrong, Nicholas? You and Hoyle were in place, how could he have slipped through the net? Was it that Lennox suspected something? Did Paxton and Gray make their move too soon? Though if they did, they paid the price for it." He turned away looking tired and drawn, each of his fifty-six years weighing on his shoulders and no doubt being plagued by his intermittent gout. "This is going to make things much more complicated and difficult."

And they were not before? Nick bit back the words. "At least we know he is somewhere in the area. We can send our soldiers to find him. If he has men we can find those and—"

Sir Bartholomew made a sharp gesture with one hand.

"We can do no such thing. The earl is mustering and preparing to march. We are summoned to Newcastle with every man we can raise. We have run out of time for such action."

One of the soldiers who had been raking through the burned-out alehouse was running towards them. He stopped a few paces away and removed his hat.

"Colonel Sir Bartholomew, sir—we found this and Ha—I mean Andrews—thought it might be important."

Something glinted in the morning sunlight, Nick held out his hand and the soldier carefully pressed what he held into the glove. It was a ring. Heavy gold, not a modern design and distinctive. Nicholas held it up for his uncle to see.

"Do you know this?"

The soldier stood by, still clutching his hat. Sir Bartholomew nodded a dismissal, saying nothing until the man had gone back to his task.

"It belonged to Lennox. So at least he will not be a problem to us, but I don't think we can count that as much success." He spoke quietly to avoid being overheard. "I was foolish to listen to your father. This would have been done by now if we had followed my intentions and not some addle-pate idea to make things right with the world. Paxton and Gray could have found some opportunity, they even told you as much, but no, that wasn't good enough for Richard. It had to be seen to be done, right through to a public execution."

Stung by this attack, Nick bridled. He thought of his father, the furtive meetings, the dangerous documents, the lifetime burden of secrecy.

"My father has always acted for the best in this. He has lived for the Covenant all his life and for all mine, he has spoken of nothing else as being so important. He always said that it needed to be finished in public so there could be no myths, no imposters. Just—just an end."

For a moment Nick feared he had taken family loyalty too far. But his uncle only nodded and took the ring from him, sliding it into his belt purse for safekeeping. Then he placed a hand on his nephew's shoulder.

"You have much of your father's strength, and I agree that in a Utopia we might hope to see things completed neatly as he suggests. But this is the real world. There are seldom tidy endings, sometimes it has to be enough to make one at all." His hand gripped tightly, willing Nick to understand. He was right in one thing at least, they needed to finish this.

"Then let me be the one to do so," Nick said. "The one to make that end."

Sir Bartholomew looked taken aback.

"This is not a task for a—"

"For what?" Nick felt a familiar resentment deep in the pit of his stomach. "A boy? I am twenty-one since May. Or perhaps you mean for a Tempest? Perhaps you want Coupland's seal placed on this deed."

The old man's grey eyes hardened into the too-familiar steel gaze.

"Listen to me. I know your branch of the family is as deep in the Covenant as mine. You are my nephew, my heir and heir to Howe—title, house and estate. In time you will come to carry the weight of that. But this is no ordinary man and you are, not yet so—so *experienced* as others."

With an effort, Nick bit back a strong rejoinder but continued in what he hoped was a reasonable tone.

"Someone has to do it so why not me? Let me stay and search. Give me a handful of men. Henry can take my place with the troop. He is old enough and he sorely wants it."

Sir Bartholomew was silent, his gaze fixed into space over Nick's shoulder. Then he cursed loudly and released his grip.

"God's wounds! Will someone deal with that?"

Nick turned. The vagrant who had been asleep under a nearby tree was now staggering around muttering to himself, heading towards them with the clear intention of looking for more drink or begging for money. Hoyle ran up as Nick grabbed at the vagrant's arm, spinning him around so he was a better target for the sergeant's gauntleted fist to the stomach.

The drunk collapsed as he made the blow, falling forward, head lolling, into Sir Bartholomew. As he did so, his legs slid from under him and caught into Nick's knees, so Nick had to take a staggering step for balance. For a moment, his face was on a level with the vagrant and he had the impression of reeking breath and a weeping sore before Hoyle pulled the man away with a grunt of disgust.

The vagrant made no resistance, muttering incoherently as he was dragged off and thrown to the ground with a few hard kicks. When he lay still Hoyle added a couple more blows for good measure then left him lying unconscious, or close to it, in the mud, as he went back to his work.

Sir Bartholomew sighed and shook his head.

"This is what England is come to. With this war we will soon see a hundred such broken men wherever there is now one."

Nick said nothing. In his opinion there were too many such already. His uncle turned away and drew Nick with him, walking back towards the horses.

"I will leave you, Hoyle, and most of the men to finish up here. I shall be at Howe making the necessary preparations to depart tomorrow. Find me there when you are done." He collected the reins of his horse and let one of his men assist him to mount.

"I'll bring you the final account before sunset, uncle," Nick promised.

"Good lad. I must to bed early as I will have to march first thing tomorrow, so don't be too late. We can talk some more about your staying here to continue the search when I take our men to the earl."

Nick's spirits rose, but that checked as he noticed something out of place.

"Uncle, your purse."

Sir Bartholomew looked down and his hand went to where the purse should be.

"God's wounds! That damned—"

But Nick was ahead of him, running back across the

uneven ground, shouting to his men as he did so.

They were already too late. The spot where they left the drunk lying unconscious was empty and a thorough search of the surrounding area found no trace of him.

Gideon woke with a groan.

Every inch of his body ached, inside and out, as if he had been trampled by a company of cavalry. The notion of horses conjured up images of the night before and he gave another groan, as involuntary as the first but caused by a pain that was not of the body. He squeezed his eyes shut hoping to block out the memory. It didn't.

Resigned, he gritted his teeth against the protests of his muscles and hauled himself free of the blanket someone had placed over him. From the vantage point of greater height, sitting up on the pallet—which to his surprise was clean and fresh—he could see the rest of the room.

It had an unshuttered, barred window and a stout-looking wooden door. Barrels and bulging sacks were stacked to one side and a few long wooden crates were set, lengthways up, against one wall. Like the pallet, everything seemed clean and neat. Which was more than could be said for Gideon himself. His hands were filthy and the stubble around his beard itched on his face. There was any amount of mud and other undesirable substances dried on his shirt and still clinging to his ripped breeches.

His doublet lay at the end of the mattress. It had been brushed clean and he could see where someone with a ready needle had repaired where a couple of genuine slashes had been added to the fashionable sewn-in ones. His boots, which stood close by, had also been cleaned. There was a shirt, linen-press fresh, new stockings and a

THE MERCENARY'S BLADE

pair of fine dark grey camlet breeches with a cassaque to match.

With an effort, Gideon pushed himself to his feet and looked out of the window. The day was well into afternoon. He was on the second floor of a building, the view out was over a track and blocked by trees and the rise of the land. No clues there—he could be anywhere. The solid oak door was newly fitted with a lock, reinforced with riveted bands of iron and looked as though it could withstand a battering ram. He clearly wasn't going to get through it until someone let him out.

Sighing, Gideon removed the worst of the mud from his face and hands with the remains of his ruined clothing then dressed himself in the borrowed finery provided and his own doublet. He then turned his attention to the stores in the room.

The lid on one of the crates was loose. Inside, packed in straw, were half-a-dozen brand new matchlock muskets. The sacks were tied and opened easily. They released the smell of new leather and contained sets of bandoliers, each wooden flask attached to the strap by oiled hemp twine, and accompanied by an attached powder flask and a small leather pouch for bullets. Under the sacks were coils of match cord, imbued with the unmistakable odour of saltpetre, and a heap of small metal jugs. The barrels were well sealed, but Gideon already suspected he knew what they would contain and had no desire to prise one open to confirm his guess.

His own experience of firearms was limited to shooting borrowed fowling pieces at ducks. But these were not for hunting, these were weapons of war. Casting his inexpert eyes over the arms cache, Gideon reckoned there were enough supplies there to equip some thirty men as musketeers. It seemed his captor was either engaged in selling arms or looking to add his own contribution to the general hostilities that were threatening to engulf the nation.

Which made it all the more puzzling to Gideon that he was still alive.

Lord had gone to some effort to bring him here. Perhaps he needed a hostage. If so, Gideon Lennox made a poor choice. A struggling young lawyer with no connections and an employer who had clearly washed his hands of him. Or perhaps Lord believed Gideon had more information to offer than he had already imparted. In which case he would be disappointed.

Gideon looked at the boxes and wondered why he had been locked in a room with weaponry to hand. Nothing was stopping him loading one of those muskets and—

A glint of light from the edge of the straw-filled pallet caught his eye. Crossing the room with a speed he would have doubted himself capable of a few moments before, he reached down and pulled out the offending shiny metal object.

His own sword.

It made no sense, why leave him his sword, leave him with muskets and powder if he was a prisoner?

Unless…

Putting the sword home on his hip, he walked to the door and lifted the latch. Unbelievably it opened and swung onto a stairway. He was greeted by the smell of fresh bread, which made him realise he was hungry— very hungry. His last meal had been a snatched bite at his lodgings the previous morning.

THE MERCENARY'S BLADE

Wondering and cautious, he went down the stairs.

They descended first to a small gallery landing with two doors and then led on down to ground level. Leaving the rooms on the gallery unexplored for now, Gideon headed down towards the smell of food.

The lowest level was a single cavernous room with a stone-flagged floor. There were signs it had once housed something large and cumbersome, but now it had been turned into a hall with trestles and boards for tables—all newly made. A stack of pallet mattresses identical to the one he had slept upon was pushed up against one wall and a tall double door stood open beyond.

He walked through the large doorway and looked back at the building. To one side a river meandered past and Gideon realised he was standing by what had once been a fulling mill, although it would have been long since this one served its purpose. Not much of the original extent remained, just the stump of the mill itself with the rooms above the fulling area and some outbuildings. The waterwheel and its housing were long gone, but the surviving stonework showed signs of recent repair and reroofing.

A young woman sat by the edge of the river, rubbing laundry. Her hair was scooped up beneath a coif and under a concealing lappet cap, but it had escaped in places to lie in bright coiling curls on her shoulder the colour of ripe peach flesh, warm as the sunshine. She had skin like an English rose. She wore a russet skirt and a man's coat, the sleeves pulled to her elbows as she worked.

Gideon was so captivated, that he didn't notice anyone else at first. It was only when he realised the woman was speaking to someone as she worked, that he saw the figure under the tree. It was a man. He had seen Gideon and was watching him intently.

The man had stepped from a woodcut of the German wars. In his middle years, dressed in practical clothes, a dull brown Dutch coat and a battered hat. He looked foreign, Italian or even Greek perhaps—Gideon was no expert—black hair flecked with grey, and the olive skin tones of one native to much sunnier climes.

As Gideon approached, he made a strange low grunting sound at which the woman turned, rose from her laundry and wiped her wet hands on her skirt, pulling her sleeves down to her wrists as she did so.

She smiled.

Gideon felt his soul rise, divide and then melt.

"I did not know you were awake," she said. Her accent seemed to continue the sound of the alien tongue she had been speaking. It was warm and exotic, like cinnamon. "Please, take a seat in the hall Mr Lennox and I will bring food. The Schiavono said you would be hungry, so we have not yet had dinner."

Reluctant, but compelled from her presence by her command, he went back into the old mill building. No sooner had he taken a seat on a bench at one of the new tables than she appeared and placed a loaf of bread, still oven warm, and some cheese before him. Then she was gone again to return moments later bearing the remains of his hat, lost, he had thought, in the scuffles of the previous night. It looked as though someone had rolled on it, stamped on it and thrown it aside and someone else had spent time and effort trying to restore it to a pristine appearance.

"I am sorry," she said, sounding regretful. "I could not get all the blood out, but it marked most under the brim at the back so will not be noticed."

"I—uh—that is fine—I mean, thank you, Mistress…?"

"My name is Zahara," she said. "Just Zahara. But I am often called Sara."

"Zahara." It was a name Gideon had never heard before. "You are Italian?"

She broke off a piece of the cheese to eat. The man who had been so watchful outside came in, placing a small stool for himself at the end of the trestle so he was sitting between them. Gideon helped himself to the food, the first salty taste of the cheese reminding him how much he needed to eat.

"No. Not Italian. I was born in Aleppo," Zahara told him.

"Aleppo?" He was unable to keep the disbelief from his tone. "In *Syria*?"

She frowned.

"There is another Aleppo?"

Gideon just shook his head, his mouth full. It seemed beyond belief that such a young woman—she couldn't be older than he was himself at most—and of such appearance could have been born in Syria. He would have assumed Surrey or Sussex as much more likely.

Between the three of them, with Gideon eating far more than one man's fair portion, the bread and cheese vanished. Zahara brushed the last crumbs from the table. She said something to the silent figure at the end of the board who nodded, rising as he did so. He gave Gideon a look that contained a clear warning, before walking outside. Gideon watched him go.

"He doesn't speak English?"

"Shiraz does not speak at all. His tongue was cut out."

"Why?" asked Gideon. "Who is he?"

"You ask a lot of questions." She softened the criticism with a small smile.

Gideon wondered if anyone before, in the history of the world, had ever had such huge green eyes. He found himself answering her smile in kind.

"I am a lawyer, it is what we do."

Which made her laugh.

"Shiraz is Shiraz as that is where we met." She gave a little shrug. "There was a bad flood. Many people died. I would have as well. I was a child. He rescued me, though he claims I saved him."

When she turned away Gideon felt as if the sun had passed behind a cloud. He realised then that from that first glance by the river her presence had ensorceled him, making him forget where he was and what he needed to do. At the door, she turned again and looked back at him.

"There is soap where I was washing the linens, should you want to use it. The Schiavono said that when you had eaten I was to tell you your horse is in the stable and Shiraz will show you to the road if you wish to leave."

There were perhaps more surprising and less believable things she could have said—such as that she was born in Aleppo.

"The Schiavono?" He thought for a moment. "You mean Philip Lord? The man who brought me here? He said I am free to go?" The notion made so little sense that Gideon couldn't grasp it.

"Of course. Why would you not be?" Her nose crinkled in genuine puzzlement.

THE MERCENARY'S BLADE

"But then why did he bring me here? What was going on last night? Why—?" Gideon broke off. He had been about to ask why he hadn't been murdered along with the rest.

Zahara stood motionless at the door, haloed by the sun, escaped strands of saffron hair catching the rays and blending to amber.

"I cannot answer your questions. I am sorry. The Schiavono said he will be back by this evening. If you wish to stay, you can ask him then."

After she had gone, Gideon took the time to wash his face and hands in the river, then looked around the mill and its buildings. There was one that was being used as a kitchen and a long stone outbuilding that had once been a store and stables for the mill. Someone had been busy though, and now it boasted several new, well-set stalls. Three of them were occupied and the occupants were all good-quality mounts.

His own chestnut mare, the one he had been riding since leaving Durham, recognised him as he walked in and he greeted her with an odd rush of emotion. It was like encountering an old friend in a strange and dangerous city. He had no treat to give her, so he spent a few minutes petting her. She had been well-groomed and the straw in the stall was fresh. Common sense suggested that he should take her now and ride. Escape before the enigmatic Philip Lord returned.

What did it matter why he hadn't been killed? All that mattered was that he was alive now. No thanks to Sir Bartholomew Coupland.

Thoughts of the baronet took him away from the quiet stable and back to the afternoon he had spent at

Coupland's seat at Howe Hall. He had not been there as a guest, but in the chamber set aside for matters of business. Unlike most such cabinets, it was a good-sized room in the house with a writing table, bookshelves, document bags and coffers.

The conversation that had reached him in snatches as he was admitted, was of the news that few could yet believe: the king had raised his standard in Nottingham and Sir Bartholomew and his brother-in-law, Sir Richard Tempest, were not the only men of substance that day calculating the cost of giving their support.

For all the political fomenting that had gone on in London over the last couple of years, no one there had truly believed that modern, educated Englishmen would ever resort to arms against each other. No one believed that the English Parliament would condone conducting war against their own monarch. No one Gideon knew, anyway. Everyone believed something would happen at the last moment to deflect hostilities and reconcile the two parties.

"But there are matters yet more pressing that have arisen as a result," Sir Bartholomew said, acknowledging Gideon's presence with no more than a nod. His brother-in-law, a few years younger, wearing the expression of a troubled man, seemed not to notice that anyone else had joined them.

"You mentioned so before," Sir Richard said. "Though God knows war is enough."

"The war will be done before Christmas. As soon as men see it harms production, trade and wealth they will come to their senses. No one wants that."

"You forget religion. That has more sway over minds

and hearts than commerce. Look at the Harvey boy, sailing with Plowden to 'New Albion'." Sir Richard made a sound of disgust. "New Albion, New Haven, New England, New Hampshire, New Cambriol. Romantic rubbish."

It had the sound of a much-expressed opinion and the look of irritation on Coupland's face confirmed as much. Sir Bartholomew gestured to Gideon.

"Mr Lennox comes to us well recommended, and I believe he may be just the man for the job we were discussing when you were last here."

Now Sir Richard looked at him, fatigue-shadowed eyes gaining something of alertness and interest.

"Lennox? That's a Scottish name."

"I am from London," Gideon said carefully. Thanks to the recent invasion, feelings towards those who came from north of the border tended to be much worse here in the north of England than at home. Even in London prejudice against his name had cost him clients in the past. Before more could be said to his ancestry he added: "I understand you have some matter in which you feel I could assist? If so, it would be an honour to be of service and I can assure you of my professional competence and discretion."

There was an awkward silence in which both men looked at him. Then Coupland cleared his throat.

"We need you to bear an important message to someone we have good reason to believe has recently returned to the country and is now somewhere in the area."

"You need me to write to someone on your account?" Gideon asked, puzzled at first.

Sir Richard shifted his position as if the padded brocade

chair he occupied was uncomfortable. Coupland simply shook his head.

"The man was—" he hesitated, seeking the right term. "He was *required* to leave England by the old king, King James, some twenty years ago, under conditions that will no doubt make him believe his return would be—"

Tempest made the sound of an impatient horse.

"Philip Lord was denounced as a traitor and had a price put on his head. He isn't likely to walk up to one he knows to be a justice of the peace and declare himself now he is returned. What sane man would? We need to find him and convince him that it is safe to do so. That he has no need to remain in hiding."

At the time, in Howe Hall, Gideon had wondered what manner of man under sentence of death would risk returning after twenty years of successful living abroad.

Now, having met the man in question, and standing in what appeared to be his stable, Gideon at least had the beginnings of an answer to that.

He must have been lost in thought far longer than he had realised, for when the sound of hooves outside drew him from reverie and back to the reality of his position, the September sun was already setting. Lord was back, calling to Zahara and Shiraz in the strange language the three of them seemed to share. The opportunity to ride away was gone. Already wondering if he had been a fool not to grab at the chance, Gideon left the stable.

"I see you are still here. That is something of a surprise."

Wearing filthy rags for clothing, the wretch speaking with Lord's voice had short-cut black hair poking out from beneath a knitted border bonnet. His skin looked grimy and coarse, he had hooded eyes and an open sore oozing on his face. In one hand he held an earthenware bottle and he stank of alcohol.

The grin that greeted Gideon seemed gap-toothed, but the mocking tone was all too familiar.

"I would have thought you'd have been charging back to Durham or Sir Bartholomew. Perhaps you are not quite so giddy as I had presumed. When I have changed and eaten, we shall talk. Until then this is for you."

Gideon accepted the proffered bottle, wondering what trick it held, then saw, unbelievably, pressed into the top was his great-grandfather's signet ring. It was something so unexpected and unlooked for, Gideon had no words.

"Save some for me," Lord said, "it is not often I have to share at the moment." Then he walked into the old mill building, singing in a light and melodic voice.

"I am mighty melancholy,
And a quart of sack shall cure me.
I am choleric as any,
Quart of claret will secure me.
I am phlegmatic as may be,
Peter-see-me must inure me.
I am sanguine for a lady,
And cool Rhenish shall conjure me..."

Gideon stood where he was, the dusk settling around him until Zahara called him inside to eat.

The ring restored to its rightful place on his hand, Gideon sat with a bowl of mutton hotpotch and a cup of aqua vitae from the bottle. The hotpotch tasted strange, flavoured through with some unfamiliar spice. Lemony, but not unpleasant. Having served the meal, Zahara sat down opposite him. She brought a sense of peace with her, as if he were sitting down to his supper at home. There was food and a cup before her but she left it untouched and watched him eat. He offered her the bottle of aqua vitae but she shook her head.

"I thank you. I do not drink strong spirits."

"So what are you doing here?" he asked. "Have you been here long?"

"We came here six weeks ago," she said, "from Holland."

"From Holland? You travel a lot."

That made her laugh softly. Laughter as sweet and natural as water bubbling from a spring.

"I have travelled all my life. Now, I travel with the Schiavono."

A sudden tug of dread pulled at Gideon's heart.

"You are married?"

The question made her glance down at the table as if to avoid his gaze.

"No. I am not married. Are you?"

Her answer lifted his spirits.

"Not yet. But then I have neither name nor fortune to tempt anyone to be my wife," he explained. "And as things are now, it is unlikely I will have for many years."

"A wife? Or a name and a fortune?"

"Both. No reasonable family would commit their daughter to a man with no solid prospects."

Zahara looked up at him then, her chin tilted. She seemed to be weighing his words with care and when she spoke it was as if she had given the matter grave consideration and was announcing a verdict.

"But love is not reasonable. Only reason always seeks a profit. Love gives and asks nothing in return."

THE MERCENARY'S BLADE

Gideon found himself smiling but whether at her intensity, her innocence, or simply because she looked so appealing, he wasn't sure.

"Which would be wisdom, were it not that profit is the purpose of marriage for any of substance. Indeed profit is the purpose for just about everything in the world."

Under the lappet cap, her eyes sparkled like emeralds set in the cameo of her oval face.

"And what," she asked, as if she was striving to learn and his answer mattered to her, "is the purpose of profit?"

It was a strange question, the kind Gideon had discussed in earnest in his student days, with his friends well in their cups. Zahara looked as though she was about to add something more, perhaps to explain or expand upon the question, when a light tread on the stair interrupted her and she stood up.

"I must take some food for Shiraz."

Then she was gone, slipping nimbly from the room.

"She is a beauty, is she not?"

Philip Lord sat down at the place Zahara had left and breathed in the steam rising from the pottage. His appearance had been transformed again, hair restored looking impeccable. He wore peacock blue calamanco, slashed with white silk. It had silver points, each studded with a single sapphire. Shoes of grey leather with silver buckles that matched the points and a fine silk shirt. It would have been adequate at court, over-dressing for dinner at a private house, but in this setting, Gideon thought it crass, especially as it must have cost a fortune.

"She is pretty," he conceded. It didn't appeal to discuss Zahara with Philip Lord, who nodded and poured himself a cup of the aqua vitae.

"She is also forbidden fruit, my Giddy One, and you would be wise not to forget that." He lifted the cup as if in a silent toast. "It is one of the few crimes for which the Lord has no forgiveness."

"Your 'property'?" Gideon asked, irritated at the proprietorial tone and angry at the assumption behind it.

Lord nodded and sat back, his gaze appraising.

"Yes. I bought her in Algiers."

Which was not the reply Gideon had expected and he found he had no answer to it, just a tightening vice of fury around his heart. Lord lifted his cup to his lips, eyes above the rim as peacock bright as his clothing, before downing it in a single draught. A second cup followed the first and then was refilled a third time, before being left full upon the table.

"Then tell me, why are you still here?" Lord gestured expansively towards the door. "The way is open. No chains restrain you. Your horse is rested and well-fed. No doubt you have friends and family eager to embrace you to their collective bosoms and make clucking noises of shock and outrage about how ill you were treated."

Gideon felt the anger grow to fill all the space beneath his ribs. It made breathing uncomfortable as he forced himself to contain it. He knew this was deliberate, the baiting. It was the same variety of taunting an opponent in litigation might offer but touching different nerves. What he couldn't fathom was the reason for it. Here he was as much at the mercy of this man as if he had a sword blade pressed to his throat.

Sipping his own aqua vitae, he put the cup down with exaggerated care.

"I don't like to be taken for a complete fool even if I

may seem one to you. We don't all live in a world where decency and honesty are playthings or counters in a game."

Lord laughed aloud and banged his hands on the table as if in applause.

"Oh but we do. Even if some prefer not to believe it. But honesty is a refreshing change and has its own value when you come to the trade." His voice shifted, shedding something of its playfulness. "And I do not take you for a fool. Lennox, I take you for naïve and ill-informed. You are clearly no fool, for you are sitting here now."

"You will have ordered Shiraz to knife me if I leave," said Gideon. "You wouldn't let me see your secret cache and walk out again."

Lord picked up his spoon and poked at the pottage as if expecting to find something in it that might move.

"Sumac," he said at last. "If you were wondering. And no, Shiraz had no orders to harm you. I asked him to protect you. If he could. He is very good at looking after people. But there *are* men waiting to kill you if you return to your lodgings in Durham and I told him only to try and save you if he was sure he could get out alive himself."

Gideon felt the obstruction in his chest freeze. He half rose to his feet.

"I don't believe you. How could you know? And who would—?"

Then he sank back down as realisation hit.

"Be glad, my Not-So-Giddy-One," Lord said. "Your wisdom in remaining has saved you. When they raked through the ashes of the alehouse, they found your ring on one of the bodies. You are already dead to the world, grieved over and mourned."

Gideon barely registered what he was being told. One thought remained in his mind.

"Coupland."

"Coupland is like the flower on the buttercup, bright and eye-catching, socialising with the busiest of bees, drawing the attention and holding it. But the true business of the plant lies in the plain green leaves, and the most important part is the root, out of sight, hidden deeply. Pick the flower and the plant yet lives, pluck most all its leaves and it will not perish," he gave a brief, chilling smile, "but cut the root and it dies."

"You make it sound as though there is some—some grand conspiracy going on," Gideon said, struggling to make any sense of what he was being told.

"You think there is not?" Lord sounded incredulous. "You must be the one man in England to think that way at the moment with the king and his own parliament at war with each other. But have it your way. Sir Bartholomew Coupland, acting alone, perhaps jealous of your youthful form and handsome face, arranged for you to be murdered by me. He then put in place an alternative plan to ensure that if by chance you escaped that fate, you would still die when you got back to Durham. I would have thought that might pique your curiosity. I know it would mine, in your shoes."

"I only have your word for all that," said Gideon, but he was shaken and knew his tone lacked sincerity.

"So take your horse and go back to Durham." Lord frowned at the spoon he was holding as if it were at some fault and set it down. Then, pulling out his knife, stabbed a lump of mutton and started eating. Gideon watched as Lord first speared and ate all the meat, then finished the rest with a spoon, finally wiping the bowl with a piece of bread. Pushing the bowl away he looked up, an expression of mock surprise on his face.

"Still here? Then since you have decided to stay with us, you will be pleased to know the room you are sleeping in has been cleared of the vast majority of its stores for your greater comfort."

Gideon shrugged, the resentment smouldering anew at how his life seemed to have been usurped by this man.

"It seems I don't have anywhere to go, at least not tonight. From what you have said for all that my life may be bound up in this, it isn't about me. This is about you. And you have the answers."

"Perhaps I do." Lord's eyes widened and glimmered with humour as if he found the situation hilarious. "But do you have the right questions?"

That was too much and Gideon's anger shattered the chains of willpower that had been holding it constrained.

"I don't know, shall we try a few and see?" The tightness in his throat made his voice a half-snarl. "Am I here because it amuses you to sit there in your arrogance and gloat? Are you bored with Zahara and finding Shiraz a bit short on conversation? Or perhaps you want a foil for your ready wit? Someone to play with who cannot bite back? Or is it to have another forced to endure your damn smug preening because you just have to be the cock-of-the-walk?"

His voice rose as he spoke and all trace of humour faded from Lord's face as it did so. Instead, Lord lifted a hand to smother a yawn.

"But of course," he said, tone mild and amicable. "Why else would you be here?" Then he drained the last from his cup of aqua vitae and got to his feet, "Since that is cleared up, I suggest an early night."

He was gone before Gideon could frame a fitting reply, crossing the room in a few swift strides and stepping lightly up the stairs. Some moments later Gideon heard a door being opened and closed and the distinctive sound of a key being turned. He wondered, viciously, if Philip Lord had to lock himself away at night to avoid being murdered in his sleep.

"He is a good man, the Schiavono."

Zahara had entered the room like a silent shadow as if she had waited for Lord to leave before returning. She crossed over to the table and started clearing away the remains of the meal. She paused and looked at Gideon, with a questioning expression on her face. It obviously mattered to her that he shouldn't think ill of Lord. Much as he would want to please her in all things, in that Gideon was powerless to oblige.

"He lies, murders, steals, blasphemes, covets what is not his, pays no respect to anyone or anything. I have known him for less than a full day and I would say there is no Commandment he has not broken in that time."

A brief troubled look disturbed Zahara's usual serenity and he regretted his words. It dawned on him that she was infatuated. The very notion turned his guts violently inside out.

"He is *not* a bad man," she insisted, before taking the plates and leaving Gideon alone with his thoughts.

THE MERCENARY'S BLADE

Chapter Three

The scream tore him from sleep.

Mind dulled by torpor and shifting dreams, Gideon woke cold and clammy. It took a few moments to convince himself that it had been a real scream and not just a part of the strange, shapeless nightmare from which it had dragged him. There was no second scream, but re-enacting the sound in his head assured him it had belonged to the waking world and that it had been female, and terrified.

Zahara.

Some primaeval instinct drove deep into his heart and exploded there as a burst of protective rage. Throwing open the door, he charged down the stairs, two or three at a time, clutching his knife—the first weapon his fingers had closed on in his haste.

The two doors on the floor below were open. From one came light, the sounds of struggle and another anguished scream, abruptly muffled. Without conscious thought, Gideon hurled himself towards the source of the sound. The scent of sandalwood and a dozen sweet and exotic perfumes met him, incongruous with the dark thoughts that filled his mind.

Within the room two bodies wrestled on a bed, one still clad in the overblown finery he had worn in the evening, the other, nightshift dragged up to her thighs, pinned beneath him. Silver and gold hair tangled together as Lord exerted his strength to hold Zahara down. A guttering candle reflected the struggle in stark, angular shadows on the wall.

Gideon heard a noise like an enraged animal. Scarcely conscious that it issued from his own throat, he launched himself forward, knife gripped in one fist, blade downwards like a fang ready to tear into flesh.

Before his headlong rush could connect, something swept his legs from beneath him and he sprawled full length. The knife clattered away as a solid weight landed on him, rolling him, with force enough to drive the breath from his lungs. He gasped for air, but a strong arm pulled his head back, choking it off. Lord's voice, from the dishevelled bed, sounded taut and long-suffering.

"Oh God! Sir Percival—seeing without understanding what he sees. Get him out of here Shiraz."

Manhandled with ease, like a wayward child, half-choked and with a blade pressed close to the skin of his throat, Gideon was bundled back up to his room and locked in. There the impotent anger burst from him, as he pounded on the sturdy wood of the door with anything that came to hand. As the military supplies had been removed, there was not much, but what there was he pulled apart. He roared curses through the soulless, unheeding wood and stone. Eventually, frustration and fatigue took their toll and he slumped to rest for a moment on the disordered pallet.

He woke much later to the sound of the key turning in the lock. It was full day. Night-clad and sword in hand he was at the door and pulling it open before any could enter. Zahara was in the doorway, her bright hair bound from sight under a plain blue linen lappet. She picked up a steaming basin of water which she must have set down to unlock the door. His hold on the sword went limp and the raised blade fell onto the blanket.

"I brought you water to wash with," she said and stepped past him, with care to avoid the chaos left by his endeavours to escape the room revealed by the bright morning sunshine. Finding a place to set the basin down, Zahara turned to leave.

"Are you alright?" he asked. "I mean—last night…"

"Last night?"

She sounded genuinely puzzled and it was then Gideon realised she hadn't even known he had tried to rescue her.

"Your screams woke me," he said, by way of explanation.

A slight touch of colour pinked her features.

"I am sorry," she said, looking down, embarrassed. She walked to the door, keeping her face from him. "It happens. You should pay it no regard."

"No regard? I can't—"

He broke off and stepped forward to capture one of her hands. But, like a shy bird taking wing, it slipped from him before he could close his own upon it.

"Listen," he said, low-voiced and imperative. "I will get you out of here. Somehow. I have friends in London who can help you. You don't have to live like this."

She looked up at him then. The kitten-green eyes expressionless, searching his face.

"You are kind. But it is much better for me here."

The pent-up anger of the night burst through.

"How can it be better with that—that *demon*?"

Gideon heard his own voice snarling and regretted it instantly. Zahara took a small step away from him, close to full flight.

"The Schiavono is good to me," she said gently, "and to you. He saved your life. He is no demon."

Memories of his mother rose to haunt him. A woman so beaten down that the fault became twisted back to herself in all things until she could see nothing but righteous wrath in the treatment she received from her husband. And even Gideon, her only son, found nothing he ever said could change that view—no argument, no reasoning, no appeal.

His fists, stiff from the damage he had done to them hammering at the door, clenched and unclenched. In his mind ran visions of the things he would do to Philip Lord should the opportunity present itself. Zahara was still watching him, her eyes now wary as if she wanted to run but still had some duty that held her.

"There is food for you downstairs," she said, "and a man the Schiavono would have you speak with. He said that since you are staying here you should earn your keep."

She turned away and ran down the stairs.

Gideon vowed then that whatever it took he would deliver her beyond Lord's reach. His every instinct screamed for violence. But in violence, as last night had shown, it would be himself who came off the worse. If that would have in any way helped Zahara, he would not have hesitated, but he was her sole protector. Her sole chance of escape from a prison whose bars she helped, willingly, to cement in place.

There were other, better, weapons than blades with which such battles could be won. Weapons in which he was well trained and of which he owned the mastery.

Before he went downstairs, he had tidied the room and

THE MERCENARY'S BLADE

become, in every external aspect, once more the composed, competent man of law: dressed in borrowed finery, washed and shaven.

Although he had been warned there was a visitor, he was still taken aback to see someone sitting at the table, clad as a simple man might be when in his Sunday best. The man's gaze as he looked up at Gideon was haunted by misery. Before his foot had left the bottom step, the man was up and hurrying over.

"You must be the lawyer," he said. "The Schiavono said you would speak with me. Please, it's my wife..."

This at least was familiar territory. Dealing with distressed clients was part and parcel of his regular day-to-day work life. It took a few words and little time to persuade the man—who introduced himself only as Dutch—to be seated and as Gideon broke his fast on bread and small beer, to draw out the cause of his distress.

"They've taken my Beth and are calling her a witch. Two nights ago she was sent for by the Widow Bothwell to help deliver a child for one of the miners' women who was in travail. As well as Beth, the widow was there with the Turner sisters. Reverend Fanthorpe took them all for witches. But, I do swear to you, sir, my Beth is a godly woman, a good mother and a fine wife. No one has ever a bad word for her, but they are saying she is consorting with demons and devils."

Gideon listened as Dutch went on with his story. He spoke of livestock found dead in the fields around the village of Pethridge, mysterious lights seen in the dark. Then the arrival of Reverend Fanthorpe, a man who claimed to be able to find witches.

"At first," Dutch said, "I was as relieved as the rest

when the witchfinder came. I hoped this might root out the problem. But Reverend Fanthorpe seems to see witches in some of the kindest and most Christian-hearted of the village womenfolk, my own Beth amongst them."

With dogged professionalism, Gideon set about establishing the facts. "Aside from your wife, who else is accused?"

Dutch scratched at his beard and looked bemused. "Widow Bothwell, of course."

"Of course?"

"She is the one any who didn't know her might mark as a witch. She talks to herself and her cats and her cottage is full of pots of simples and ointments. And not a bairn for miles around that was born without her help these last thirty years. But the other two are just girls. Sisters. Leah and Ann Turner. Leah turned nineteen last month. Anne must be a year younger. Their mother's long passed on, but their father raised them well, before he caught a fever last winter. They have the land out past my place. Leah is betrothed to one of the Lamb boys, she's a good catch for him too and sharp as a knife. But Ann is a bit simple. Widow Bothwell—her cottage is on the other side of the Turner's—she's always had time for Ann, which is likely why the girls were with her when they were taken."

To Gideon it all sounded innocent enough.

"If there is no evidence and no confessions there may be something that can be done," he said.

Dutch shook his head. "But I have no way to pay you. I don't know what you would charge or how I can—"

"There will be no charge for you to meet," said a new voice. Philip Lord entered the room from outside. Framed in the doorway, he had an aurora of sunlight about his white hair, like the icon of an ancient saint. Gideon tasted bile in his mouth and, fists clenched, he mentally rehearsed all the good reasons he had for restraint. Any concern he might have held for Dutch and the women of Pethridge was consumed in a moment.

Dutch rose smiling. "Thank you, thank you, sir. My Beth—the bairns... I can't begin to tell you what this means to us. When word came you were here Schiavono, sir, I knew you'd find a way to save my Beth. You have done so much for us in the past."

Lord walked over and clapped Dutch on the back, as a comrade might. "You must go home, my friend, look to your children and tell them their mother will be coming home soon." Lord's words calmed the flow of effusive gratitude. "We will come shortly and do whatever may be done. You have my word."

"I will go with good heart and certainty, thanks to you, sir. And thank you, too, mister lawyer."

Dutch managed a bow to Lord so deep that it seemed a reverence, then had a lesser bow for Gideon and took his leave, escorted by Shiraz.

Lord crossed to the table and helped himself to bread and beer whilst Gideon found his own appetite suddenly diminished.

"*From ghoulies and ghosties and long-leggedy beasties, and things that go bump in the night—Good Lord, deliver us.* Or maybe," Lord said, his tone speculative, "this time it should be 'Good Lennox'?"

Had Gideon spoken the words that crowded upon his tongue there would have been no way back. It required all his training in the testing ground of the law, from the exercise of extremes of self-control to the rational application of internal rhetoric. That and the knowledge that the hardest fight could only be won by the clearest mind.

He drew a brief but steadying breath and pitched his tone as if addressing a dog. "If you are looking to rely on my legal skills, you should know they are not cheap and you should also understand that I know next to nothing of the law as it relates to maleficium. It's not something I have ever needed to deal with in London. Besides, for all I know these women are guilty. Until I have more than the pained words of a troubled man, I cannot promise any 'deliverance'. Then he added, with calculation: "It may be Dutch has been deceived himself, for we are told that even Satan can take the outward form of an angel of light."

Lord set down the mug of small ale and brushed some crumbs from his sleeve before replying.

"You will receive your fee, no need to concern yourself with that, for are we not also told, the labourer is worthy of his hire? And for the rest..." He sat back and surveyed Gideon thoughtfully. "I knew someone—one of the cleverest men I ever met—who held fast to the conviction that witches had nearly killed himself and his wife. He wrote a book about it. But even he would question all such accusations and dismiss most as superstition. Few rational men in this day and age would give credence to tales of the devil stalking the earth and talking to mad old beldames who love cats so he can help them curdle their neighbour's milk."

It was no real surprise to find Lord looking to defend the infernal through denying its existence. It was enough to make Gideon set aside all his own usual scepticism about such happenings.

"The church teaches that witches are amongst us. With the state of the world as it is, few rational men could doubt that the devil must have his minions on earth, working their evil on his behalf." Gideon heard his own voice sounding primly pious and disliked how much it reminded him of his father's preaching, so he added pointedly: "But an *atheist* might have such doubts."

"An atheist might," Lord agreed, "but so might a man of faith who uses the wits God has granted him. Besides, whatever is troubling Pethridge is not the work of Beth Sawyer. I have known her since before she married Dutch, and to accuse her of consorting with demons is as heretical as to suggest the Virgin Mary was an adulteress."

A character reference couched in blasphemy from Philip Lord didn't strike Gideon as any good grounds for removing suspicion.

"If you think so, then maybe you should handle it with your usual finesse," he said. "I am sure a few more dead bodies wouldn't lose you any sleep."

Lord sighed with extravagant exasperation.

"I have yet to lose any sleep over a single dead body. Only the living plague me."

Gideon rose leaving his food unfinished, all reserves of control exhausted. He felt unable to trust that he might not do or say something that would betray his true mind to his tormentor, the end result of which would undoubtedly be fatal. His feet carried him out of the main mill building and into the fresh air. He went in search of Zahara, needing to remind himself that something good and true resided here.

He found her sweeping out the fireplace in what passed for a kitchen. She looked as fresh and untainted as a dew-touched rose.

From the rafters above her hung bunches of herbs, small sacks of vegetables and cooking utensils. There was a well-scrubbed oak table that looked as though the rest of the kitchen had been built around it. The cooking hearth, with an oven to one side, was much as it must have been when a wealthy fuller's wife was baking there a couple of hundred years ago, before the mill race became a slow ooze.

Zahara turned as he entered her eyes storm-dark as if she was troubled but they lightened when she saw him.

"You will help that man and his wife?"

"Er—yes," he said, though in all honesty he had it half in mind to decline the task simply because Lord had demanded—no, worse, *assumed* it of him.

She nodded and brushed at the stone floor of the hearth. "It is not right for innocent people to be wrongly accused and punished. I am glad you are here to help them. The laws of the land must defend the weak against the rich and powerful."

Gideon wondered where in all that to start.

"It is the rich and powerful who write the laws," he told her. "But this—" He paused, shaking his head. "This is a law beyond man, it is a law of God. Men and women of all ranks have been hanged for witchcraft."

That prompted her to frown.

"But this woman is innocent. The Schiavono said—"

"He has no grounds to be so sure," Gideon spoke more sharply than he had intended. It would give him no small pleasure to be able to prove the man unarguably wrong in Zahara's eyes. "We all know the devil is clever and no one is safe from his wiles and false promises."

The emerald eyes widened, then she turned back to her sweeping. Gideon instantly regretted his tone. It was not her fault, after all, that she gave too much credence to Lord's words. He would have to earn her trust.

"I will look at what has been going on in Pethridge," he promised, wanting to sound conciliatory and chastened. "You are right. The innocent should not be falsely accused and left undefended. Nor should the guilty go free to benefit from their crimes and strike again."

She continued brushing the hearth, but half-turned her head towards him and gave a small nod. Then she stood and stooped to pick up the straw-lined basket of fine white ash. Gideon stepped in and lifted the basket from her. She glanced at him with suspicious surprise, before leading him out of the kitchen and showing him where to set the basket down on a small tub. There she poured a bucket of water over the ash to let the lye seep out into the tub below. When she was done she wiped her hands on her skirt and looked up at him.

"The Schiavono is right," she said quietly. "He told me you are a good man."

Zahara turned away and walked back into the kitchen.

Struck speechless by her words, Gideon didn't follow her. The time for talking about this was over. He needed to act.

At least his plans ran with those Lord had in mind, even if his motivation and intended outcome were completely different. He tried to recall all he knew of the law as it related to witchcraft. In most cases, as he recalled, conviction was based on confession, and if such was forthcoming on this occasion it would save him a great deal of effort. But even if not, the women had been arrested so there must be witnesses to condemn them and some proof of their deeds. That meant a visit to Pethridge was needed. Little as he wished it, he would have to speak to Lord.

Infuriatingly, the thought seemed more than enough to conjure the man.

When Gideon crossed back towards the main building, Lord was emerging from the stables holding the bridles of his own powerful mount and Gideon's slighter chestnut mare, as if they had already arranged to meet and ride out together.

"For I am formed from smokeless fire and named 'The Whisperer' amongst men." Lord tossed the reins of the chestnut to Gideon as he spoke. "Mount up, Giddy One—we have a people to deliver from bondage. Pethridge is not too far westwards into Weardale."

They were setting out shortly before mid-morning, the path Lord chose took them through less populated land, avoiding roads and well-used tracks. They rode in silence. Lord in front and Gideon making little attempt to keep close so long as he remained in sight. But sometime after they set out, at the edge of a coppice, Lord reined in and waited until the chestnut drew up to him.

There was a dipping valley to their right, well-tended land. At one end was a bustling village and at the other, set against the opposite slope, a large, fortified manor which showed distinct signs of recent rebuilding. Gideon knew the house at once.

The walled courtyard and kitchen gardens were

surrounded by dug ditches, with raised banks of earth. The old stone gatehouse was mounted with two small cannons, their sweep covering the only approach to the house which didn't require scrambling up a steep slope from the river that wound through the valley below. To Gideon, whose knowledge of military engineering began and ended with a fraught tort case over a lost ship carrying supplies to The Hague, it looked impregnable.

"Howe Hall," Lord said. "Ancestral home to the Coupland Clan, descended from a long line of rustlers, reivers and professional feuding folk, who became civilised gentry under the first Henry Tudor. Having enjoyed the passing privilege of knighthoods, they were finally established by a baronetcy, purchased with wealth achieved through generations of theft, extortion and blackmail." He paused as if considering. "I suppose that makes them the epitome of a successful family, were it not that the last of the line seems reluctant or unable to father the requisite heirs. Although who knows. He may yet engender a new generation of little Couplands should a beautiful enough estate with a virtuous dowry capture his heart." Lord fell silent and stared at the house for a moment, his expression unreadable. Then he shook his head. "Not that it matters. Through careful marriage the family has already assured an heir and a spare in nephews, with the eldest secured to the right of inheritance by letters patent. I speak, of course, of the redoubtable Tempest tribe, who can bring all Coupland's finer qualities and graces to the table, but no title beyond the occasional humble knighthood and substantially less wealth."

"And they all want you dead," said Gideon, with

powerful satisfaction. His tolerance for Lord's verbose whimsies at that point worn to a nub.

Lord shook his head, shivering the feathers on his plumed hat.

"No," he said, with total assurance. "They *want* much other than that. But being pragmatic to the core, it is what they will settle for. I have been keeping them from the opportunity to sin in such a manner, by the simple expedient of not being here. Let us pray that their souls may be delivered from temptation to that evil, now that I am again come amongst them."

"You should be praying for your own soul," Gideon said, stiffly. "To my mind it stands more sorely in need of rescue than Coupland's."

Lord laughed and turned his horse along the fringe of trees where they could ride invisible to those in the house.

"You are, perhaps, not wrong. But you will have to forgive me if I differ."

And that was all their conversation as they rode on, across ground that had never tasted the plough. Trees became increasingly sparse and the land was higher, bleaker and wilder. The only living creatures aside from themselves seemed to be sheep, until the outskirts of Pethridge came into view.

To Gideon's urban eyes, it was a village as any other—a church, a huddle of houses cowering together, and braver out-riding farms still cusped within the parish bounds but standing alone or with a sole companion close by.

If it was also a nest of the devil's minions there was nothing to betray that. No stench of sulphur. No ominous dark clouds overhead. No hideous screams or evil cackling and no grotesque familiars scuttling through the hedges. All looked peaceful in the soft golden light of mid-afternoon, on a September day that still harked back to summer rather than looking ahead to autumn.

"So how to proceed?" Lord asked as they neared the place and stopped by a stand of trees. "Do we beard the lion in his den like David? Or seek out the lie of the land as Caleb and Joshua?" He sounded guileless, but the goading needed no herald. As he had before, Gideon ignored it.

"I need to find out the exact nature and extent of the accusations. Hearsay from the accused woman's husband tells me little of the real value."

"Then you can be David and I will be Caleb," Lord said. "I will be in the copse of trees here when you are done. Try not to get yourself into too much trouble, Giddy One, and remember that the Lord is watching over you."

He turned his horse towards the hills and headed off at a brisk trot, leaving Gideon alone by the main road into the village.

Chapter Four

In his hunt for Philip Lord, Gideon had become adept at riding into communities like Pethridge and asking searching questions. Where many a London man might have needed an interpreter who could speak the strange northern dialect, with its language as close to Scots as to English, Gideon had the advantage of a Scottish father who often fell into such speech, leaving him able to understand enough to get by.

In this case, he barely needed to ask. The whole community was eager to share the news. All the people he spoke to seemed shocked and excited and many were more than a little frightened.

He learned the witchfinder was lodged with the vicar, who was an ailing man by all accounts and much overwhelmed by the events. The constable kept the accused women securely in his house until they could be moved to the gaol in Durham.

But, Gideon was told, there would be no point seeking out Reverend Fanthorpe at the parsonage. He was seen riding from there this morning, with one of those men of his and that nice Mistress Goody. They were out towards the Bothwell place to search for signs of witchcraft. That made the villagers wonder if Mary Bothwell was indeed by the way of being a witch. She did have all those cats she spoke to, and she had been a widow now these eighteen years, never looking to marry again. Not to mention she had a fearful temper and was much given to cursing at those who crossed her. And it was true, sometimes, those she had cursed at had taken harm, like Will Ridley who broke his leg and Agnes Bright who had lost a bairn the following summer. But then it had been Mary who had delivered her next safely and he was now a strapping lad.

As for the others, the villagers told him, who was to say? Beth Sawyer was an incomer. Dutch had brought her back from who knew where in his wild days. That said, she was a good neighbour, always happy to help. But who knew about her really? The Turner girls, poor motherless bairns they had been and run a bit wild no doubt. Leah was a good lass at heart, but she did have a tongue on her and always too pretty and knowing it. Ann could, for sure, be led astray. She was sometimes near wanton the way she talked to the boys. Some said she would never tell them no if her sister were not around.

Gideon listened to all the willing gossip then hesitated about continuing with his original intention of speaking first with Reverend Fanthorpe. A word with the constable might be of some value, but for now he had no wish to speak with the accused women. If guilty, they might find a way to influence him—and if innocent, then their inevitable tears and protests would do nothing to help him uncover the truth.

Constable Fulke Brierly lived in the largest house in the village: a fine stone-built, slate-roofed structure with two floors, a gated stableyard and an enclosed vegetable garden to the rear. It was known locally as the Priory. Just over a century ago it would have housed an outlying religious community, but now it was a pleasantly modernised family dwelling.

Constable Brierly himself wasn't at home but his mother made Gideon welcome, especially upon hearing he was a lawyer from London, there with a legal interest in the witchcraft problem. He declined her offer of food, but she still took him into the hall, perhaps thinking it unfitting to entertain a man alone in the parlour.

"I have no mind how to deal with this whole thing," she said, sitting by the big hearth, her hands moving as she spoke. "Demons, devils and dead animals. Terrible business, Mister—?"

"David," Gideon supplied. The constable's mother gave a vague smile, her grey head bobbing. She reminded Gideon of a rabbit. Small and slight, dark-eyed, with grey-flecked light brown hair contained under a lace-edged cap.

"Indeed. Mr David. We've not been here long, my son received this lovely house when he was appointed to deputise the work of moormaster last year, so I cannot speak for or against these women. But they always seemed nice enough to me."

"Moormaster?" Gideon had heard the term before somewhere, but in the moment it escaped him.

"Oh yes—he has charge of the lead mines and the smelting for Sir Bartholomew Coupland who handles the rights to the mines on behalf of the Duke of Richmond. A most important job, every piece of ore must be accounted for. Of course the bishop sends his own man as well to see he gets his share, but the chief part of the work falls to my Fulke. That's where he will be now. Tis not easy for him going all up and down the dales, but Sir Bartholomew thinks highly of him and will trust no other to do it."

THE MERCENARY'S BLADE

Gideon remembered then. It was one of the matters he had touched on with the Hostmen in Newcastle. Some who had interests in coal also held an interest in lead. If he recalled, the moormaster was entitled to grant the right to each lead mine and would have rich profit on the ore extracted, as it had to be sold to him for smelting.

He was thinking how wealthy that must make Coupland when the constable's mother spoke again.

"Does your wife not miss you, being away so long?" The enquiry came with a small rodent smile.

"I am not married," Gideon said, a moment before the sudden predatory gleam in her eye made him realise his mistake. He countered quickly with a distraction. "There have been no confessions from these women accused then?"

The constable's mother shook her head with a hen-like jiggle.

"No. Not a one. But Reverend Fanthorpe says that it may take a while for them to be brought to see the need to do so. In the meantime, he seeks the evidence in their homes and questions their families and friends. But he is quite sure they are witches. Quite sure."

"Why is he so certain?"

"Well, that is it, you see," she said, hands fluttering. "I am not sure how much is known and I am not one to gossip."

Gideon nodded gravely, thinking that if he had a groat for every time he had heard that kind of thing, he would be a rich man. But he knew the game and how to play it.

"That is to your credit," he said, as sincerely as he could. "I applaud your reticence and discrimination.

Common tongues can wag rumour into ruin. You are right to say nothing about it to anyone."

The constable's mother blinked and looked put out. Then no doubt seeing a path ahead, she smiled again.

"Yes. But you are a man of law and these matters are not just idle chat to you, are they? I am sure I would be duty bound to pass on to you what little I know, so that the courts can hear the truth."

Gideon had made no claim to anything other than an interest in the matter, but he didn't trouble to remind her of that. Instead, he repeated his grave nod and murmured agreement about the courts needing to know the truth. It took some gentle, round-about questioning and a little reading between the lines, because Mistress Brierly was neither that well informed nor someone used to reporting things in any orderly manner, but he pieced together the story and filled in patches with things he had learned from Dutch.

Since the end of August, an uncertain number of sheep—some said six or seven some said more—had died with no known cause. Each had been found with the severed head of a dead cat close by. Someone as yet unknown, for Mistress Brierly swore it wasn't herself or her son, had sent for Reverend Fanthorpe. He was a Puritan parson turned out from his living from looking more to Geneva than Canterbury for his spiritual guidance. The exact location of his previous benefice was unknown but was 'somewhere down south'. He had arrived in Pethridge a week before with his two men and Mistress Goody and examined the places where the sheep were found.

THE MERCENARY'S BLADE

Then two nights ago, Reverend Fanthorpe and Mistress Goody woke the constable's household, he being then at home, and asked to place four women in security in the house as they had been overheard planning further acts of witchcraft. They claimed to be assisting at a birth but there was no trace of any woman in labour or any recently delivered and no one knew anything of a messenger arriving for Widow Bothwell with word of such a woman in need.

In Mistress Brierly's opinion, it all seemed sure evidence against the four taken up by the witchfinder.

Gideon nodded and agreed it seemed most strange. Indeed, in his own mind, unless there was something missing from the tale, it sounded damning. These women might truly be servants of the devil. A shiver of apprehension lifted the hair on his forearms when he realised they were held in this very house.

"You're not troubled at being alone here with these witches?" he asked.

"Oh no. I'm not alone with them at all." She sounded eager to reassure. "Reverend Fanthorpe leaves Mistress Goody to tend them and she is well versed in the finding and containing of witches. She sees to all their needs. She prays with them, exhorts them to confess and repent so they may save their souls. And if ever she is gone, a man is left to guard the locked door."

Gideon was surprised such a task should be entrusted by Fanthorpe to any assistant, especially a female one, when surely the soul-saving was part of his work.

"Who is Mistress Goody?"

The hands fluttered. "She is so well named. Such a caring person. She kept house for Reverend Fanthorpe before he was removed from his place and held such faith in him that she followed him into his new calling. She wants to bring peace to the torment she says these witches must suffer at the hands of their imps. Reverend Fanthorpe regards it as unfitting for a man to make examination of a woman, until the charge is certain, and he trusts her to do that. Oh, but you should see her distress when the poor women are screaming their innocence. She cannot do enough for them in their misery, asking me for blankets and warm food so she can take it to them with her own hands. Even a small brazier so they wouldn't catch the cold when she must examine their bodies for witchmarks. And she will let no one but herself be with them and wait on their needs."

"Is that not rather dangerous for her?" Gideon was thinking that for four women to overpower one, even without the aid of demonic magic, would not be too difficult.

"Mistress Goody is secure in her faith, And when she is with them Reverend Fanthorpe's two young men will always be close by the door." She lowered her voice as if worried someone might overhear her "I know the good woman has had to call them in at least the once, for I took them refreshment last night and they were not standing outside the door—and the sounds from within." She covered her mouth and drew back. "And above it all Mistress Goody praying as loud as she could."

Gideon tried to recall what he knew of witches and how they were accused and proven.

"And has she found marks of a witch on any of them?"

The Constable's mother fluttered her hands and shook her head.

THE MERCENARY'S BLADE

"Well, that I don't know, for she has not said. Reverend Fanthorpe did tell me that it might be the marks only appear when the imps come to feed. I think they were intending to try to capture one of the cats that live with Widow Bothwell, which is why they have gone that way today."

There was little more Gideon felt he could learn here. Thanking his hostess, he took his leave, although she insisted on escorting him to the stableyard and took the opportunity to tell him of her daughter. An uncommonly attractive young woman of a gentle nature and modest demeanour, as yet unmarried but well of an age to be so, who was staying in Newcastle with a relative. It was safer in these more troubled times, at least until all the talk of war was past. But if Gideon came again, as he must to talk with her son over this matter of witches, they would be sure to meet.

Gideon disentangled himself with a vague promise to arrange a date to do so on some future visit to the village and was glad when he could mount the chestnut and head away from the house.

The path to Widow Bothwell's was easy enough to find. By then it was getting late into the afternoon and he was regretting not having accepted the offer of food. As well as hunger, his thoughts were poor companions for the ride.

He knew very well that the enmity of neighbours was an easy explanation for many accusations of witchcraft, but there was no evidence that these women were hated. All he had heard in the village so far, and from the constable's mother, was the sort of things people will always say when someone they know is accused of a crime. The same mix of disbelief mingled with over-examination of minor failings that would have earned no comment if the individual hadn't been under suspicion. It told him nothing of their innocence or guilt, except that no one had accused the women of any link to witchcraft before they were taken.

The shadows were getting longer when he heard voices.. A small group was making its way along the path behind him, some mounted and some afoot. It was not hard to identify the leader of the group.

Reverend Fanthorpe looked morose, much more so than was required for professional purposes. He sat heavily in the saddle, face thunderous as if a dark storm cloud rode with him. Behind him and on foot came a broad-shouldered man, armed and dour. He was leading a piebald mule, on which sat a large woman with apple cheeks, who by her dress might well have been the matron of a pious Puritan household. The rest of the party was made up by half a dozen of the village men, some of whom Gideon had spoken with before his visit to the Priory. They looked uncomfortable and ill at ease, as if undertaking a task that they would much rather avoid.

Gideon introduced himself to the witchfinder under his assumed name, indicating that he was known to Constable Brierly's mother and had just been to visit her. He was rewarded with a terse nod.

"Is witchcraft right enough," said Fanthorpe. "Clear marks of it. When I am done they will have no defence to call upon except their devils and those have no power over true Christian souls."

Behind him, the woman on the mule shook her head and sighed as if the whole matter was a personal tragedy.

THE MERCENARY'S BLADE

"The ones you accuse have confessed?" Gideon asked.

"Not yet. But they will when they see they have nothing to gain from withholding the truth." Fanthorpe's tone of conviction was absolute.

Behind him, the woman sighed again.

"The poor lost lambs. I beg them on my bended knees in heartfelt prayer to confess, repent and open themselves to God's forgiveness. They are weak flesh, and ignorant. Why they would soon as say 'Ave Maria' before 'Our Father'. 'Tis no surprise they have fallen into such sin, such could engulf the whole nation soon enough with the king half-way to Rome led by his popish wife."

Fanthorpe said nothing, his lips tightening into a harsh line. The villagers looked uncomfortable, but then the words probably pared them too close to the bone.

"There is much evidence?" Gideon asked.

The woman sniffed and wiped at her eyes. Fanthorpe nodded with a short upward jerk of the head.

"I would be interested to know what it might be."

"Why would a London man be quite so interested in this affair?" The question came from Mistress Goody and seemed to hold much doubt that his interest was genuine or impartial. But it was a question Gideon had expected someone to ask him at some point and he was prepared for it.

"There are too many today willing to scorn God's word and set witchcraft aside as foolish superstition. The last case I know of, eight years ago, although the witches were found guilty under law and each condemned a maleficium, they were then brought to London and examined by physicians who declared that they had nothing wrong with them and so went free."

This was clearly not news to Mistress Goody, who nodded, but one or two of the village men looked shocked to hear it.

"I do not wish to see that happen here," Gideon explained. "A jury of physicians should never be allowed to overset the judgement of the law." He paused to add the simple truth. "I believe there may well be witchcraft at work and I want to be able to prove so."

Fanthorpe stared at him intently, as if he thought Gideon might have something to conceal that could be revealed to observant eyes. Whatever it was he looked for he seemed satisfied because he nodded.

"We are going to the place we believe was their meeting house. A village lad saw lights up there some evenings. He came by and saw it lit up within and the women enter. He held his tongue until today, but God showed him he should speak. Ride with me. Let me reveal to you something of what we are facing here."

"Gladly," Gideon said. "It is important I see the truth of this."

He joined the small cavalcade and would have ridden alongside Fanthorpe, had Mistress Goody not called to him.

"Mr David, might I ask what brings you from London?"

He slowed and let her mule come up beside him. It wasn't happy to be made to walk by his mount. It flattened its ears and would have even tried a nip had the man leading it not cuffed its head and pulled it away. Gideon steadied the chestnut with a reassuring hand before answering.

"I have some business in the area and heard of this case. Having an interest, I thought to see what was going on."

THE MERCENARY'S BLADE

It was not enough of an answer to satisfy, but Mistress Goody would be hard-pressed to probe further without seeming rude. She let it lie. Instead, she said:

"There are those who believe that if a witch is but arrested and detained by due process of law, it will break the enchantments. The old way was to scratch her. Shed her blood to finish it. That always worked."

Gideon felt as though he was being tested.

"If the bewitchment requires that the witch is free and able to consort with minions and familiars, then it would stand to reason confinement would end it," he said.

"But why then only legal confinement?"

"If the confinement isn't legal then how can any be sure it is either adequate or deserved? It can never be right for anyone to kidnap and imprison their neighbour on mere accusation. Who is then to say the deed is not done from malice? The law is needed to ensure justice and the effectiveness of the confinement."

Mistress Goody fell silent for a while as they went on. Fanthorpe turned along a side track which seemed to lead away from where Gideon had been told the widow's modest cottage could be found.

"Who was it who summoned you here so timely?" he asked.

"Constable Brierly."

Something Brierly had not bothered to tell his mother.

"He must have been sorely troubled by these events."

Mistress Goody nodded. "Indeed so. He is a God-fearing man with care for the woes of his neighbours and the work of the Lord. Tis a shame we couldn't have been here sooner, to stop the worst of the evil."

Something in the way she put emphasis on her words sent a tingle of apprehension down from Gideon's shoulders to where his hands gripped the reins. Beneath his shirt, his forearms prickled as the hair on them lifted.

"The worst?" He echoed.

"Reverend Fanthorpe believes we have yet to discover what manner of foulness they practised in this den of theirs."

"What manner...?" Gideon didn't finish the question. He was suddenly far from certain that he wanted to hear the answer. The fast-fading afternoon carried a cold breeze, but that was not the reason he felt a slight shiver.

"We shall see," Mistress Goody said firmly. It was clear she had no doubt in her own mind that they would find something damning in the place they were headed.

The track had grown steeper and the land bleaker, until they could look back down to the church and houses now small enough to fit in two cupped hands. Fanthorpe stopped below the brow of the hill and dismounted. Gideon did likewise, and the man leading Mistress Goody's mule helped her from its back, before collecting the reins of all three animals.

The sun was barely visible now, although its light was still enough to see by. Fanthorpe gestured to his small flock of villagers who gathered around him in awkward silence. Mistress Goody moved to take a place beside him, whilst Gideon found himself standing apart from the group to the other side. Fanthorpe stood very straight and closed his eyes, lowering his head as if his neck was too stiff, and clasped his hands.

"Oh Lord, keep your watch over your servant that I may do your work as is your will. Amen."

THE MERCENARY'S BLADE

Belatedly, Gideon bowed his head and joined in the murmured 'amen'. Fanthorpe continued with no pause for breath.

"Oh Lord, if thou shouldst but enter into judgement with us, and search out our natural corruption, and observe all the cursed fruits and effects that we have derived from thence..."

The prayer went on for a long time and Gideon again joined in with the 'Amen.'

The small group then joined with Fanthorpe as he went on to recite the Lord's Prayer. Somehow, standing in that bleak spot, high above a village riddled with witchcraft, it seemed a fitting thing to ask to be delivered from evil. It certainly satisfied Fanthorpe, for his demeanour had changed.

"We leave the horses here. I'd not wish to take any mindless creature where we are going. Who knows what could possess them. I will tell you now that I was today at the house of one of the witches—the one called Bothwell. Her house is the run of imps and familiars in the form of cats, many in the village have told me that. That house was full of evil brews, jars and pots, poisons and potions, but this place may be worse. Quiet now."

As he finished speaking Fanthorpe led the way over towards what Gideon would have taken for a long-abandoned cottage. Only the unmistakable bite of fresh burnt peat in the air gave any clue that this might have been recently occupied.

They walked the last part of the way with Fanthorpe's broad strides setting the pace, Gideon beside him. On the edge of an overgrown vegetable garden, he thrust out a hand across Gideon's chest, like a barricade.

The building was uncannily silent. Gideon felt as though even in the fading light of the afternoon, a darker darkness was curled up inside, watching them. He noticed—or thought he noticed—the door that was standing ajar, move a little wider of its own accord. The sun, which had dipped close into the horizon, was swallowed abruptly by a cloud and a cold breeze stirred.

Despite himself, Gideon shivered and he heard Fanthorpe draw in a sharp breath. The hand that had been a barrier moved to his shoulder, fatherly and reassuring.

"Wait here. I sense a presence of evil and will proceed with prayer."

Gideon murmured a few prayers of his own as the black-clad man strode past the tumbled-down garden wall, looking like a prophet from the Old Testament. Gideon had heard the phrase 'armoured in righteousness' used by his father when he preached, but this was the first time he had seen someone fit the words. It gave him some small reassurance and comfort to see the confidence of Reverend Fanthorpe's stride.

The witchfinder's tall-crowned hat was too high to let him walk straight into the hovel, and he stopped on the threshold. He pushed open the door to look within. A trail of smoke coiled out from it as he did so, the smell reaching Gideon's nose a moment later. It smelt of decay and sulphur.

He saw Fanthorpe take a step back. Even sheltered by his extreme faith, the physical effect of the stench must be hard to endure. The expression on the witchfinder's face was one of slight puzzlement rather than fear, but he seemed less certain than before when he approached the door a second time.

THE MERCENARY'S BLADE

If Fanthorpe's certainty had given Gideon courage to face the unknown, his obvious hesitation began to erode it. A single coarse crow called, sudden and insistent, from behind the cottage and Gideon felt shadows reaching out towards him. Whatever he may have held by way of doubt was being stifled with each extra moment he stood there.

The witchfinder stepped into the cottage.

The yell that followed wasn't Fanthorpe's but was very human and frightened. It broke the spell that had frozen Gideon in place. He crossed the ground at a run and entered the dark hovel.

The only light within came from a crude peat fire in the old hearth and the stench came from it too. The dull glow was sufficient to reveal an almost empty room—empty aside from a half-rotted table, too solid to have yet decayed away and too big to have been salvaged easily. It was supported by a heap of debris beneath. Close beside the hearth was curled a ragged figure, by all appearances roused from sleep with the intrusion of Fanthorpe.

"What are you doing here?" Fanthorpe demanded, his voice harsh. The only answer was a whine and the human bundle curled itself tightly. Fanthorpe directed a hard kick into the rags, his face distorted in fury and by the shadow.

"What is it Reverend Fanthorpe?" Mistress Goody asked from the doorway. She held a covered lantern which cast more brightness in the gloomy interior. "What devilry is there here?"

She stopped and looked shocked by the sight of the vagrant. Beneath the brim of her hat, her eyes glanced to the table then back to the human rag-pile in disbelief.

"What is he doing in here?" she demanded.

Fanthorpe shook his head, turned and pushed his way from the room, the dark, brooding anger still about him like a cloak. Gideon stepped aside to let him pass. Maybe a man who came armed to fight demons could feel so cheated to discover them absent. A couple of the village men had come in.

Mistress Goody pointed at the creature curled in terror by the hearth. "Maybe that is one of the witches."

The man nearest the hearth bent over and pulled at the bundle, which quivered and made mewling sounds of terror. With help from his companion and a few hard blows they managed to unravel the figure, despite his wailing pleas which intensified as his shirtless torso emerged. Gideon got a glimpse of filthy skin, purpled with bruises and old scars ridged into the flesh. This wasn't the first time the unfortunate had fallen foul of his fellow man. The man who had uncovered him dropped him back to the floor where he remained half-naked and shivering.

"Never seen him before, Mistress, looks like he's a simpleton and half out of what wits he still has."

She took a step closer to see for herself but Gideon's sense of propriety was faster.

"It is not a fitting sight for any woman," he told her. "There is no need for you to be here."

"Aye, mistress," one of the other men agreed. "If there is anything to be found out from him we will do so, be sure of that."

THE MERCENARY'S BLADE

For a moment, Gideon thought Mistress Goody was going to protest. But then she nodded and let Gideon take her outside. The other village men were clustered around the door. Two of them took the chance to go in, whilst the rest stood uncertain as Fanthorpe hovered like a bird of prey, beyond them.

"There is nothing here," he said as the men moved aside to let Mistress Goody pass them. "Nothing at all." His tone was vexed, as if the lack of demons was a personal affront to him. Mistress Goody was silent, her expression invisible under the brim of her hat.

"That vagrant should be whipped," he added with coldness, gesturing at the house from which pathetic whimpers could be heard. Gideon found himself perturbed at the idea of venting anger on the pitiable creature he had glimpsed.

"You are sure this is the place they met?" he asked. Fanthorpe gave him a dark look.

"So I was told."

"Then perhaps the women did no more than meet and plot here. You said you had found much evidence at one of their houses. Perhaps that was where they did whatever they did."

Fanthorpe gave a non-committal grunt and glanced at the woman.

"What are your thoughts, Mistress Goody?"

Her thoughts remained unknown, because the men came out of the cottage with news. It turned out one of their company could vouch that the half-wit had arrived in the village that very day and another had seen him begging for bread. He claimed someone had told him he could find shelter for the night here.

"He knows nothing of witches. Thought it was just an old empty place."

"As it is," Gideon observed dryly. There was a short, taut silence.

"We have seen all there is here," Mistress Goody agreed. "Should we not be letting these good people return to their own homes, Reverend Fanthorpe? And Mr David, tis getting late to be riding far, I am sure there could be room found for you in the constable's house."

Gideon thanked her and declined the offer, then stood in thoughtful silence as Fanthorpe said some long-winded prayers. After, as he mounted the chestnut mare, Gideon observed a brief conversation between Mistress Goody and the man who had led her mule. It could have been about the behaviour of the vile-tempered animal, but Gideon doubted that. By the time the group approached the path where they would turn to the village, Mistress Goody was managing the reins of the mule with her own capable hands.

Compassion and curiosity nudged for attention in Gideon's mind, both in the same direction. He made his farewells, saying his fastest way lay in a straight ride, not one through Pethridge. Then he took a moment to be sure Fanthorpe's small flock were headed away before wheeling back along the path. The chestnut was tired but not unwilling and gave a good burst of speed so that he was back by the abandoned building only a few minutes after he had left it.

THE MERCENARY'S BLADE

Chapter Five

A moving lantern outlined the figure of a man walking towards the doorway of the ruin. The figure turned to glance back, then ducked into the building. Looping his horse's reins on the bushes by the tumbledown garden wall, Gideon wondered if he was being foolhardy or maybe simply foolish. The thought was enough to make him hesitate, but not to hold him back.

"Hello?" he called. There was no reply, but now the door glowed from within. That at least made Gideon feel braver about approaching. With light inside he would be able to see before he entered, and that was much more comfortable than stepping into a dark enclosed space.

The scene within was innocent enough. The ragged figure they had first found sleeping by the hearth had pulled itself into the nearest corner and was curled up and rocking slightly. The man Mistress Goody had sent back seemed to be ignoring his presence and was looking around the empty room as if seeking something lost.

When Gideon's shadow filled the room he turned, unsurprised, all expression closed on his life-hardened face.

"You," Gideon made the word sound like an accusation. "You're Fanthorpe's man. You were leading Mistress Goody's mule. What on earth are you doing back here?"

The voice of confident authority made the other man shift his weight uneasily, but he wasn't cowed and had an answer ready.

"Mistress Goody sent me for charity's sake," he said, gesturing to the wretched creature in the corner. "She asked me to see to him."

Gideon let the face value of that claim shine to advantage.

"Then your mistress and I are of a mind," he said. "The men were none too gentle with him in asking their questions. Though I admit I have little enough about me that would be of any use. Did she send you with anything?"

The other man shook his head, his eyes uneasy.

"She just said to see how he was. And, I will do so, sir, there is no need for you to trouble yourself over it."

Which was Gideon's clear cue to take his leave in relief, having shed the burden of unwanted guilt onto the shoulders of another. Instead, there was an awkward silence as he remained standing by the door. He let it hold for a few moments then made a slight shrugging gesture.

"Don't let me keep you from your task," he said. The man looked uncomfortable.

"I am thinking that there is little more I can do anyway, sir," he admitted.

Gideon let himself appear thoughtful.

"You have been charged to look to this poor creature's wellbeing. It isn't a long way to the village and your coat would serve him well. Leave him that for warmth."

"My coat?" the man sounded disbelieving.

Gideon nodded.

"Well, I can hardly leave him mine." He reached for his purse. "Here, this will go some way towards replacing it, and your mistress will be sure to see you are not the worse

THE MERCENARY'S BLADE

for charity done on her behalf."

For a moment he saw blank refusal in the other man's face, but then the coins were snatched from his hand and the man shrugged himself out of the coat, which was well worn enough that he should have been glad of the price Gideon offered him for it. He dropped the coat over the shivering heap in the corner and picked up the lantern, ill-hidden resentment clear on his face.

"I'll be going then. The reverend and Mistress Goody will want me to look to their mounts. I can see you safe to the village, sir."

Gideon shook his head.

"No need, my way doesn't take me there. You go back to your duty and your rest."

The man looked unhappy but lit the way back to where Gideon had left his chestnut without protest, and helped him to mount, before making a final, rather surly farewell. Gathering his reins, but not riding off, Gideon watched the lantern's glow make its way along the path until a turn took it from sight. He wondered how far the man might go before returning to complete whatever task he had in mind and the retrieval of his coat. He also wondered what on earth he himself was thinking he could achieve in the dark in this place, and indeed if his whole reasoning for returning at all was flawed.

He glanced back at the cottage, a humped outline with no features. Then the hairs on the back of his neck bristled as if a sudden chill had touched the exposed flesh. But it was not a physical cold. A new glow of light, much fainter than the lantern but much more than could be given by the embers of the fire, shimmered and then was extinguished. Had he not stood within the walls himself scant minutes before, the images of demons and witches with which this place had been invested would have taken full hold. As it was, he needed to grip the steel surety of his own memory to silence the clamour.

Gideon slid from the chestnut again, who snuffled at him, wanting to be away to her own food and rest. Making her a silent promise that it wouldn't be much longer, he left her and made a stealthy approach to the cottage door. He was right outside it when a familiar voice spoke softly from within, holding a trace of mocking laughter.

"He that has pity upon the poor gives unto the Lord; and that which he has given will he pay him."

Gideon's heart lurched in his chest with a grimness that contained anger and understanding in equal measure. Philip Lord was wearing the coat Gideon had just purchased for him, his hair, brought out from under the concealing knitted border bonnet which had disguised it so well, held a living shimmer of silver in the light of the candle stub that was set on the table. He was crouched over something that he was retrieving from concealment beneath the pile of rubble under the table.

"You should come and see. It was a masque designed for you after all. Or if not for you, for whoever else Fanthorpe could inveigle here. You handed him the perfect witness—a London lawyer whose word no one would doubt."

He knew it was going to be unpleasant, but Gideon was still unprepared for the gruesome array. Spread out on the cloth of the fine shirt Lord had been wearing when they set out from the mill, now ruined by spoilage from its use beneath the rubbish under the table, were the grisly relics

THE MERCENARY'S BLADE

of some unknown demonic rite. Three cat's heads—eyes glazed in death, a clay figure, with its scalp decorated by a lock of human hair. And, in a basin of congealing blood, was something the size of Gideon's fist. Tiny, with perfectly formed fingers and toes.

Gideon took a moment to recognise what it was and then he was out of that place and vomiting violently. Over and over until nothing more could emerge. The spasms passed after a few minutes, but the trace-stench of peat smoke brought back the image of the horror in the bowl and his body wracked itself some more with dry retching.

The moon had risen and worked hard to soften the world around him, blending shadows in a pallet of greys. Skeletal bushes, bearing banners from the lost battle for summer, clutched at the star-speckled sky. A dog barked in the distance. Nearby a horse snorted. Gideon stood, breathing hard, his throat burning and his stomach sore. Facing away from the cottage because the sight of it was unbearable, he felt as if part of himself had been voided with the vomit.

"We must leave. Our friend may well have gone back to the village, but he might also decide to return. It would be awkward if he were to find us here." Lord stood holding the chestnut's bridle.

A body without a will of its own, Gideon accepted the reins of the little mare. Lord led the way on foot, around the village of Pethridge. Questions kept forming in Gideon's mind, like bubbles in a pan set to boil. But before he could quite give them form and purpose they were gone again. A large part of him wanted to mount up and ride hard away—anywhere, no matter where, but far away from the horror. However, the ruling part of his mind had developed a stubborn need to know, to bring someone to account for what he had seen.

"Schiavono." Dutch's voice came from the shadows ahead and then the man himself was beside them. He led them to a stone-built shed from which the light of a covered lantern gave a welcoming glow. Lord's horse was tethered outside.

"It's the old bulb store," Dutch informed them. "So is warm and dry. It was always out of sight and no one comes here. I brought a lantern and have left food and blankets but couldn't do much more. I'd stay but our Pippa, for all she is a good lass, I don't like to leave her to mind the rest of the bairns alone for long. You'll be safe here though—the dogs'll set up a terror of barking if anyone comes."

As he spoke he went to Gideon's horse and would have begun the work of removing the saddle, but Lord put a hand on his arm to stop him.

"Go to your children, We will look after the horses. And thank you."

For a moment Dutch seemed half inclined to argue, torn between duties, but then he released the leather girth and stepped back.

"No need to thank me, sir. You are doing all this for my Beth."

Then he was gone into the night, needing no light to find the way on his own land. Lord removed the saddle, pulled some dry grass and began to rub the chestnut down. He pulled some more after the first handful seemed no more use and thrust some at Gideon who felt as empty as a ghost—aware of, but not engaged with what was going on around him.

THE MERCENARY'S BLADE

"Please tell me you know how to look after a horse?"

The tone stung Gideon back to some sense of reality. He snatched the grass and tended the mare. Once he had checked and cleaned her hooves, he took her to drink from a trough that lay beside the shed.

When he went inside, Lord was already sitting on an upturned tub in the small pool of light provided by the lantern, eating what Dutch had provided. A bottle of some unknown spirits was set on the ground beside Lord, the reek of it already on his breath. His posture looked stiff as he gestured to another tub nearby, tipping his hand to suggest that Gideon make his own seat from it. As he did so Lord took a deep swig from the bottle and held it out. Gideon shook his head. His stomach was too raw to face food, let alone anything stronger.

"This place was a small gold-mine for Dutch once," Lord said amiably, lifting the hand with the bottle to gesture to the room they were in. "That is how he got his name. He grew tulips. He would ship the bulbs to a trader in Haarlem who made ten or a hundred times as much again on them. But Dutch made good enough money from it. It was the height of the United Provinces' expensive love affair with the tulip." He paused to take a pull on the pottery bottle before going on. "They'd built an invisible market around the bulbs, not just buying and selling the tulips themselves, but a market of promises to buy and sell them—promises which themselves could then be bought and sold. Fortunes were made."

To Gideon it seemed too incongruous to be talking about tulips with the horror of what he had seen still stamped in his mind. So he said nothing and after a few moments Lord went on speaking.

"Dutch would ship them from Whitby on a smuggling vessel I owned. That was where he met Beth, she was a Whitby tavern keeper's daughter. Half the men in that town and a fair part of those who sailed in and out of there set out to woo her, but it was Dutch who carried her home."

The memory must have been a good one, because he smiled as it came to him. And the smile had a warmth that Gideon had never yet seen on that brutally controlled face, melting the uncompromising mask into brief humanity. Then, even as it was born, the warmth and the smile vanished again and Lord gave a shrug.

"Four years ago, one winter morning in thirty-seven, no one turned up to buy the promises and tulips were just flowers again." Lord took another pull on the bottle and sighed. "Since then Dutch has struggled. There is not so much money to be made running a few sheep on Weardale."

For the love of God, what was with the man?

"That would explain it then," Gideon said. He was sure now that all this was an effort by Lord to distract him from what they had seen in the tumbledown cottage, as if not talking of it would make it any less terrible.

"Explain what?" Lord sounded nonplussed.

"Explain why his wife would turn to witchcraft, because what I saw in that place *was* witchcraft," Gideon said, grim now and sure of his ground. "Whatever false part Fanthorpe may be playing in bringing it to light, that is the place those women met. They were seen there by a witness—and I will see them hang for it."

Lord groaned as if with a pain that couldn't be contained. He buried his face in both his hands, from where his voice came muffled, close to the edge of endurance.

"For the love of God, Lennox. You saw the blood." Lord lifted his face, gaunt and riven by shadow. "It was *fresh*."

Then in a single smooth movement Lord rose and crossed to the door, slipping into the darkness as an otter into water. One moment he was there in the room and the next Gideon was alone with the remains of the meal Dutch had prepared for them.

The wind was fresh from over the Durham Dales, fresh enough that Nick Tempest worried about his hat. It wouldn't impress these men to see their new commander's fine plumes cartwheeling away over the grass and mud of the bailey. He had been explaining the need to find Philip Lord in terms such men could understand—that they hunted a wanted man who was desperate, dangerous and unlikely to submit peacefully.

The men he had been given, twelve of them hand-picked by his uncle for the task, were a curious mix of the capable and the unsuitable—or at least unsuitable at first impression. But Nick had been told that amongst mercenaries, the fashion was for overdone apparel as a mark of their success. If that were indeed the truth, then he had some extremely successful soldiers in the group before him.

There were also some who were simply a pox inflicted upon him.

"So we need to find this lad afore he turns to murdering?"

The one they called Mags—not given to showy clothes,

but much given to opening his mouth and asking awkward questions. If it were not that the rest of the men seemed to defer to him with reverence and follow his lead in all things, Nick would have dismissed him and been done. He had been a late arrival the previous morning. Just after Sir Bartholomew had ridden out with the pick of the men of Howe and surrounding Weardale lands, Mags had appeared and offered his services.

Having been accepted, he then came close to causing a revolt, stirring up an argument about overdue pay. Nick resolved that problem by handing out the boots his uncle had commissioned to provide for his personal troop, but which had arrived too late. Much too fine for the rag-tag of men left to him, and of a size that meant most needed to stuff them with cloth or straw to ensure a fit, they had at least fended off a crisis, prompted by Mags, which could have seen Nick deprived of even this small command.

"He's already turned to murder."

The cold voice from behind Nick seemed to hold criticism of himself for allowing a question. It was also an unwelcome reminder that although this was nominally his independent command, in truth he still had his uncle's eyes upon him in the form of Sergeant Hoyle.

He had hoped Hoyle was gone with his uncle for he hadn't been around the Hall yesterday. But this morning Nick woke to find him returned. He had put into Nick's hands a note from his uncle to the effect that he should heed well the advice Hoyle should offer. Which really meant Nick should obey him in everything or have a good reason for failing to do so.

"We need to find Lord and stop him," Nick said, doing

his best to ignore the interruption. "Lord's agenda is to prey upon the inevitable confusion of these troubled times.Whoever finds him, your purse will be much the heavier for it."

Mags nodded good-naturedly. "I'm always happy to have something heavy swinging down by my thighs that will please the women."

Laughter rippled and spread.

"Have a care," Hoyle barked, and mirth evaporated into a resentful silence. Nick allowed it to stretch for a good few moments longer than was needed, in order to assert his own authority. Then he spoke quietly, so the men needed to keep the silence to catch his words.

"There is someone out there who knows where we can find this man. Maybe the whore he slept with last night or the farrier who tended his horse." As he spoke Nick paced along the line of men, making eye contact with each, though most looked down or away when he did so. "He must eat, drink and sleep like the rest of us, and that means he will have to leave a mark somewhere. If you hear word of a stranger seen passing by, or an unknown guest staying at a house, follow it through."

After he had dismissed the men and they were making final preparations to ride out, Nick remained by the brooding walls of the bailey which surrounded his uncle's house, a house which would one day be his. Hoyle found him there.

"That was well enough done, aside you allowed Mags his head. That one is a troublemaker. Too sure of himself and too popular with the men. He needs taking down a peg or two." Nick fell back through time to the days when Hoyle had been given the charge of educating him in the use of sword and firearms. But Nick was no longer twelve years old, and he was no longer willing to allow a man such as Hoyle to rule him.

"Thank you, sergeant," he said, coldly.

Hoyle nodded then carried on talking in the same over-familiar manner.

"I'll be happy to see to it, if you give me the word."

Irritated, Nick's gaze passed over Hoyle and to the figure approaching behind him. "I will speak to him myself."

Hoyle turned, following Nick's gaze. The man they called Mags was sauntering towards them in an unhurried way, heavy wool cassaque flung back over one shoulder revealing the well-worn buff coat he wore beneath. The faded sash tied around it held a pistol, and a long-bladed sword swung as he walked. Like the others in the troop, he was wearing the new boots, rolled down from their protective length into bucket-tops. From under the drooping brim of his hat emerged long brown hair, flecked through with a peppering of grey. His weather-beaten face was half hidden by a crudely trimmed beard.

As he reached them, Mags swept off his hat, revealing a patch of scarred flesh on his scalp where the hair could no longer grow. He replaced his hat with a muttered apology and looked up at Nick.

"I can find the man you are hunting, sir."

"Finding him is what you are being paid for," Nick agreed.

Mags scratched at his chin and glanced at Hoyle.

"Maybe I could speak with you privily, sir."

Nick liked the thought and made a dismissive gesture of the kind he had seen his uncle use.

THE MERCENARY'S BLADE

"Fetch my horse, Hoyle."

For a second he saw outright refusal in the sergeant's eyes, shifting into glowering resentment as the big man stalked away towards the stables. No doubt he was already thinking of ways to make Nick's life more difficult in revenge, but for now at least he was cowed.

"What is it you wish to tell me?"

"I know the man you seek. I know his ways. Our paths have crossed a few times. If you want him found that badly, give me enough coin, and I will find him for you."

Nick bridled at the demand.

"You've been paid already and the prize money, should you find him, is more than enough."

The older man sucked on his teeth and shook his head.

"You get me wrong, sir. I'm not asking more for myself, but if you want the people I could ask to tell what they know, they will need some reward for it." He paused and spat in the grass then wiped his mouth with a grubby shirt sleeve. "You see, this isn't like hunting a regular criminal. Of those who might know where he is, half are terrified of him, and the other half would burn in hellfire rather than give him up." He gestured towards the rest of the troop. "Your men there will find no word—save false directions. That I can promise you."

Which was probably true enough. Lord seemed to cast an enchantment over those he encountered. Nick's father had said it was the power of the devil himself. Still, true or not, the man standing in front of him now, for all his brazenness, had no appearance to inspire confidence.

"They call you Mags," he said.

"That they do, sir. For Magdeburg."

"*Magdeburg?*"

Nick couldn't keep the surprise from his voice. Magdeburg, the city of Protestant martyrs. Over twenty thousand men, women and children, put to sword and flame by a Catholic army ten years before. He had grown up with the story of it.

Mags hawked and spat. "That's right. I was at Magdeburg with Tilly and his butchers. I watched the city burn and the Elbe run red with blood."

"You fought for *Tilly*?" Nick struggled to grasp the notion. Tilly had been the Catholic general.

"I could tell you the tale of the storming, it makes a fine story but not what you want to hear right now, I'll warrant."

"Before God—you are not telling me you fought *for* the emperor?" Nick was unable to keep the horror from his voice. As a boy he had pictured the power of the Hapsburgs as a hideous colossus straddling Europe, with one foot planted in Spain and one in the German lands of the Holy Roman Empire. It reached out clutching claws westwards to snatch ingots by the shipload from the Americas and feed the ever-hungry maw of their Catholic war machine set on the eventual domination of all Europe—England included.

Mags spat again. "Back then I'd have fought for Satan himself if he had paid for my sword. Not that we got paid. Mostly took what we could. I met him there, the one you're looking for."

"Lord? He was fighting with the imperial forces?"

"No. Funny thing that. He wasn't fighting at all, just wanting to get into Magdeburg a while before we stormed it. I never did find out why."

"You dislike him then?"

THE MERCENARY'S BLADE

Mags shook his head and gave an impatient shrug, as if he felt Nick was missing the point.

"I liked him well enough. Even if he was too pretty and too clever for his own good. Still is, I hear."

"You like him but you'll hunt him down?"

Mags looked puzzled.

"It's not as if he is kin now, is it? That would be different. You always look out for kin as much as you can. But you're promising me a wage for the work and I've a good pair of new boots from you now as well. I'll hunt you down the Archangel Gabriel if you pay me fair for the task."

Nick was uncertain whether he felt more disgust at the amorality or the lack of compunction in hiding it which Mags displayed. He swallowed the feeling and tried to think what his uncle would do in the same situation.

"What makes you believe you can find Lord and no one else can?"

"Not saying no one else can, but these men won't. I know them. There's some that could if they set their minds to it, local lads like me, but they wouldn't place your prize money against their own skins or, for a couple, the berating they'd be getting from their womenfolk."

"And you can—because?"

"Well, the way I see it, the man can't be hunting me down if he's dead and with that money you're paying, I can be a good way out of the county or the country if need be, afore anyone takes it upon themselves to look for me."

At the far side of the bailey, Hoyle was standing with two horses, staring across at them with a glower that crawled over Nick's skin.

"What do you need to do this?" he asked.

"Give me two men and that purse you carry. I'll find where he is within the week."

Nick nodded agreement, an idea suddenly large in his mind.

"Very well. But you will need just one other man. The purse I shall carry myself."

Mags' head bobbed. "Of course, for sure, sir. It will fill the hearts of our lads to see you take such a course, there being no finer figure in the county. Though sad to say some with the knowledge we need might shy from talking with us, your uncle being a local justice and all."

Nick sucked in his lower lip. He had the vision of himself finding and rooting out from some desperate hideaway the man who had dominated the life of his family for as long as he could remember. It was too sweet and tempting an image for him to discard.

"Then I will ride as one of you," he said promptly. "My face is not so well known as all that. Dressed the part, I believe none would think me a Tempest.

Mags looked thoughtful and then gave a brief grin.

"I reckon I could find something for you to wear. It'll not smell so well mind, and we'd be needing to muddy you up a bit, to look the part. At least you're not so dainty as some gentlemen, but if you speak, it'll make no difference how you look."

Nick shook his head. Almost welcoming each obstacle for the satisfaction of overthrowing it.

"I shall be there just to pay what needs paying and to bring in the man we hunt, when we uncover him," he said. Then, thinking he saw some trace of doubt in the other's face, went on: "For the rest, you shall have command of what must be done."

"As you say then, sir. And might I suggest we take along Shadrack Heron? There's few paths and places hereabouts he won't know and he's a good man in a fight."

Agreeing, Nick headed back across the bailey to where Hoyle waited. The sergeant would object, of course, maybe even send word to his uncle. But by the time he received it, Nick would already have Lord safe under lock and key—or failing that, even more safe under six feet of earth.

Chapter Six

When Lord woke Gideon at dawn's first blush, he was wearing his own clothes once more, with a borrowed shirt no doubt. Or maybe he'd had the foresight to bring one rolled in the leather bag Gideon had noticed strapped behind the cantle of his saddle.

"You must make your escape from Morpheus' arms." Lord looked and sounded as fresh and untroubled as if he had slept the night in a feather bed with nothing to cloud his conscience. Where he had slept—or even if he had—Gideon had no idea, for he hadn't returned to the bulb shed. Gideon's own discomfort, within and without, had kept him awake for a long time.

He rose, dressed, and brushed down his clothes, then used the water from a stone trough beside the bulb shed to wash. As he did so, the horror seen by flickering candlelight rose unbidden into his mind as it had into his restless dreams when sleep finally claimed him. But Lord's words of the night before held a terrible truth. The blood had indeed been fresh. Whoever had placed such an abomination there must have done so that day. It could not have been Beth Sawyer or any of the other women being held under close keeping by Fulke Brierly.

Yet Fanthorpe had been certain there was something to be found in that cottage that would condemn the women. He had been furious when nothing was found. And Mistress Goody had sent her man back to look again. It was hard to take that information and still see only an

THE MERCENARY'S BLADE

accusation of witchcraft. To Gideon it suggested rather that the witchfinders were as vile as those they hunted—or maybe that they believed that any means was justified if the end was the destruction of maleficium. Literally any means.

Lord's voice cut into his thoughts.

"There is still food left to break your fast. Or we can ride without."

Despite himself, Gideon realised that he was ravenously hungry and the remains of the meal Dutch had provided the night before seemed little enough to satisfy him. Then, fortified by the food, he risked a sally at Lord, who was preparing the horses.

"Do you keep a steady supply of stinking rags to hand, or was that your regular dress and this the exception?"

Lord laughed then caught on the laughter and took a sharp breath.

"I am found out," he said. "The clothes were from Dutch, not his secret finery, but some he had long worn out and to be cut up for cloths."

"How did you know that there would be anything at that abandoned cottage?"

Lord didn't even look up to answer.

"Dutch told me he had heard Fanthorpe talking of a meeting place. He was not certain where was meant, but it stood to reason it would be somewhere isolated where a scene could be set and not revealed until the paying audience arrived."

"And the—the—?" Gideon started, struggled, but was unable to complete his question.

"The stage settings?" Lord looked up then, malice bright in his eyes. "There's a ready euphemism for you to avoid stating the truth of it."

Gideon wanted to think of a cutting reply, but none came. The revulsion returned, turning the food in his mouth flavourless and he had to force himself to swallow it down.

"I would think we would need to look first to the players to find the source," Lord said, turning back to his task. "If indeed they knew what was there."

"How could they not?" Gideon asked, puzzled.

Lord finished tightening the saddle on his mount, shook his head and made a wry smile.

"It is not always the actors themselves who set up the stage."

"Meaning?"

"Meaning we have more work to do—lawyers work."

Gideon brushed away the crumbs and went over to where Lord was waiting with the horses which were now ready to go. A new bruise purpled the side of Lord's chin from where Fanthorpe's enquiries had taken their toll. He handed the reins of the chestnut to Gideon together with a question.

"So tell me, are these women illegally held?"

Gideon clenched his jaw.

"Only if they have no formal charge made against them."

Lord looked thoughtful. "*Habeas corpus*?"

The very idea made Gideon laugh.

"For a bunch of village women who stand accused as maleficium? That would be ridiculous. Besides, it requires a writ from a court—it isn't something to be conjured up by a mere lawyer on his own authority. I could petition Coupland for one, if you like."

THE MERCENARY'S BLADE

His sarcasm was wasted on Lord.

"Then who has the power to release them?"

Gideon sighed. "Right now? The constable himself would have. But since they are detained under Constable Brierly's own roof and it was he who summoned the witchfinder here in the first place, I can't believe he would be much inclined to do so."

Lord looked at him sharply. "It was Brierly who brought Fanthorpe here?"

There was a small spark of satisfaction in that for Gideon. He had found out something Philip Lord had failed to unearth. And he hadn't needed to roll around on the floor in rags like some mummer's apprentice to do so.

"Why not? His role is to police the peace of the parish," Gideon pointed out. "If the people I spoke to yesterday are to be believed, then there were many whispering about witchcraft even before Fanthorpe arrived."

"And yet no one pointed fingers at anyone until Fanthorpe came," Philip Lord observed. Then he pulled himself onto his horse and looked down at Gideon with an amused smirk. "But I quite like Preacher Fanthorpe. He is given to loud and long prayers about delivering the innocent from evil, which the Lord heard and answered. Without those prayers it is entirely possible the innocent could have been condemned."

He pulled his horse around and began walking it out to the road, his body stiff in the saddle. Gideon mounted and followed. He couldn't help but turn over in his mind the various ways he could achieve what Lord wanted. It was a legal problem, and despite his own feelings on the matter, his professional instincts were stirred. However, all of the ways he could think of ended at the door of a justice and that was a door barred against them.

After the conversation they had as he ate, Gideon half-expected they would be returning to the mill. They had accomplished all they could here so far as he could see. Even had he wanted to help find a way to free the women, Gideon could think of none except an armed assault on the Priory, which he wouldn't put past Philip Lord. So he was surprised when Lord stopped by the small stand of trees by the track to the village and turned in his saddle.

"I'll wait for you here, but I need you to go back and talk to Brierly."

"About what?"

"I'm sure you'll think of something. You are a lawyer after all. Talking is your trade."

"It would help to know what you expect me to achieve."

The longsuffering look returned to Lord's face.

"My words were all spent in vain. What have we been talking of?"

"A way to free the women," Gideon conceded.

"A *legal* way to free the women. Maybe you can persuade the constable to do so. Yes, I could pluck the roses from the briers, nothing easier, but I have no wish to see them stand condemned because of my intervention. Were I to act, they would be seen as confessed of guilt by the fact they flee. However, you can achieve their freedom another way, a legal way, by which means they can remain with their reputations unsullied."

Safely immured in his antipathy, Gideon met Lord's gaze.

"Whatever may be Fanthorpe's part in this, yesterday Brierly's mother told me that the women held in her house were possessed by demons. She heard them screaming obscenities. They needed to be restrained by the men with Mistress Goody. Those don't sound like innocent women to me."

Gideon saw Lord's eyes flash with anger before he looked away and laughed. It was a bitter sound with no trace of mirth or humour.

"As a dog returns to his vomit so the Giddy One returns to his giddiness. You must be indeed the fool if you cannot solve that simple cypher." Then his tone hardened further. "But if you are so much in love with the law you should at least adhere to its most basic of principles. *Item quilbet presumitur innocens nisi probetur nocens.* The guilt of those women has not been proven, so their innocence should be presumed. Except now whatever innocence they had has doubtless been ripped from their bodies thanks to the attentions from those loyal and godly men of our most pious Mistress Goody."

Gideon felt the blood drain from his face as the meaning of Lord's words sank in. He wanted to protest it, but yesterday he had seen the compassionate Mistress Goody order a man to kill. A fat worm of doubt turned the solid earth upon which he had been building his walls of certainty.

"That doesn't change the fact I have no legal way to free them, innocent or no."

Lord lifted his chin.

"Go as Moses," he advised. "Maybe pharaoh can be persuaded."

"Without plagues?"

"Plagues," Lord said prosaically, "can be provided."

Whatever that was supposed to mean. Gideon had to wonder why a man like Lord was putting so much of his time and effort into the fate of these women. For one insane moment it crossed his mind that Lord was in truth a demon incarnate trying to free his fellow minions. But the weight of evidence pulled his mind back from that brink.

"I'll go," he said at last. "But not because I believe they are not witches, and not because you ask it. I'll go because what Fanthorpe is doing is a clear abuse of the law."

Lord rewarded him with a flash of white teeth.

"And no doubt you also go as a quested knight, Sir Percival. Whom does the lawyer serve?"

Gideon tasted bile in his mouth as anger constricted his throat. It was only when he saw there was curiosity not mockery in Lord's gaze that he was able to fight it down. He was being baited with a purpose and whatever that purpose might be, he would not give Lord the satisfaction.

"Yes. I gave my word to Zahara that I would help if I could."

Lord's expression remained unchanged.

"Then you ride to the lists wearing her favour."

Grinding his teeth, Gideon turned his mount and headed back towards the village. Then, after a short distance he changed direction so that his path would take him first to the scene of the vile play acting of yesterday. There was a brisk breeze on the open hillside, and by morning light the tumbledown cottage appeared sad and abandoned. Driven by a need to lay to rest the spectre of what he had seen, Gideon approached the ruined building.

Slipping from his horse, he noticed the sinister shroud

of mystery and evil which the place had conjured in twilight was replaced, in the brilliance of early morning, with an air of simple dilapidation. Even so, Gideon felt his stomach clench at the trace of the stench which greeted him as he reached the open door. He wondered what had been added to the peat to make it smell so vile. Summoning courage he crossed the threshold into the darkened room.

Even before his eyes had adjusted to the gloom, he knew there was no one there and nothing to see. The room was empty. All traces of the atrocity that had been there were gone. The old table still held its place, but its surface bore nothing more than the stains and grime of age. The hearth had been raked out and there was less surface dust than might be expected. But nothing here hinted that the building had been host to anything more suspicious than a chance traveller who had made use of it for shelter on a rainy night at some point within the last couple of weeks.

For a time, Gideon stood in the shadowed room, light pouring in through the door and a small window, wondering if he had imagined what Lord had shown him. The things laid out on a shirt and the unspeakable horror in the bowl of fresh blood. Had that even been there? Been real? Or some simulacrum homunculus, carved from wood or stone? He was no longer sure he could consider the witness of his own senses reliable and that was not a comfortable conclusion.

As he left the cottage he looked back and then stared, as something gave him pause. For a few moments he had no idea what it was. The garden remained, scarcely visible and overgrown, its harvest days recalled in traces.

The house itself, stone walls still solid. The wall about the garden, dry stone, part tumbledown. But something had changed since he had seen it before. He waited, patient with himself, for the difference to be recalled.

Cottage.

Garden.

Wall.

Like the ghost of a vision, his memory overlaid the outlines from yesterday onto the reality of today, past forming over present.

There.

That was it.

There by the corner of the wall. A small cairn, resembling the natural displacement of stones so well that even a wild rose pushed through them—or had been led to do so.

Making no move to trouble the stones but feeling sure he knew their purpose, Gideon turned away and walked back to where he had left his horse. Scooping up the reins he mounted and took the path to Pethridge.

So it had been no simulacrum. And it was a strangely tender gesture from a man of Lord's ilk that seemed not to fit with what Gideon knew of him. That uneasy thought stayed with him until he reached the village.

Gideon's arrival at the Priory was met with delight—at least on the part of Brierly's mother.

"I am so pleased you came by," she said, showing him into the hall with its linenfold panelling and large warming hearth. "You must stay to eat with us. My son came home last night and would like to meet you, I am sure. He is out on a matter of business right now but will be back shortly."

THE MERCENARY'S BLADE

The attractive image of Lord waiting and wondering in the woods while he enjoyed a good meal held a powerful allure. But the price of spending several hours in the company of the constable's mother was too high. So he made a non-committal response and allowed her to engage him in polite conversation for a short time before bringing up the reason for his visit.

He realised that he only had one-way forwards. He had to decide for himself whether these were indeed witches, or whether Lord was right and they were victims of calculated malice. And that meant he would have to speak with them himself.

"I was hoping for the opportunity to speak with Mistress Goody. Is she here?"

He had every expectation that she wouldn't be, which would allow him the opportunity to talk to the accused women alone. What he didn't expect was the reaction he got to his enquiry.

The woman's hands flew up to her mouth.

"Oh, of course, you will not have heard." Her rabbit-like nose twitched and her hands fluttered as she spoke. "Poor Reverend Fanthorpe, he died last night. Such a terrible shame."

Gideon realised he was gaping at her.

"He—died?"

"Yes. He had a fall from his horse. Horrible. He was found after dark not far from here. So unfortunate! Poor man hit his head on a stone. Mistress Goody tells us that he was no great horseman. She is beside herself, of course."

Gideon let the implications seep into his mind and rearrange the neat theories into new patterns. He would have appreciated the opportunity to question further, but that was denied by the unceremonious return of the master of the house. Brierly bundled himself into the room and politeness demanded they both gave him their full attention.

Fulke Brierly was perhaps four or five years older than Gideon and had inherited little of his appearance from his mother. He was sturdy, where she was slight, and had dark brown hair, worn at an awkward compromise between fashionably long and workmanlike short. At least his demeanour and style of dress were professional. As his mother made the introductions, Brierly's expression shifted from distracted politeness to sudden interest.

"Mr David," he said, putting the slightest pressure on the name. "The lawyer from London? My mother mentioned your previous visit. And by coincidence I come fresh from speaking with an acquaintance of yours, Joshua Cale? He did mention you might well be here."

Gideon felt his chest tighten. So much for 'I'll wait for you here'. The shrewd gaze was fixed on his face.

"You don't like Mr Cale?" Brierly guessed. "I am certain I do not. But business makes strange friends for us. He even took the time to caution me against trusting you. If I had my say, his kind would have no place in my affairs."

"Indeed," Gideon agreed weakly, wondering what role he had just been set up to play, and why he couldn't have been given decent notice of it and a chance to prepare and learn his lines.

Brierly turned to his mother. "Ruth was asking for you as I came in. I believe there's a crisis in the kitchen—or it might have been the laundry. Perhaps you should go and see what needs to be done, hmm?"

His mother opened her mouth and seemed about to protest, but then appeared to think better of it, bobbing a brief curtsey and begging Gideon to excuse her. Brierly watched her go. When he turned back his expression was fierce.

"Let me be brief and clear, Mr. David, this is not a good place to be pushing your interest. My sister isn't so much of a catch as my mother might have led you to believe and besides, she is soon to be spoken for."

Gideon blinked. It seemed everyone was bristling with assumptions about him.

"I am sure your sister is a most charming and modest young woman, but I assure you any interest in her on my part lies purely in the mind of your mother."

That provoked a thin smile.

"My mother would see Prudence settled," Brierly agreed, his tone more amiable than before. Gideon suspected he had his own plans for his sister and felt a moment of pity for the absent party.

"So," Brierly demanded, "are you sent here from London, as Cale claims, to investigate shortcomings in the accounts on behalf of Bishop Morton? A replacement for Mr. Tindell, hmm?"

What was it Lord had said? *Plagues can be provided.*

"I was told you were sent a letter to expect me," Gideon said. "Has it not arrived? No? Then that indeed makes things more difficult. I can assure you, however, I am not a permanent fixture. Merely a visitor. I shall be returning south to make my report when I have finished here."

Brierly rubbed at his beard.

"I can understand the need for discretion in these troubled times. So if you were able, upon your return to London, to inform the bishop that all is well with his share, there would be no need to disturb Sir Bartholomew with it all. He is much involved in preparing for war and I wouldn't wish to distract him with such minor matters at the moment."

So Brierly was crossing Coupland in something. That was a dangerous line to walk. Gideon managed an obliging nod, an idea forming in his mind.

"Your mother mentioned you are holding some women who have been accused of witchcraft?"

Brierly's expression froze and he turned away.

"That is no matter of mine," he said. "Though the murder of Reverend Fanthorpe might perforce make it so."

For the second time since his arrival at the house Gideon realised he was gaping.

"Murder?"

Brierly nodded, still not looking at Gideon. "He was killed by a blow to the head. The reverend's assistant, Mistress Goody, would have it that it were witchcraft."

Gideon's thoughts took him back to the ruin.

"Perhaps imps can throw stones?" he suggested.

Brierly turned back to face Gideon.

"For all I know of it they may, but a man killed Reverend Fanthorpe, unless demons wear boots now." His lips drew into a tight line as if that thought touched some inner nerve. "He was found by the brook. It would be on his way back to the parsonage. The ground is soft there."

"When did it happen?"

THE MERCENARY'S BLADE

"Sometime yesterday evening or night. He was found early this morning."

Up to that point Gideon had assumed that Brierly was in the same camp as Fanthorpe and Mistress Goody.

"You were the one who summoned Reverend Fanthorpe?"

"Yes. I had—er—received word he was in the area and with the village all talking of witches it seemed..." He broke off. "But you were saying something before. What is your interest in these women, hmm?"

Gideon wondered if his idea was so wise in the light of the news he had received. But he had a feeling Lord would make no allowances, so he pressed on.

"You will have heard of the Boy of Bilston?"

The other man pushed out a lip in thought then lifted his head and nodded a few times.

"That was a good while ago, down south somewhere. A lad who claimed he was possessed and accused a neighbour of bewitching him?"

"Yes, and he'd go into fits when anyone read certain verses from the gospel. Bishop Morton was the man who unmasked the deception. He read the verses in Greek and the lad threw his fit at the wrong verse."

For a moment Brierly stared at him as if trying to catch some deeper meaning in the words.

"You are saying the bishop himself might take an interest in these witches? But he is in London and—"

"And still a man for uncovering supernatural pretence and deceit."

"But I—"

Having wrongfooted the man Gideon took advantage. "If I were to have the opportunity to speak to the women myself, I could report back to the bishop and assure him that on this occasion there is no pretence. Or perhaps save you from making a mistake that might earn his wrath."

Brierly looked at him intently.

"You have yet to tell me why you are here. It can't be the witches. They were only arrested a couple of days before you showed up."

Gideon said nothing, just stared back. Brierly was a clever man in a cunning way but lacked the ability for clarity of thought that Gideon's training had given him. Left to himself the man would make his own plagues.

Sure enough, he did.

"You are here to ensure the bishop is getting his due share of the proceeds from the lead mines. You'll want to see the accounts then. So this with these witches? How does that…?"

"If the bishop knew you were ensuring another injustice was avoided, he would think well of you for it. It is even possible he would wish to examine the women himself if they are indeed to be arraigned for witchcraft."

Brierly took a small gulp of air and nodded.

"Come by tomorrow afternoon. I will arrange it so you may see the women and the accounts."

It was not unreasonable to require time to gather and organise all the necessary documents for such an audit.

"Very well. I will be here soon after noon. I trust the women will be well cared for until then."

Brierly's lips tightened again.

"My word on it."

Riding away from the village Gideon found his sense of achievement watered down by other thoughts. Fanthorpe had been killed. But why? Whatever their motives, those who wanted the minister to find Beth and the other women to be witches would have no reason to see him dead, far from it in fact.

The only candidate Gideon could think of amongst the villagers was Dutch himself. Was it possible he had followed Fanthorpe after the incident at the ruin? God knows, he would have had reason enough to strike against the man he held responsible for tormenting his family. And Gideon knew from his own experience of those who did murder, that no matter how mild a nature a man might have, there was no one who could not be provoked into bloodshed given circumstances that pushed them beyond endurance.

But it was still easier to paint Lord's face into the picture—even without his own prejudice Gideon could see that. Lord had the perfect opportunity and a clear reason for wanting the witchfinder removed. Lord had been back to the ruin last night after he left Gideon sleeping in the bulb shed and so was out and about at the right time and not far from the right place. It would have been easy enough to kill Fanthorpe, leaving the body near the brook, especially if you were a man like Philip Lord for whom killing was no more than a job of work.

Lord was waiting where Gideon had left him, sitting beneath a tree and munching on an apple as if he had been nowhere else all morning. He got to his feet and stretched as Gideon approached.

"You were successful." It wasn't a question.

"You set me up to be so," Gideon said, refusing to meet the other man's gaze and focusing on checking over his mount. "I am to see the women and the accounts tomorrow afternoon. And I have led Brierly to think he might protect himself from issues with the bishop through the women, so they will be well treated."

"Well done. And I merely acted as your herald," Lord said, his tone pious. Then he frowned. "But something is gnawing on you."

Now Gideon looked the other man full in the face.

"Fanthorpe was killed last night. Murdered."

Whatever reaction he might have expected it wasn't the one he got.

"Murdered?" Lord echoed the word, at the same time filling it with delight. Then he laughed as if Gideon had made the best joke. "Someone murdered the murderers' crow? Now that is a sweet irony. But who? Who might it be? Oh. You think it was me." That made him laugh even harder and Gideon felt his anger slip its leash.

"Yes, I think it was you. I went back to the broken cottage and I saw that little cairn of stones, so I know you were out last night. And, you know, for a while after I saw that I thought you might have a sliver of decency buried somewhere in your soul. My mistake."

Lord seemed to find nothing in that to stop his laughter and he was still chuckling as they mounted and headed away from the village.

Chapter Seven

Philip Lord clearly believed something had been accomplished by the visit to Pethridge, because once he had stopped laughing, he spent much of the journey back humming to himself. It was the same tune over and over. They were not too far from the turn off the main path that led down to the mill when in exasperation Gideon kicked his chestnut to catch up.

"If you didn't kill Fanthorpe who did?"

At least Lord had to stop humming to answer.

"Now that is the question. *When thieves fall out, honest men come by their own.*"

"But who are the thieves?"

"I think the bigger question," Lord said, his tone reflective, "is 'who are the honest men?'"

Gideon thought about that and was about to reply that he had no idea, when Lord reined hard and made a sudden gesture for silence and stillness. Gideon obeyed but could see nothing ahead on the tree-lined track, until a musket-bearing, buff-clad man moved from the shelter of the trees beside the turning. Another joined him and they shared a brief conversation looking back along the road towards them.

Had Coupland's men found the mill in their absence? Gideon felt a sudden cold rush of fear for Zahara. He tried to comfort himself that whilst mute, Shiraz was not deaf or blind and had a care for her which would have seen them both away before they could fall into the hands of attackers. Beside him Lord seemed preternaturally still, almost without breath. Then as suddenly as he had frozen, he relaxed and moved on, even breaking into a trot. Still uncertain, Gideon followed. One of the soldiers on the road shouted—a welcome, not a challenge. His skin was dark and his greying hair hung in long braids from under his bonnet.

"By all the saints," he greeted them, "do you know how hard this place was to find?"

"Not hard enough," Lord said, a rare warmth enriching his voice. "You are early, Matt. I had not expected you for another two days at the least."

"Well, we can leave again if that's what you wish. Take another pilgrimage to all the quarters of the county. Heaven be my witness, I think we saw the Roman wall."

Lord laughed and slid from his horse to embrace the one he had called Matt as he might a brother. Then they walked together, Lord leading his horse, down the wide track towards the river and the mill. Gideon followed, still mounted, and so had a better view of what had happened in their absence.

Where the mill had been quiet it now bustled with life. Two large wagons were backed together making an informal gate and some men were working on a short length of crude ditch and wall between mill and bank on one side. Others were cleaning muskets, pouring boiling water, being brought by women from the kitchen, down the barrels of their guns. Near the stables, a farrier was checking the hooves of one horse and another horse was being held ready for his attention. A small group of children splashed at the edge of the river whilst some older boys were working with the men carrying stones to

THE MERCENARY'S BLADE

build into the wall. On a bench set by the mill, two young women sat sewing repairs in clothes and beside them a soldier was mending a belt.

Even to Gideon's unpractised eye it was clear these were not recruits but men whose business was war. All the work was being undertaken with an easy competence that needed no direction, familiar and sure.

Zahara was there, coming out of the main building with two other women, all three carrying baskets. Zahara looked alive and animated as she chatted. For a few long breaths, Gideon had no other awareness save of seeing her and gratitude that she was there and safe.

From his vantage of height, he also witnessed the moment the new household realised their patron had returned. Like a wave of wind through grass, the awareness spread and everywhere men and women stopped working and stood to see or drew nearer. Even the children sensed something special and came from their play to discover what their elders were about. It was like a strange family reunion, the sense of completeness that comes when a long-absent sibling or parent returns, the subdued or expressed delight as tangible as an embrace.

As they reached the makeshift gateway, one of the men stepped up and took hold of Gideon's bridle. Taking the hint, Gideon dismounted, thanked the man, and walked between the wagons. By now he was a good distance from Lord, who had handed his own horse off to another and was moving through the men, greeting some with a few words as he went. To Gideon it appeared akin to a royal progress. These men, who looked as though they had fought their way through every battle of the German wars, seemed in awe of Lord as he passed through their ranks. The pleasure those honoured received from his personal interest glowed from their faces as he spoke to them.

The progress stopped abruptly when Lord reached the mill. A man stood there who looked out of place. Perhaps in his early thirties, he was dressed in a manner that spoke to the professional rather than the military. Even if his clothes looked a little travel-worn, he had made some effort with his appearance. His light brown hair was combed through, his face shaved and beard neatly trimmed.

As Lord reached him, there was obvious curiosity amongst those watching as to how this encounter would play out. Even those returning to their work kept an eye on what was happening beside the mill. Matt, who had stood back whilst Lord had greeted his men, now moved forwards to stand beside him. The well-dressed man swept off his hat and held it before him as a supplicant might.

He spoke with a German or Scandinavian accent. Gideon wasn't sure which as the only language he knew himself apart from English, and of course Latin, was French.

"Anders Jensen. I have come a long way to see you, sir."

"Really?" Lord asked, a note of cold reserve in his voice. "How far exactly?"

"I am from Denmark, but I studied at Padua and travelled widely since. Most recently I have come from Paris and London."

"Mister Jensen joined us at Coventry," Matt said

explained. "He seemed to know a lot about you. I thought you would want to meet him. He has been the perfect guest in our company." Something in the way Matt used the word 'guest' lent it a different weight from usual usage.

Philip Lord turned a charming smile upon the Dane.

"Padua? You are a student of medicine then, perhaps? A physician?"

Jensen inclined his head. "That is what I studied there, but I am not allowed to be accounted as such here. I have the skills and the knowledge, but I am no longer granted a licence to practise."

His words brought Lord's eyes to narrow in speculation.

"There is some crime for which you have been banished? A patient of standing who perished under your care? Did you mis-sell some remedy? Or is it more political—a disagreement over the rules of engagement within your craft?"

Jensen gave the same slight nod as before.

"I will be open with you, sir," he said. "I was accredited in London for a time last year, I worked with William Harvey the Royal Physician, but I am not in agreement with the division in medicine that is made between physician and surgeon. I have skill in both, and I would seek work where I am free to use all my ability, not just part of it."

"And what makes you believe I would be a man to disagree with the wisdom of the ages and not demand of you the same distinction?"

"Your reputation."

Lord made no sign of either conceding or rejecting the claim. Instead, he made a dismissive gesture. "If you seek employment, we can discuss it later. Until then you may continue here as my guest." On the final word, he turned, eyes seeking and finding Gideon and beckoned him to join them. Reluctantly, Gideon complied. "This is Mr Lennox, who is also my guest for now. The two of you will be sharing a room."

Gideon felt himself flush with embarrassment as his status was laid out publicly, as if he were a naughty schoolboy. Every eye moved to take in his appearance, lingering long enough to be sure to know him. That matter settled, Lord made to pass on but Jensen spoke again, this time in a voice pitched so as not to reach beyond Lord, though Gideon, close beside him, heard it also.

"I can see you are injured, if you would allow me to…" Philip Lord frowned. The Dane broke off, then added even more quietly: "If I might say so, sir, alcohol is no panacea—there are better remedies for pain and better ways to deal with its cause, so no remedy is needed."

Gideon watched as Lord's gaze turned to Baltic ice and cut into the other man with a soul-freezing intensity before he turned away.

"Come, Matthew, we have much to discuss," Lord said, cheerful again, clapping Matt on the back and drawing him away and into the mill, hand resting on his shoulder. The pace of activity picked up once more, leaving Gideon and the Dane the only two who were not busily engaged.

"So that is the Schiavono," Jensen said softly.

"It is what his people call him," Gideon agreed, delighted that someone other than himself had suffered Philip Lord's unique style of hostility. He made a slight bow to his enforced companion. "Gideon Lennox, lawyer. I am from London and stranded in this northern county by circumstance rather than my own will."

Jensen looked at him thoughtfully and inclined his head.

"Ah, you are not a 'guest' by choice then? That must be an uncomfortable situation in which to find oneself. You have my sympathy. Although, after this first encounter, I may be in your position before much longer."

"I couldn't advise you there," Gideon admitted ruefully. "But perhaps you can advise me."

"A medical matter?"

"More as 'guest' to 'guest'."

"Ah. I think I understand." The Dane smiled. "You are guest here at another's will, whilst I—at my own. This may place certain limitations upon such advice as I can afford you without prejudice. But I will do my best."

Gideon was finding it difficult not to like this man.

"Are you sure you studied medicine and not law, Dr Jensen?"

"Anders, please. There are few enough here who will use that and it is warming to hear ones given name spoken by a friendly voice."

"I would be delighted. I am Gideon."

Anders looked at him with an open and level gaze. He had hazel eyes, warm in expression.

"Then tell me, Gideon, what advice can I give you?"

"I have known Philip Lord for two days and found nothing in him to like or admire. But you seek him out. What is it others are seeing that I am not?"

The Dane considered the question for a few moments before replying.

"I am not sure I can answer you. For myself, I see an

employer who will allow me full practise of my skills and the chance to learn more of military medicine. But in the ports of the Mediterranean and across France and Germany you will hear men speak of the Schiavono as they might speak of an irresistible force of nature. It is known that if he sets out to do something then it is as good as done. If he sets out to win a battle, the battle will be won. If he sails to take a ship, he will sail back with it. If he declares he will kill a man, that man is dead."

"They follow him because he succeeds?"

"That might be so." Anders gestured to the hive of activity around them. "You would need to ask them. Or perhaps he succeeds because they follow him?" He shrugged. "We have a saying in Denmark, that there is often a royal heart under a tattered coat."

Gideon laughed. "I have seen him in a tattered coat. However I have yet to witness any sign of a royal heart. But either way, as guest to guest, there is something you might want to consider before asking him to employ you. Philip Lord was declared a traitor nearly twenty years ago, and that leaves a man with no rights before the law— no right to title or property, to liberty or even to life."

"Naturally," Anders agreed. "How could it be otherwise? However, if a man still thrives despite enduring these trials, might not those who would wish his goodwill, perhaps think it polite not to remind him of his status?"

Gideon said nothing. It seemed pointless to observe that voluntary association with a condemned traitor was to share in his crime and his fate.

"I will say," the Dane continued, "it is an odd name they give him, 'Schiavono'."

"It is strange," Gideon agreed. "I think it sounds Italian, maybe?"

"Ah, there you may have it. You will have seen the sword that our mutual friend wears? With its broad double-edged blade, basket-hilt and cat's head shape of the pommel? That is known as a schiavona. I suspect his informal title has arisen on that account, for he is a master with that sword, is he not?"

For a moment Gideon recalled the alehouse where he had met Philip Lord and the way when the Lord drew the blade it had seemed to become a fluid extension of his body.

"I wouldn't know," he said. Something flickered on the edge of his thoughts, to do with something Anders had said—or was it the sword…?

But his attention wavered because Zahara and the women she had been chatting to were coming towards them. From the first awareness of her approach his senses were being filled with her presence and his mind shed all other concerns. When she saw him and smiled, his soul slid sideways.

"Dr Jensen, a patient needs you." The speaker was the oldest of the three women. She had a marked Irish accent and sounded confident in her authority to summon the doctor to his patient. "Dun has been asking for you. He says the pain is worse again."

Anders inclined his head to her. "Ah. I thank you, Goodwife Rider. I will look to him." He turned to Gideon. "It has been a pleasure to talk with you. I hope we will have more opportunities for conversation in the days to come."

Then with a polite acknowledgement to Zahara and the

other woman, a younger version of Goodwife Rider but with dark skin where her mother's was fair, Anders walked away in the direction they had come.

"Mr Lennox," Goodwife Rider said, seizing Gideon's attention. Her bright blue eyes held him in a critical vice. "We've not been introduced, but I have heard much about you. I'm Máire Rider and I'm the one in charge of organising the camp. If you are without work, I can always find you some. There is no need to be standing around watching others."

She made a sound of disapproval and swept past him. The younger woman offered a brief smile of sympathy and followed in her mother's wake. Zahara hesitated, as if uncertain whether to go with them, but stayed and looked searchingly up at him.

"Did you find a way to help those people?"

He wondered how he could even begin to answer her.

"Not yet."

"But you will." She spoke with certainty.

"I will try."

Which was enough to earn him another smile.

"Be patient," she said softly, "and persevere. As a wise man once said, it is rain that grows flowers, not thunder."

Then she slipped past him and into the hall, leaving Gideon alone in the middle of the crowded yard.

Through the course of the afternoon, as he observed the new arrivals, the niggling sensation that he had failed to pick up on something important remained with him. Gideon counted somewhere over forty men, nine women and a small gaggle of children who did not stay still long enough to be counted. There were a rich variety of accents and appearances from across Europe and well beyond. They looked and acted like a disciplined body of soldiers. But whatever discipline held them, it was needed. He had seen a scuffle break out over nothing and turn to drawn blades in a moment. Those who stood by and watched had done so with the eager intensity of men at a cockfight.

Only the arrival of the man Lord had called Matt, who seemed to hold some authority amongst them, had prevented bloodshed. He stepped between the two like a schoolmaster separating squabbling children. They backed off at once, but even then one spat towards Matt as he turned away. The older man turned, took a calm step towards the offender as though to reprimand him. But the turn didn't stop and the force of it was carried with an elbow into the man's stomach, whilst his other arm swung a solid fist into the undefended jaw hard enough to drop him to the ground, followed with a booted foot once he landed there. Then Matt walked off, to an ironic cheer and harsh laughter at his victim's expense.

This was what war was bringing to England—a rule of anarchy and violence with the only law being that of fist, boot and sword. Sickened, Gideon took himself as far away from the mill as he could. Walking along the river to where a large dipping willow allowed him some sense of separation and privacy. The last three days of his life had contained more in depth and breadth than the entirety of the previous twenty-three years put together. A part of him yearned to return to the known and steady life he had before, but he was disturbed to realise that a small rebellious corner of his soul was finding it exhilarating.

Not for the first time he wondered what he was doing there and why he didn't take his horse and ride south.

Even if Durham was closed to him, there were other places where he could go and from where he could arrange his return to London with relative ease.

But then there was Zahara. He stayed for Zahara. But perhaps also it was that he was unwilling to test the word of Philip Lord who said he was free to go unmolested.

As if to underline that point, when he made his way back to the mill at sunset, he saw the silent figure of Shiraz watching him from further downstream, crouched by a rocky outcrop, still and intent. A cat ready to pounce if the mouse came within reach.

That evening there was a buoyant gathering.

Work over for the day and reunited with their adored leader, the men were in a mood to celebrate. Much of the main room had been changed to resemble the common room of a tavern. At the other end, some of the pallets Gideon had seen were already laid out to offer sleeping space for the company. A handful of them were already occupied, although how anyone could sleep with the amount of noise there was, Gideon had no idea. More pallets were stacked, ready to be pulled to the floor when the boards were pushed back at the end of the evening, whenever that might be.

There were jugs on the tables. Enough beer to soothe throats, but not sufficient for anyone to wake with a headache the next day. Everyone seemed to be laughing or smiling, but to Gideon, the convivial atmosphere was too much akin to a thin silk cloth laid lightly over naked steel.

Philip Lord had no table set aside. Instead, he broke bread and shared beer alongside his men, moving places several times. His whereabouts were easy to track by the focus of laughter as much as by the peacock plumes he had placed in his hat, or the garish crimson doublet he now wore, slashed with fabric that matched the plumes.

After a bit of searching, Gideon found himself a space at the end of a table where Anders Jensen was talking with Matt. The older man had a small clay pipe between his lips which he puffed to keep lit. Anders greeted Gideon with warmth as he sat.

"You must eat. The food is good."

The food was bread and chicken steeped in mutton pottage and Gideon was serving himself when the Dane stood up to go stifling a yawn.

"Forgive me, fellow guest, I need to retire. I hope you will not mind sharing your room with me? I undertake not to snore if you do likewise." He looked serious as if Gideon's response was of great moment to him.

"I will draw up a contract," Gideon promised. "There will be a punitive indemnity for breach of it."

"Ah, God gives the will and necessity gives the law. It is a good thing that I know a man of law who can advise me," Anders said with a smile, inclining his head in a half-nod, before turning to Matt. "I bid you a good-night, captain, and again my thanks for your consideration."

Any reply was lost in a sudden burst of laughter from across the room. The Dane had left and was halfway up the stairs before it subsided. Gideon wondered if Anders had called Matt 'captain' as a casual form of address between acquaintances, or specifically as that was his military rank.

Someone started a song. A vulgar one with a loud chorus that involved much foot stamping. It was followed by another, then a shout went up demanding the

Schiavono sing a turn. Lord was laughing and bounded onto a table, making of it a stage, to give them a song of war.

"He that may lose the field,
Yet let him never yield
Though thousands should be killed,
Let soldiers try it."

His voice was strong and clear and the men thundered out the chorus in a noise that must have been heard by the sentries watching the road at the top of the track.

"When cannons are roaring
And bullets are flying
He that would honour win
Must not fear dying!"

They were not satisfied when it finished and demanded more. Playing at reluctance, Lord eventually consented. He reached down and drew one of the men up beside him—one who boasted a broken nose, taggle-bearded chin and an almost toothless grin of embarrassment at being singled out.

Dropping to one knee and sweeping his hat into a lavish bow, Lord sang a gentle ballad, a song of undefiled love. His voice rising and falling with flawless expression, full of the grace of devotion that the words contained, his face the image of devout sincerity as his gaze remained fixed on his victim.

"And I will make thee beds of Roses,
And a thousand fragrant poesies,
A cap of flowers, and a kirtle,
Imbroydred all with leaves of Mirtle."

Gideon felt disgusted and looked away. It wasn't so much a parody as deliberate sacrilege. When the song finished, he had no idea, for long before it did, the volume of laughter and shouts of raucous glee made it mercifully impossible to hear any singing and the press of bodies about the table blocked the singer from view.

Then Lord stood up and the laughter became loud shouts of approval, which only subsided when he stepped from the table, drawing four of those who had been in his audience aside to talk about something which seemed to hold their serious attention.

"You must think us a strange company, Mr Lennox," Matt said when the room had settled again. He tapped out his pipe and put it away, eyes bright against his dark skin above a full beard. "Or if not strange, then perhaps misguided?"

Which was not the kind of question Gideon had anticipated.

"I don't think I'm qualified to judge," he said, picking his words with care. "I have not spent too much time with men who fight just for money."

"You think?" the older man sounded amused. "Well, some do for sure. Take Bela Rigo there, the farrier? He keeps careful accounting of each hoof he lifts, written up in a ledger. And Tom Garland—he's the bald one with his face half-broken, he was only today telling me how he'd be leaving us to go home and take up lace-making if it came up short a penny on his reckoning."

"You are saying you are not here for money?" Gideon made no attempt to keep the disbelief from his voice.

Matt seemed to give the question some careful thought.

"If there was no money, I wouldn't be here," he said at last. "After all, a man has to live, to feed, shelter and clothe his family. And my family is all women, saving myself and young Liam, so they take a lot to clothe according to their fancy. Saying 'nay' to my Brighid when she has her heart set on a new shawl or when little Nessa wants some ribbons, I'm not sure I have the strength that needs." He broke off as if struck by the dreadful gravity of the thought and shook his head.

"I can see why you get on so well with Philip Lord," Gideon said, sourly.

"You learn a lot about clever talk if you stay about him," Matt agreed without rancour. "I used to be as mild as mother's milk, back in the day. We all were."

"I wouldn't know," Gideon said, nettled. "Most of this company seems to have taken pains to avoid speaking with me."

The older man leaned forward as though sharing a confidence.

"If you will keep looking daggers at the one man everyone here respects the most, you can expect to find more than a few will turn you a cold shoulder in one way or another. Not that you need me to tell you that."

"So why do *you* bother talking with me?" Gideon asked, his anger kindling.

Matt leant back again, picked up his beer and drank some down before he replied.

"Well, partly because me being seen talking with you in a friendly way will make it a lot less likely that I might need to waste any of my time tomorrow pulling your body out of the river. But mostly because Sara thinks well of you, and she is someone who sees further into people's hearts than anyone I know."

It took him a moment to remember.

Zahara—but I am sometimes called Sara.

THE MERCENARY'S BLADE

The anger which had quickened to a blaze at the first part of Matt's answer, turned inside out as he finished. Gideon felt his face flush and covered the moment by taking a swallow of beer. Matt, if he noticed at all, gave no sign. His gaze was sweeping the room like a farmer overlooking his fields.

Lord had started a game of dice and a fair number of the company were now gathered around to watch or play. A loud whoop announced a winning roll, with groans from the loser. When Gideon looked across, Lord was pounding the winner on the back and laughing. As the next man shook the dice, Matt Rider's wife appeared in the doorway beyond them, coming in from outside, and looked at the gamers with pursed lips. Lord saw her and moved from his place to take her hand, making a bow over it as if she were a lady of the highest rank. He tucked her arm under his own and led her, resisting, over to the game. By the time they reached it her face was struggling to keep its stern look of disapproval and she burst out laughing.

"He certainly has the common touch," Gideon muttered grudgingly.

"Is that what you see?" Matt's tolerant tone sounded strained. He stood and picked up his ale mug. "You should get some sleep soon, Mr Lennox. We rise early."

Gideon watched as the older man made his way across the room. He stopped by each small group he came to, said a few words then moved on. By the time he had reached the gathering around the dice game, the first of the groups he had spoken with had drained the dregs of their drinks and risen to begin moving the tables and bring out the rest of the pallets which were stacked by the walls. Matt spoke a few words into Lord's ear, who shrugged lightly, surrendering the arm of Mairé Rider, but still intent on the game. Released, the woman exchanged a look with Matt, which Gideon took as exasperation, then moved off to help collect the jugs and mugs, gathering Matt's own as she went.

Matt persisted in his task, moving around the dicing group and saying a brief word to this man or that. Most nodded and got up. One or two scowled before complying. One though just shrugged off the hand on his shoulder and when Matt insisted, he grudgingly turned to answer. Gideon recognised the sullen featured individual who had caused trouble earlier in the day.

It happened so fast that Gideon almost missed it since his own attention had been taken by the appearance of Zahara. She was there with Matt's older daughter, Brighid, and had started to help clear the pots. He was following her progress and wondering if he might offer to help when he saw that the troublemaker was back watching the game. Matt was beside him, one hand on his arm. Sidestepping the fist aimed at him, Matt caught the arm and twisted it back, moving in to look the man full in the face and say something brief and harsh before releasing him again.

The rest of the room either didn't notice or considered the matter too unimportant to merit a second glance. The dice game, now a tight knot of six or seven around Lord, were all absorbed in the rolls. Those clearing the room went about the task unconcerned. It was, Gideon realised, far from an unfamiliar event for these men.

The troublemaker looked pale. Whatever Matt had said to him carried a burden of promised punishment. Matt added a final word, his face unyielding, then moved on. Subdued at last, the man glanced back at the game before turning away, drinking down the dregs from his mug and pushing it at Zahara as she passed by.

Which was why Gideon saw what happened next, because the movement was neither sharp enough nor fast enough to be eye-catching. There was the slightest shimmer as the knife was drawn, before being turned in the hand at belt level. Before Gideon could finish taking the breath he needed to shout warning, it was already thrusting into Matt's back.

But he hadn't, after all, been the only one to see something. Before the length of the blade could sink fully its wielder jerked back, a beer mug hitting him in the face. Close behind the thrown mug was Philip Lord, holding no weapon in his own hands but fast and sure.

Matt made a dark gasping sound and staggered, held upright by those around him who realised what was happening as the blade came out with blood. A woman screamed, which one Gideon couldn't tell, but he did see Zahara running not away from but towards the danger, and then he was on his feet and running too.

Chapter Eight

By the time Gideon reached Zahara, his hand was on his sword, ready to defend her. But by then there was no need. Philip Lord, face carved from marble, had already followed up the thrown mug and floored the knife wielder. A moment later Lord's sword was at his throat. The man was still dazed, but he knew what was happening and spat defiance, a single word that Gideon couldn't understand, before the sword thrust and he gurgled, choking on his own blood.

Gideon had never seen one man kill another before, though he had witnessed enough brawls and injuries. Despite his training in law, he had avoided the spectacle of criminal execution. He saw it much as he saw cockfights and bearbaiting, slaking the public taste for blood—a taste he had never shared. At least, as everyone knew, the animals didn't suffer as they had neither souls nor ability to feel, but the poor wretch on the scaffold could and did. Until then the one death he had witnessed at close hand had been of someone so weakened and spent with disease, that the exact moment their final breath escaped had been missed by those present.

Now, faced with this reality, Gideon felt nothing except cold relief. A human life extinguished before his eyes, but with less impact upon him than a faked death at the height of a grand tragedy played out on the stage of the Globe. The only thing that mattered was that Zahara was no longer in danger. Zahara was safe.

THE MERCENARY'S BLADE

"Fetch the Dane."

Gideon wondered if others noticed the rasp in Lord's voice or the fact that his hand trembled as he wiped his sword on the dead man's clothes and restored it to its scabbard.

It was Zahara who turned and pushed her way through those who had risen to their feet the better to see. Mairé Rider was bent over Matt, her complexion the same shade as the linen of her coif as she worked by the light of a candle being held for her by one of the men. Gideon couldn't see Matt behind the spread of her skirts but he heard the grunt of his voice.

"You fret too much, woman." But the groan that followed gave the lie to the words.

Lord had already begun clearing the room, ordering the removal of the dead man, and sending those who yet remained to their beds. He grasped Gideon's arm as his men moved to obey, eyes for once devoid of either malice or humour.

"This is work for Hippocrates of Kos, not Corax of Syracuse—leave us to our exigency."

It was true and there was nothing to say. Gideon cast a final glance back and saw Lord had dropped into a crouch by his fallen friend, clearly confident that all would be done as he had commanded without his need to supervise.

Gideon turned to leave but had to wait for the dead man to be carried out. He had no idea what they would do with the corpse. But he was certain that this was not the first these men would have handled, nor would it be the last.

Matt's warning words came back to him as he caught the gaze of the dead staring eyes. *I might need to waste my time tomorrow pulling your body out of the river.*

Despite the warmth in the room, he felt gooseflesh pock his skin.

Before he could escape from the scene, the stairs were occupied. Anders Jensen came down them, hatless, dishevelled and clad in shirt and breeches, a large leather bag under one arm. He gave a brief nod to acknowledge Gideon, but his focus was on the group across the room. Lord had come to his feet the moment Anders appeared and intercepted him with three swift strides.

"If you wish to enter my employ, this is your test physician-surgeon."

Anders spoke softly, the words reaching only Lord—and Gideon as he was close beside them. "Each life I am called to save is my 'test', sir. I need no other inducement." Then he moved to kneel beside Matt, asking questions as he undid the buckles that held his bag.

Philip Lord stood for a moment like a stag at bay then noticed Gideon and his eyes changed, the rime of frost forming.

"Still here? I—"

But whatever he might have intended by way of wounding words remained unspoken as Zahara returned and passed between them, bearing a bowl of steaming water. Under the cover of that distraction Gideon made his escape.

Sleep eluded him and the more he tried to chase it to covert, the more it evaded him, his thoughts bounding over open acres of speculation. It was a relief when the latch lifted on the door at last and Anders came in. His shirt was stained with blood, and he held the final remains of a candle in one hand which illuminated his face, drawn with fatigue.

Gideon sat up as the Dane placed the candle on the window ledge, then pulled off his shirt and without replacing it got into his bed.

"How is—?

"Captain Rider is still alive, though that was mostly his good fortune the knife missed any vitals. If he is alive this time next week—if—*that* will be my doing."

Then Anders rolled onto his side, snuffed the candle with a thumb and forefinger and within a minute his breath had altered into the slow pattern of sleep. Gideon mustered a brief envy which wilted when he considered what the Dane had been engaged in to earn his rapid rest. It occurred to him that he wouldn't want to be in the shoes of Anders Jensen should his patient not survive.

Sleep ambushed Gideon soon after and he woke to the sound of activity without, and the absence of Anders. The sun had barely broken the horizon and the light coming in through the window was thin and pink, picking out the shadows in many shades of grey. It chanced on the discarded shirt at the end of Anders' mattress. The patches of blood looked black on the linen. As if reluctant to face the real implications, Gideon's mind entertained itself for a moment with the idea that were he Anders, whatever terms of employment he might accept he would wish it to include an extra allowance for laundering shirts.

Gideon might have sat there for longer, but the door opened and Anders himself came in, neatly dressed and with no mark of blood on his fresh shirt.

"Ah, you are awake. Our Lord and master was asking for you. I have a feeling his patience is somewhat intemperate today. Lack of sleep is never good for a man no matter how strong he might be."

"He was up drinking late?" Gideon hazarded as he pulled on breeches and found his boots.

"I would not be able to speak to what he drank, but there was no smell of such on his breath this morning. He was sitting at the bedside of Captain Rider much of the night so myself, Goodwife Rider, and Sara could sleep by turns." There was the slightest trace of reproach in Ander's tone and Gideon was reminded again of their different guest status.

"How is Captain Rider?"

"He has survived thus far. We will have to see if my needlepoint and that of Sara will be enough. Then, if the wound does not fester, he should make a full recovery."

"Zahara helped you?"

Somehow the notion was not at all surprising.

Anders nodded and splayed his hands. "My hands are as shovels, placed next to hers. She was stitching where my fingers would not even fit. She is a brave woman—she and Goodwife Rider." He bent and picked up the blood-stained shirt. "Which reminds me I must burn this before either of them takes it in mind to seek to save it. You should hurry—his lordship is not in a patient mood."

Gideon finished pulling on his boots after Anders had gone and thought that he cared little for Philip Lord's moods either way.

He found his host showing no sign of a second night with scant sleep. Lord was dressed in fresh clothes and the only remarkable thing was that his sword was not at his side. It lay on the table where he sat eating some bread. He wasted no time on any pleasantry, not even a greeting.

"I won't be going with you back to Pethridge today. You will ride with Shiraz. I have other matters I have to see to. I am sure you can manage the lawyers' work you have there."

Gideon's first reaction was relief. The notion of having time away from the oversight of Philip Lord was one he welcomed. But then it meant having the silent menace of Shiraz as his shadow instead.

"I'm sure I will manage," he agreed, tightly.

"You will need to set off soon. Keep well away from Howe." Lord pushed himself to his feet and picked up his sword, sliding it home in its scabbard at his thigh. Gideon's gaze was drawn to the intricate weave of its basket hilt and the oddly shaped pommel, crowned with a curve between two raised points.

Cat's head.

That had been how Anders had described it. That was what Dutch said had been found at the site of all the witchcraft sheep killings, and there had been more than one in the ruined cottage.

Lord had already turned away, his business with Gideon done.

"It's *you*," Gideon said and Lord turned back, frowning.

"I will admit the charge. I am indeed myself. What of it?"

Gideon shook his head.

"No. I mean, all this with Dutch. The witchcraft. The killings." He had Lord's full attention now. "Don't you see it? The cat's heads—your sword. Your name…"

He trailed off because the reaction his revelation received wasn't the one he had anticipated. There was no look of surprise on Lord's face. Instead, he looked impatient.

"I applaud your epiphany," he said. "Perhaps now you will be more assiduous in your enquiries."

Gideon was furious at that.

"If you knew, why didn't you tell me?"

Lord's attention was taken by a call from someone outside, he lifted a hand to indicate to them that he would be there momentarily before he replied.

"Because I thought it too obvious to mention. Besides, if I had, you would have taken it as further proof of my own involvement and seen the presence of the heads as some kind of signature proving my demonic prowess. Which is, of course, how Coupland wishes it to be seen."

"You seem very sure Sir Bartholomew is behind this."

Lord released a long-suffering sigh and sank down to rest his weight on the table boards.

"Yes, I am sure. Just as I am sure when the leaves change green to gold that winter is around the corner and that the glow on the horizon of each dawn will presage a day. If there is some turn of events that strives too hard to make of me its focus, a Coupland or a Tempest or one of their ilk, will be behind the stage turning the wheels and blowing smoke in the audience's eyes."

"Why?"

Lord closed his eyes as if close to despair.

"Why does the wind blow? Why do men lust? Why does a Lennox ask questions?" He opened his eyes, the turquoise gaze benign. "You are the lawyer, oh Giddy One, you find the answer. Meanwhile, if you can find some common reason why those women and not others were picked to be condemned, then mayhap we'll see the hand moving the pieces. But to be honest, I am less concerned with any 'why' and more concerned with a 'how'. How you can have Beth Sawyer, Widow Bothwell and those two young maids, Leah and Anne, set at liberty with no taint left against their good names."

"Because you fear they might condemn you if they go to trial?"

Lord laughed and was already striding away, his final words thrown back over one shoulder without so much as a turn of the head.

"I might. If it actually mattered."

Gideon found his hands tightened into fists.

"You have eaten?"

Zahara stood beside him holding a bowl of bread and cold meat. Appalled that he had failed to notice her approach, Gideon wondered how much of the conversation she overheard.

"Thank you, but I'm not hungry," he said. Any appetite had been stifled to nausea by the arrogance of Lord.

"You have work today. You should eat," she insisted, then she smiled and sunlight filled the old mill. "Would you eat if I join you?"

That was more than incentive enough. Gideon sat at the table Lord had vacated, but even before Zahara could take a seat opposite, Anders Jensen slipped in beside him. Gideon quelled an annoyance he knew was unmerited and unworthy.

"My quest was successful," Anders explained, tearing a piece of bread from the loaf on the table. Gideon looked at him blankly.

"Quest?"

"To ensure I disposed of the shirt before any of the

women took a mind to attempt its salvation." He accompanied that with a wink.

"It was a good shirt," Zahara chided. "I could have cleaned it for you. Mr Lennox helped me prepare the lye for our laundry." She rewarded Gideon with another smile and the day became more beautiful.

"It was a shirt," Anders agreed, between mouthfuls. "Not one worth saving. I have two others."

"That is not the point," Zahara said, her expression serious. "It could have been washed, not wasted. If you had not wanted it, there are others who would." She looked between them. "Do you know how much work goes into making a shirt? From growing the flax to sewing the woven cloth?"

Gideon shook his head. He had never given a moment's thought to how his shirts might be made, but somehow Zahara made him feel ashamed he had not.

"I accept my chastisement at your hands," Anders told her. "I promise I will grant you all my spoiled shirts in the future." He reached a pocket. "Here. This is what I promised you. Perhaps it will be some small recompense for my poor behaviour with regards to the shirt. I have looked into the problem and found some hope in the works of Paracelsus. As ever, God feeds the birds that use their wings."

Zahara seemed not to hear his words, her attention was on the pouch he held which she picked up and opened as he was speaking, looking inside before her gaze moved back to the Dane.

"What is the dose?"

"A pinch as an infusion before sleep if there is need. You will want to sweeten it with honey or it will be too bitter to drink."

"Thank you. I appreciate your kindness," she gave him a smile edged with gentle mischief, "and will repay you with a new shirt."

Gideon felt an unreasonable stab of envy at the smile and the warm look of gratitude that went with it.

Anders made a slight bow towards her.

"It should bring relief and that is reward enough. But if you wish to repay me further, then put words of praise for me in the ears of your man, Philip Lord."

The smile faded into a slight frown.

"The Schiavono is not mine," she said gravely, her words lifting a weight from Gideon's heart.

Zahara turned on the bench as someone called her name, then got up.

"I am sorry. I have to go after all." She gave Gideon an apologetic look. "Please eat, even if I am not here." At that moment he could forgive her abandonment, or anything else. She had denied Lord and his heart sung.

"A remarkable young woman," Anders observed, as he watched her go. "A faster study I have not seen. She needed little explanation and showed much skill in assisting me. She knew of Avicenna, though by another name Iben-something-or-another and even argued Hippocrates to my Galen, though I doubt she knew she did so—and Hippocrates was right, of course."

"Of course," Gideon agreed, though with no real idea of who Avicenna might be or why Hippocrates should be thought of more highly than Galen, who all knew was the father of medicine. But he was keen to be obliging to the Dane as there was something he needed to know, a sudden worm of worry burrowing through his thoughts.

"Was that some remedy you passed to Zahara? Is she ailing?"

The Dane looked at him sideways.

"That is not the most polite of questions to ask me, even as guest to guest. I am sure your clients seek confidentiality in the matters they bring to you and I accord the same privilege to mine."

Gideon felt his face grow warm at the rebuke.

"Truly, I didn't mean to pry, I—"

Anders took another mouthful of the bread and chewed it, talking before he had swallowed it fully.

"I am sure you did not." He chewed a bit more then swallowed. "I can assure you that to the best of my knowledge she has no physical illness, if that is what concerns you. For the rest, as I said, you should ask her what the remedy is for."

Gideon got to his feet with every intention of doing that, but one of the men appeared as he stood up, saying that Shiraz was waiting for him outside. He would have to find Zahara when he got back. Making a hasty farewell to Anders, Gideon realised he had still barely broken his fast and was now indeed hungry, so he scooped up some of the bread, eating it as he went out.

Shiraz was already mounted. On one side of his saddle was a pistol, but hanging from the other was a curiously shaped bow and a quiver of arrows. Gideon was sure he had seen similar weapons in images depicting wars with the Ottoman Empire. He would have liked to ask about it, but Shiraz, being mute, wouldn't be able to explain. So taking the reins of his mare from the outheld hand he mounted and led the way from the mill.

THE MERCENARY'S BLADE

Nick had begun to wonder if Hoyle was right about Mags. This was the second day of searching and he seemed to be taking his time chatting over an ale discussing the state of the nation, women, the weather and the best way to serve mutton.

On the surface, he seemed capable and showed Nick a cooperative face, agreeable and amenable. But Nick had to wonder if Mags was taking unnecessary advantage of his own role as the lead in their expedition.

Nick challenged him on it when they were alone, riding between the inexhaustible supply of alehouses and taverns Mags seemed to know in the area.

"You can't expect to walk up to people and ask them straight out," the mercenary told him, "It's a sort of game. You have to play by the rules or you stand out more than a wherry on a duck pond."

"You should have a care," Nick snapped. "Your attitude has very little of respect in it that I can see."

Mags was quick to climb down. "Sorry, sir, I mean nothing by it. As I said before we set out, this isn't work you would be used to. And, begging your pardon to remind you, but you did say you would be guided by me in this."

Which was all very well except the amount of time they were wasting in alehouses wasn't getting them anywhere in Nick's view. But without breaking with the role he had been assigned and rashly accepted, Nick had no way to change that. So, perforce, he sank back into a subdued but frustrated silence.

In the end, the first possible lead they found wasn't one he had expected.

They must have cut across the path that Lennox had

taken on his ill-fated search, because several of those Mags spoke to replied that they were not the first to be asking after their prey, although none of them could offer any more than that.

"It is strange though," one man offered. "So many lawyers from London hereabouts of a sudden."

"You have seen more than the one?" Mags asked him.

"My cousin said there was another one in Pethridge yesterday, the place they found all those witches. He was a red-haired lad too. If you like that for coincidence."

"*Yesterday*?" Nick couldn't help himself. The word spoken before his thoughts had caught up enough to remind him that was not a good idea. Their drinking companion shot him a frown. It was his first contribution to the conversation and it broke all his promises to Mags not to speak. But the thought that a man he had assumed dead three days since might be alive had taken him off guard.

A ring found by a body too burned to be recognisable was perhaps not entirely conclusive. But even if Lennox had somehow survived, somehow escaped, what earthly reason would he have to be in Pethridge? It had to be a coincidence.

"Aye, that's a terrible business those witches," Mags said, though Nick would have sworn it was the first he had heard of them. Then Nick caught the sideways look. Of course, Mags had no knowledge of Lennox or his role in events, but the mercenary was no fool and mention of a lawyer seeking Lord wouldn't have escaped him.

Twisting his voice to a close approximation of the local dialect, and adding a rasp to disguise any lack, Nick said. "Witches? Around here?"

THE MERCENARY'S BLADE

Their informant gave him an odd look and nodded. "They say so. I always did wonder how Ben Sawyer's lad had managed to get the money to rebuild that old place of his. If he married a witch it would stand to reason she'd have ways to make them rich."

Mags agreed it would. They might have got more but the man rose right after and went to relieve himself. He didn't come back.

"And that, sir," Mags murmured in an undertone, "is why I am the one doing the talking."

Nick wasn't troubled. His mind had already moved forward with the strange coincidence that two red-headed London lawyers were to be found at the same time on the same side of the county, especially as the first was presumed dead by the hand of Philip Lord.

"We're going to Pethridge," he told the two men with him. Heron said nothing, his straight black hair hanging down either side of his face, but then Nick could count on his fingers the individual words he had heard the man say since they set out.

Mags nodded, sage and eager.

"Of course we are, sir. Witches can't be left unlooked at. I'm sure it'd not be wasting more than a day or two of our time at most. And with fair fortune, the trail won't be too cold by the time we get back to it again."

"Exactly," Nick said soberly, pushing down the nagging feeling that Mags was either being wilfully insubordinate or making deliberate fun of him, despite the fulsome sincerity in his voice. "And I am sure there will still be some ale here when we do."

"Ale, I wouldn't doubt, but fresh news of the man we seek, that might be harder to come by then. And this lawyer, you know of him?"

There seemed little point in spinning a lie.

"My uncle hired a lawyer to try the same task as we now undertake."

Mags sucked air through his teeth. "Not a word against the wisdom of Sir Bartholomew would ever pass my lips, but as I see it, that was akin to setting a hen to catch a fox."

"So it turned out," Nick admitted.

Mags said nothing to that, but it was hard to miss the speculative glint in his eyes.

They left the alehouse right after, and Nick took the opportunity to return to Howe Hall. He was keen to find out if there was any other rumour yet brought in of Lord's possible whereabouts. The downside of such a visit was it meant running the gauntlet of Hoyle's disapproval. Steeled to face it, Nick was surprised to find Hoyle absent when they rode into the bailey.

There was also no further news of Lord. Although several of the search parties had checked in and left again, each had drawn a blank. One reported encountering a body of armed men which turned out to be a Danish physician and some troops heading to Newcastle to join the earl.

Having slept the night at Howe, Nick abandoned his disguise and, lacking any other escort, took Mags and Heron west to Pethridge.

THE MERCENARY'S BLADE

Chapter Nine

Gideon was glad there was no need to make conversation with Shiraz on the ride to Pethridge. His mind was too full of thoughts and ideas, each needing urgent attention. He welcomed the opportunity to try and sort them all out and put them in perspective.

Foremost in his thoughts was the revelation that the repeated appearance of a cat's head linked the events in Pethridge with Philip Lord. Of course, as Lord would claim, it could be an attempt to cast the appearance of guilt onto him. On the other hand, a small voice within still whispered that if Lord were indeed the demonic master of these witches, then surely in his arrogance he would wish to leave his sign.

Setting aside his own prejudices, Gideon considered the other possibility. If Coupland were seeking to somehow implicate Lord, and if indeed as Lord claimed Coupland was behind all this, then who would have murdered Fanthorpe and why? Gideon was fairly certain now it wasn't Philip Lord, if only because, by his nature, the man would have spoken of it and justified it without a qualm.

He shelved that mystery too for the time being, because the words Lord had spoken when Gideon challenged him sprang unbidden into his mind. *Seek some common reason why those women and not others were picked to be condemned.* If there was any conspiracy of the kind Lord seemed to think existed, then there would have to be some link between the women. Again he had the sensation that something he already knew held the key. It nagged at the back of his mind but refused to be lured into the bright light of conscious thought.

On an impulse, he rode past the turnoff that led into Pethridge and pushed his chestnut off the track, retracing the way he had ridden with Lord from Dutch's bulb shed. Shiraz followed without protest, making Gideon wonder what orders he had been given. Belatedly, he realised that if Lord had decided an uncooperative London lawyer was too much of an embarrassment, Shiraz would offer a way to relieve himself of that.

Past the bulb shed, the way opened onto a vegetable patch, a sty with a fattening pig, and the view of a stone cottage beyond, which bespoke a comfortable level of prosperity now fallen away. The sound of dogs barking came from within. A young girl was scraping some leftovers from a bucket into the pig's trough. He could see little of Dutch in her. She had a small, heart-shaped face and her hair, which was tied back, was much the same colour as Gideon's mare. She straightened up as she caught sight of them.

Aware that two armed men would be intimidating for any child, Gideon dismounted. Handing the reins of his mount to Shiraz, he walked over, stopping a short distance from her.

There was wariness but no fear in the girl's face. She clutched the leather bucket in front of her chest. Gideon struggled to recall the name Dutch had given for his eldest child. Then he remembered and the flesh chilled along his forearms. Pippa, Dutch had said. And Lord said he had known Beth Sawyer before she married.

"You must be Philippa Sawyer," he said gently. "I'm a

friend of your father's and I need to speak with him."

The girl's expression remained wary.

"Me da's up widda sheep."

She unclutched the bucket enough to point with one hand to where a narrow track led up the hillside behind the cottage. Then, as if considering she had done her duty, she turned and ran back to the cottage, shutting the door behind her.

Sometimes, faced with the human consequences of the legal issues he had to resolve, Gideon had felt such a lurch in his stomach. He tried to ignore it, took the reins from the patient Shiraz and, having remounted, led the way along the track the child had indicated.

In fact, Dutch wasn't with his sheep. He was repairing a wall, fitting the stones together with care and using no mortar. He glanced around from his work as Gideon rode up, then setting the stone he held carefully in place, he used a smaller chip of stone to brace it before he turned nodding his head in greeting.

"You've word for me, Mr Lawyer?"

"Not as yet," Gideon admitted, "I wanted to ask you something, if I may?"

Dutch looked at the length of fallen wall, then tilted his head back and heaved a sigh.

"Will it be long?"

"No. Just a couple of questions. I'll not keep you from your repairs." Gideon found this impatience strange when the life of his wife was at stake. "I wanted to know who might have some reason to want your wife, the Turner girls and Widow Bothwell to be accused and arrested? Someone with a grudge, someone with something to gain?"

"Now that's a question I've been giving much thought to," Dutch admitted. "I am not sure I have an answer."

The strange tickling of something gnawing at the edge of memory began again. Gideon was certain it had been something Dutch said he was trying to bring to mind—something...

Gideon blinked.

"You told me that the Turners are neighbours to Widow Bothwell?"

"Aye, on the other side of her land from us."

"So your land, Widow Bothwell's land and the Turners' run together?"

Dutch nodded.

"And you own the land?"

Dutch gave a brief, hollow laugh.

"Only two men own land in Pethridge, Sir Bartholomew Coupland and the bishop, and even much Coupland land is held from the bishop. I had the copyhold of this place from my da, which I now hold from Bishop Morton."

"And Widow Bothwell and the Turners?"

"The same. Though Widow Bothwell has no heir and the Turners have yet to pay their fine and be confirmed as tenants. In normal times they would do that at the halmote court session next month. But with the troubles we have now, who can say when that will sit again?"

"Could they afford the inheritance fine?" Gideon knew such charges could be high. Sometimes it might be the farms best animal, or an extra year's rent or two.

"The bishop's fines are light," Dutch assured him. "Were they not so, few here could afford it. We've got land scarce fit for sheep, not rich crops like others." He glanced at the unfinished wall then up to the heavy grey clouds overhead. "But what's this to do with the women being accused of witchcraft?"

"I'm not sure," Gideon admitted. "It strikes me as strange that the women taken were from three farmsteads that run together."

Dutch avoided his gaze and stared out over the rolling hills.

"Well, that's as might be, but I'm done. Soon as my Beth is free, we're leaving." He turned back to the wall and started selecting a stone.

It was a different man to the one who had begged Gideon to help him or the one who had offered himself and Lord shelter in his bulb shed. That man had been desperate, full of fear and anger, grateful for any help offered. This one was resigned and evasive.

"Something's happened, hasn't it?"

Dutch paused in his work, back to Gideon and lowered his head. "I haven't any more for you than I've said."

Gideon felt his lips tighten in frustration. "There is something more, though, isn't there? Something you are withholding."

Dutch's back seemed to tense but he said nothing.

"You can't just abandon your tenancy agreement here," Gideon said. "There would be legal ramifications."

The words made Dutch turn sharply, the walling hammer in his hand now gripped as if it were a weapon. Gideon's mare stepped back at the sudden movement, her front feet dancing. From the corner of his eye he saw Shiraz bring his own mount forward, reins held in one hand, the other on his bow. It was enough for Dutch to shift his hold on the hammer, then throw it to the ground at the base of the wall.

"When I went to the Schiavono, I thought he'd bring my Beth home. Well, it's five days she's been gone now and he's done nothing except sleep a night in my bulb shed and send you. And you, for all your fine-sounding words have done nowt. My Beth is still not home and word in the village is they are talking of sending her to Durham for trial. She'll be hanged, for sure." As he was speaking the over-brightness in his eyes had become liquid and a tear tracked, unnoticed, through the dust on his face. "What is it to me to keep this—" he gestured at the land around them, "if the price of it is her life?"

Gideon felt a stir of pity and against his will the image of the child feeding the pigs, her closed face hiding her heart, crept into his mind.

"Who has told you they can save her if you leave?" he asked.

Dutch gave a tight laugh that transformed partway into a throat-catching sob, but he still avoided Gideon's gaze.

"If they take my Beth, they take my heart and soul. That's why I'll not stay."

It wasn't a lie, Gideon was sure, but it was also not the whole truth.

"If you can tell me who is making you promises, I might be able to act," he said, realising how weak that must sound against the imperative pounding in Dutch's head like the tuck of a war-drum. "I will be speaking with the constable today and will see your wife. If I am able—"

Dutch shook his head and interrupted before Gideon could finish.

"Go to your work then and leave me to mine."

THE MERCENARY'S BLADE

He picked up the hammer again and began attacking the stones. For the first time that day, Gideon regretted the absence of Philip Lord. Perhaps if he had been there Dutch would have been more open and cooperative. As it was, bar physical violence, he could see no way to get more from the man. Something, or someone, had bridled his tongue with false promises and fear. Which thought brought a sudden start of fear to Gideon too.

"You didn't tell anyone you have spoken to Philip Lord?"

"I've said nowt to none. Not you, not...." he drew a breath and swung the hammer, "anyone."

Gideon left it at that and turned his horse back towards the village. If Dutch was lying and had betrayed the whereabouts of Philip Lord, there could be an attack on the mill. Even with armed men about her, Zahara could be in danger.

He stopped in the same small stand of trees where he had left Lord on the previous day, turning to put his mare in the path of Shiraz's mount. The other man tilted his head a little in enquiry.

"I think," Gideon said, "someone should warn Lord that his whereabouts might have been betrayed."

Shiraz frowned and lifted his chin, then gave a wary nod.

"I need to stay here and see the Constable," Gideon explained. "Can you take word to Lor—the Schiavono?"

The steady brown gaze held his own for a moment, then Shiraz inclined his head in assent before pulling his horse around. With the merest flex of his leg muscles, he put the creature into a ground eating pace. Belatedly Gideon wondered how a man without a tongue could pass on any message or warning.

Nick was as sure as he could be that he had never been to Pethridge before.

It might lie within half a morning's ride from Howe Hall but it was not on any road he had ever needed to take, and the only road beyond was the high track to Allendale. He set out early to ride the miles from Howe with Mags and Heron as his sole escort and spent the time thinking about what he would need to do and say once he reached his destination.

The thin autumnal sun picked its way through the last swirls of a lifting mist, making the dale appear grey and insubstantial, a ghostly vision made solid by the reassuring sound of the three horses' hooves.

Passing the first cottages, there was a lot Nick could find familiar in the huddle of houses and outlying farms. It was like any other such community in the area. All he knew of the place was that his uncle had land interests there and it was one of the links in the chain that connected the scattered lead mines and funnelled their profits. Nick had no interest in the lead business. Time enough to learn the workings of it when he became master of Howe one day. Aside from the mines, there was nothing else to bring a man of substance to Pethridge.

He had it from his uncle's steward that Coupland's man in the village was one Fulke Brierly, the constable, who was also employed to ensure the money from the lead mines flowed into Coupland coffers. Nick tried to recall if he had ever met Brierly. No face sprang to mind to match the name. But as constable he would be the man to know if any lawyer had been involving himself in the

THE MERCENARY'S BLADE

witchcraft case in the village.

He was given directions to the Priory, by a man clearing a ditch, and found it easily enough. Leaving his two men in the stableyard, confident that the ever-loquacious Mags would secure hospitality for them both, Nick was greeted by Brierly himself, freshly returned from some errand. From the first he seemed to ooze obsequiousness, showing Nick into the hall and introducing his mother in passing, before sending her off to arrange refreshments.

Soon they were sitting at a table near the hearth in the hall, well supplied with wine and cold mutton pie.

"An honour and a pleasure, sir, honour and pleasure," Brierly said when Nick thanked him for the refreshments. "You are sent on business by Sir Bartholomew, hmm?"

Nick shook his head.

"My business here is my own, my uncle has nothing to do with it," Then fearful the man might launch into talk of tax and administration, added quickly, "Nor have I anything to do with his affairs in Pethridge. This is another matter altogether."

Something flickered in the astute brown eyes and Brierly dropped his gaze. The man was probably relieved he wouldn't be expected to account for himself.

"Then how may I help you, sir?"

Nick swallowed down the mouthful of pie before he replied. It wasn't badly cooked at all.

"I wanted to ask you about a visitor you may have had here, a day or two ago—a London man, red hair, who may have been calling himself Lennox and travelling as a lawyer."

Brierly sat for a few moments looking thoughtful.

"There was a man here such as you speak of, sir, said

he was from London, red hair and a lawyer, but the name he went by was David. He was an extraordinary surveyor from the bishop. From what you are telling me though, I should suppose that's not certain, hmm?"

"It is very possible that is not so." Nick had to hide his sudden excitement. He had feared the journey would be as much a waste as Mags had implied it would be. "When was he here? I am trying to find him."

"He was here yesterday and the day before that, taking much interest in a matter of witchcraft."

A coal in the hearth popped and Nick took a breath.

"*Witchcraft?*" He was pleased with the delivery. To his own ears it sounded a fine mix of surprise and outrage.

Brierly's eyes widened.

"There is no need to be alarmed, sir. We have the witches secure. All is in order. But yes, the man was asking some questions about the witches as well as about the lead mines he was here to assess."

This revelation threw Nick into a morass of fresh doubt. Why would Lennox have any interest in lead mines or witches anyway? What if this was indeed a different man—the bishop's man as he claimed to be?

"What interest did this lawyer have in witchcraft?"

"He led me to believe that the bishop would take a poor view of ill-founded charges."

"Then he may indeed be all he says he is," Nick admitted. "Or again he may not. And this I need to clarify. Urgently."

Brierly leaned forward as if to share a confidence. "Should he come by again, would you want me to let you know?"

"You don't know where he is staying?"

THE MERCENARY'S BLADE

"He never said, sir, and it wasn't my place to ask."

He would have to check the local inns, although of course if it was indeed the bishop's man he could be staying at a private house.

Nick wondered how delicate he needed to be. To be granted the position of authority Brierly had within the village and entrusted with oversight of the precious alchemy that turned Weardale lead into gold to fill the coffers of Howe, he had to be a man his uncle trusted. But even so...

"I need to speak with him," Nick said. "If he is the man I seek, he has information which could be vital to my uncle's interests." And that was no lie at all.

Brierly blinked and rubbed at the end of his chin.

"Forgive me, sir, but did you not tell me you were *not* here on behalf of Sir Bartholomew, hmm?"

He had too, damn the man for remembering. But then Brierly couldn't be a fool and keep his place.

"This isn't connected with his interests here. It is a separate matter." Nick tried to think how to make it clear that this was not something to take to his uncle, and yet somehow leave the solid pressure of Coupland authority behind his demands. Then it occurred there was, perhaps, a simpler way.

Nick reached for his purse. "Send word to me when he is here." He tipped the gold coins onto the table exposing the image of an angel on each. "And there will be more of the same when I get to speak with him myself."

Brierly's eyes took on the covetous gleam of cupidity and Nick's shoulders relaxed a little. He had judged the man well. In a small way that helped restore his faith in himself, a faith which the uncomfortable conversation had set at a tilt.

The coins had already vanished when Brierly spoke. "I shall make sure you know if he comes here again. Should I send to you at Howe Hall?"

"Yes. Send written word to me saying you have procured my purchase and if any should ask—anyone at all—tell them I am negotiating to buy some of the local lead for the manufacture of bullets."

Brierly's expression was dour.

"I am a man of discretion, sir, but should Sir Bartholomew ask he will have the truth from me. You understand I am *his* man, hmm?"

"Of course," Nick said. "That is never in question."

It wasn't a thought that concerned him too much. As far as he knew, his uncle would be with the men mustering with Newcastle and not anywhere near Pethridge for the foreseeable future. He stood up, brushing a few stray crumbs from his cuffs.

"I must take my leave. My thanks for your hospitality."

He was shown out much as he had been shown in, with the same ingratiating smile. Mags and Heron were already waiting with the horses. Nick ignored the questioning look Mags gave him. He had no intention of admitting that he was no longer sure the lawyer who had been here was Lennox. Mags would never use the words 'I told you so' but his demeanour would speak as loudly.

They were more than half-way back to Howe when he remembered something. He reined in and turned to Mags.

"Where might a man of some substance stay the night close to Pethridge?"

Mags rubbed his chin. "I'd say they would be looking at a place in Wolsingham. The Pack Horse most likely.

THE MERCENARY'S BLADE

Some king once slept there centuries back and they've not stopped boasting about it since."

"But Wolsingham is further than Howe from Pethridge," Nick observed.

Mags said nothing.

Reluctantly, Nick turned his horse for the market town.

"I'd not be wanting to question your wisdom, sir," Mags said, "but I don't see—"

"You don't need to," Nick snapped.

There was a weighted silence in the wake of his words, filled by the rhythm of their horses' hooves on the hard ground.

"I was going to say you are not *dressed* for making those enquiries, sir," Mags said mildly.

Nick curbed his horse so hard the creature protested. Damn the man, but he was right. If they rode to Wolsingham asking after Lennox, a place where Nick was known, it would be the gossip of the town. He pulled his horse's head round hard until he could see the road to Howe between its ears.

It was some while later Mags spoke again, raising his voice to carry.

"A terrible thing that murder," he said.

What was the man on about now? Nick glanced round to see Heron, the apparent target of the comment, nod agreement.

"Murder?" Nick asked, unable to keep the edge from his voice.

"The man brought in to hunt out the witches. Fanhope, Fanshaw or something, he was killed. Though Brierly is putting it about it were an accident. Word in the kitchen was he didn't want to have to deal with it as a murder—

and that's not the first time. There was one of the miners who—"

"I don't pay you to repeat baseless gossip. Constable Brierly is loyal to the Couplands. Servants' stories are always ill-informed. How can they know the real thoughts of their masters and betters?"

"Right you are then sir," Mags said, his tone pleasant and respectful. "I don't suppose you'll be interested to hear the rumour then that a red-headed lawyer was expected to talk with the Constable in the afternoon today."

Nick had his horse at a standstill again, staring at Mags, who met his gaze with an open air of innocence.

"Brierly said nothing about that."

"Well, he'd told his mother to expect him and she was chivvying the kitchen to serve something special as it seems she has her eye on a London lawyer for her daughter—that's the constable's sister. But I had that from the cook, so it must have been more of that baseless gossip and you shouldn't be paying it any mind."

"God's Wounds!" For the third time Nick jerked his horse's head around, but this time he put it into a canter back the way they had just come from Pethridge, careless whether Mags and Heron were following him or not.

Chapter Ten

Gideon had an uneasy feeling as the gates of the constable's stableyard were closed behind him. Brierly was there, fingers working at each other between his clasped hands. Now and then one hand would stray to rub at his beard as he waited for Gideon to dismount. But once Gideon had alighted, he was courtesy itself.

"Mr David, I am so pleased you have returned." He sounded sincere and the words were matched with a deferential bow. "I have all prepared for you. If you would come inside."

It had rained in the night and the stableyard was pocked with puddles. Gideon had to step with care as he preceded his unexpectedly welcoming host into the house. The hall was as it had been the day before, although the table near the hearth, which Gideon had expected to find piled with the documents and rolls he had asked to see, was empty. But Brierly would have a private cabinet to keep such things and perhaps he intended to take Gideon there.

What he hadn't expected to find was Mistress Goody standing holding the backs of her hands towards the fire to warm them through thin gloves. Her two men stood by the far wall. Gideon assumed they were awaiting orders to bring the witches out when asked.

So it was to be the witches first, then the accounts. Gideon drew on his reserves of self-control and readied them. It was something he knew he would find difficult.

"Is this the man you saw?" Brierly asked.

Gideon blinked. "Which man?"

The words were spoken before he realised the question wasn't directed at him—Brierly was addressing the two men standing away from the fire. One stepped forward, looking at Gideon through narrowed, assessing eyes. It was the man he had parted from his coat in the ruined hovel.

"That's him," the man said. "I recognised his mare. He must have followed me back down to the village and seen Reverend Fanthorpe riding alone, cut across the back field to reach him before he got to the vicar's house. He's the one who killed the reverend."

Gideon felt his jaw drop open, for a moment deprived of words. Brierly watched him with hard eyes and Mistress Goody stepped away from him as if fearful.

"I knew it," she said, "I knew when I first set eyes on him he was up to no good. Poor Reverend Fanthorpe, and him just wanting to keep the village safe from the devil's minions."

"What did you see him do?" Brierly asked the man who had spoken, ignoring Mistress Goody completely.

But Gideon's powers of speech returned with a rush as if a dam had been breached.

"What is this, Brierly?" he demanded. "I came here to see your accounts and spare you some needless embarrassment with the bishop, and you greet me with wild accusations of—"

"Of murder," Brierly said, tone sharp. "And not wild. We have witnesses who accuse you, Mr David—if indeed that is your name, hmm?"

Gideon's blood froze as an invisible band constricted his breath. He had to gamble that since these witnesses were lying, Brierly had no certainty that he wasn't who he was claiming to be. Fortunately, the outrage and anger were real enough, he had only to shape them to the task.

"What game are you playing? When the bishop hears of this, he—"

"The bishop is in London and as things stand, I believe it unlikely he would be in a place to send an extraordinary surveyor such as you say you are. But whether you answer to David or some other name such as Lennox, perchance, I have two men who are willing to swear before a justice that they saw you kill Reverend Fanthorpe."

How in God's name did he learn who I am? Gideon knew his face must have lost colour at the mention of his own name, but he schooled his features, hoping the paling might seem more to do with the unmerited accusation of murder.

"If there is anyone speaking falsehoods here it is that man." He pointed at his accuser. "Why would I have any reason to harm Reverend Fanthorpe?"

"I am sure that will come out in time," Brierly said, his tone making it clear that he had no real interest in either the question or its possible answer. That chilled Gideon. It meant Brierly had his own agenda, and truth, fact and evidence were not going to count. "For now I am more concerned to discover where you have been staying these last two nights. Not in the village and no one has seen you take the main road."

Gideon had to think fast. He could not keep his persona as a man serving the bishop and claim to have slept rough. To name Dutch would be to condemn the man, and to offer the name of any local inn would be a lie easy to expose.

"I stayed with Mr Cale," he said with no hesitation before his answer. "He and I travelled together from London and he had a friend in Killhope. I never met the man. He was away and allowed us accommodation in his absence."

The speed and certainty with which he delivered the lie clearly rocked Brierly's confidence and for a moment Gideon thought he might have a chance yet to talk himself free. But his brief flare of optimism was short-lived.

"No matter." Brierly lifted a dismissive hand. "The fact remains that we have sworn witnesses accusing you of the murder of Reverend Jeremiah Fanthorpe. As such it falls to me in my official capacity as constable to detain you. You are a man of law, or so you claim, therefore you will know I have the right—nay, the *duty* to do so under such circumstances, hmm?"

This was getting serious. Brierly had both the legal standing and the force majeure to lock Gideon up and hold him, then present him to the local justice, Sir Bartholomew Coupland. After the way Coupland had treated him to date, Gideon was in no doubt where that would lead. He rounded on Brierly.

"I am entitled to know the names of all my accusers."

"In good time," the constable told him. "For now, I must ask you to put your sword on the table and, tell me, you are here alone, hmm? That is a strange way for a man of your status to travel."

Gideon didn't answer. There was no point he could see to do so. The presence of Mistress Goody's two men made it clear that any refusal to cooperate in full would result in violence, and from the expressions each wore he had the impression they would appreciate the opportunity. Instead, he drew his sword from the frog at his belt and set it on the table.

"I have little alternative," he conceded, doing up his now empty belt. "You have me at your mercy at the moment, both in legal and practical terms. I shall consider myself your house guest for the foreseeable future. You have my word I won't abscond."

"But whose word would that be, hmmm?" Brierly asked. "Mr David's? Or that of Mr Lennox? You do see my problem?"

Gideon opened his mouth to answer, then closed it again and sighed. "I have no proof of who I am. I told you a letter was sent."

"And that is very convenient in itself. Surely were you here from the bishop as you say, you would carry his warrant in some form, hmm?"

That wasn't hard at least.

"If my business could be moved openly, then yes, but you would know how delicate matters can become and with war stirring the need to secure vital resources, such as lead, for the right—"

It was Mistress Goody who interrupted him. "All this is beside the point, Constable. This creature has murdered one of the most pious and upstanding men in the kingdom." Her voice trembled and beneath the black broadcloth of her bodice her ample bosom heaved in anguish. She put a cloth to her face and blew her nose noisily. "I cannot bear to breathe the same air as that— that *fiend*. He must be in cohorts with the witches, sent to see them freed. He travels alone, appears from nowhere, has no good account to make for himself, seeks to inveigle himself into your affairs—*can you not see what he is?*"

There was an odd silence and her gaze locked with Brierly's. To Gideon's surprise it was he who looked away and turned to the fire. Which of them was the one in command here?

Brierly rubbed his hands together as if washing them in the heat, before looking past Gideon to where Mistress Goody's two men were waiting.

"Put him in the room at the back," he told them. "I will question him later."

"He should be questioned now. We need answers." Their gazes locked again in silent commune—or battle. This time it was Mistress Goody who looked away with a terse nod, as if admitting something. "Of course, Constable Brierly. As you say."

The words of Philip Lord returned to Gideon with full force.

When thieves fall out…

And his own question that quotation had provoked stood in sudden need of an urgent answer.

But who are the thieves?

He was allowed little time to consider as the two men seized him and hustled him from the hall.

The room he was taken to sat at the end of a passageway towards the back of the house. It had a sturdy wooden door, set deep in the wall and Gideon realised it had once been the wall of an outbuilding before the expanding house caught up with it. As they reached the door, the man Gideon had spoken with in the ruined cottage pulled him around and dragged his doublet back over his arms.

"You owe me a coat. This will serve."

"He won't need it in there. Less clothes the better. You're doing him a favour, Jacko."

"I paid for that coat of yours," Gideon protested.

"So you did," the man called Jacko agreed. "A good purse you had then too and—oh look, you still have." His hands moved. "Had." He held up the money pouch so Gideon could see it and grinned.

"Won't be needing that no more," the other man agreed. "Got to pay for your comforts like any other prisoner."

They both laughed at that. It struck Gideon that whatever their mistress might claim to believe about his possible demonic origins, these men suffered from no such superstition.

Then he was propelled through the door so hard that he stumbled and fell to his knees, hands out to keep his face from hitting the ground. Before he could recover, the door had slammed and there was the solid sound of a key turning in a lock.

The reek was vile. Human urine and excrement. It assaulted his senses before he could take in any other details. He got to his feet feeling the cold and damp, one hand pressed to his nose in a vain attempt to staunch the stench and looked around.

It had been a grey afternoon, but in this room dusk had already settled. The sole illumination came through the gaps in a boarded-over and barred window high up in one wall and some thin lances of light from above. Looking up Gideon saw raw rafters and gaps in the roof above them where tiles had come loose and now admitted both sun and rain. This was a storeroom that had probably once opened into the stableyard, before being swallowed into the main house. The poor maintenance of the roof having made it too damp for other purposes, it now served as storage for reluctant guests of the Constable.

"You're not with *them*, are you?"

He had thought himself alone and the voice from the shadows in the corner made him start. A female voice, wary and hoarse. He swallowed the cold saliva in his mouth. It had to be one of the witches.

"No," he admitted, trying to see the speaker, but she had stolen the deepest shadows leaving him at a disadvantage.

"Then who are you and why are you here? You a friend of Brierly?"

"No. I am no friend to the constable. He put me here. I am falsely accused."

"Thank God for that," she said, relief stark in her voice. "I prayed so hard, but was sure it would be more of the likes of Len and Jacko." She spoke the names with disgust and Gideon had no need to ask why. "What do they say you've done? Not a witch, is it?" Her voice grew stronger as she spoke, losing the rasp and edge of fear and gaining a bitter bite. "Or is it something else to Brierly's profit?"

"Not a witch," he agreed, "but to what profit, or whose, I have no notion. You are one of those he holds on a charge of witchcraft?"

"That's what they said. Witchcraft." The contempt in her tone silenced his next question. He had intended to ask if the charges were true.

"You have no idea why these charges were brought against you?"

"I can guess well enough. There were many jealous of

how my John once made good money, Fulke Brierly among them. No. Stay there. They took all my clothes."

Gideon had made a step towards the dark corner and her words stopped him on the spot.

"All?"

"All." She gave a mirthless laugh "I'm like Eve in the garden, though I hope she was a bit warmer."

Brierly had locked him in a room with a naked woman.

Half torn between flight and simple human compassion, Gideon struggled for words. Then realised words were not enough and began unfastening the laces on his shirt.

"Not you too?" There was real misery and desperation in the woman's voice and her words ended on a hopeless moan.

"No," Gideon protested, appalled. "Please, don't think…"

He pulled the shirt up and fought the cloth over his head, before folding it into a ball.

"Here," he said, throwing the bundled fabric as best he could to where she hid, shadow-clad for modesty. "I regret it means you must endure the sight of my chest, but better that I am half exposed to you than you are fully revealed to me."

There was no sound from the corner for a moment after the shirt had vanished into the darkness there. Then he could see slight movements in the clinging shadows and hear the sounds of flesh against cloth. A few moments later a woman stepped into the centre of the room, her face lit by the threads of light that had stolen their way in.

His shirt was huge on her, falling well below her knees,

legs and feet bare below its hem, and she had laced it tightly, almost to her chin for as much of modesty as she could achieve. She looked up at him and was studying his face as if it might hold some secret or the answer she needed to an urgent question.

He had already guessed, of course, but seeing her confirmed it. Her heart shaped face, with chestnut hair still glorious despite being filthy. He had seen her mirror, in much younger form, a scant hour or two before

"Goodwife Sawyer? Elizabeth Sawyer?"

The scrutinising expression shifted as if she had made some profound decision about him and she nodded.

"That's who I am, but who might you be?"

Gideon turned his head to glance at the door, hoping she would get his meaning.

"I am a lawyer from London."

It was hard to see in the dappled lighting, but he thought her mouth lifted a little as she nodded understanding.

"I'd not worry too much. They've not heard me shouting these last two days. They put me in here when they saw I was the one giving heart to the others. That door's stout enough."

"Even so…"

How much could he say, *should* he say?

"What are you accused of?" she asked.

"Murder."

She nodded, as if it was not any kind of surprise.

"Who are they saying you killed?" There was no accusation. She didn't believe he was guilty.

"The witchfinder, Fanthorpe. They even have witnesses willing to swear to having seen me in the act."

It hit him then. This was exactly what had happened to

the women arrested for witchcraft, and he had been party to it by believing in their guilt. It was only now, made victim by the same process, that he knew for sure they were as innocent of the charges brought against them as he was himself.

But Beth Sawyer seemed not to notice.

"That bastard deserved to die," she spat the words with venom. "He wasn't even a proper minister. Just an actor hired to play the role. I heard them laughing about it. Are you sure you had no hand in his killing? I'd be the last to condemn you if you did." She sounded as if she wished he had.

"No," Gideon assured her, quickly. "It was nothing to do with me. If it was, I'd not be so surprised to find myself here."

"Then it seems to me we'd be wise to think who profits from these false charges we both bear. From where I'm standing it looks like it could be the same person."

If Gideon had ever thought to wonder how it was that a man like Dutch would have dreamt of making money from tulips in Weardale, the intelligent gaze that held his own answered the question.

"That is possible," he agreed. Then he thought of the way Brierly and Mistress Goody had exchanged looks. "Or it might be an unholy alliance."

"Oh, I'm sure it's that," Beth Sawyer agreed. "The real question is who's holding the whip?"

Searching his memory, Gideon found nothing. Had he been asked between Fanthorpe and Mistress Goody he would have vowed that the reins were held by the one who should have been the servant. But between her and Brierly?

"I have no answer for you. Although it might also be that the two we have seen are yoked and driven by another."

Her eyes widened.

"Or that. I'd not thought… But you've still not said why you came to Pethridge in the first place?"

And that was hard. He was as sure as he could be she was no witch. Aside from anything else a witch would have tried to use her nakedness to seduce him, bind him to her will. Beth Sawyer was uncomfortable even now, although his shirt covered her decently. However, that still didn't make it safe to share with her why he had come. She might be questioned by Brierly and at present, as Gideon read the situation, his own safety rested on the thin sliver of uncertainty Brierly still had around his identity.

It wouldn't look good to have a genuine emergency surveyor who had been sent by Bishop Morton left in a ditch with his throat cut. Far better to have such a man accused of murder and detained until they could be sure who he was and if, by mischance, it turned out they had indeed misjudged then he could be released and restored with many apologies.

"Well?" Beth Sawyer prompted, waiting for his reply. "It must be something Brierly thinks hurts him?"

In the thin light he caught something in her expression that gave him pause. She had a wary, appraising look and it occurred to him that all the time he had been trying to decide how far he could trust her, she was making a similar assessment of himself.

"That I unwittingly led him to believe," Gideon admitted, reluctant to place any lies between them. "But in part it was so I could gain the opportunity to speak with you and the other women, to get to the bottom of these charges of witchcraft."

She drew in a sharp breath.

"You came to help us?"

"I wished to avoid any miscarriage of justice," he said, wondering even as he spoke if it was caution or cowardice that guided his tongue.

Beth Sawyer threw back her head and laughed.

"Maybe it's different in London, but around here justice gets carried around by men of wealth and power in the same basket as they keep greed. They use it as a stick to beat the likes of us."

He had no answer to that. Or no good answer.

"In London that is true most often as well."

"Then maybe we shouldn't sit around and hope the law will save us."

There was something in her tone that made him pay attention.

"There is another choice?"

She hesitated and again he could sense both her need to trust and her reluctance to do so. It was enough to push him one more step, to tell a truth he was sure she would never betray.

"I came because your husband asked me to do what I could to get you set free. I knew you on sight because I saw your daughter Philippa this morning when I went to speak to him. And before you say anything, you should know your husband now seems to think something he has done will see you set free without my aid."

It was hard to see her reaction as she had looked away at the mention of her daughter's name.

"John is a good man but ever a fool. He'll have said 'Aye' to whatever they promised and never thought it means nothing to what they'll do to me." Her voice caught and she pressed the back of her hand to her mouth as if to stifle what might follow her words. She recovered herself quickly and when she spoke again there was new steel of resolution in her tone. "If you have the courage, I may have our way out. It would be beyond me alone, but the good Lord answered my prayers and sent you, so now we may both have a chance."

The invocation made Gideon think of the man at whose behest he was in this place. Philip Lord would surely hear of his plight and effect a rescue.

Except…

Except Gideon knew the whereabouts of his quarters and could give a good account of the number of men he commanded. Lord couldn't afford to risk his betrayal.

He would come—he had to for his own security. But whether in time to redeem or with intent to destroy, Gideon was far from certain.

So he listened with close attention to what clever Beth Sawyer had in mind.

THE MERCENARY'S BLADE

Chapter Eleven

The first Nick knew of the ambush was a shout from behind.

He had outpaced Mags and Heron in his impatience to get back to Pethridge and confront Brierly. As he rode he ran over the conversation he would have with the constable, for once happy to invoke his uncle's name.

The yell from Mags made him turn in the saddle.

Which was maybe the worst thing he could have done. The road here looped through a small stretch of woodland. It meant he was looking the wrong way when a figure dropped from the trees and bowled him from his horse.

The force of impact drove the breath from him. Landing on his back, gasping, for a moment he could do nothing to defend himself. His assailant, dark against the sky, had reached for a knife, its blade catching the light.

Nick reacted. The moves were wrestling moves learned from hard, impersonal and painful sparring sessions with Hoyle. At the time, Nick had seen little purpose in mastering the art of rolling around in the mud. But now those hard-earned lessons came into their own, and the endless bruises were a price worth paying.

He fought with fury hoping he was hurting his attacker at least as much as he was being hurt. Then a force like a battering ram drove into his stomach and he folded, half gasping, half vomiting and collapsed forward onto the ground, helped on his way by a stunning blow to the back of his head.

"Try not to kill him, Shiraz." The lazy voice sounded not much concerned if the words were obeyed or not.

Pressed face down to the earth, a knife blade against the side of his throat, Nick gave up when his hands were pulled behind him and secured with what felt like matchcord.

"How dare—?" His mouth filled with peaty loam and he broke off, spitting and choking.

"Turn him over. Let's see the side that talks, unless he's like a flounder with his eyes on top and mouth all askew." The words were mocking but there was a hardness under the humour.

The men holding Nick rolled him over and he found himself staring into a cold aquamarine gaze. He had never met Philip Lord but he hadn't the slightest doubt that this was he. The white hair, patrician nose and those eyes that chilled like winter frost. Nick felt as if he had swallowed an ingot of lead and a cold sweat prickled on his skin. His life could be counted by breaths if he were recognised.

If.

They had never met, there was no reason to think he...

Lord gave a sudden grin, mirthless and feral.

"Ah, a Tempest—or at least a squall. But which one? It is breeched, so no longer in the nursery, which rules out, Mark and James. Beneath the mud I see the trace of what might one day make a beard, so I think it cannot be Louise or Elizabeth. Which leaves a choice, does it not, between Nicholas and Henry? And we know Henry has ridden with the Coupland cavalry to join my lord of Newcastle, which means…"

THE MERCENARY'S BLADE

Nick tried to speak, appalled that the man knew so much of his family, but the breath he drew was tainted with leaf mould and instead he wound up coughing and choking.

"Which means," Lord went on with a note of satisfaction that boarded on glee, "what we have here is the proudest scion of house Tempest. The best loved bud on the family shrub. The undisplaced Esau, sole legatee to not just Tempest tenure, but the whole crown of Coupland glory. In short, my friends, this is not *a* Tempest, this is *the* Tempest—the Tempest heir."

Finding the ability to speak at last, Nick pulled himself to sit upright. The fear that had gripped him before blasted away by devastating anger.

"If you are going to kill me, have done with it. At least then I'll not have to endure more of your insults."

The jewel-cold eyes that watched him widened with mock surprise.

"So quick to own your identity? Foolish child. You could have claimed I was mistaken, had some story to explain your likeness to the Tempest-Coupland clan. Something creative and believable, a distant cousin or a misbegotten bastard, perhaps?" Any pretence of humour vanished and the ruthless eyes were viewing him along the length of a sword blade. "But no, that would cut too close to the bone, wouldn't it? Because every Tempest that breathes the air is a misbegotten bastard."

The sword flicked and the cloth of his doublet over his heart, through the lining and shirt below, were cut away to expose flesh. The pitiless gaze held an unquenchable hatred which hungered for his death and the blood in Nick's veins ran as cold as the River Wear. He swallowed hard and stiffened, heart thudding behind the frail protection of his ribs, vividly aware that the meagre strips of flesh connecting them were all that stood between it and the blade in Lord's hand. He knew then his time had come. But he refused to so much as blink, determined he would not give this man the satisfaction of his fear.

Lord turned and hurled his sword away. It flew straight and true to land upright, like a woodland Excalibur, stuck in the ground by the roots of a tree.

"You *will* die," Lord said, turning back, voice allowing no doubt, "but I need to know some things from you first and I don't have the leisure or privacy here that requires."

Lord spoke in a low tone to the man who had first attacked Nick, the one he had called Shiraz. It was a language Nick couldn't understand in full, but seemed to contain the odd word in French, Spanish and Italian alongside others, as if Babel had fallen and the languages of mankind all flowed back together. What Lord said sounded something like: "Keep him away from me. I might not be able to help myself."

They were interrupted by horses approaching. For a half-dozen wild heartbeats, Nick hoped it was rescue. But his captors showed no sign of alarm and a few moments later the four riders were with them. One dropped from his horse and swept off his hat, wiping a hand over his hairline.

"We lost them, sir." The man sounded bitter and embarrassed. "They just disappeared from the road. One moment they were in front of us, then they were gone."

For the first time since he had been ambushed, Nick had a thought to spare for Mags and Heron. Mags had shouted the warning, albeit too late, then he had turned tail and ridden off. Somehow Nick wasn't surprised Mags had made good on his own escape.

Lord's back was to Nick, but he could see the faces of the men reporting to him. They wore looks of shame. Men who had failed their own expectation of themselves.

"An easier task then, perhaps," Lord said, his tone like a whiplash. "Far be it from me to strain your abilities too far, gentlemen. If you can manage to lose two mounted men on an empty road, then maybe you can manage not to lose one already bound and held." The eyes of the four men moved to Nick and he felt his skin tighten.

Lord spoke again in the same strange mix of tongues, ordering Shiraz to find Mags and Heron and make sure, by any means necessary, that they didn't get back to Howe.

Nick understood then why Mags had run and that it had been far from an act of abandonment and cowardice.

"They are not Coupland men, they are mercenaries," he said, loud enough to catch Lord's attention. "Pay them and they will be as loyal to you as any here."

Lord turned and his gaze snapped with surprise to Nick's face. Nick suddenly regretted speaking.

"Most men with their own land to hold raise their own crops," Lord said, his voice gentle. "Kine and sheep, beans and oats—children and fighting men. Trust a Coupland to buy in what others grow and nurture for themselves." That cut was too sharp for Nick to miss, though he doubted any else present would have marked it. Lord turned away and gestured to Shiraz, who was on his horse in a moment and riding off. Lord glanced back at Nick with a mocking smile. "But take comfort, tender-hearted child, if they are indeed soldiers of fortune they will know full well the stakes for which they play."

Then they were on the move, ten men including Lord and Nick. They were on the approach to the village, its cottages and small stone church still invisible beyond the rise when Shiraz reappeared alone. There was no way Nick could tell from his demeanour how he had fared. After a brief conversation with Lord which was too quiet for Nick to overhear, but involved a lot of hand gestures, he rode off again in another direction, heading past the village. Lord turned his own mount back and reined in beside Nick and his personal guard, picking out two of the four.

"Hassan. Bell. There is an abandoned cottage above the village. You will see it from the top of that rise. Take our guest there. The locals think it is haunted so they will stay away. Anyone who does come by..." He didn't finish the sentence, just pulled his horse around and started giving terse orders to the rest of the men.

Nick called out, "If you harm the constable you will answer for it. He is a crown official."

The white-haired man looked back, his face creased into a look of bemusement.

"The *constable*? Why might you think *he* is in any danger from me?"

Nick cursed himself silently.

Lord's smile held no trace of humour.

"Your expression betrays you like a puritan caught lingering by the door of a whorehouse. Do not concern yourself. Your uncle's interests are quite safe. Brierly is a Coupland placeholder. Much as you are. And as easy to replace as you will be." The eyes were alive with malice. "How is brother Henry? I wonder what he will do to celebrate his promotion in the inheritance ranks."

The skin on Nick's forearms felt raw and overexposed as gooseflesh pricked along them. Despite himself, he shivered.

"Whoreson," Nick snarled, as angry at himself for his own folly and weakness as at Lord for his words.

The other man shook his head.

"Oh dear God, if only you knew how often I prayed that might be so, but it is your misfortune that I am not."

Lord gestured to those holding Nick. "Stop his mouth and get him out of my sight." The man holding the reins of Nick's horse turned the beast sharply and, hands roped to his saddle tree, Nick was powerless to resist as cloth was forced into his mouth.

When it was done, his two-man escort closed about him, riding in the direction Lord had given. The rest of Lord's men, Nick saw, followed their leader along the road towards Pethridge. Nick kept his head high and his back as straight as a new made polearm. He would not give his captors the satisfaction of seeing him so much as sway.

If he was going to die, then before God it would be in a way worthy of a Tempest. His ancestors had fought and died in the Crusades. One lay entombed in the church near his home, carved in full armour with sword drawn and a stone lion at his feet. That same strong blood flowed through his own veins. It was his father's favourite saying and the family's informal motto—*It is our bloodline that defines us, makes us who and what we are*. Tempest and Coupland, two branches of the same stout English oak and Nick himself heir to both.

A lone crow called from somewhere nearby as they

went, its harsh throaty cry the sole sound aside the hoof steps of the horses and the wind which had picked up to bring the occasional smatter of rain. The world they rode through was grey. From the clouds to the drystone walls. Even the sheep were grey fleeced, watching the three riders from a distance, jaws working tirelessly, converting useless grass to valuable wool.

The two men with him seemed to have no need to converse. They were alert to their surroundings and yet in some way communicating without need for speech. He had seen Mags and Heron do the same and had been irritated by it. It was something that drew them together and locked him out.

Right now, he hoped that Mags and Heron had somehow evaded the attention of Shiraz. If they went for help to Howe, Hoyle could muster maybe twenty to thirty men quickly enough and outmatch Lord's band. The bitterness in that remedy was the thought of Hoyle leading the rescue party.

The place he was being taken to must once have been a home but was now abandoned. A stone-built cottage surrounded by a tangled garden with a broken wall.

Lord's two men manhandled Nick from his horse and into the building, setting him on the filthy floor and lashing his ankles when he tried to kick out at them. One—Bell, he assumed, as the man had brawny English hands and a florid face—ploughed a meaty fist into Nick's midriff. Then, as he struggled to breathe, smashed a second into his jaw, leaving him dazed. It dawned on him belatedly that Lord hadn't told them to be careful with their prisoner. His mind still running on the hope of redemption by Hoyle, he decided it would be bad enough having to be rescued, but a hundred times worse to do so having been beaten to a pulp.

Gritting his teeth to wait, but determined to keep alert for any opportunity he might have to free himself, Nick sat with his back against the rough stone and tried to ignore the cold and damp already seeping through his clothing. By the sullen grey light that crept in through the empty window he appraised his surroundings.

Someone, it seemed, had used the place for shelter recently. There was a hearth which had fresh ash in it, but the place smelt dank and rotten, as if something had died and been left too long. The only furniture was a table standing in a corner that must have been too big to take out through the door. Most of the rubble and detritus had been swept from the stone flags and pushed into a heap under the table.

Alone inside the cottage, Nick heard the men outside tending the horses and talking in low voices. Then there was quiet again broken by the lone call of a crow, the slight scrape of harness and the sound of the horses pulling at the forage. A few small flies, attracted by the bad smell, danced in circles, adding a low buzzing hum to the background.

Despite his best efforts and the discomfort he was in, Nick found his mind wandering. He had no idea what questions Lord would wish to ask of him or why. What did the man not already know that Nick did? If he could, in some way, anticipate what that might be, perhaps he could use it to his own benefit.

It had to be something to do with the documents. If he was asked what was in them then Nick in all honesty, could not say. He'd been shown the bundle of copies, sealed and secure, that Sir Bartholomew held. He knew as well as Lord must what they were said to contain, but he could neither confirm nor deny the truth of any of it. More likely, it might be that Lord would ask where the documents he sought were being kept. In such a case, Nick could claim—with some justification—that he could take Lord to retrieve them better than he could describe where they might be found. That might buy him more time for Hoyle to mount some kind of rescue. But then again—

A slant of shadow fell through the doorway and one of the two men guarding him came in. The one Lord had called Hassan, whose dark eyes took in the fact Nick hadn't moved. He held Nick's gaze for half a breath, then looked away with less interest than if Nick had been the worm-eaten table in the corner. Hassan settled himself by the door with a view both through it and across the room, then tilted his hat down over his eyes as if he was planning on sleeping.

It was an illusion. When Nick moved to ease his muscles, the hat brim lifted.

Which was when Nick began to feel the first faint tendrils of fear, like the fibres of some clammy fungal growth, weaving a tight web around his heart.

He was a fool to think Hoyle would come. Even if Mags and Heron made it back to Howe, by the time they could gather sufficient men and set out it would be near nightfall. Lord would have finished whatever business he had in Pethridge and have returned. When Nick refused to answer his questions—which he would both because he would betray nothing of the Covenant being vowed to it and from the deep pride that he carried in his family

THE MERCENARY'S BLADE

name—Lord would kill him. If Hoyle ever came, he would find only a dead body here on the floor of this stinking hovel.

Like a leech, the fear drew the bravado from him. *Damn Philip Lord. Damn him to the deepest pit of hell.*

Except he undoubtedly already was.

If Nick's mouth hadn't been stopped with cloth he could have told Hassan things about the man he served which would make even a hardened mercenary flinch. He could have offered the two set to guard him a golden alternative as the key to his release. Instead, he had to sit trussed like a plucked fowl awaiting the attention of a careless cook.

It started to rain and the drops drummed on the slates overhead. Then came a sound from beyond the wall, a sort of muffled groan, like the moan an old man might make when rising with his aching joints.

The effect on Hassan was dramatic. He was on his feet instantly, a wicked-looking knife gripped in one hand, and a pistol appearing in the other. Thumbing the lock back on the pistol he then stood very still, looking through the doorway, head lifted like a hunting dog, listening.

Nick felt his own heart shift to a higher tempo. Whatever was going on had the man rattled and that had to be to Nick's benefit.

Something flew in through the window and the sound of it skittering on the flags of the floor drew Hassan's attention for a moment. That was enough. A small knife sprouted suddenly in Hassan's arm, and the pistol clattered useless to the floor. At once, a human cannonball erupted through the door, impacting the mercenary. But even then Hassan might have prevailed, flooring his attacker, his knife scything down for the kill. But a second man came through the door and grasped the arm in the instant before it struck, turning the blade.

Nick, struggling now to get his feet under him, could only watch as Hassan fought in grim silence for his life, but the men he was pitched against were as feral as he and a few moments later it was over.

Mags stooped to pick up the pistol, fingered the lock to restore it to be safe and pushed it into his own belt. Beyond him, Nick could see Heron working through the other possessions of the man they had killed, relieving him of a purse and claiming the knife that would have taken his own life had Mags been a little slower.

Grinning, Mags crouched to cut Nick free, starting with his hands.

"Sorry, sir, we were a bit delayed. I needed to be sure that your friend Lord was well away with his people before we came."

Nick needed a moment to get the circulation back in his hands. Then he finished pulling off the gag Mags had cut loose from his mouth, spitting out threads and fluff. Anger flared on the tinder of his relief.

"I will slice him open and pull his entrails out through—"

"Of course you will, sir, as soon as we have him. But right now we need to be going. There's no telling how long he'll be in Pethridge and the two of—three of us wouldn't be any kind of a match for the eight of them." Mags offered a hand to help Nick to his feet, saw the blood still on it and wiped it on his breeches before offering it again. But Nick knocked it aside, grim determination pulling him to his feet.

THE MERCENARY'S BLADE

"We could take Lord here," Nick snarled. "If you had sent to Howe we'd have the men to do so."

"And rightly so," Mags agreed, placidly. "But I was put in the place of weighing your life against the chance we might take Lord. I see now I made the wrong choice. I hope you'll forgive me, one day—though that's something you'd not have been in any place to do if I'd ridden for Howe."

A low whistle came from outside. Nick realised Heron had finished looting and left the building. Mags' lips tightened.

"That means we must go now, sir." His tone held the bite of urgency and command and by instinct Nick found himself complying. It was still raining, the horses stood ready and Heron was mounted. His horse and Mags' were caked with mud under their bellies and up to the shoulder.

"They got a mite clarty when we hid them in a ditch," Mags explained as he helped Nick to his horse. Then the three headed across the sparse slopes of Weardale at a brisk canter, Bell's and Hassan's mounts trailing behind. Nick, seeing them, thought with satisfaction of their masters now staring with unseeing eyes at a darkening sky.

It left a message for Philip Lord that he made a mistake tangling with a Tempest.

Chapter Twelve

Gideon listened as Beth explained and studied the rafter she spoke about. It was a good four feet over his head, solid oak and running from wall to wall of the room.

"So let me get this straight. I help you get onto that rafter then you can go along it to the wall and reach the roof. There is—you say—a place where the water has weakened the lathe battens and if it has, then you will be able to work the slates loose to make a hole large enough for us to fit through."

Beth nodded. "I've been here two days and it was the first thing I noticed when I looked for a way out, that the roof was weak there."

Gideon, whose understanding of the way roofs were constructed came somewhere around his level of understanding of how shirts might be made, could only see a small slant of light through the tiles at the place Beth was indicating.

"I will take your word for that, but even if you can break through, how would I get up there after you?"

"I don't know. Unless…"

"Unless?"

"Your shirt is strong. Perhaps, if I—"

Gideon held up a hand. "No."

"You'd prefer to sit here and wait for them to come for you?"

"No. If that were the only way I would agree, but I have my belt and maybe if I jumped…" He looked again at the

THE MERCENARY'S BLADE

rafter and realised that if his belt was put around it there would be little slack for him to climb. "And if not and either of us need to go naked, then it will be me."

She held his gaze for a moment, her own doubtful, then nodded.

"I hope it may not be needed."

"Me too. But right now I think the most important thing is to see if you can get up there and through the roof."

It was easier than Gideon thought it would be. She wasn't heavy and was agile enough to pull herself on to the solid crossbeam when he lifted her up. But it had got even darker as clouds closed in, threatening heavy rain. There was so little light he feared she wouldn't be able to see her way. Watching lighter shadow move against the darker shadow, he resisted the impulse to call out to her.

Despite Beth's reassurances that no one would come even if he shouted, the thought of drawing any attention to themselves was not a pleasant one. She had said she was sure they would be left alone until after dark as that was how it had been for her each day so far. But who knew when Brierly might come to question Gideon as he had threatened?

From above came small noises of stone on stone and a brief silence.

"I'm not strong enough to do this." Beth's voice seemed to drift out of the darkness. Then she had wriggled back to the crossbeam and spoke more quietly. "There is good news, though. The roof overlooks the back of the house. If we can get out, we can drop down into the vegetable garden."

That would be better than the well populated stableyard with its heavy gates.

"I will try and get up there," he said, undoing his belt, looping it in his hands. "Can you catch this?"

It took two attempts as the first time he didn't throw it hard enough, fearful of catching her with the buckle. The second throw was after she had scolded him in a few quiet words for treating her as a fragile thing.

The first real luck they had was when she found a notch in the wood of the beam. Perhaps where it had been cut to fit the rafters but needed alteration after. She threaded the belt through the gap and the buckle held on the notch. Now it was in easy reach and right beside the wall, which should, in theory, give Gideon some purchase for his feet to support his climb.

But when he tried, he found himself swinging out from the wall on the belt. Cursing he dropped down and tried again, this time twisting his body, so he wasn't pushing with his feet away from the wall but more sideways onto it. That worked better. The stonework provided a sort of staircase. He had his fingers pressed against the rafter when, unable to pull himself higher, he slipped again.

Dropping back, he shook his head.

"I can't get high enough to get over the rafter. The belt lies too flat on the wood."

"Take your boots off," Beth suggested, and wriggled herself flat on the rafter, reaching down towards him. "Then grab my arm at the top."

Doubtful, he removed his boots and knotted the laces, throwing them up for Beth to place over the rafter. Then he tried a third time, using what he could now feel as toeholds on the rough stone. The grip of Beth's hand was stronger than he had expected, and a moment later he had a hold on the solid bar of the rafter and was heaving himself onto it beside her.

"I need more practice at that," he said, feeling as blown as if he had been running. "Perhaps we should do it again?"

The laugh was momentary, but it was laughter and he felt more hopeful than he had since Jacko and Len had pushed him into the room.

Navigating along the beam, he reached the point in the roof where he could see subdued daylight. Already a good half dozen of the tiles had been moved and were now lying on the ledge where the roof met the wall. Removing some more would make a space big enough for them to get through. But he could see the problem. The tiles might be removed, but the wooden batten to which they had been secured was still in place. He tried the wood, but although old, it was still solid. He could break through it with his full weight, but then he would risk tumbling through the roof. What he needed was something to weaken it—to saw through it at least a little and damage the wood enough that he could break it.

Moving back to get a better view his hand caught the edge of a broken slate. The cut was slight, but the idea…

Voices outside sounded sudden and loud. Gideon nearly dropped the slate he was holding.

"Seven men. Armed. They were seen heading in the way of the Sawyers' place."

He didn't know that voice, but he recognised Brierly who spoke after.

"Nothing to say whose men they were?"

"No."

"Then it is possible they have no business in Pethridge, they could well be taking the track to Allendale. If I were going that way I'd want a man or two at my back as well. I think you…" Brierly's voice faded and a door closed silencing it again.

Gideon wasn't sure if what he felt was apprehension or excitement at the news. An anonymous body of armed men riding towards Dutch's farm could mean only one thing. But whatever the arrival of Philip Lord might presage, he had no intention of waiting on it. Shifting his grip on the slate he started using the rough edge of it to saw at the wood. Had he needed to cut clean through it would have been a long and difficult task, but once he had a decent notch cut into the lathe, he shifted his attention to the other side of the gap in the tiles and started working on the wood there.

Behind him and to one side, perched like a dove on the rafter, Beth Sawyer watched his efforts. The slate was almost as hard on his hands as on the wood. It came to him to regret that his hands were not hardened from manual work, but soft-fleshed from wielding pen and ink.

"Here," Beth said, touching his arm to get his attention. She held a strip torn off the bottom of his shirt and wrapped it around the hand he was using to saw with the slate. After that it was easier to work and a short time later, with rain now falling heavily, he managed to apply the strength of his arms to break the batten.

"We did it," Beth Sawyer's voice was breathy with exhilaration and Gideon found himself smiling at her, feeling much as he had been when he won his first legal case.

"We did," he agreed. "Now we just—"

He didn't need to say anything more. One moment he was right beside the hole and then he was through it, bracing himself on a roof slick with rain and exposed to the full force of the downpour. The bare skin on his chest and back felt more like jelly than flesh under the freezing assault. He looked down, taking in the view of the soft earth of the vegetable garden, maybe eight feet below the bottom of the roof, and trying to see where there might be a place to drop down.

A jutting corbel on the corner.

If he could work his way over to it…

Beth was beside him scant moments later. Her chestnut hair plastered to her face. The shirt had begun to cling to her naked body in the rain, revealing more than Gideon would have liked of the curves beneath. He looked quickly away and focused on reaching the corbel, moving crablike on the slick slates. Beth seemed to slip less. Her bare feet had better holding than his own, which were encased in woollen stockings.

At the corner of the roof, the corbel was difficult to grip, smooth with age and slick with rain that washed from the tiles. He twisted his body, feeling his hands lose grasp, and then dangled for the briefest moment before his weight pulled him free. Landing heavily in the middle of several rows of spinach, he fell forward to measure his own length in the mud. Fortunately, the brief moment hanging from the corbel had been enough to break his fall and the final drop did no real harm. By the time he was on his feet, caked in clay, but ready to help Beth Sawyer down, she had landed beside him, with much more agility than he had been able to muster. She took off running right away, keeping close by the wall, oblivious to the rough, muddy ground and her lack of footwear.

Gideon followed as fast as he could, feeling every stone

and the suck of the mud, cursing himself for his folly in leaving the boots swinging on the rafter. It was scant comfort to tell himself that even if the boots had been around his neck there would still have been no time to put them on and he'd have had to run without them just the same.

As fortune had it the jutting wall of their erstwhile prison protected them from being viewed from the house. But that advantage would not last long. To reach the gate at the far end of the walled garden they would be in view of the upper floor of the house and anyone glancing from one of the windows would see them. The hopelessness of even attempting this escape uncoiled like a serpent in his guts. They should have waited until it was closer to dusk.

As if in confirmation of his worst fears a shout came from the direction of the house. Glancing back, his heart jumped into his throat as he realised that there were two men working in the garden. He hadn't noticed them before, even from above, because they were concealed close behind a high trellis of beans. One was grey-bearded and made no move to intercept them, standing arms akimbo in evident disapproval, but the other, younger, started running towards them, holding a long-handled garden tool.

Beth Sawyer was already by the small gate and was pulling at the bolts. Gideon prayed for a miracle and ran. He reached the gate paces ahead of their pursuer, as the last bolt gave way. Beth waited for him to reach it then stood her ground in the gateway.

"Joseph Carter, you stop right there. Bolt this gate behind us and forget you saw me." Her tone was so imperious that Gideon wondered anew if she was indeed

THE MERCENARY'S BLADE

a witch and had the power of command over others. But then she went on. "You and your da wouldn't even be living in Pethridge today if my John hadn't stood by you. Don't you dare try and stop me and don't you dare say a word to the constable. I'm thinking I'll tell him you're a witch too."

The man mumbled something which Gideon couldn't hear, but the tone of voice sounded hostile.

"Oh don't you worry, I'll not be staying here now. You'll be safe enough 'cos I'll be gone."

Then she pulled the gate shut and ran followed by Gideon. To his surprise she was laughing as they ran into the trees.

"His face. He really believed me." Then she sobered. "He's right though. We can't stay here now, me and John and the bairns. But someone needs to get the others out."

Gideon realised in their own desperate escape he had forgotten the other three women, somewhere in the house, being held as Beth had been held.

"We'll get them out," he vowed as they ran on. "By legal means or whatever it takes."

And that was when it came to him.

The whole picture with everything in place.

But he could do nothing about it on his own, so he followed Beth Sawyer as she ran.

They were out of sight of Brierly's house when Gideon recognised they were taking the way he had ridden earlier to reach Dutch's farm. The intense rain had slackened when he saw an orderly group of riders topping the rise ahead. His instinct was to hide, but they were in open ground and they couldn't hope to outrun mounted men. He hesitated and was going to try and flee anyway...

But Beth Sawyer was already running—and running *towards* the riders. They had turned off their path and headed towards her, the man in front reaching down to swing her up to sit behind his saddle despite the mud. With one hand the rider released the cloak he had been wearing against the rain so Beth could wrap herself in it. As the rider did so a sweep of white hair caught the silvered sunlight.

Gideon, half-naked, soaked, bedraggled, and coated from head to foot in mud from where he had landed in the spinach, waited for the horsemen to reach him.

"Behold, a creature formed entirely of clay," Philip Lord said by way of greeting. "Do we need to take the *aleph* from the *emet*? Oh, wait. It breathes so it cannot be a golem. What then might it be? A lugworm?"

Gideon had no resources to respond as the jibe deserved, so he ignored it.

"We need to get the other women away from Brierly," he said instead.

The gaze resting on him became a little less hilarious and a little more appraising.

"The Star Chamber has reached a final judgement in favour of the accused?"

"If you are asking do I believe the women are innocent of any charges of witchcraft, then yes. Brierly is holding them for some nefarious purpose of his own, which isn't entirely to do with you, although I believe he is using the excuse and cover of that to serve his own ends, too."

Now he had Lord's full and undivided attention. This was what had come to Gideon suddenly, as they were running—the solution, shining, pristine and complete, with the reasons trailing behind like oriflamme, to justify

THE MERCENARY'S BLADE

it.

"You need to tell me," Lord said, then glanced in the direction of the Priory, the tops of its chimneys just visible from where they stood. "But not here. Let us get Beth back to her family and see if we can find you something to wear that does not appear to belong more to a potter than a lawyer."

He gestured to one of the men to offer Gideon a mount, who reluctantly obliged, preferring to give over his horse rather than share a saddle with the mud-caked Gideon.

Less than an hour later as the afternoon was beginning to drop into twilight the rain had stopped. Under the watchful eye of Shiraz, Gideon had endured amused looks and comments from four of Lord's men as he cleaned up. Finally, he rinsed the mud from his hair in the trough outside Dutch's bulb shed. He was dressed in clean clothes which looked well-worn and fitted badly. But for all that he was grateful for them.

As he finished his transformation, Lord, who had ridden on to the Sawyer's farm with Beth, reappeared from that direction in company with a short procession. First came Beth Sawyer, fully clad. A sturdy toddler curled against her shoulder, capped head showing from beneath her voluminous cloak. Beth walked beside Lord, who was leading his own horse.

Dutch, holding the rails of a good-sized hand cart, packed high, came after. He was followed by a small, high-sided cart pulled by a hardy-looking black pony which was led by the slight Pippa Sawyer. In the cart sat three much younger children, all of their father's sturdy build, perched on another pile of belongings. Two dogs ran alongside them.

"You are set on this?" Lord asked, looking at Beth.

"It is for the best," she said, untwisting the fingers of the child from her hair. "If we stay, they may try again. I won't allow that to happen to my family." She spoke firmly and behind her Dutch nodded.

For once it looked as if someone was not bending to Lord's will and Gideon found his high estimation of Beth Sawyer rose some more as she held her ground against him.

"If Brierly were made to recant—"

She didn't let him finish. "It would be the same. People would always look at me wondering and the children would suffer. I always was the outsider here, anyway, tolerated more than accepted even after all these years. No. It's better this way. For us. Even John knew it. It's why he'd packed up already."

Dutch nodded again, but this time added his voice to his wife's. "I signed the papers. The land is no longer ours anyway. All we can do now is go."

"Those documents can be found and challenged or destroyed," Lord told him. "You were under duress."

"I took the money they offered me," Dutch said in a low voice avoiding Lord's gaze. "They said that proved it was consenting. Besides, what have we to stay for anymore?"

Beth Sawyer sighed and looked over at Gideon.

"You should travel with us," she said. "We go to my family in Whitby and you'll be welcome to stay with us there until I can find you a reliable ship heading south."

The offer was as generous as it was unexpected. It was too much to grasp and consider in a single moment. Gideon realised he must be gaping at her. With an effort, he gathered his wits and started thinking.

THE MERCENARY'S BLADE

"If I flee, my guilt will be assumed. Especially if it is discovered that I took a false name and identity."

"But it would save your life," Beth pointed out. "There is no shame in it. You'd not be the first, nor likely the last." She sent a meaningful look towards Lord, who returned it with an untroubled gaze.

"The man Fanthorpe deserved nothing else. Whoever did the deed has my thanks for one and I'd not see anyone suffer for it." Dutch said, stoutly.

"Go back home to London," Beth said. "Even if they condemn Mr Whoever-you-said-you-were here, your true name is still an innocent man who can return to London and go back to his work there."

Dutch was nodding.

"You should listen to my Beth and we would welcome your company on the road. She has the right of it, wouldn't you say so, Schiavono, sir?

Philip Lord didn't answer at once. He narrowed his eyes at Gideon, as if weighing his worth.

"It is not my choice to make," he said, then shrugged as if shedding any responsibility for the matter. "The offer is there for you to go. But if you wish to remain, it seems I now keep open house to take in waifs and strays. One more or less is no great issue."

The temptation to walk away from the last few days—to make them as if they had never happened, was almost irresistible. It was true that an accusation was unlikely to follow him back to London and with the winds of war blowing ever stronger, he had little to fear from it. But then a single face and a promise he made rose like a ghost to fill his thoughts, and he bowed his head accepting the burden that he knew he must carry.

"Goodwife Sawyer, your offer is generous and much appreciated, but there are matters here I cannot leave unfinished including that of this witchcraft charge and the women still caught in it."

She smiled as if pleased with his answer despite all she had said.

"You have work here then, Mr Lawyer—those girls and Widow Bothwell have no one else who can help them as they most need. But a clever man could find a way to make the confessed words of a frightened child stand for nothing."

"They have confessed?"

"Just before they moved me Anne signed their words—well put her mark to them as she can neither write nor read. And who could blame the girl, more than half out of her wits already, with those men using her, nothing to eat and that evil bitch tormenting her day and night." She levelled her gaze on Gideon as she might level a musket barrel. "It was a confession to murder. To witchcraft. To killing sheep and unborn children. A man good with a sword might cut them free. But they are not like me. They have no other home to go to and would wither like vines snapped from their roots if they had to leave. They belong here. Leah is set to wed Drew Lamb next spring, my John says he has been one ever protesting her innocence. Few in the village are convinced of their guilt. If any, tis myself they would see blamed. But only a lawyer and a clever one can unsign those words, show the women as innocent, and expose what has been done here."

Gideon wondered how he was supposed to effect such a miracle whilst under condemnation for murder on his own account.

THE MERCENARY'S BLADE

"I can try."

"Then let me tell you what else I know," she said, handing the infant to Dutch who held the child close as she reluctantly relinquished her grip on her mother. "I'd speak it to a justice if I didn't have the little ones to think of—and if the justice wasn't a Coupland."

"They don't seem well respected as a family around here," Gideon observed.

Beth made a snorting sound.

"I suppose you're come from London, so you have that as an excuse," she said, as though being from London was akin to being from Bedlam. "Around these parts the only law that counts is that of Coupland and every man of law hereabouts dances to the tune he plays. Any who disagrees he either buys or buries—or both."

Dutch nodded and when he did so his daughter made a grab for his beard as it came within reach. The small fingers gripped tightly. Gideon saw the tiny fist and turned his head away sharply, caught out by the memory of what he had seen in the ruined cottage. It was a reminder, if he needed any, of why he had to act.

"These people are no true seekers of witches," Beth said, "They spoke of how Fanthorpe was come from Leicester and hired to play-act the role. It might be that Fanthorpe is murdered, but the one to watch is that woman, Goody. She is the one who led him."

"And who is she working for?" Gideon asked.

"Well that they were not kind enough to mention. But as I said before, it doesn't take much to know who would do such around here," Beth said. "The only thing else I can tell you is that they were not the ones making things seem like witchcraft. Fanthorpe and Goody met with someone who told them what had been done and where to go to discover it."

"No names?"

"No names."

By this time the child in Dutch's arms was becoming fractious and the other children sitting in the pony cart were getting loud in whatever game they had made for themselves.

"We must go," Dutch said firmly and passed the wriggling toddler back to his wife. "We need to get a good way before it's too dark to travel."

"You'll have two of my people to see you to Whitby," Lord insisted. "It's not safe to travel unguarded in these times."

Beth Sawyer accepted with obvious reluctance and after a brief farewell, the family began their trek to a new life.

"You could have gone with them," Lord said as the small procession disappeared into the gathering dusk, taking the direction away from Pethridge. "No one would have blamed you or held it against you, least of all Zahara."

Mention of her name made Gideon look at Lord sharply, but the expression on the other man's face was one of simple curiosity, as if wanting an explanation.

"When I know the location of your sanctuary?"

Lord smiled.

"My 'sanctuary' as you put it, may well have outlived its intended purpose already. I came here seeking some information and, thanks to a fortuitous encounter, I expect now to have my hands on it very shortly. After that," he pulled himself up on his horse as he spoke,

THE MERCENARY'S BLADE

"well, after that, *all shall be well, and all shall be well and all manner of things shall be well.*"

Someone had found a horse for Gideon, one that seemed to dislike him, as it flattened its ears and tried to bite when he clambered on.

"And now?" Gideon asked.

"Now you tell me what you have discerned and deduced regarding the intrigues and machinations of Clan Coupland and their allies, and then we shall go and revisit your nemesis, redeem your horse, and David may slay Goliath."

Under darkening skies, they set the horses towards the Priory, Lord's remaining four men and Shiraz as their escort, while Gideon explained.

"As I see it, the plan was to use this accusation of witchcraft to stir local ill-feeling against you—that part would have been Coupland's without a doubt—and someone of his has been doing the sheep killing behind it and," he hesitated, "and setting the scenes. Brierly may have said he sent for the witchfinder, but I suspect that to have been at Coupland's behest, and people of Coupland's choosing are working hand in glove with whoever of his had been doing the killing before they arrived."

"You think this is all at Coupland's door?" Lord asked. Then he laughed. "How refreshing to have you agree with me at last."

"All that I said, yes. But I believe, the choice of victims was down to Brierly. Coupland would trust him as a local man best placed to make such a choice. I think Brierly saw in it an opportunity to use this all for his own gain. You see, the holdings of the accused run together and each small parcel is struggling. The Sawyers only made enough money while they had income from the tulip trade and they had the largest and best placed of the three. No doubt the constable thought to combine the plots in his own name. Together they might be profitable for grazing."

"Or perhaps," Lord suggested, "he knows of something to be found beneath the farms which he would be hard-pressed to lay claim to if the land was titled in lease to others. There are lead mines all around here."

Lead.

That was something that Gideon hadn't thought of, but it made a lot more sense than Brierly thinking it worth killing to gain more grazing for his sheep.

"Or that," he agreed. "But whatever the incentive, it was his plan to have the women accused and then purchase their copyholds. Beth Sawyer was the only real problem as the land wasn't in her name but Dutch's."

"Oh, Brierly had that well in hand," Lord told him. "Yesterday after we left, Dutch was approached by two men and told that if he signed over his farm, they would release Beth today and if he chose not to she would be sent to Durham for the next assizes and they would make sure that she did not survive to the trial. That is why he was packed and ready to go. They even gave him four pounds in crowns to purchase all the livestock and chattels. Much less than their worth, of course."

Which explained Dutch's sudden change of heart, but...

"Then why did Brierly not release Beth Sawyer?"

"Why should he once Dutch had signed? He had what he wanted at that point. And he still had to carry out what Coupland had charged him with."

THE MERCENARY'S BLADE

"I think," Gideon said carefully, "Brierly recognized she knew too much of his scheme—enough to fear that she might tell someone, and then Coupland might realise his loyal constable had been working on feathering his own nest, using Coupland's scheme against you for his own ends. I think much of what we see: Beth Sawyer not being freed, the power that Mistress Goody seems to wield, perhaps even the murder of Fanthorpe, but certainly me being accused of it, all come from Brierly fearing exposure. My arrival must have taken him close to panic—which was why he forced Dutch to sign and told him to leave."

Lord considered that for a time.

"You may have the right of it, I encountered one of Coupland's people on the road who seemed most solicitous for the welfare of the constable."

"Well, we do know someone who wasn't Brierly was setting the traces of witchcraft. A Coupland man no doubt. Perhaps that was who you encountered?"

Lord's grin was brief and feral.

"That would make things interesting. But for now." He removed the hat he wore and pulled something around inside the crown, then grabbing and twisting his hair, pushed it back up under the hat, letting a long fringe of black curls now lie visible in its stead. "For now, in company with an armed escort, flying the prince bishop's banner and preceded by hautbois and clarions, Mr David shall prove his identity as said bishop's extraordinary surveyor and secure the release of the women still held."

"I am sure you will tell me how. And how the small matter of the men who perjured themselves to condemn me will be resolved."

Lord laughed.

"*Doubt thou the stars are fire,*
Doubt that the sun doth move,
Doubt truth to be a liar,
But never doubt…

…but never doubt that these things are in hand."

As they rode on it occurred to Gideon that this was the first conversation he could recall having with Philip Lord in which he had been treated as an equal. Something had changed, he was unsure exactly what, or what had led to the change, but it felt as if the man he rode beside had discovered some reason to offer him a modicum of respect. Which was perhaps why he asked something he had been wondering about ever since he had seen the two talking.

"Tell me, Beth Sawyer, what is she to you?"

Lord didn't even glance at him before replying.

"A friend."

"And Philippa Sawyer?"

There was nothing of Dutch in the child, unlike the others who were of his sturdy breeding. Lord favoured Gideon with a look, but one that held something which he found hard to interpret in the growing dusk.

"And Philippa Sawyer is the daughter of a friend." Lord brushed the black curls back from around his face with an impatient hand. "If you must go digging with the bones of children at least have a care for the ground you choose. I can't be hurt by anything you might say or any claims that flow from it. But you, of all men, should know the power accusation can have to form the illusion of truth—especially in those predisposed to believe. The Sawyers have enough troubles already without being

THE MERCENARY'S BLADE

pursued all the way to Whitby by the twin demons of rumour and gossip."

"Is that an admission?"

"An admission of what?" Lord reined in hard, so his mount cut in front of Gideon's and the bad-tempered beast objected with a sharp buck. Lord was looking at him with a cold expression. "It was a statement about the way of the world, the nature of humanity and the fact that any that dare call me 'friend' are invariably subject to calumny. Now, is there any purpose to your line of questioning, or is it something designed to assault my *amour-propre*?"

Gideon, caught in a swirl of tight anger, had to wonder the same himself.

"I asked because I want to know how far you plan to go in any attempt to free the other women. Beth Sawyer might have a call on your loyalty, but those women are nothing to you and I don't want to find myself walking out on a limb only to turn around and discover I am left balancing there on my own."

It was too dark to see the details of Lord's face, but the laughter was harsh. "It seems whatever I do or do not do, it makes little difference in your giddy mind. There is dew on the fleece and there is dew not on the fleece—here, Jerubbaal..." and something glittered in the air, ignited by the last light of the day. Gideon caught it instinctively. It was a gold coin. "There is your angel too. And now you are in my paid employ, under my protection, and thus sure of my investment, perhaps we can go to work?"

Lord turned his mount back to the track and broke into a fast trot. Urged on by Shiraz and the men around him,

Gideon had very little choice but to follow.

Chapter Thirteen

As they reached their destination, Lord said something quietly to Shiraz who turned his horse away from the house on whatever mission he had been set.

The constable's house stood peaceful in the twilight. Far from hautbois, clarions and banners, their arrival was uneventful. Remarkably so, because Gideon had suspected they would find the place much like a wasp's nest that had been beaten with a stick. Brierly should surely have sent someone to check on his prisoners by now. Finding the two people who could do him and his scheme great harm missing, would surely leave the Constable frantic.

But they were ushered into the house by one of the household servants with no sign of unease or dismay. As Gideon and Lord waited in the hall with Lord apparently admiring the sagging hangings and the parchemin wainscoting they partially covered, Brierly's mother appeared, head bobbing like a hen, hands clasped high on her chest as if she was about to use them to cover her mouth. It was Lord she greeted.

"Oh Mr Cale, I am pleased to see you. But my Fulke..." She broke off, her hands fluttered like nervous pigeons.

"There is something ailing the constable? I trust he has not been taken ill?" The voice Lord spoke in was unlike his own, burred and less penetrating.

"Oh, no. No. Not at all, but..." Then she seemed to become aware of Gideon and the nervous head movements stopped for a moment as she smiled.

"I am glad you have come too, Mr David. My daughter is expected home in a day or two and I am *so* sure she would like to meet you."

"If I am able to be here I shall look forward to that," Gideon lied, "but your son?"

"Oh, he isn't here. He went with Mistress Goody to the funeral of poor Reverend Fanthorpe and has not yet returned. I sent a man to enquire and was told he had left for home well over an hour ago, but he has not come. Mistress Goody returned, but before I could speak with her, she and her two men—"

Her words were silenced by the door slamming open and Brierly stormed into the hall shouting. "Who gave those men in the stable yard permission to furnish that chestnut mare and who the hell are they?"

Gideon instinctively looked to Lord who gave the slightest nod and stood in shadow with his arms crossed as Brierly advanced on his mother.

"And who in God's name…?"

Gideon moved so his face was illuminated by the candle on the table. Brierly saw him, blanched and drew a sharp breath.

"You, sir, should be…"

"I should be considering how to frame my letter to Sir Bartholomew regarding the behaviour of his Constable towards a representative of Bishop Morton," Gideon said in his best legal voice.

"I have witnesses," Brierly snarled, then turned to his mother and grabbed her arm hard enough that she squeaked. "Get out of here, woman, this man is dangerous."

THE MERCENARY'S BLADE

He pushed her towards the door but before she had taken more than a few nervous steps, Lord was beside her, an arm out in a solicitous manner, turning to both block her passage and confront Brierly, his voice level.

"There is no need to concern yourself, Widow Brierly, it is quite safe to remain, I promise." He spoke over her head, gaze fixed on the Constable. "Incidentally, where are Mistress Goody and her two men?"

"They are not here?" Brierly turned to his mother who stood beside Philip Lord, wringing her hands as if they were a rag she needed to squeeze all the water from.

"I was just telling Mr Cale, they came back then left almost at once," she said, her voice little more than a whisper. "I did not get to speak to them."

"But—" Brierly had lost his choler.

"Mr David," Lord said, "came to me in a bad state and told me a tale of being detained by you. I did not believe him, of course."

The constable's whole body stiffened.

"What was I to do, hmmm? Mistress Goody, her two men, they were willing to take an oath they saw this man murder Fanthorpe."

"Of course," Lord said. "Isn't it obvious? If they were the ones who killed him, it would be in their best interest to place the blame elsewhere."

To Gideon that made a terrible sense.

Brierly frowned. "Why would they want him dead?"

"Maybe he was thinking to try blackmail," Lord suggested. "Or perhaps simply because he was not one of their own. Perhaps it was a convenient way of removing someone they could not be sure of and Mr David here as well. They will have noticed he was getting close to the truth of their activities."

Something within Brierly faltered. The sense of solidity he projected seeped away, like a waterskin that had been punctured. He took a small step backwards and dropped onto one of the chairs.

"I—I had to speak with someone after the funeral. I didn't think…"

"Didn't think what?" Gideon asked, wondering at the sudden change.

"That Mistress Goody and her two helpers would leave Pethridge," Lord provided helpfully. "They will be well away by now."

Gideon stifled a groan. Mistress Goody and her bullies must have returned, found himself and Beth Sawyer gone and realised they were about to be exposed.

Brierly shook his head and seemed to come to himself again. He got to his feet and made a form of bow, lowering his head and shoulders towards Gideon.

"I owe you an apology, Mr David. I was misinformed."

"Misin—?" Gideon found himself fighting down sudden fury.

"I think the word you meant is 'misled'." Lord's voice in its disguised tone reminded Gideon he was there to play a role, not to speak as he felt.

Brierly looked at Lord as if wondering whether he was being offered a rope to cling to or to hang himself.

"Yes. That is what I meant. Misled. And I apologise. Wholeheartedly. You must permit me to find you some more suitable clothes before you leave, Mr David, that's the least I can do, hmm?"

Gideon opened his mouth to refuse, but Lord answered for him.

THE MERCENARY'S BLADE

"Thank you. Perhaps your mother?" He turned a charming smile on the terrified woman. "Would you be so kind?" When she had nodded her agreement, Lord stepped aside so she could scuttle out of the door. Gideon heard a loud sob as she closed it behind her.

"Now, my good friend Mr David can explain to you what he needs you to do to resolve the legal and financial aspects of his business here," Lord said in the same patient tone.

"Yes. Yes, of course." Suddenly eager, Brierly gestured to the table. "Please. Sit. Tell me what you need."

It took Gideon all his strength of will to swallow his fury and keep in his role as extraordinary surveyor. Focusing his questions on the mines and the money as he would if he was indeed the bishop's man.

He worked through the key points as quickly as he could, demanding more detail, more documentation—receipts and chits against which figures could be checked. At some point Brierly's mother came in with a pile of clothes, including a fine pair of boots that Gideon suspected were Brierly's best and left them on the table, before rushing off again. She didn't return but a servant appeared with wine and goblets.

"I will find all you ask for and see to the destruction of the false confession," Brierly assured Gideon, by now wringing his hands very like his mother.

"You need only to produce it," Gideon told him. "I will see it destroyed myself."

"As you wish, of course, but this will take time, hmm? If you can give me until tomorrow…"

Not wanting to delay the resolution longer, Gideon had his mouth open to refuse, to see it all done there and then even if they had to wait half the night for him to find it all. But Lord had got to his feet and put down his goblet which was still more than half-full.

"We have covered the main business and will leave you to arrange matters. I am sure you will see the women who have been wrongfully accused are well tended. We shall return upon the morrow to oversee the end of this and then Mr David here can go back to the bishop with all the financial details and a glowing report of your role in preventing a vile miscarriage of justice."

Gideon wanted to protest. The last occasion he had given Brierly time it had gone badly. But Lord's iron grip on his arm served to keep him silent. Fuming, but silent.

Brierly nodded rapidly. "As you say, Mr Cale, of course."

The constable showed them out in person, waiting as their horses were brought round and despite his ill mood, Gideon felt a brief warmth when his chestnut mare nickered as she recognised him.

"Mistakes are made sometimes," Brierly said as they were mounted. "I am glad you understand. Tomorrow all will be set right. Hmmm?" Then he looked around as he realised something wasn't as it should be. "Mr Cale, your four men…?"

"Will be staying here tonight," Lord said, "You may have problems if Mistress Goody and her companions decide to return. They will be here to keep you and your mother safe."

He didn't allow any time for Brierly to protest, leading the way from the stableyard and out under the clearing sky where the field of stars now shone cold. The moon was bright enough to bestow the gift of limited vision to those travelling in the dark.

"As soon as we get back to the mill," Lord said. "I give you my word I will send some men to try and find the Goody woman and her bravos although I suspect there will be no trace of them. They could be miles away by now."

Gideon barely heard the words.

"Why did you say tomorrow?" he demanded. "We could have had those women free this night if we had waited."

"We could," Lord agreed in a pleasant tone. "But the bishop's extraordinary surveyor and especially the man who represents the interests of the Duke of Richmond would not be so concerned in the fate of three women as in the possible misappropriation of funds from the mines. So we were not going to sit there and ask it of him over and above those things."

Gideon struggled hard to work with that. Struggled and failed.

"I don't understand you. Being so gentle and careful with the man. What does it matter what he believes once the women are free and safe?"

"As I already mentioned and Beth Sawyer was at pains to point out, these women are not wild adventurers or those with the means to uproot and resettle. Nor like the Sawyers blessed with family elsewhere who will take them in. They need to be able to stay here and live in peace."

"How does that involve Brierly?" It seemed stark and simple enough to Gideon. "What he has done would earn him a death sentence if it came to light."

"*And almost all things are by the law purged with*

blood; and without shedding of blood is no remission." Lord shook his head. "If that were the best solution, don't you think I would have taken it? But, think on it: Brierly is a vile maggot of a man, but he is also a Coupland placeholder. If he were replaced it would be by another man of like kind or worse, willing to do whatever Coupland asked of him. And that man would not be one we have a hold over. So do we kill him too? And his successor? How would that protect these women?"

"Once the charges against them have been quashed they would be deemed innocent. We could have forced Brierly to provide what we needed there and then and freed the women."

"We could," Lord repeated, his tone still amiable, "and left them exposed to be harassed on the same grounds or new ones when we were gone, because he would then know for sure we were not who we claimed to be. This way they will be safe as they will have the hand of the prelate himself raised over them in their protection—in the mind of Brierly at least."

Somewhere a dog fox cried into the night and they went on a few paces with the sounds of the horses' hooves soft in the air.

"In real life," Lord said, "problems are not solved with neat cuts and straight edges. We live in a make do and mend world, with small and practical, if rather grubby, dealings patching over the gross abuses to achieve what help we can. If you want noble restitutions where good rides triumphant and evil falls, go read Thomas Malory or Chrétien de Troyes." He stopped speaking and drew a breath which escaped as a sigh. "Besides, as much as I understand you men of law have values that the majority of humanity finds strange and hard to fathom, I for one am not that happy about terrorising innocent middle-aged beldames in their own home by threatening and torturing their sons before their eyes."

Gideon's anger slipped its leash, careering free and he had no mind to recall it. How dare this man, a man with no morals, lecture him on such things?

"No? You terrorise innocent *young* women in their beds." Gideon snarled.

"And just as we were getting along so well." Lord let out a breath with exaggerated energy. "Then let me put it another way. Much as I am sure you would like to return to Zahara tonight bearing all three liberated prisoners upon a single elephant, garlanded with lotus, jasmine and red hibiscus, there to lay them at her feet as offerings, I promise you, being who she is she will be better satisfied by a more prosaic, effective, if less dramatic result."

"Leave Zahara out of this."

Lord laughed. "As I recall you were the one who brought her into the conversation. I am attempting to show that whilst you are accusing the rest of us of whatever calumny you might perhaps care to study your own motivation." He paused for a moment and when he spoke again his voice had changed and was back to the brisk, impersonal tone he had always adopted with Gideon before, the same tone he used with his men. "As soon as we rejoin Shiraz and those he has with him we will be riding fast. I want to get back. It may have slipped your mind but I have a friend who might be dying. Have no concerns. My men will ensure Brierly keeps his word, we can return tomorrow to collect them and see to it the women have been set free. If you—"

He broke off as Shiraz joined them, somehow silent and invisible even on horseback.

Gideon couldn't see much but he was aware of Shiraz's hands moving in brief gestures illuminated by the scarce moonlight. Then his hands were still and Lord drew in a sharp breath. He turned his mount towards the slopes above the village in the direction of the abandoned cottage and when he spoke his voice was flat and bleak.

"With me, Lennox. It seems we have other work to see to this night."

And for once there was nothing of humour, malice or cleverness in his words.

Nick knew what he should do was to send urgent word to his uncle about what had happened. But with the events now in the past and the sting of shame lingering in the present, he stayed his hand.

On their return to Howe, he forbade Mags and Heron to speak of what had occurred. He even sat and ate with them so he could ensure they understood. Mags rubbed at his beard and looked doubtful.

"Well, you see, sir, your uncle, Sir Bartholomew, he pays my fee, when indeed it is paid. So were he to ask…"

It was a conceit as Nick knew full well that Mags had never spoken with his uncle. He had arrived the day after the men had marched for Newcastle and been taken on because of the recommendation of the others of his own kind who seemed to hold him in much respect. Impatient, Nick slid a gold unite from the purse at his belt, more than a month's pay for the man. "Here."

Mags left the coin where it sat on the table between them.

THE MERCENARY'S BLADE

"Is that for my silence or my hire?"

Fuming, Nick added two angels, then as Mags' gaze shifted to Heron, who was applying himself to his food as if oblivious to any conversation, took another twenty-shilling coin and added it to the pile.

"I don't need to buy the silence of a man who never talks," Nick said.

Mags scooped the four coins up in one hand and laughed.

"You have the right of it there. He's not the world's greatest gossip." Then he grew serious and leaned over the table. "You do know Lord is going to be hunting you now? Two of his men dead on the dales, he can't ignore that. Can't afford to."

The flesh between Nick's shoulder blades seemed to shrink.

You will die.

It had the feel of a dark prophecy.

"Then I will have to find him first," Nick said tightly and rose from the table. "We will resume the search tomorrow."

Mags released a breath that puffed from his cheeks.

"You might be needed here, sir. Sergeant Hoyle being absent still, if you were thinking to gather the men as they come in—"

"I can leave word they are to remain," Nick said, a gnawing certainty of the real reason for Mags' reluctance spicing his words with sharpness.

"Of course you can, sir. But then if we were to run into Philip Lord again, the result might not be so different from today. And today we had a stroke of luck that meant me and Heron could get free and hide. The next time we might not and you can be sure Lord will be much more careful now he knows he underestimated us."

Nick tightened his lips and dropped back onto the bench.

"So we remain cooped up whilst Lord struts like a rooster all over Weardale?"

Mags spread his hands. "Not at all, sir. You can order me and Heron to keep searching, while you are assembling the men for when we might know where to go."

Heron had finished eating and now looked between the two of them with the mildest interest.

"What is to stop you returning to the alehouses and spending those coins and the rest of the money you will no doubt ask me to provide you?"

Mags made the same outbreath as before, but in a lesser key.

"The time of visits to alehouses is done with, much as I am sad to say so. Our man was riding with a company and the horses were still fresh—a lot fresher than ours that had been ridden hither and yon. That means he must be quartering them somewhere in the area, somewhere that isn't a tavern, an inn or an alehouse."

Nick hadn't considered that at all.

"You mean Lord has a house nearby?"

Mags lifted a shoulder,

"That could be. He was born hereabouts."

Nick was very tired after what had been by any standards an exhausting and trying day. The words took him off guard and he spoke before he thought.

"He was born at Mortlake but raised here at Howe."

"Mortlake? That'll be some place down south?"

THE MERCENARY'S BLADE

Nick realised then what he had said and cursed himself. Not that it mattered, a man like Mags wouldn't understand the significance. So he nodded as if it were nothing. "Near London."

"Then what did—" Mags stopped himself, as if having second thoughts. "Why do you think he had business in Pethridge?"

Nick tried to make his overtired brain think.

"He was after Lennox, perhaps, as we were?"

Mags nodded and looked thoughtful.

"You could be right, sir. Maybe you should send for the constable to see what he knows? It might not be safe for you to go to him, but he can't refuse a summons here. It seems to me he wasn't properly open about it all when you spoke with him today."

And that was the uncomfortable thought Nick took with him to his bed.

Riding back to the mill, exhausted and with the bodies of two men slung over the horses, Gideon felt as if all the victories of his day were swept away. It didn't help that Philip Lord was entombed in an anger so cold it could shatter rock and had no time for what he derided as Gideon's 'legal frills and ribbons'.

But despite that Gideon tried.

"They are dead," Lord told him. "No amount of law will restore them to life."

"We should be reporting this as murder."

"Who to? The constable?"

He had no answer to that.

"They were my men," Lord said tersely, "and I will ensure they have justice as they would have wished."

"That's not justice, that's vengeance," Gideon protested.

"And what precisely do you think 'justice' is?"

Gideon said nothing. Not that he had no reply. On the contrary he could have replied at length and in great depth, but there would have been no point. He had been forced to step into a world where the values he nurtured and had been nurtured in were disregarded as irrelevant.

He was used to an England where law was respected, where the vision of justice and revenge as held by great men like Thomas Aquinas or Francis Bacon held sway. An England where it was a given that *'Revenge is a kind of wild Justice; which the more Man's nature runs to, the more ought the Law to weed it out'*. Lord had dragged him into an alien England, where there was only what Bacon called 'wild justice,' an avowed enemy to true justice and the law.

Refusing to answer Gideon's questions as to what his men had been doing in the cottage, Lord rode hard across the night-embalmed land.

What little Gideon could gather of what had happened to the two men came from overhearing a brief conversation as they dismounted outside the mill. It was between Lord and a man whose name Gideon had yet to ascertain, but who seemed to be taking on the leadership role Matt Rider had held.

Lord, he learned, had chanced upon Nicholas Tempest on the road and taken him prisoner. Tempest had been bound, gagged and held in the abandoned cottage with two men left to guard him. Gideon wondered, but didn't ask, what Lord had intended with him. A hostage against Coupland, perhaps? But whatever the plan might have been, it had ended in blood. The blood of two of Lord's men.

"It was not the Tempest brat," Lord said. "Even unbound he could not have overcome one of them, let alone both. But he had two men with him when we ambushed him. I assumed, being outnumbered, they would head back to Howe for support, giving me all the time I needed. It seems they didn't."

"You'll not take the blame for that from any here. Hassan and Bell were both born with eyes and ears."

"You tell that to their families," Lord said bitterly.

"Thankful I am that's not my job, Schiavono sir. Now, you should know, there's somebody here asking for you. She's been waiting a while..."

Gideon heard no more. The two moved off and he was left standing alone outside the mill, holding the bundle of clothes he had been gifted by the Brierlys.

Even at night the mill slept with one eye open. As he made his way from the stables to his room he was challenged twice. The second time was by a man guarding the stairs in the main room, who was kind enough to offer him a candle stub so he could see rather than feel his way upstairs.

To his chagrin the room was locked and he had to bang on the door. Had he been less tired he might have thought to go back down and sleep on one of the pallets, but he had reached that point of fatigue where his focus had become single-minded and alternatives were too much to consider.

Anders let him in.

"I apologise for the door, but I wished to speak with you upon your return and knew that as I would sleep it was the best way to ensure you would wake me."

Gideon felt his guts sag and he sat on his bed to begin working off the borrowed boots.

"Can it not wait for morning?"

"It can, but I think you might prefer it did not."

Which could mean only one thing. The jolt of adrenaline brought him to his feet, one boot off.

"Zahara?"

Anders lifted both his hands. "Is well."

The relief left Gideon even more exhausted as he sank back. An odd tic began in the corner of one eye.

"But it is about her that I wish to speak. This afternoon she asked me something about the medication I gave her and as she was talking freely on the matter with others present, I asked if she wished the matter kept confidential. She told me there was no need to do so as it was well known to all here, just most had the delicacy not to speak of it."

"She is ill?"

"Hear me out," Anders said. "I observed to her that you had no knowledge of her problem and she said that was not so. You most certainly did. She was most insistent and surprised that I thought otherwise. But that was all the conversation we had on it as I was called away."

Gideon tried to trawl through anything Zahara had said to him about her health, but there was nothing. Nothing at all. Anxiety and fatigue hazed his thinking.

"I don't understand," he said at last. "I can't think of anything…"

"I am not sure I understand either," Anders agreed, "and she did not elaborate. But if she already believes you know, it would not be breaking any confidence for me to

THE MERCENARY'S BLADE

tell you. On some nights Sara is subject to violent fits which can come on when she sleeps. When she relives her past. Unless she is restrained, she has been known to do herself harm, throwing herself around quite violently. The medication I have given her should help. If not, I have a distillation that might."

It was a night for revelations.

"Fits?" For a moment Gideon was back in that bedroom, the soft scent of sandalwood, the guttering flame of the candle throwing crude shadows on the wall and Lord, fully clothed, pinning the night clad Zahara beneath him.

Oh God! It's Sir Percival...seeing without understanding what he sees.

His whole being felt as if a mighty hand had picked him up and turned the world around before setting him down again, so he could view it all from a new perspective.

"Seizures, if you prefer," Anders was saying, apparently oblivious to the impact of his words. "Brought on by a distortion of her humours where her dreams become too real to her sleeping mind."

"Seizures," Gideon echoed, flatly.

The Dane must have mistaken the reason for that reaction because he leaned forward and clapped Gideon's shoulder with one hand.

"You should not worry, my friend. I think—and she agrees—that it comes more by an ailment of the mind than of the body, a trauma she suffered in the past that haunts her sometimes when she sleeps. A wound never heals so well that a scar cannot be seen, but with my treatment which should rebalance her humours these fits may pass completely. She is not in grave danger from this." He sank back on his bed and pulled the blankets up over himself. "And now kind words don't wear the tongue, but you will excuse me if I go back to sleep."

"Of course. Thank you, it was most considerate of you to tell me." The words came out anodyne. The implications were too much to process and in his exhausted state Gideon didn't even try. He felt numb. He lay back on the pallet and had the presence of mind to snuff out the candle before sleep took full possession of him.

He was still reeling from the full meaning of what Anders had said the following morning. Dressed in the gifted clothes he went down for breakfast. He had risen late so had to make do with the remains of what had been brought to the table an hour before. Since Anders had been up and gone when he woke, he ate alone. There was no sign of Zahara or of Lord himself. The mercenary company went about their business, paying Gideon less heed than one of their horses. If they were a bit more subdued than they had been, he didn't notice it. But then loss of comrades had to be something such soldiers took in their stride. From their conversation, though, he gathered men had been sent out to look for Mistress Goody. Philip Lord had kept his promise.

And now Gideon knew, thanks to Anders, that he had been wrong about him.

That changed everything.

He should be getting ready to head back to Pethridge with Lord, but suddenly, the desire to be alone was unbearable. Instead, pushed to a place beyond thought, he walked. Taking the path along the riverbank, letting the peace of the river sounds seep into him. The autumnal sunshine was welcome after the rain and a fresh breeze scudded grey clouds over the sky.

He reached the willow, stooped on the bank by the path, branches trailing to kiss the water. Stepping under its shelter he sat, his back against the trunk, trying to let the turmoil within fade.

Perhaps he needed to recast Philip Lord from demonic monster with few redeeming qualities, the man as described by Sir Bartholomew Coupland and Sir Richard Tempest, into Philip Lord—the Schiavono—as seen through the eyes of Zahara, Shiraz, Beth Sawyer, Anders Jensen and Matthew Rider. Perhaps Lord might be a fundamentally decent human being who Gideon, by his own actions, was pushing into behaving in ways that made him seem the monster.

A voice spoke suddenly and close by

"I will miss you."

Gideon froze. The voice belonged to Lord and it was on the other side of the willow from the direction of the mill. Lord was speaking in French. Then there was a second voice. A woman's voice, rich and sultry answering in the same language.

"I wish I could stay, even one more night, but there is no time. The devil rides south and I must follow."

"My loss is surely his gain. He is being a hard master?"

The hair over Gideon's forearms rose.

Just when he had begun to convince himself that he had been wrong about Lord…

The words of long-familiar prayer ran through his head. *Deliver us from evil.*

"Anything but," the woman said. "He is perhaps the only one in all creation except you who appreciates what

I can do for him that no one else can." She laughed, then went on in a different tone. Lower, more urgent. "He wants you, though of course he would never say. Will you be long at your affairs here? He still intends that you join with him."

"He sent you to ask?"

"He sent me for a thousand reasons, that was not one. I ask because he would want to know."

"And I have already given him my answer. Nothing has changed."

There was a strong silence and despite the cold sickness in his stomach, Gideon was overwhelmed by a desire to see the scene he could only hear. If he moved a little...

With exaggerated care he got up and tried to peer through the veil of hanging branches. The broken twig seemed as loud as a pistol shot and he froze again, but at least now he could see Lord standing with a man who had his back to Gideon. A man who was booted and wearing a dark blue cassaque, sword visible from beneath the cloth. A bay gelding of evident quality tugged at the grass nearby. Of the woman he had heard speaking there was no sign.

Mercifully, Lord seemed oblivious to Gideon's presence.

"Tell the prince I will come when I may." Lord stepped forward as he spoke and drew the other man into a close embrace. "He knows as long as he keeps you by his side, I must do so. What are his intentions?"

The prince. The Prince of Darkness?

"If he has his way he will push south. He believes London is everything."

Gideon blinked. When the figure spoke he realised it

wasn't a man. It was the woman he heard speaking before but dressed as a man. He drew a breath sharp with astonishment.

Lord was smiling at her. A tender smile.

"As long as he keeps you safe."

"It is my work that keeps him safe."

They kissed then, in the way that those who were old lovers might kiss, lips parting at the end slowly, reluctantly. Now Gideon could see the woman in profile. Had he not heard her speak he would never have guessed her gender. She was tall, slender-hipped, her hair loose beneath the broad-brimmed hat, its dark red curls matching male fashion and her face comely, though marred by a deep scar which puckered the flesh from eye to ear on the side of her face he could see.

She walked away towards the horse, her stride as bold and broad as any man. Lord followed but offered her no help to mount and it was clear she needed none. Her final words were soft.

"Take care, Philip. I would not wish to walk a world without you in it."

It was the first time Gideon had ever heard someone use Lord's given name to address him and it sounded beyond strange to his ears.

Lord had caught her hand and kissed the fingers before relinquishing it.

"How can that ever be when you hold my soul in your keeping?"

Gideon couldn't catch the rest of Lord's reply to her as it was spoken too softly. Whatever it was made her laugh and brought a sparkle of pure mischief to light her face, revealing a beauty her masculine disguise was hiding.

Then she touched her hat in farewell, looking every inch the man she pretended to be and rode off, pressing her horse into a canter along the river path.

Lord stood still, watching her go and Gideon realised he would need to go too. When Lord headed back to the mill it would be along this path.

"*And that which ye have spoken in the ear in closets shall be proclaimed upon the housetops.*" Lord spoke to the empty air then he turned and looked directly at Gideon. "You may as well come out now, I would not think it a lawyer's work to lurk in bushes and eavesdrop on private conversations."

Feeling both angry and ashamed, Gideon pushed through the fringe of foliage.

"How could you know for sure it was me?" he demanded, moving onto the attack to avoid having to defend the indefensible.

"How could I not?" Lord asked, his tone acerbic. "It had to be someone who had my permission to be there or Shiraz would have dissuaded them from taking the river path and of those, you are the only one who has both an unhealthy fascination with my affairs and the habits of a duckling flying after its mother, calling 'peep'. It did not take theurgic powers or the examination of entrails."

"Who was she?"

Lord shook his head.

"If I had intended to introduce you, I would have invited you to join us. Whatever your curiosity, you will have to be satisfied with what you witnessed and whatever speculation you may make from that. But you would be well advised to have a care as to what you might choose to say next. The lady's honour is in my keeping and I will defend it."

"What honour can there be in those who admit to serving the devil?"

"The—?" Lord's bemusement seemed genuine but then his expression cleared and he started laughing.

Gideon felt a familiar knot grip his stomach and despite being cropped short, his nails dug into the flesh of his palms with tightening fists.

"You mock everything decent and sacred," he snarled, all the goodwill he had so recently tried to muster for Lord dispersed. "I despise you."

Still caught up in his mirth, Lord managed to control himself and stifle the laughter sufficiently for speech.

"And you, most vertiginous of Giddy Ones, are shying at shadows. If you must leap to conclusions with all the exuberance of a wild he-goat, then at least be sure you have studied the ground upon which you will land." Lord turned away, making of the movement a dismissive gesture as he began walking back towards the mill.

Gideon was left with little option but to follow. He had committed himself to see through the matter of the witches, and his promise to Zahara was a binding oath.

Chapter Fourteen

Although Nick wasn't about to admit it, Mags' words were responsible for his decision to send for the constable. He was also waiting impatiently for Hoyle to reappear and for the men out hunting Lord to return. Then he could reassemble his small command to seek out and exterminate whatever rat's nest Lord had contrived to furnish for himself.

But to roust out Lord and whatever force he might have with him, he would need to have more men. So he had been over the carefully prepared muster roll left by his uncle for the defence of Howe in the event of an emergency and arranged to have word sent to all those on it who had a horse that they should be prepared to answer his summons at a moment's notice.

That done, time hung on him like a waterlogged cloak. He sat in his uncle's private cabinet, booted feet resting on the desk and eyes fixed on the panelling on the wall opposite. It had been in this very room last spring that he had learned the truth about his own family and the Couplands.

All his life Nick had known they were set apart from others by some greater responsibility. Known he had to grow up fast and grow up well to be able to take on that burden when he came of age. He'd heard words like 'covenant' and the name of Philip Lord from the day he arrived at Howe after his mother's death and the need for silence regarding any matters relating to the family and its affairs had been impressed on him with brutal force.

Then, last spring, in this room with his uncle and his father, he had met two other men. Men he had never seen before or since. Men he was told he had no need yet to know by name. They watched him in silent judgement as they asked him questions. Questions that made no sense even now, ranging from what languages he could speak through to his religious convictions. He had given them the catechism he had been raised in, though he had it more by rote than by belief. The two men heard him repeat it and were pleased. One had even leaned forward and gripped his arm.

"You are given the hardest of tasks, for to you falls the ending of what was begun. These are troubled times and all of the Covenant men must be ready."

He hadn't understood of course. But he had felt the cold chill of responsibility the words placed on him. Then, having spoken the words of an oath to bind himself to whatever it was they wanted of him, he sat in silence as his uncle, voice ringing with pride, spoke of his family history. How Sir Bartholomew's grandfather had built a false wall into this chamber and constructed the chambers beyond to serve a great purpose. A purpose that lay at the heart of the Covenant and which had been the highest of trusts given to the Couplands and their close kin the Tempests.

It had remained a closely guarded secret since.

Nick thought back to the times he had stood in this room to receive praise, or more often a strap for poor behaviour from Sir Bartholomew. Unaware then of the secret that lay behind the wall, concealed within the fabric of Howe only accessible to those who held the key.

He swung his feet to the floor and crossed to the wall. He was now one of those holding the key. He bent so his fingers could reach into the small, invisible hole where bookshelves became wainscoting. The catch was there and he pulled on it, gently. From somewhere in the wall came a loud click, metal hitting metal as in a clockwork. Where there had been wall panels now was a door. But not a door one might walk through. To enter one had to crawl.

Pulling the door fully open, Nick crouched and stared inside. It was dark, but not damp. There was a lantern set by the door with flint and tinder ready to light it. Nick could tell from the lack of dust and the faint smell of beeswax and linseed that it hadn't been long since his uncle had been in here. Part of him wanted to light the lamp and go in. See if it was as it had been, if his memory had played him false. But sense prevailed. If he did, his uncle would know.

Footsteps were coming along the galleried landing towards the room. Nick straightened up, swung the panel back in place and managed to reseat himself before there was a sharp rap on the door.

"Come," he called, matching the tone his uncle used.

It was Mags.

"Sorry to disturb you, sir, but I thought you'd want to know. Sergeant Hoyle's returned—he'll be making his way to speak with you."

That brought Nick to his feet again.

"God's wounds. The last thing I need is Hoyle lurking like an extra shadow when I speak to Brierly." And the man would always find some reason or justification to do exactly that.

THE MERCENARY'S BLADE

"You want me to distract him, sir?"

"No." Nick knew that Hoyle could not fail to notice if he had a visitor and who it might be. "I want you and Heron to keep the constable from coming here."

"That won't be a problem, sir, Ben Chainy only set out with your message a half-hour ago. He had to wait on the farrier."

"Then if you are quick, you could catch him."

"Did you want me to go see the constable myself and ask him—"

"No." Nick didn't let him finish. Brierly would have to wait and he wanted Mags out of Hoyle's way too. "Just make sure the constable will stay in Pethridge and then continue your search."

Mags nodded.

"As you wish, sir. I'll come back soon as I have news. Shouldn't be too long."

For some reason Nick had no doubt whatsoever that Mags would indeed find Lord.

After Mags had gone Nick looked around the room, making sure there was nothing out of place for Hoyle to criticise. He rescued one of the document bags that was half off its hook and swiftly rearranged some books he had moved to place his feet on the table. As he did so he glanced over to the wall and realised the catch on the secret door had not caught fully and a faint line of shadow showed its outline. Relieved he had spotted that before Hoyle should notice, he closed it firmly.

He was sitting with the account's ledger open and a sharpened quill in hand when Hoyle knocked briskly and came through the door without waiting.

"We need to speak, young master, and in private."

Nick felt his fists clench at the use of his nursery name. He threw down the pen so that ink flicked over the page, spoiling the neat columns of figures.

To his surprise Hoyle ignored it.

"It's about something your uncle set me to do. Some plans he wanted kept secret, but it looks to me that if I don't tell you they will be in ruins—if they're not already."

Nick frowned. It didn't surprise him in the slightest that his uncle had left the sergeant secret instructions. But he was surprised Hoyle wanted to talk about any of them. Especially with Nick, whom Hoyle still seemed to see as barely worthy of being in breeches.

"What plans?"

Hoyle stood with his hands behind him, rocking back on his heels as he spoke.

"The traitor you stayed here to hunt."

Nick felt a pulse of excitement.

"Philip Lord?"

"That's the one," Hoyle cleared his throat and then coughed. "You see, Sir Bartholomew had this notion that it was needful to make sure Lord became someone those hereabouts would fear and have no time for. He said that Lord was too good at cozening folk to his way of things. That's true. He always was."

The implications of that last comment nearly passed Nick by, but there was something in Hoyle's expression that drew his attention.

"He always was?"

Hoyle shuffled his feet. "He was a boy here, too, like you were."

Nick had known that for a long time. But now it struck

him what it meant. All the same things that Hoyle had taught him, he would have taught Lord. All the same things Nick had hated about Hoyle, Lord would have gone through. All the same things…

"Anyway, Sir Bartholomew said that the people need some reason to hate him. To show that he was capable of the greatest of evils. A worshipper of Satan, making sacrifices to the devil."

"You mean this of witchcraft in Pethridge?"

Hoyle clamped his lips together and nodded.

"It were what your uncle ordered. He arranged for some people who he told me could be trusted, to come and sort matters. I was overseeing it all. He said it would lead to someone who knew where Lord might be found coming forward to say."

And that sounded exactly like the kind of thing his uncle would do. With ruthless disregard for any caught in the net of deceit. 'You do not,' Sir Bartholomew had often told him, 'go to a battle and spare the brats and whores.' Nick wondered if the people summoned belonged to the Covenant. That was usually what his uncle meant when he said someone was worthy of trust.

"Then what has gone wrong that you need to tell me about it?"

"Fulke Brierly," Hoyle said. "He didn't keep to the original plan."

"What was my uncle's plan?"

"To accuse an old woman and have her admit to the crimes and blame Lord. But the constable added his own ideas. He decided that it would carry more weight if there were more witches."

"And you agreed?"

"It was already done when I heard of it," Hoyle told him, scowling. "Sir Bartholomew's people had agreed to it in his absence. They thought it was a good idea, better than the original one. I had to make the best of it. And maybe it might have worked out, but something went wrong. The evidence I put in place for the village to find, to convince even the doubters, was removed by someone before it was seen."

"What was removed?"

"The things they should have found..." Hoyle trailed off and one of his meaty hands swiped across his face. "Well, *things*. Things I'd put there. Proof of witchcraft and things to mark it as Lord's work."

Nick wondered why Hoyle was being so coy about the nature of the proof.

"What happened?" he asked.

"They had taken a visitor to see it. One of the bishop's men, there about the accounts for the mines. Someone who would make a good witness. But when they got there nothing was where it was supposed to be."

"Who removed that proof?"

Hoyle shook his head. "We don't know. The man paid to play the part of a witch hunter accused the others of betraying him and that led to an argument and he wound up dead. The constable will have told you."

Nick drew a sharp breath at that. "No. But I have spoken to Brierly." He wondered if it was wise to go on. But perhaps it would show Hoyle that he was not the only one who could deal in such secrets. "It is possible Brierly might have seen the lawyer Lennox, alive."

That made Hoyle's features darken. "The lawyer's dead in that fire. We have witnesses and there was a ring. Sir

THE MERCENARY'S BLADE

Bartholomew—"

"—isn't here and is not in possession of the most recent facts," Nick said. But the certainty with which Hoyle spoke shook Nick's confidence in the idea a little more.

"I'm not sure you are either, sir," Hoyle said in a tone that suggested he wasn't surprised Nick should draw a wrong conclusion. "I spoke with Constable Brierly yesterday after the funeral for the witch hunter. He told me of your suspicions and that he had the lawyer under lock and key for you. He intended to send word to you as soon as he had questioned the lawyer."

"So he thought the man was Lennox too?"

"He was uncertain, you see the man had been vouched for by someone he knew. I told him he was right not to be sure. That he should release the bishop's man and make fulsome apologies for his mistake. But after I left Brierly, I met your uncle's people on the road. They were leaving. It seems the lawyer escaped and took one of the witches with him."

"And you are telling me of this because?"

"Because the constable, in doing what you asked, has crossed your uncle's plan by involving the bishop's man. No one will listen to a woman escaping a charge of witchcraft, but a respectable London lawyer is another matter. He is to meet with Brierly today, travelling from Killhope and if word ever gets back to the bishop…"

Nick stood up.

"Then we'll have to make sure it doesn't, won't we?"

Gideon spent the morning impatient to leave, waiting for Lord to summon him. But it was gone noon when his mare was fetched from the stables. Someone had left a cheap hanger sword looped on a baldric over the saddle tree, his own having been stolen by Jacko and Len. He expected Lord to appear, but of the three other horses which stood waiting, none was Lord's fine mount.

"It looks like the rain may hold off for the rest of today," Anders Jensen said as he emerged from the main door of the mill. He had his large leather bag under one arm and proceeded to strap it behind the saddle of one of the horses. "If we are fortunate, we might avoid even a shower."

With him were two of the men from Lord's company. As they mounted Anders introduced them as Roger Jupp and Turk Nelson, who, despite his name, was clearly both English and from London.

"You are coming with me to Pethridge?" Gideon asked Anders.

The Dane pushed his hat back and nodded.

"Our host deemed it wise. He told me there are three women who have been detained against their will and abused, one of whom is not young and the others perhaps too young. It is his wish that I should be in attendance in case they require the care of a physician or—God forbid—a surgeon."

Gideon found himself without words for a moment. Each time he found good reason to cast Lord in the villain's role, it seemed something would happen to make him question that all over again.

"And is Philip Lord riding with us?"

Anders answer was to push his horse through the crude gates that had been built at the entrance to the mill leaving Gideon to follow. The two men sent as their escort closed up behind. Lord had obviously found something more important to do than see through his promise to Beth Sawyer.

"I have heard great things of your adventures," Anders said when Gideon drew level with him. "That you rescued a damsel in distress from captivity single-handed and that your legal prowess is what is freeing these women we ride for today. Our host speaks of you as something of a worker of miracles."

"Then he talks me up for reasons of his own," Gideon said, wondering at the same time why Lord should bother.

"Indeed, he does seem to enjoy theatrics. He has a very dramatic temperament—which is strange as by appearance he is phlegmatic although Avicenna did say that no matter their humour, each individual is themselves uniquely."

"I prefer not to speculate on his temperament," Gideon said, rather grimly.

"Oh? I find him an interesting subject of study. For example, what do we know of his reasons for being here?"

That made Gideon look at the Dane. "You know something of them?"

Anders shook his head. "I have not the first idea beyond camp gossip—and that seems a little far-fetched to me."

"What does camp gossip say?"

"It would have it that he is here seeking some heirloom, a treasure of great value, stolen from him by a notable family hereabouts when he was a child in their ward."

"And the local family—is it Coupland? Tempest?"

"I am not sure the gossips have a name for them, but it sounds to me as if you might."

It was a gentle invitation and Gideon could see no harm in sharing some of what he knew. So he told the tale of how he came to be a guest of Philip Lord and had the satisfaction of seeing Anders become thoughtful.

"Perhaps there is something in the camp gossip then. It sounds to me as if there is a long-standing enmity there." Then Anders' face cleared and he gave Gideon a friendly nod. "I thank you for that, it has given me something to consider."

"You mean you might not remain with Lord?"

"On the contrary, I am now more curious about our host than before. Did you know he had a woman with him last night? A woman who came after dark and was gone first thing."

Gideon wondered how he could answer that politely.

"I find I would be very pleased," he said, "if I didn't have to have anything more to do with Philip Lord. Ever."

Anders looked puzzled.

"But he told his men this morning that as of yesterday evening you were in his employ."

Gideon remembered a jibe and snatching a flipped coin out of the air.

"Lord jested about it last night—I never thought…"

"That is something to note about our host—or perhaps now I should refer to him as our patron since at the same time he confirmed me as having a place in his company too. He never does anything in jest. Everything I have seen him do has been with a fixed and certain purpose even if clad in motley. It might be wise for you to keep that in mind, my friend."

"There is a lot to bear in mind when it comes to Philip

THE MERCENARY'S BLADE

Lord," Gideon agreed, "and unless he has drawn up a proper and enforceable contract of employment, I'd be wary to take him at his word on even that."

Anders smiled. "Spoken as a true lawyer, but to circumstances and custom, the law must yield. Which brings me to another enigma around our new employer. Equipping and maintaining his own troops cannot come cheaply."

Gideon recalled his own thoughts about the cost of the careful military provision he had found waiting at the mill when he first arrived. "Perhaps he has a wealthy employer."

"Perhaps. But who?"

Their speculation was interrupted by the pounding of hooves on the track behind them. Jupp and Nelson turned, reaching for weapons, but then stayed without drawing them.

The horse closing fast towards them carried Shiraz and sitting pillion behind him was Zahara, her arms holding fast around his waist. Shiraz reined in, stopping beside the group. It was, of course, Zahara who spoke.

"Dr Jensen, you must return at once. Captain Rider has taken a fever. I am concerned for him and my skills are not as yours."

"You were sent to fetch me?" Anders asked, frowning.

"No. The Schiavono is not there. I came on my own account. By my own judgement. You must go back."

Gideon was surprised at the note of command in her tone and he had a terrible feeling the Dane might refuse simply because of that. But Anders was nodding.

"I trust your judgement, I will go back with you." He turned to Gideon. "My apologies, but our discussion will have to wait. If any of the women you go to assist need my aid, I will come as soon as I may."

"There is no need, I shall go in your place," Zahara said. "It is better so. If any of these women have been violated, she may be unwilling to have a man touch her."

Her plain-speaking silenced them both.

Anders inclined his head. "Then I will leave them to your care," he said, made a rapid farewell and set off back to the mill at speed. Shiraz nodded to Nelson, who turned and rode off after him.

Zahara shifted a little in her pillion seat.

"We should go on."

Gideon realised that he had been staring after the departing riders and came back to the present moment with a small shock. He was heading into a dangerous situation and he had Zahara with him.

"There is no need for you to come with me."

Zahara met his gaze.

"There is a need or I would not be here." Then she gave him a gentle smile. "*The duty was allotted, mad as I am, to me.*" She was clearly quoting, but who or what Gideon had no idea.

Gideon glanced at Shiraz for support, but he looked as if he was waiting for Gideon to ride on. Roger Jupp seemed to have found something of overriding interest in his horse's mane. Resigned, Gideon turned his mount's head in the direction of Pethridge.

For a while, they travelled in what was, for Gideon, a tense and frustrating silence.

"I don't see how I will explain your presence to the constable." It was the one possible argument he could muster without impugning Zahara herself.

THE MERCENARY'S BLADE

"There will be no need, I will wait with Shiraz and you will send for us when the women are free."

She made it sound simple, and perhaps it was. After all, this time there could be no possible danger as he would have five of Lord's men on hand. He pushed that worry aside and tried to think of a way to repair the distance he had created between himself and Zahara.

"I didn't know you were skilled in the healing arts," he said at last.

"You have not asked."

Gideon felt the gentle rebuke and was suddenly at sea. It was true. If anyone asked him what he knew of Zahara he could say almost nothing. But in her presence, he never felt the need to know more. It was as if by being there she answered every question about herself he might ever have.

"May I ask you now?"

"Of course," she said, meeting his gaze with a smile. "I do not live in shadows. I prefer the sunlight."

"Then why would you stay with one who makes his whole life there?" He had not meant to mention Lord, had wanted to take this chance to ask about Zahara herself, her past, her hopes and dreams, but even in his absence and against Gideon's will, Lord's presence came between them.

Zahara looked away, but not before Gideon had caught the disappointment in her eyes.

"Some people have no choice in how they must live," she told him. "They are thrust into the shadows and bound there by powers they cannot control."

"And make no attempt to free themselves," Gideon said bitterly. "Even revel in it."

There was no immediate reply to that and after a short while Zahara sighed.

"There are those who live in shadow because they have no choice. They see the sun, know its warmth and yearn for its embrace, but must deny themselves for the sake of something greater. It is, perhaps, the highest form of sacrifice." She paused and then seemed to choose her words with care before she went on. "And then there are those who fall into shadow because they have no way to tell a guiding sunbeam from a dancing firefly or a will-o'the-wisp." She broke off with a gentle smile. "But as a wise man once said: *Your heart knows the way. Run in that direction.*"

Her words were so strange, Gideon found himself frowning at her.

"Lord is no saint. He didn't even keep his commitment to ride with me today to make sure these three women are freed."

"The Schiavono is no saint. No," she agreed. "But he is a good man. The parents of Walter Bell live near Healeyfield. That is not too far. He went to see them, to take to them their son's body for burial and to speak to them of his courage and loyalty, return his possessions together with all the pay he would be due until the end of the year and a bonus for his service. He was their only son, they are humble folk and will need it to get by. If the Schiavono did not have faith in your ability to see through what must be done, then the Bells would not have learned of their son's death today, or maybe not for many days."

In another man Gideon might have admired the courage and compassion, facing the parents of a man who had died following orders he had given. But in Lord, he found it hard to see it as anything more than the desire to ingratiate himself with his remaining men rather than to bring any comfort to the family of one who had died in his service.

"I find I have had enough of talking about Philip Lord," he said, grimly.

"Then why do you keep choosing to do so?"

Gideon looked sharply at Zahara, but her expression held a guileless and genuine interest. He opened his mouth to deny that he did, then thought back over the conversation and closed it again.

They rode on a little, passing through the edge of a small wood, the trees still waving the tattered rags of their summer finery. A scattering of beech masts and horse chestnuts covered the track where the leaves were also drifting, making it hard to see where the road ran.

"I would ask you something if I may?"

Zahara spoke quietly and Gideon felt a sudden uplift within.

"You have no need to make such a request, you may ask me anything, at any time."

She met his gaze and smiled.

"I will remember that when I have need of someone to help me light the fires before dawn tomorrow."

Gideon felt himself flush.

"If you wish," he said, and meant it.

"Thank you." She rewarded him with a full smile. "But I will let you sleep. That is my work, not yours and I rise for prayer anyway."

The thought of Zahara choosing to rise for prayer before beginning her work for the day was one that touched Gideon deeply. When he had been a student he had done so too. It had made dealing with whatever came each day seem more blessed. But that was a habit he had found the world of work had worn away. Early rising had become essential to take full advantage of every moment of daylight for composing, copying or reading. But perhaps he should try to get back to it.

"What was your question?" he asked.

"I would know why you have decided to stay with us?"

"I want to see these women freed."

"And then?"

She was looking at him with a quiet expectation and he found it hard to meet her gaze.

"And then—I don't know."

"You will stay?"

Now he met her gaze. *I will stay forever if you ask me.* But he held the words back behind the barrier of his lips.

"I don't know," he repeated.

"I hope you will stay," she said, and his soul sang, making up his mind for him in that instant. "There is much you could do. We have—"

Shiraz reined abruptly, looking into the trees, lifting one hand in a sudden, urgent gesture.

]

THE MERCENARY'S BLADE

Chapter Fifteen

Shiraz made more rapid gestures and Jupp nodded, drawing his pistol. Zahara slipped from the pillion as Shiraz looked with purpose at Gideon, making a stepped gesture indicating he wanted Gideon to dismount.

Still with no idea what was going on, but understanding it was both serious and urgent, Gideon swung his leg over the chestnut's quarters and dropped down to the ground. He reached for the cheap hanger and as his hand closed on the unfamiliar grip, wished he hadn't lost his own sword to Mistress Goody's bullies.

Zahara took the bridle of his mare and was leading her into a small stand of trees, warded by brambles. Shiraz had snatched up his bow from where it hung from his saddle, and Jupp held his pistol ready as they plunged their horses into the trees on the other side of the path. A moment later there was a shout.

Standing inside the fringe of undergrowth, borrowed sword in hand, Gideon tried to follow what was happening. As far as he could judge, the two men on horseback were chasing two or more on foot, who were slower but had an edge in navigating the terrain because of the trees. Gideon could see nothing but could hear the plunging rush through branches and undergrowth and skirling of leaves kicked up under hoof and foot and then a single pistol shot.

With the echo still in his ears, he nearly missed a much

smaller sound close at hand. He would have disregarded it had not a movement in the corner of his eye alerted him. The man was levelling a pistol as Gideon turned and it was the turning that saved him. The bullet scorched his doublet. But Gideon had no thought for that, no thought for himself at all. His sole awareness was that behind him, unarmed and as vulnerable as a child, Zahara was hiding.

The man threw the now useless pistol at Gideon who had to deflect it, and reached for the long-bladed dagger he wore. Gideon fought as he had never fought before, in earnest and in desperation. His senses were sharpened by a rush of energy that set his heart pounding and lent wings to his reactions. The unfamiliar blade responded to the techniques his sword master had made him practice. He tried to keep in mind the advice his teacher said would save his life. Use only the simple moves he knew well.

It was clear the man he fought had never set foot in a fencing school. His dagger was double-edged and sharp, and he fought with feet and fists in a style no sword master would teach. The evil blade managed to cut through the fabric of Gideon's left arm, drawing blood. But even though that hurt, it was as if it happened to someone else. His whole world was caught up in the fight. Nothing existed beyond it.

In the end, the trees fought for him. As Gideon attempted a lunge, the other man sidestepped, heavy knife blade sweeping in towards Gideon's undefended throat forcing Gideon to pull back and avoid it. His opponent stepped in to compensate, but his feet caught on a root concealed by the litter of leaves and momentarily put him off balance. Gideon's thrust cut deep and a dreadful gush of red spewed from the wound as he withdrew his blade.

The man fell back and thrashed in the leaves. Then he lay, chest heaving, eyes fixed on Gideon, holding silent accusation, until that faded and they held nothing at all.

If there had been another attacker Gideon could have done nothing about it, because where before there had been fire and unbelievable strength, now his limbs were palsied with weakness. He staggered and had there not been strong arms supporting him, would have fallen to his knees beside the body of the man he had killed...

He had killed a man.

A black void opened in the core of his heart that he was sure could never be made well.

Thou shalt not kill.

His first fully conscious thought was that he was going to throw up, but the arms that supported him moved him away from the horror and then he was sitting with his back to a tree, gentle hands pushing his head forward, between his knees.

When he sat up again, the world no longer spinning around him, he realised it had been Zahara who had held him and helped him. Now she had pulled back the slit sleeve from the cut on his arm and was focused on the wound. Behind her, he could see Shiraz and Jupp. They looked unharmed but grim-faced.

That was when Gideon realised he must have passed out for a short time and felt a shiver of shame that he had done so. To these men of war what he had done was much as pursuing a tort case against champerty and maintenance might be to himself—an unpleasant job of work that had to be done sometimes. Or maybe not even unpleasant for them.

"You are lucky, it is not at all deep," Zahara said as she worked, taking a small pot of some salve from a small bag beside her which, when she opened it, smelled of myrrh. "It might scar though, but if God is willing you need not fear worse than that."

"Thank you," The words took real effort to speak, but there was more he needed to know. "Are *you* all right?"

She finished applying the salve, then sat back on her heels and studied his face as if wondering why he might ask.

"I am well. You were very brave."

Her words sent a tremor of fragile joy into the dark cavern his heart had become and somehow made him whole.

"They were Coupland's men," Jupp said, as Zahara wound strips over the linen pad she had pressed on the wound. "The Schiavono told us to look out for them. He's heard they have taken on mercenaries. But those were no mercenaries, they were locals."

"How can you be sure who they served?" Gideon asked.

Jupp scratched at his beard, his expression hard. "We asked the one we caught. Well, I asked him, Shiraz persuaded him it was a good idea to speak up."

Then Jupp laughed as if at a good joke and Gideon felt his flesh creep.

Wild justice.

This was what happened when there was no true justice. They had lost two of their own, so taking the lives of any who served the Coupland-Tempest clan was justified.

But what right had he now to condemn their violence?

He too had killed a man. Pushing that knowledge down he tried hard to think beyond it, to think about what needed doing now.

"Did you find out why they were here?"

"They'd been told to watch the road for any sign of you."

"Me?" Gideon heard the pitch of his voice rise on the word.

Jupp shrugged. "So he said. I think the lad who you killed was hoping to get you back to Howe while we were chasing after his friends. He was thinking a soft London lawyer wouldn't put up much of a fight. You did good."

Somehow the praise didn't warm Gideon. Zahara completed her work and stood up, brushing the leaves from her skirts.

"We should go," she said.

Gideon could not agree more.

"We must get you back to the mill."

He struggled to his feet and accepted the hand Shiraz held out to help him rise.

Zahara was looking at him, momentarily puzzled, then she smiled.

"I meant that we should go and ensure those women are free and well."

Gideon shook his head.

"It's too dangerous."

Shiraz clearly agreed and made some curt urgent movements with his hands, face stern, gaze on Zahara.

"These were the only men sent from Coupland?" she asked, looking between Shiraz and Jupp. Both men nodded, Jupp with strong certainty, Shiraz giving a single, reluctant chin lift. "Then where is the danger? We have four men waiting at Pethridge to give us escort back, and we must be much nearer the village than the mill."

Shiraz let the breath leave his lungs through his teeth and made a spreading hand movement outwards and upwards, and turned to check the pillion was still secured. Jupp was grinning.

"You do have a point there, Mistress Sara."

Gideon started to marshal arguments then stopped.

"Of course," he said, "You have the right of it."

"Thank you," Zahara said and rewarded him with a smile. She let him help her mount, and Gideon was grateful that she was oblivious to the effect that supporting her body and touching her ungloved hand, even if so briefly, had upon him.

In fact, they had barely set off again before they were joined by the men they had hoped to find waiting for them in Pethridge.

"We heard a shot," the man leading them said by way of explanation.

So when Gideon arrived in Pethridge it was with an escort of five armed men and wearing a red coat, borrowed from Jupp to cover the damage to his doublet. Shiraz and Zahara waited in the stand of trees nearby to be summoned when needed.

When he reached the Priory, Fulke Brierly was obsequious in his welcome.

"I am so glad you arrived safely, Mr David. When we heard shots and your men rode out, I wondered, hmmm?"

Gideon managed to keep his stride a confident swagger, although his body felt as if several horses had trampled over him.

"I heard it as well," he said, surprised how matter of

fact he could make the words sound. "But, as you can see, I am fine."

"That is good indeed," Brierly said and added a smile that had no warmth.

He kept Jupp and two of the other men with him as he strode into the hall, earning a frown from Brierly, but after his previous solo experience of the constable, Gideon wasn't about to take any chances.

Everything was as it had been the day before, except for the heap of documents that was now on the table. Brierly gestured to them.

"You can see I have found out all you asked for. My mother asks you to forgive her absence but she has not been well since your last visit."

"I am here," Gideon told him frostily, "on behalf of Bishop Morton and the only women under your roof who I have an interest in are those presently detained by you on charges of witchcraft."

The smile changed its quality, becoming colder and more brittle.

"As you say, Master David. And those women have already been released in the absence of any now accusing them."

That was news.

"I am pleased to hear that. But there is the small matter of a signed confession."

Brierly pushed one of the documents over the table in reply. Picking it up, Gideon read it to assure himself it was not some forgery, walked quickly to the hearth and consigned it to the flames.

"I will send one of my men to make sure the women you released are safe and well," he said and nodded at

Jupp who he knew would understand he was to inform Shiraz and Zahara.

"Of course," Brierly said smoothly. "Let me send someone to show—"

Gideon held up both hands.

"If you don't mind, constable, I think my man will ask direction to their houses himself. The presence of one of your people would only disturb them."

Brierly managed a taut nod, his whole body bristling with objection and Jupp left.

"If that matter is being undertaken to your satisfaction, please, be seated." Brierly gestured to a chair set by the table. "All you need is here."

Gideon sat and went through the motions. The detailed sheets of accounts were kept in an immaculate hand and his eyes glazed as he went over them. He had never enjoyed this aspect of his work and was glad it wasn't often he needed to spend time perusing accounts. After the best part of an hour of looking through various ledgers and making random checks on the calculations, to the point that it was all beginning to blur, he saw something that snapped him back to full focus.

"Where is the report mentioned here?" He tapped the entry and Brierly peered at it.

It referred to a series of payments for a survey of land which from its description was land which he knew to be that held by Widow Bothwell and included some land owned by the Turners and the Sawyers.

Sweat appeared on Brierly's brow. It was clear he had hoped the entry wouldn't attract any attention, buried as it was in a list of other such expenses related to his work.

"I am not sure," he said quickly. Much too quickly. "It

showed nothing of interest, I do recall that."

"Then perhaps you would be kind enough to take me to where you keep such documents and I will look for it myself. I wish to see that report."

The Constable had begun to wring his hands in a way that he must have acquired from his mother.

"I am not sure where it might be. It was some time ago. I—"

In that moment Gideon's sheer disgust at the man, at what he had done and at his deliberate turning of a blind eye to what was being done by others, overspilled into anger. He shot to his feet so fast the chair teetered on its back legs and then fell back with a crash. Both Lord's men had hands on their swords as if he had given a signal and Gideon knew, with a chilling certainty, if he required it of them, they would kill Brierly in his own hall.

That knowledge hit him as a bucket of icy water might and he drew in a sharp breath.

Wild justice.

That was what these times, this wasting war, was bringing to all of England. Even before the first bodies might pile up on a battlefield, the corpse of Justice herself had been flung careless and broken to the ground. Grown men—intelligent, educated and civilised men—were grabbing swords and muskets, pikes and pistols to settle their disputes with blows.

So wild justice was all he could bring to Pethridge. And it made him sick to his stomach that Lord was right in what should be done. Gideon had no wish to leave a creature like Brierly in office. But with no appeal to true justice possible, he could see no other way to protect the women.

The door swung open and Judd came in.

"Mr David sir, the women are all safe and in their homes. They have friends and neighbours tending to them. From what I can gather, a few in the village seem to be calling 'no smoke without fire', but most maintain that if the women have been released they must be innocent—especially when they see the state of the poor girls." As he was speaking Jupp's gaze moved to Brierly and Gideon was surprised to see the coldness and anger in it.

"The girls are injured?" he asked.

Jupp's jaw tightened.

"In a manner of speaking. But they are being tended."

Zahara.

Brierly paled before the mercenary's glare. He might not have laid a finger on the women himself, as Beth Sawyer's account upheld, but he was darkly guilty of suspecting what had been happening under his own roof and closing his eyes to it.

With an effort, Gideon thanked Jupp and pulled himself back to the task in hand, an idea forming as he did so, spurred by the aching need to see more done for these victims of injustice.

"I wish to see that report," he repeated. "If not, I will commission a further one on my own authority. That would mean I should have to remain here whilst it is done and if I were to then discover that you had been keeping the findings hidden from the bishop about his own land…"

If Brierly had paled before, now his face was grey and the knuckles of his hands stood out bright red where he pressured the locked fingers together.

THE MERCENARY'S BLADE

"May we speak of this privily?" His voice had a hoarse rasp. "I assure you it is in no interest of the bishop for this to be something known more widely. That's why I have kept it under lock and key upon advice from Mr Cale."

That brought Gideon up short. For a moment his mind stopped working, unable to fit the incongruous into the pattern he had been so sure of up until that moment.

"*Cale?*"

"Of course, he has advised all my dealings since he arrived in June."

Brierly had to be lying or at least playing around with the truth.

Or did he?

The doubt was enough to make Gideon agree to the request and to follow the constable upstairs to his own cabinet. If Lord had any involvement in this, then Gideon had no wish to allow his men to know it before he understood for himself what was going on.

Brierly's cabinet was a comfortable and well-appointed room, much of the kind Gideon himself had maintained for his own work in London. There were a number of leather and canvas document bags marked with dates, and wooden boxes no doubt holding archived bags. Beside Brierly's working desk, hanging on the wall, were the active files. The papers pierced and held on a lace secured with a clip.

It was well organised and bespoke a neat and diligent man—traits that Gideon would normally admire. Except they counted for little as Brierly was not an honest man.

Brierly went straight to one of the archive boxes, a locked one, and after searching within it for a short time pulled out a few papers, tied together. He went over to his working table and cut the knots, letting the pages fall open so Gideon could see them.

Knowing little of the work of such a survey, although in his role as Bishop Morton's man he needed to pretend he did, Gideon picked up one of the pages and read through. Then he looked at another which had a sketch map with marks on it. One word hit him with near physical force and, disbelieving, he read on through other pages, making sense of most and suddenly understanding why Brierly had taken the risks he had.

Silver.

The report declared the lead ore found was 'richly argentiferous'—high in silver.

Now it all made sense. But the final page contained the biggest shock of all.

It was countersigned by Joshua Cale.

"What was Cale's role in this?" he demanded.

Brierly gave him an odd look.

"I thought you would have known. I told you how much I misliked his kind. Leeches."

"That is a fine judgement coming from you. But what was it he was doing?"

"Bleeding coins from me for nothing. He told me I needed his signature against every document and he charged me for the privilege of providing it."

No wonder Lord had been keen not to press matters. The familiar fury began to rise and Gideon had to fight it down. There would be time later to thrust it into Lord's face, with Zahara as his witness so she could see the tawdry nature of the man she idolised. But for now he would be damned if Lord and Brierly should profit from this and, wild justice or not, he would use the power of law to prevent it.

"I need paper, parchment, pen and ink," he said, glaring at Brierly to such effect that the man swallowed hard and moved to find what he wanted, "and I hope you are a fast copy or we may be here some time."

It took longer than Gideon wanted, but when he left soon after dusk, Brierly was a sombre looking man.

Gideon carried with him the report, complete with the sheet that bore the flamboyant Joshua Cale signature countersigning Brierly's own cramped mark. He also had a copy of a document he had drawn up in tight legal phrasing. Brierly signed it in his capacity deputising as Moormaster, agreeing that any wealth from minerals taken from the lands held under copyhold by any other party would be shared with them. They were to be shared half and half, once the portions due to the Duke of Richmond and the bishop had been tallied and deducted. In addition any destruction done to the land making it unfit for other use would be made good to the copyholder from Brierly's share of the profit.

Brierly had protested that the terms meant that it wouldn't be worth his while making any investment to mine the ore, which was, of course, what Gideon intended. He ensured the document was witnessed. A contract between Brierly and the copyholders of Pethridge. And as long as Brierly held his post it should provide legal chains to keep him from being tempted to take any such measures against the people of Pethridge again. Especially as he believed the copy Gideon held was to be lodged in Bishop Morton's archives.

Whether it would hold up to a full and intense legal scrutiny and challenge, Gideon doubted. But, combined with the belief that the bishop would be displeased were there any more false accusations of witchcraft, it should be sufficient to shackle Brierly and keep him from further such illegal excesses.

By the time they were heading back to the mill it was fully dark. They headed across country, led by Jupp, who seemed confident of the way. With an escort of six capable fighting men, Gideon felt Zahara should be safe. She was close beside him in the middle of the group on her pillion.

"How were the women?" he asked

"They are in no danger of their health, or their lives," she told him, "but their souls are wounded. The widow is a strong woman and she will find her own path to managing what has happened. Leah and Anne have those about them who will help them heal." She shook her head. "Of course, we cannot be sure yet if there will be more consequences."

"There will be no more accusations," he assured her. "I have put paid to that."

Zahara was silent for a moment.

"I am sure so, and you did well," she said quietly. "But I meant one or both might be with child. The world is not kind to women with a child born out of wedlock, even if one forced on them against their will by a man."

Gideon had nothing he could say to that. It was true. And every moment he had left the women in Brierly's keeping, the two men Jacko and Len would have been free to abuse them. The thought made him sick to the stomach.

"If that happens," Zahara went on, "I will see the Schiavono does something for them."

Gideon had to bite on his lip to avoid retorting that her precious Schiavono had known of and maybe even colluded in the machinations that led to those women being imprisoned. But it would wait. Wait until the man himself was there to answer the charge in person.

Chapter Sixteen

"Have you decided to stay?"

Zahara's question came after a long silence on the ride back.

Gideon wondered what to say. He could no more leave Zahara with Lord than he could take his own heart from his body and set it aside. He would bide until he could persuade her to leave with him. But, of course, he couldn't say that. Not in front of Shiraz and these others of Lord's men.

He must have taken too long to reply because she spoke again. "I can tell you why I stay, if you would like to know?"

"If you don't mind telling me, I would love to know."

It could be the key to unlocking the shackles that bound her to Philip Lord.

"I would not offer if I minded." He could hear the smile in her voice when she said it, even though it was too dark to see her face clearly. "I will tell you."

She was silent for a few moments as if uncertain where to begin or how to phrase what she wished to tell him. When she spoke her voice was calm and free of emotion.

"A Venetian ship I was travelling on fell victim to Algerian privateers. I was enslaved along with most of the rest of the passengers and crew. The commander of the privateers took me from amongst the spoils and kept me in his house for a year."

She stopped talking and drew a small breath. It struck

Gideon that she was speaking of a time that had been unbearable to her. That was why she gave him only the baldest of facts. When she went on her voice had a different timbre, a warmth, as if she spoke of something that was still close to her heart.

"The Schiavono was in Algiers, and Shiraz, having no money, pledged himself if the Schiavono would purchase me. But the commander refused to sell as I should never have been enslaved in the first place and he was afraid of the consequences if that came out. The Schiavono became stubborn, as he does when thwarted in what he sees as right, and he used all the influence, power and wealth his name and reputation could muster, to bring pressure on the commander until he was forced to sell me. But the price of that was high. Because of it, because he chose to help me, the Schiavono lost his wealth, his good name and nearly lost his life."

Gideon shook his head. He knew well the misery caused by the Barbary Pirates, who sometimes raided the coast of southern England, taking innocent families from their homes and shipping them to a life of slavery. He had nothing but admiration for those who worked to ransom those victims. But this was not that. What he was hearing in Zahara's history was a power struggle between two pirates, not a noble tale of deliverance.

I bought her in Algiers.

The moon slipped behind a cloud and it felt suddenly colder.

"You and Shiraz are *owned* by Lord?"

He was about to add that was no longer possible. As soon as they had set foot on English soil they were freed. No Christian could be enslaved under English law, but

Zahara was already talking.

"No. What he did was unconditional." She spoke gently as if explaining something to a small child. "His reasons were his own, but he set nothing of it upon me. I have never been his slave. Nothing compels me to be here. Or Shiraz. We stay with him from friendship."

Gideon struggled hard with that idea and then thought of what Matt Rider had said about the men he had brought to the mill—that they were not there just for the money.

"Philip Lord seems to have a lot of friends," he said bitterly.

The moon emerged again from the shrouding clouds to grant them some better illumination. Zahara was grasping Shiraz's belt with one hand, with the other she caught an escaping lock of her hair, transmuted to silver by the moonlight, and pushed it back into her coif.

"He has many who claim to be so, for their own ends and when it suits them," she said. "And there are those who think highly of him but would not make any claim to friendship. And some who will offer friendship, to their own understanding of the word. He is kind to them because of it. But he has few true friends, those he can be at ease with and be himself with and trust to hold his interests as they hold their own."

It was much later that Gideon realised Zahara was not only telling him something about Philip Lord when she said this. She was telling him something about herself. At the time, there seemed nothing he could say to it without also saying much more than he wanted about his view of the nature of Philip Lord.

The rest of the journey passed in silence and they reached the old mill without any incident. After the day

THE MERCENARY'S BLADE

Gideon had fought through, emotionally, physically and intellectually, his sole desire was to see Zahara was safe and then get to bed. Tomorrow he would enjoy challenging Lord with his Joshua Cale signature. The report it was attached to held safely in a leather bag. But first he needed sleep. He took the time to make sure his mare was well settled and was emerging from the stables when he was informed the Schiavono wished to speak with him.

He was even less happy when, upon answering that summons, he was told the Schiavono was not able to see him right away. He would have ignored the demand and gone to his bed, but the guard by the stairs refused to let him go up. So he had no choice but to wait in the main room of the mill. On one side of it were snoring men; on the other sat the few who had yet to retire or were going out on duty. They sat around a table, sharing the light of a single candle, faces mostly concealed in shadow.

The past couple of days since their arrival Lord's men had ignored Gideon or, if compelled into acknowledging his existence, had been coldly polite. But now one lifted a hand to encourage him to join them.

Gideon would have preferred to sit alone, but he had no wish to antagonise these men by refusing. So he crossed to the table and took the seat offered.

The man who had beckoned him over was one of those who had been his bodyguard in Brierly's house. Gideon fumbled for a name. Olsen. A big man with a thatch of golden-brown hair and a slight sing-song Swedish intonation as he spoke in an unsophisticated French.

"This man is one to watch." He put a heavy hand on Gideon's shoulder. "He has a mind like a fox—not just the pelt of one." Olsen gestured to Gideon's hair. "He had that man Brierly on a hook."

"It is what I do," Gideon said. "My training is in the law."

"Yes, but how many lawyers do we see using their skill to do something like that?" Olsen asked and the others at the table nodded and agreed it was rare. One made some uncomplimentary statements about the legal profession, profusely punctuated with foul language. The others agreed, resulting in a spate of lawyer jokes. Gideon grinned at the ones that were actually funny but began to wish he hadn't chosen to join the group after all.

"He killed a man who would have attacked Mistress Sara, so Jupp was saying," another man put in as the jokes wound down.

Someone filled a mug from the jug on the table and pushed it towards him. Gideon found himself colouring under the shift of mood.

"I had no choice," he said, but before he could explain there were some knowing looks around the table.

"Sweet on Mistress Sara, are you?"

He looked down at his hands where they were both curled around the mug, wishing the floor could open beneath him, but unable to deny something so profoundly true.

"No matter," one of his new companions told him, "It's nay secret. It's you and every other man who e'er clapped eyes on her. But be careful, mind. One step o'er the line and you'll have Shiraz slit your throat for you."

"That'd be right after the Schiavono cut out your balls and made you eat them," Olsen added helpfully. "In fact, if you didn't swallow fast, they might come out the gash."

THE MERCENARY'S BLADE

Gideon was about to make it very clear that the last thing he would do was step over any line when it came to Zahara, when an amused voice called from the gallery above.

"If you have done corrupting my innocent men with your lawyer's wiles, oh Lennox the Fox, I would like to speak with you." Lord leant with careless elegance on the rail. His face, lit from below, was stricken by odd shadows lending it a demonic appearance that matched his nature.

As he excused himself from the table and made his way upstairs, Gideon wondered how much of the conversation Lord had overheard—and how long his new boon companions had known Lord was there.

He hadn't before seen within the room Lord had set aside for his own use. There was no trace of it being any kind of bed chamber. A heavy canvas curtain formed the back wall, which he assumed concealed that aspect of the room. The part that was visible seemed sparse to the point of spartan, though much was lost to shadow.

Aside from a high-sided, travel desk perched on an old piece of ironwork and graced with a stool, Gideon could see four chests of no huge size, each fitted with straps that could be slung over a pack mount. These, he assumed, would hold everything from Lord's personal weaponry to his spare shirts. The wall with the desk was dominated by a hearth and the one opposite, by a shuttered window. The boxes and barrels that had been in Gideon's chamber were now stacked neatly beside it.

Lord stood by the open desk studying a document set out on its writing surface. He was less than his usual immaculate self, wearing clothes that showed signs of travel. His hair fell forward in uneven strands as he read. The room smelt of aqua vitae.

Lord straightened up, eyes over brilliant and Gideon realised he wasn't sober. He was anything but.

"*We few, we happy few, we band of brothers;*
For he to-day that sheds his blood with me
Shall be my brother; be he ne'er so vile,
This day shall gentle his condition."

Lord walked to one of the chests and flung it open as he spoke. "I hear your condition has been gentled this day and we are now as brothers."

The short rein Gideon held on his anger slipped and drew a steadying breath.

"I can't think of any day on which I might call you 'brother'," he said.

Lord pulled something long from the chest, wrapped in cloth.

"Oh?" He sounded amused. "And what if you discovered I was brother to Zahara?"

Gideon felt the blood drain away from his face.

"Are you?" he demanded hoarsely.

Lord laughed and held out what he had picked up, shaking the cloth from it as he did so.

"I have no idea," he said, "which makes life complicated when looking to decide whom to bed and whom to pass by. It would be damnably awkward to wake up having spent the best hours of the night in the throes of lust, only to learn I had done so with a previously unknown sibling. Here, this is for you."

His demeanour changed on the last words. The humour evaporated, leaving something warm but sombre in its wake. Lord was holding a sword in a well-used scabbard, the grip behind its curling metal hilt and guard showing signs of wear. He pulled the blade free in part, so the fire and the candle flame glinted on the sleek metal

Gideon stared at the weapon. It was solid craftsmanship and made the sword he had lost look little better than the hanger he still wore and with which he had taken the life of another.

"I don't want your sword," he said, tightly.

"Oh it's not mine, but the gentleman it belonged to has no further use for it."

"Someone you killed, I assume?"

"In a manner of speaking," Lord agreed. "It belonged to a man called Watt Bell. Perhaps if he had been wearing it when he needed it most, things might have been different, but the grip needed repair, so he was wielding another. His parents told me to take it and give it to someone who would use it as well as their son had done." Lord paused as if in thought or remembrance. "Take it. And use it better than he did."

Gideon made no move. He recalled what Zahara had said about Bell's parents.

"You should sell it. Give them the price of it."

"I don't think there is a price to be put on parental love for a son or their pride in him," Lord said quietly and, for a few moments, the only sound in the room was the spitting of flame in the hearth. "You need a sword and they wanted to gift it. It comes with no oath or deed attached."

He hadn't wanted to do it here and now. He had wanted an audience, Zahara, to see once and for all the perfidy of this man, but this nauseating act was more than he could bear.

"And what of your oath or deed? You who say you knew nothing of a plot when you were fist in glove with Brierly to make money from his scheme."

Lord stood still. The sword, half-naked, held in his hands, his expression unreadable. Then he slid the sword home and stepped back to lay it with care on top of the chest.

"You'd better tell me," he said.

Gideon dropped the bag he was carrying onto the table beside him, undoing the straps and pulling out the tied papers of the report. He flung the packet on the open desk, sending pen and ink flying to splash blackly on the heavy curtaining beyond.

"There, explain how your signature as Joshua Cale is on that report detailing the existence of silver-bearing lead ore on the lands tenanted by the Sawyers, the Turners and Widow Bothwell. *You knew*. All along you knew."

Lord looked at the packet and shook his head.

"I didn't know. How could I have?" His voice sounded flat and weary as if the excesses he had been indulging in were catching him up in fatigue. "If I'd had any idea what was behind…" He broke off and picked up the bound papers and stared at them.

"How can you say that when you put your signature to it and were even *paid to do so*?" Gideon demanded.

Lord glanced up, a sudden animation in his look. He thrust the report at Gideon.

"Open it. Then apply your wits if not your legal mind. Look at the page the signature is on. For God's sake, you are a lawyer. You must be awake to such fraudulent practices."

THE MERCENARY'S BLADE

Gideon cut the strings and turned to the back page where Lord's signature as Joshua Cale could be seen. There was a reason why most vital legal documents were written on a single sheet where possible. Signatures could be removed or amended more easily if not. But this was a survey report, not a legal agreement, so no such care was needed. Aware of Lord standing in front of him, arms folded as if to stop himself from taking any action, Gideon studied the final sheet and the others. There were a few lines of the actual report on the page, before the concluding formalities and the signatures.

Looking closely now, he could see what in his anger he had missed before—those lines were in a hand that was ever so slightly different from the rest. This writer preferred to flatten their letters where the other liked to embolden them. Gideon had seen enough of Brierly's hand that day to know he much preferred the neater, flatter style.

As he studied the pages Lord began talking. He sounded achingly weary.

"When I began creating Joshua Cale I needed to have Brierly convinced Cale was no threat to him. A man of weak morals. A man he had a hold over at need. So that Cale could come and go and not be someone for Brierly to worry about. Men like Brierly always have their schemes and backdoor money-making enterprises that they keep from those they should be serving and he would have been concerned Cale might trip over one." Lord stopped and Gideon glanced up to see he had pressed both palms against his forehead, closing his eyes as if he had a blinding headache. After a few moments, he lowered his arms, drew a deep breath and went on talking. "I sold him ten sheets with my signature on it for him to use as he might, to confirm things were known and approved by myself—and through me, by my supposed principal. I assumed he would attach one to something incriminating to hold over me at need, but it made no difference to me what he might use them on. Joshua Cale does not exist, after all."

It was plausible, probable and the evidence of the sheets Gidon held in his hands added proof. He stared at the signature and felt only a sickness within.

"I don't know about you," Lord said quietly, "but I'm finding this game of doubt and counter somewhat exhausting." He stepped forward and took the report from Gideon's nerveless fingers. "I had hoped to have a full account of what you achieved with Brierly, although I know from others that you succeeded. I also know that you have never killed a man before today and that you will be feeling as if a portion of your soul has been drowned in his blood. You will ask yourself a thousand times if things could have worked out some other way. I promise you, they could not have. You had no choice and you did what you needed to do to defend yourself and Zahara."

Gideon stood, head bowed, hearing the words of absolution but feeling nothing. Lord pushed the sword into his hands and closed his fingers over the leather.

"The sword is yours. If you wish to sell it and send the money to Watt Bell's family, I will see they get it, but I promise you it is not what they want. They want to be able to think their son's spirit will somehow live on in another brave man and this is their way of doing that."

This time Gideon didn't resist. He held onto the sword

and managed to glance up and meet Lord's gaze. What he saw there was compassion, so alien to all he believed he knew of the man that his breath caught in his throat. A moment later the look vanished and the gemstone eyes were cool and indifferent.

"*There's time to speake much, time as much to sleepe.* I think the speaking of today is done. Go sleep. We will talk more tomorrow."

Barely aware of how he got there, Gideon found himself climbing into bed. But he slept with troubled dreams, and something terrifying stalked him through the shadows of sleep, something never seen, implacable and faceless.

Nick was proud of his plan, one worthy of his uncle. But more than that, for the first time in Nick's life Hoyle had come to him with a decision to be made that was above a sergeant's authority and had treated him with the respect due to his status. For the first time, Hoyle had seemed impressed by his decisions and acted upon them.

But then the idea was brilliant.

A simple but effective way to remove the bishop's man and let the blame for that fall at the door of Philip Lord. It dawned on Nick that right now anything he wished to achieve that might fall outside the trammels of the law could be conveniently blamed on that man.

During the course of the day, most of the men he had been left by his uncle and who he had sent to search for Lord had returned. As Mags had predicted from the start, none of them had any news beyond the vaguest of rumour and gossip. Nick was also hearing dark rumbles from some of the men that those yet to return were not going to. England had a crying need for fighting men and those who were willing to travel could expect to find employment easily. And, thanks to Mags, all the men had new boots which made travel that much easier.

Now as the day neared its end, he sat impotent and impatient, chewing on his lower lip, watching the fire burn down. The Coupland men Hoyle had sent out to deal with the lawyer David had still failed to return. He was left facing the possibility that the plan had failed. That the bishop's man had taken another road or been delayed. He decided to send someone to recall the men sitting in ambush and was thus, by chance, in the stableyard when Mags and Heron rode in with a grisly cargo of bodies.

A sombre group carried the three dead men into the house and a few minutes later there was a cry of keening grief torn from a woman's throat. A reminder, if Nick needed any, that these were not mercenaries like Mags and his ilk, paid to fight and die in defence of Coupland interests. These were their own: people of Howe, fathers, brothers, sons and friends, carried home to the grief of those who loved them.

The burn of fury rose from Nick's stomach to his throat and his eyes stung with rage. This had to be the work of Lord, seeing the chance for revenge for the loss of his own men.

"Where did you find them?" he demanded.

"Not too far out of Pethridge," Mags said. "Maybe three miles. One was by the road, he took a sword thrust. The other two looked like they had tried to run. One took an arrow, the other…" He stopped talking and spat. "I'll just say that whoever did this will now know for sure who they were, what they were doing there and anything else they cared to ask."

"*Whoever* did it?" Nick heard the sharp bark in his own voice. "Is there any doubt who did this? It will have been Lord. An act of vengeance. This was aimed at me." Then he closed his mouth, aware that they would be overheard. "Come with me," he snapped and turned back into the house.

Oblivious to any social niceties or the mud being trailed by the two men over stone floor and rushes, he took them to the privacy of the parlour with its friendly fire and warm hangings. Then, having armed himself with a restorative warmed wine, he had them repeat the exact circumstance of their discovery. Or at least Mags did so whilst Heron stood with his eyes on the floor, occasionally giving a nod to confirm some detail.

"How did Lord know?" Nick demanded at the end.

"I don't think he did," Mags said. "Is more that they were found."

"By chance? But how—?"

"They were local men you sent, sir. Familiar with the area. But they were not soldiers."

"You are saying it was my fault?"

"What I would say, sir," Mags spoke quickly, not answering the question, "is Lord has a fair number of people with him. Perhaps thirty men or more. That means there can't be that many places he could be around here."

"How can you know how many men he has?"

"Yesterday he had maybe ten men with him and the moor," Mags said, lifting his hat to scratch a little at his head. "But they were an escort, not his full complement. That was very obvious. No. He's got something bigger going on."

Nick had dreamed last night of cold dark eyes and the blade at his throat.

"The moor?"

"He travels with a moor and a woman, who they say he bought on the Barbary Coast. It would have been the moor who killed with an arrow. Now, he is someone I'd not like to have out hunting me."

Nick digested that for a moment as another thought occurred.

"You say you'd met Lord outside Magdeburg. But that isn't the only time you met, is it?"

Mags shifted his feet and glanced at his boots.

"It's no secret. We've fought on the same side and on different sides. That happens sometimes in the German Wars."

"How can I be sure if you find him you'll stay loyal? He might pay you more."

"Because I killed his men to save you," Mags said, his gaze steady now. "If I were after making myself a friend to Lord, I'd have left you with him."

The thought sent a shiver down Nick's spine. He couldn't shake the feeling there was something in this conversation that he was missing, something important but nebulous. Nick felt suddenly tired. Perhaps he was seeing ghosts where there were none.

"You are sure you can find him?" he asked at last.

Mags dropped his gaze, coughed then hawked and spat in the fire.

"I told you I would and I shall."

"And when you do?"

"I'll bring him to you one way or another. You paid me to do so, after all."

THE MERCENARY'S BLADE

Chapter Seventeen

Gideon woke early, his mind heavy as if with dread.

The first birdsong was starting outside and darkness was barely paling. He felt a profound need for familiar comfort and recalled what Zahara had told him of her own pre-dawn habit of devotion and decided he would do likewise.

From the settled breathing that came from the other pallet, he knew Anders was sleeping. The Dane had been absent when Gideon had gone to bed, tending to Matthew Rider and others in need of his care. Not wanting to disturb him, Gideon rose and dressed with care. As he picked up the gaudy red coat he had been loaned by Jupp, his hand brushed the sword Lord had given him. For a moment he felt disoriented. None of this was any part of his familiar world.

He couldn't wear the sword he had used to kill with and to go without a sword in this company was akin to walking naked. With some reluctance, he put it on. Now he looked more like one of the mercenary company than the sober lawyer he had been but days ago.

Walking quietly downstairs he noticed the door to Zahara's room was ajar with a soothing murmur coming from within. The fact the door was open seemed an invitation and Gideon found himself drawn to it, thinking he might join her devotions. He paused on the threshold, one hand lifted to knock softly. Then froze.

On small soft carpets laid over the floor, Zahara and

THE MERCENARY'S BLADE

Shiraz knelt a distance apart on either side of the room. Zahara was speaking softly, the flow of words clearly as familiar and beloved to her as they sounded alien and dreadful to Gideon. He could see the look of utter peace that suffused her face as she bowed forward on the floor to touch her head to the ground between the palms of her hands. When she sat back on her heels, her eyes were closed and the inner tranquillity flowing from her seemed to fill the room like the lingering trace of incense. Gideon was aware then of Shiraz, whose eyes were not closed and whose gaze came to rest upon him watchfully, but without hostility.

Gideon stepped away in turmoil. He had hoped to find a familiar source of peace. Instead, he was met with another disconcerting mystery. Lost in a labyrinth where every turn brought strangeness and confusion, he turned and fled back up to the room he shared with Anders. With the sleeping Dane his sole companion, Gideon dropped to his knees, head bowed over hands that clung to each other, and tried to pray.

Nothing had changed. The birdsong grew to full chorus and light blossomed from the unseen horizon. Sounds reached him of preparations underway to meet the needs of the day. Still on his knees, Gideon felt numb. Every time he tried to turn his thoughts to God, to his own sins and the desperate need there must be to account for them, all he could see was the beatific expression on Zahara's face, as if her spirit had been uplifted to a place of grace.

He prayed as he had been taught to pray but felt nothing from it. Instead, he gave in to the moment and let his troubled mind seek its own way. Slowly, like the sun rising, it came to him that there was a profound truth in the knowledge that nothing had changed.

Nothing had changed in his heart at all. Through all the desperation of his prayers and his hope for some shift or banishment of his feelings towards her, the fact remained that whatever she might be or not be, she was still Zahara.

With that, there came a kind of peace, of acceptance. If not of what she was, then of the fact that how he felt about her was never going to change. And from that grew the sense of certainty: he would find a way to cope with it—one day.

It was hunger that eventually made him get up from his knees. That and the shift in breathing of the sleeping man which presaged his awakening. He left the room quietly.

The company was already at breakfast and today, far from cold-shouldering him, Gideon found himself greeted with terse but friendly nods. He took his usual place apart from the rest, but after he had been eating for a while, Jupp came over and clapped him on the shoulder and slipped into the seat beside him.

"I was to tell you our men found no trace of your Mistress Goody, though they searched high and low about the place. No one likes what those two bastards did to those poor girls." That was a blow, but not an unexpected one. "Oh, and you can keep the coat. The lads all call you Lennox the Fox for your cunning. So you need a red coat."

Gideon was uncertain how he felt about that. Even if Lord's men were more friendly towards him, he still felt little affinity with them. He had seen their delight in violence, their harsh judgements. Their values were not his.

Thanking Jupp, he was wondering what more to say

THE MERCENARY'S BLADE

when Anders joined them. He gave a warm smile to Gideon, before fixing his attention on the other man.

"There is good news of your Captain Rider," he said, helping himself to the food that was on the table. "I was with him last night when his fever broke. Today he is sitting up, protesting his health restored and presently being fed honey-sweetened frumenty by his good wife. God has been kind and he will live."

Jupp banged Anders suddenly and hard on the back so the Dane choked on his food, then banged some more so he could breathe again.

"It is good to have a doctor and a lawyer." Jupp grinned with delight and scooped some bread from the table, clapping Gideon on the back again before swaggering away across the room.

"I see you have a new sword," Anders gestured with a piece of buttered bread. "One I recognise, I think."

"Philip Lord wished me to have it."

"You are honoured, my friend. That will change things for you here. There was much speculation as to whom he would present it after word spread about what had happened with Bell's parents. I would never have thought it would be you. Most thought Matt Rider's son, Liam, but I think our valiant leader still sees him as too young to take his place with the fighting men."

"I'm not planning to join Lord's fighting men," Gideon said.

Anders considered that as he chewed his food, then gestured with one hand to indicate the whole company as he swallowed it down.

"You will have no notion of it, but these are some of the finest professional soldiers in all Europe—diamonds in the rough. Most here are not Philip Lord's regular soldiers. They are of his best. They could name their fee with any of the commanders on the continent—Conde, Torstensson or Piccolomini. Any one of them, had they been born the son of a nobleman, would be leading their own regiments and winning battles. If they bite and snarl, that is because they are curs who have the hearts of purebreds and have been kept chained perforce on leashes too short for their full talents. Here it is different. Here they can be all they are capable of being. You need to understand that since you are staying." He leaned in and lowered his voice. "You see, whichever faction our employer decides to favour, be it the king's or that of his parliament, will find it holds a fearsome weapon in its hands. Most men who are taking up arms here in England have never done so before or have maybe drilled with their trained bands at best. This is probably the most powerful body of fighting skill and expertise in this country at present. Added to any army it would be like yeast, making the whole to rise."

Gideon understood then why Anders had raised the question the previous day of where the money came from to pay the company.

"You are telling me that you think that Lord has the power to determine the outcome of this conflict?"

The Dane nodded.

"That is exactly what I am saying. Interesting, isn't it?" He sat back and helped himself to some more bread from the table. "I don't see why else he would be here."

"Seeking that family heirloom?" Gideon suggested.

"If it even exists. And if it did, why would he need all these men in full fighting readiness—and more coming

THE MERCENARY'S BLADE

as I understand it—to find a family heirloom?"

Gideon considered that for a moment. "He might if it were in a well-defended fortress."

"What are you thinking?"

"Considering his enmity with Coupland, Howe Hall, perhaps? To take that might well need a small army, but I wouldn't know. I am not a military man."

Anders gave him a broad smile.

"You soon will be, my friend, you soon will be. The ink is barely dry on my contract and already I have been told I am required to do weapons training. When I protested I was here to heal not harm, our patron informed me that were we to be attacked he would expect me to be able to defend myself so as not to be a liability. He even has the women trained in loading firearms and using a knife in their own defence."

Gideon found his hand on the hilt of the sword he had been given, fingers running over the smooth metal of its guard and wondered if the message it gave to those here was truth or lie—he wasn't sure.

He was no longer sure of anything.

Except the lodestone of his own heart.

Your heart knows the way. Run in that direction.

As if the thought of her had conjured her presence, Zahara slipped between the tables, clearing them as the men went to whatever duty the day held for them. Gideon found it impossible to watch her work—and impossible not to. She laughed and exchanged words with everyone who spoke to her. She seemed at home in this world of crude fighting men, but untouched by its crudity herself. Gideon realised with almost physical pain that he no longer had any idea who she was if indeed he had ever known.

When she approached him, she smiled as she did for everyone and he wondered if he was imagining that the smile was warmer for him than for any other.

"When you have eaten, I need to look at your arm," she told him, picking up an empty bowl and balancing it on those she already carried. "Unless you trust Mr Jensen's care over mine?"

Shiraz had somehow told her.

Gideon felt a flush of heat in his neck rise to his ears. There was no accusation, anger or even upset in her tone and when he managed to meet her gaze, he found it as open as always, simply wanting to know his answer.

Nothing had changed.

"Thank you," he said. "I have finished eating already."

She smiled then with a warmth that set his soul aflame.

"If you would be kind enough to help me carry these out, I will be free to tend to your arm."

Making a rapid farewell to Anders, Gideon allowed himself to be piled high with bowls, pots and dishes, then guided in Zahara's wake, went out to where a group of women were cleaning and stacking them, ready for the next meal.

Zahara sat Gideon at a small table in the room they were using beside the kitchen area to store and prepare food. With expert fingers, she removed the old dressing, examined the cut and declared her satisfaction that it was healing as it should be. But what Gideon had witnessed that morning remained as a ghost hovering between them.

"You speak English well for someone who was born in Aleppo," he said.

THE MERCENARY'S BLADE

"That is because my mother was English."

"And your father?"

"Was a merchant from Aleppo."

The answer drove him back into silence. Zahara took a clean strip of linen and covered it with a lotion that smelt of honey and herbs.

"Shiraz told me you saw us praying today."

He had not expected her to speak of it, but there was no awkwardness in her words. She might have been speaking of him having seen her doing the laundry. Suddenly his throat felt thick and he had to clear it before he could reply.

"I did," he admitted.

"And what did you think?" She placed the strip of honey-soaked linen with care, her eyes on her work as she did so.

"At first I didn't know what to think," he said, answering with as much honesty as he was able. "Then I thought that it must be hard for you." Which was less honest but more what his heart was telling him to say.

"It is not hard for me here," she said. And he had seen that for himself. No one in this company held her in anything less than the highest regard. "There are some things that do not need to be pulled apart and examined. Sometimes it is enough to know and to accept. To say: 'You have your understanding and I have mine'."

Perhaps she was right and that was enough. He was far from certain, but he had no wish to pull apart and examine his feelings on the matter. Instead, Gideon watched her swift, neat, fingers working, aware of their gentle pressure on his flesh and he distracted himself by thinking of what Anders had said of her knowledge of medical skills.

"Is this a healing technique from the wisdom of Avicenna or Galen?" he asked as she finished winding a bandaging strip around his arm.

"Neither." She glanced up to meet his gaze before restoring her attention to his arm. "This is from the wisdom of Máire Rider."

He hadn't expected that.

"Not all the wisdom of the world is in books," she said, "nor yet is it the sole province of men."

He was spared having to think how to answer her because Goodwife Rider herself bustled in, and the conversation went to whether there were enough spoons, and if they could find extra blankets for those who were asking. Gideon realised then that Lord ran his victualling in the same way as a huge household, and largely under the control of the women.

His arm redressed, Gideon was shooed from the kitchen area. With a pulse of relief, he remembered that for the first time since his arrival he had no need to ride to Pethridge that day. But what he couldn't avoid was another confrontation with Philip Lord.

It struck him that he cast all his dealings with Lord as confrontations. For the first time, he began to wonder if he was right to do so. Lord had saved his life when he could have left him to die in the flames of the inn. He had provided him with a place of sanctuary and offered him good use of his skills, in what Gideon had come to see was a worthy cause. He had taken Gideon's rebuffs and accusations in his stride and not once responded as he could have so easily, with ultimate violence. Then, last night, he had given Gideon a tangible mark of his esteem.

THE MERCENARY'S BLADE

On the other side of the balance, Lord was high-handed, seldom open, and mocked everything Gideon valued. He set his own brand of justice above the law of the land—and he was an attainted traitor, his assets and rights forfeit to the crown along with his life.

So when he was told Lord wished to see him, Gideon went with some trepidation and encountered Olsen emerging from Lord's room looking pleased with something.

"Mr Fox," Olsen said in salutation, grinning as he headed down the stairs. The name was sticking and Gideon wasn't at all sure how he felt about that.

Lit with daylight and no longer hung with shadows, Lord's room had an even more austere atmosphere. Lord himself was dressed for once like a military commander, in a sleeveless buff over a blue wool coat and a plain collared shirt. His sword sat as ever by his thigh, the complex weave of its hilt close to his hand.

"It appears to be," he said as Gideon entered, "my day for bold advances, for soothing ills, and for speaking of things that are tender and unpleasing. The only question is which is needed where. I read your fine work binding the upstanding Fulke Brierly in his own traces and *cadit quaestio*. If I may make a bold advance, I would like to offer you a place in my company. I promise you will not be the poorer for it, but I cannot promise you will find it an easy or comfortable employment." He gestured to a document lying on the open escritoire. "I am sure you will want to read before you sign. The key point is that in all things as long as you are in my employ the final decision on any action taken is mine. That may not appeal. But if you wish to remain here, you do need to sign."

Gideon had little knowledge of the world of mercenary soldiers but he was pretty sure such legal niceties were no more needed than between a labourer hired at a Martinmas Fair and the man doing the hiring.

"Do you make all your soldiers sign contracts?"

"Of a kind. It gives them a feeling of security and—they believe—legal grounds to slit my throat if I don't pay them what I promise, but theirs is admittedly more akin to a muster roll. I keep individual contracts for my senior officers and non-military experts such as yourself and Anders Jensen. It is the best way, I find, to ensure we are clear on the nature and duration of our relationship and the expectations of both sides."

Gideon hesitated before crossing to pick up the document. "I want to stay," he said without reading it, "but I cannot sign this."

"And so to things tender and unpleasing then." Lord leaned on the wall beside the hearth and folded his arms. "I'm sure you have good reasons and I am sure I am going to hear them. Let me guess, it will be some variety of *dura lex sed lex*?"

"To enter into any arrangement with a traitor would place me in a dangerous legal position."

"I think you crossed that particular Rubicon a while ago," Lord said, seeming unconcerned. "It is *ex post facto* by a few days now."

"Except that this," Gideon picked up the document, "would have no value as a contract anyway. It has no enforceability. You have no ability to seek legal recourse because you are condemned as a traitor so could not press the case. Equally, I would have none for the same reason as all your property is already forfeit to the crown."

Lord smiled at that.

"You will not sign because I am a traitor?"

"I will not sign," Gideon said carefully, "because my signature being on it means no more than my signature not being on it. This is not a legally enforceable contract."

"Very few are, in my experience. At their best, they seem more statements of goodwill and good intentions, and at their worst an excuse for one party to abuse the other with a sheen of respectability."

"And which is this?" Gideon waved the contract in his hand.

"That is an honest attempt to offer fair recompense for services rendered."

"I don't see how that requires a formal written contract when neither party is in a place to call upon it in any meaningful way should the other default."

Lord held his gaze, something new in the gemstone eyes, something Gideon was not sure he could put a name to, but which seemed to mark a shift in the way Lord perceived him.

"You wish to stay?"

"I wish to stay."

"You wish to stay and I find myself in need of a good lawyer." Lord straightened up and crossed to Gideon, taking the contract from his hands, tearing it across and across again, then dropping the pieces into the hearth where they flared on the bed of embers. "And so on to soothing ills. You may stay. Uncontracted. I am sure I need not lecture you on confidentiality or advise you that you are under my authority as much as any of my men."

Gideon nodded.

"I understand that." Chains of paper and ink were not the real force that held people here, himself included. "You find yourself in need of a lawyer, what for? Writing new contracts?"

Lord was watching the ashes of the burning contract collapse on the embers, but it was clear his eyes were not seeing them. It seemed to Gideon that he was making a profound decision. When he spoke he turned and held Gideon's gaze.

"I am hopeful that some documents may soon come into my possession. Documents I need to authenticate. To be sure they are not forgeries or a sham." His mouth closed on the final word as if concerned he might have said too much.

It was familiar ground for Gideon—a client bound up in legal coils with much riding on the outcome of how some deed might be assessed under the law.

"These are documents regarding an inheritance?" That was the most usual, but it seemed unlikely as they both knew Lord could no more legally inherit than he could legally remain in the country.

"Of a sort," Lord conceded.

"Where are they? Do you need me to recover them for you?"

Lord had crossed to the window and was looking out, something holding his attention.

"I wish it were that simple. If I knew for sure I would recover them myself."

Gideon recalled what Anders had said about camp gossip.

"They are concerning a family heirloom of some kind?"

That made the other man laugh.

"That would be one way to describe it."

"It must be something of extreme import for you to risk returning to England to find it."

"It is. And this present state of unrest affords me a chance to act which otherwise I would not have."

"Since you intend to allow me to study these documents in detail when you find them," Gideon said, "why such secrecy now around what they might contain?"

Outside, there were some voices raised as if in greeting.

"It is information. Information that will make a profound difference to me, but those who presently hold it believe the implications have far wider consequences. I disagree, but perhaps they are right. Either way, I am reluctant to let word run ahead of proof."

Gideon thought about that and tried to imagine what kind of information it might be.

"Is it to do with your heritage?"

Lord stopped looking out of the window and crossed the room swiftly to open the door.

"It is to do with my heritage," he agreed. "But right now is not the time to discuss it." Lord held the door open, one arm flung out to indicate he wished Gideon to leave with him. "For now, let us *prepare for deeds; let other times have words.*"

Gideon realised that whatever had caught Lord's attention through the window had now reached the open ground before the mill. He followed Lord, who took the stairs two at a time and strode out of the main building.

There was a small crowd of men talking excitedly to and about someone at the centre of their group.

"Have a care, gentlemen, I am sure there is work most of you should be doing." Lord's voice acted like magic and the cluster of men broke up, leaving just five. The man in the middle stood still and scratched at the back of one hand.

He wore clothes less flamboyant than those of the men who flanked him. An old cape covered a leather buff and his light brown hair was greying and lank. He lifted the hand he had been scratching with and tilted the brim of his battered hat, revealing a patch of puckered flesh on his scalp above the hairline. His face was weathered, making it difficult to put an age on him, but Gideon thought he would have to be at least as old as the century itself.

From where he stood, Gideon was the only man able to mark the slight widening of Lord's eyes and hear the involuntary pause in his breath when he saw who it was.

"I heard you were hiring," the newcomer said, in an accent that belonged somewhere between the Tyne and the Wear. He and Lord were much the same height and their gazes locked directly. Like swords crossing.

"I heard you were in Breisach."

The man hawked and spat. "I was. But unlike you, I never could thole the French. So I went with Mercy. But there was a misunderstanding, and as things were moving to war here, I thought I'd get myself home. Didn't think to find you here though."

"*Abroad the sword bereaveth, at home there is as death*. We are all creatures of habit who like salmon return to our spawning sooner or later. I assume you returned to yours?"

The other man ignored the question.

"That from the Bible? Well then, I have one for you: *Thou shalt not bear false witness against thy neighbour.*"

THE MERCENARY'S BLADE

Gideon wondered what this was about. Lord's four men behind the newcomer had a tension about them as if expecting something to happen, something violent. The new arrival seemed unconcerned that the frog where his sword should hang was empty.

"*A man that beareth false witness against his neighbour is a maul, and a sword, and a sharp arrow,*" Lord said quietly. "Not my way, Mags and you know it. Don't say things you don't mean just to frighten the children. Unless you have come to call me out?"

There was absolute silence in which it seemed to Gideon even the breeze was holding its breath. Then the newcomer laughed and stepped forward, open-armed. There was the barest hesitation from Lord before he did the same and the men embraced briefly, Lord stepping back first, but still smiling. The tension had been broken and the men who had been standing behind Mags were grinning.

It took a few more minutes before those men went back to whatever duty they had come from and Gideon alone heard the conversation as he followed Lord and Mags into the main mill building.

"So why have you come? Is Europe not entertaining enough for you anymore?" Lord's tone was still pleasant but had a harder edge than had been there before.

"It's entertaining enough. Forbye, I've had my time there. I thought to be one of the first back, to pick the ripest apples. I get here and find my name means next to nothing." The last was said with bitterness.

They had reached the bottom of the stairs and Lord hesitated.

"*Sith that no greater joy there can be had, Then to*

restore thy selfe unto thy blood. You went home then?"

"I went home. There's none that remember me there. But after so long..."

There was a silence and something passed between the two men, something Gideon felt but could neither see nor interpret. Then Lord was nodding and a moment later they were going up the stairs talking of old battles. Then the door to Lord's room shut behind them.

"Who was that?" Anders asked, arriving late to the events.

Gideon shook his head and then shrugged. "I'd say it was an old friend of Lord's but I'm not so sure.

Jupp, who had been one of the men in the group outside and had followed Anders into the mill, was more than happy to enlighten them.

"That, gentlemen, is one of the legends," he said. "He's a great commander, a fine swordsman—some say one of the best, and if you name any major battle of the last twenty-five years that man was there carving his mark. He is a man any of us would be proud to serve under."

Gideon wondered why such a man would be travelling alone and dressed as he was.

"Who is he then?"

"They call him Mags. Rumour has it he was some wealthy family's by-blow."

"Mags?" Anders echoed. "That is a strange name for a man."

"It is, but what I heard was he earned it for leading a whole group of women and children to a church in Magdeburg when it fell. Guarded it with his own men too. Shame what happened."

"What happened?" Gideon asked, dutifully.

THE MERCENARY'S BLADE

"There was wildfire everywhere, the whole city was burning, and he'd locked the church to keep the people safe. They were all roasted alive like chestnuts."

"That's horrific."

Jupp shrugged. "That's the kind of thing as happens in sieges sometimes. Thing is he tried. Most were too busy lining their pockets. That makes him a good man in my book."

There was a powerful silence and Gideon found his fists had tightened. With an effort, he relaxed them and tried to turn the conversation. "I thought you needed money and a title to be a military commander? Or at least money."

"Oh, he had both for a time. He were made graf of somewhere or other by Wallenstein, then lost it all when Wallenstein was murdered. Fought under the big names. Wallenstein of course. Tilly. Gallas. Joined Saxe-Weimar after Rheinfelfelden."

Gideon was pretty sure those were all commanders on the Catholic side of the wars in Europe. But loyalties here seemed to run to things other than just religion, even if that was what the rest of humanity was fighting over. Which was one more way that this strange life inverted all he knew about the world.

"Then what is he doing here?" Anders asked.

Jupp shrugged.

"Fallen on bad times. There were rumours he'd sold out his employer, and some other old stories were being retold with him as the villain in them. Never heard there was any proof, but mud sticks. After that, he must have found it hard to get any work at all."

"He is friends with our Lord and master?" Anders

asked, doubtfully.

"Everyone likes Mags. He is a living legend. But there's something between them. People say the Schiavono had a woman who was in that church, you see."

Gideon saw all too clearly and his gaze locked with Anders'.

"Mr Fox?"

Gideon looked back to Jupp and tried to ignore the raised eyebrow on Ander's face.

"I was thinking it would be a good idea for you to get some practice with that sword you carry. Maybe I could give you some advice."

Gideon had no excuse to offer. After what Anders had told him about every man in the company being expected to be able to fight at need, he knew it was something he would have to do.

"I am sure I have much to learn," he said, "and if you would be willing to teach me, I would be most grateful. Though I need to be careful not to reopen the wound on my arm."

"Perhaps I might join the class too," Anders put in, "if that is acceptable?"

It was, and soon the two of them were stripped to shirts and breeches. They gained a small audience offering running commentary on their stance, the way they moved, their grip on their swords. There was much good-humoured amusement at what must have seemed to the mercenaries an incapacity of two scholars when it came to the real world.

A bit to Gideon's surprise he found he was a better swordsman than Anders. Although what he lacked in style and skill, the Dane could provide in confidence and strength, which meant they matched well.

They were interrupted by a messenger saying the Schiavono wished to speak with Gideon immediately. Flushed with the exercise and a certain pride in how well he had carried himself through it, Gideon scooped cold water over his face and pulled on the gaudy red coat to cover the sweat stains on his shirt, before heading upstairs again.

He was met by a burst of laughter as he reached the door and the tail end of a very crude joke greeted his entrance. Whatever differences the two men might have, they had reached some understanding. Someone had provided them with wine. It seemed strange to Gideon to see the immaculate elegance of Philip Lord, half-sitting on the sill of the window, legs extended, compared with the gnomish figure of Mags, who occupied the stool set by the now closed desk. Mags had a clay pipe and was filling the room with the pungent reek of burning tobacco. His sword had been restored to him.

"Ah, we are no longer Utopians for we have a lawyer among us—pay heed in case matters are disguised and laws wrested in crafty ways." Lord stood as he spoke and gestured Gideon to the table by the wall. "There is a perch to be had or stand if you would prefer. The one seat has been taken by the old so he can be distinguished from the young."

"You mind who you are calling old," Mags said without rancour and then broke off coughing.

Gideon stayed where he was.

"You wished to speak with me," he said, sensing there were undercurrents he was missing and unwilling to yet again be made to act a part in a play where he had no notion of the script.

"I wish to avail myself of your knowledge and quick apprehension, since you are not so dull as the generality of man. It is odd," Lord said, picking up a sheet of paper from the sill beside where he had been sitting, "how someone can so denigrate a profession and yet hold in esteem the intelligence of those who follow it." He held the page out to Gideon.

The sketch was a simple one, freshly executed in charcoal. A circle with another inside. Hatching marks representing letters filled the space between the inner and outer circles. Two crowned figures sat side-by-side, a man holding a sword and a woman holding a sword-like sceptre. Their hands met, resting on a cross-topped orb. Above them was some poorly indicated heraldry which was itself also crowned. Gideon took one look and handed it back.

"That is a great seal that was used by Queen Mary. It shows herself and her husband King Philip of Spain. Your namesake."

Lord gave a brief nod and took the paper back, looking at it for a moment.

"My namesake," he echoed. "So anything this was attached to would have been known to the queen?"

"Not necessarily," Gideon said, "but in theory, yes. Her great officers of state could have used it on something she had approved but not read in detail. Of course, in theory, it could have been used without her permission by them too. But that would have been treason."

Any trace of the previous levity had left the room and Lord turned to Mags, still holding the paper with its charcoal sketch.

"Tell me again where you saw this."

"On the neck of a document bag in old Coupland's cabinet. Afore he went to Newcastle I went to see him to offer my services leading his men. He told me he had enough legitimate support not to need that of someone like me." Mags nodded at the paper. "He'd not have realised I marked that."

"Coupland took the bag with him?"

"I was thinking so. Until I was in the cabinet again yesterday. You see, I signed on after Coupland had gone. Some lads left behind spoke up for me—men left with his nephew, Nicholas Tempest. Nasty piece of work that one." He spat in the hearth, the saliva sizzling before vanishing in a tiny whiff of steam. "Anyway, I was speaking with Tempest in his uncle's cabinet and saw there was a small door hidden in the panelling right by the bookshelves. It hadn't been closed properly."

Lord had sat back on the sill again, his expression intense.

"We both know what that means," he said softly.

Mags nodded.

"I thought it might interest you."

"You went back and looked?"

"You make it sound as if that would be easy."

"For you it would be," Lord said, and Mags made no reply.

Gideon wondered if he had any part to play in this conversation. The other two men seemed to have forgotten he was even present. Lord's gaze on Mags was expectant and challenging.

"Oh, I went back," Mags said. "But if there were a way

to open it without an axe, I couldn't find it."

"So you bring it to me?"

"Who else would it have any value to?" Mags made a dismissive gesture pointing in the air with his pipe. "Besides, I've been out looking for you these past few days past on behalf of the Tempest lad. He had us all out hunting. Seems rare keen to lay hands on you."

There was a sudden stillness and to Gideon it felt as if the temperature had dropped. So much so that he shivered.

"You were with Tempest when he rode to Pethridge two days ago?" Lord asked, his tone conversational, one hand fingering the scrolls of metal on the hilt of his sword.

"I heard about that," Mags said easily.

"And you know who freed him?"

Mags nodded and tapped out the burnt remains in his pipe. "Of course I do. You'll remember Shadrack Heron? Him and a Welshman with a name I couldn't say without a mouthful of pebbles and spit."

"I'm sure Heron will be able to say it," Lord said, his tone sending ice down the back of Gideon's neck. Then he drew in a short breath and smiled. "But for the moment we come to talk of trade and huckstering—*a trade not for gold, silver, or jewels; nor for silks; nor for spices; nor any other commodity of matter*—but in this case for knowledge."

"I can get you in if that is what you're wanting," Mags said, taking a tobacco pouch from his belt and refilling the pipe, tamping down the leaves with his thumb.

"And out again?"

"Of course."

THE MERCENARY'S BLADE

"And Heron?"

Gideon felt all the hairs on his forearms stand up at the way Lord spoke the name.

"And Heron will maybe be there. If not, I can lay hands on him for you." Mags sounded close to indifferent. "But if you want the Tempest brat, I can't make you any promises."

"Of course not. For naturally, *blood will to blood be kind*. Which," Lord said thoughtfully, "only leaves us with the question of how much?"

Mags took the time to relight his pipe with a taper from the fire and puff more smoke before he replied.

"You have a sweet set up here," he said at last. "Very sweet. But you could do with someone like me. The skills I could bring."

Gideon could read nothing in Lord's expression to say what he felt about that.

"You want to join my merry men and play Robin Hood with us?" Lord suggested. "Lennox here could be our Alan-a-Dale. Who would you be? Friar Tuck, perhaps? Or were you thinking more of Little John?"

"You don't trust me?"

Lord got up and stretched like a lazy cat.

"I think we are done. I have a simple trade for you. You will get me into Howe Hall and if all is as you say, then we will talk of what comes next. If not, I have a feeling these men you wish to join will be less than merry and asking you to account for it."

Mags rocked back on the stool and puffed some more on his pipe considering.

"Just you and me to go in?"

"I want Lennox there too—to be my witness."

Gideon drew a breath to protest, but a glimpse of the pale skin, drawn tight over Lord's face silenced him.

Mags laughed. "You, I can do. You're canny enough, but if you think I can get a lawyer in…"

"Oh, I think you can," Lord said. "In fact, I'm sure of it."

The laughter died and Mags was left with a half-grin. He shook his head. "You are brain-sick and belong in Bedlam."

Lord looked thoughtful then nodded.

"You are not the first to say that and you could well be right," he said.

Chapter Eighteen

The afternoon was half done when Hoyle strode into the parlour of Howe Hall, something Nick knew he would never have dreamt of doing if Sir Bartholomew had been there.

"Heron has come with news. Says he'll speak only to you, so you'll have to talk with him."

Nick was incredulous. "You should have brought him straight to me to report."

Hoyle's expression was bemused, and with growing fury, Nick realised it hadn't even crossed the sergeant's mind to take such a course.

"Bring him now," he commanded.

Hoyle tightened his jaw.

Heron must have heard the order as he pushed his way past the burly sergeant, silent as always, a bruise visible on his face.

Nick had endured enough of Hoyle. He wished he could send him to Newcastle and promote Mags to fill his place. At least the mercenary was competent, obedient and deferential which was more than Hoyle ever managed.

Heron had taken off his hat, clutching it in both hands.

"You have news for me?" Nick asked.

"I found them," Heron said curtly. "Me and Mags we'd split up searching. So I came to you. You need to be fast. Tonight. They may move on in the morning."

Nick's blood pumped hard and, unable to keep still, he

strode across the room and back, resisting the urge to leap up and dance a galliard on the table.

"Where are they?"

"An old fulling mill on the river."

"The old mill?" he echoed. "But the place is a ruin near enough."

"Seems it's been patched and made good,"

"How many men are with Lord?"

"Thirty, maybe a handful more."

Nick did a quick calculation. With the men he had been given for his search, together with most of the garrison of Howe and those of Coupland's tenants he could muster, that should be more than enough to deal with the numbers Lord had with him. He was about to give the requisite orders when Hoyle spoke up.

"We should check those numbers before we commit. If we act too quickly, we risk making a mistake. If they have a camp they'll likely be there tomorrow and the next day, no matter what Heron says."

Not everyone, Nick yearned to say, moved at a snail's pace like an ageing fat man. But he needed Hoyle in reasonable humour, so resisted the urge.

"We must not chance losing Lord." Seeing Hoyle open his mouth to repeat his protest Nick added: "Heron can show the way to five men who can count. I'll gather the rest and follow."

Hoyle frowned at that, no doubt seeing the blank space Nick was painting for him. But then Nick had no intention of allowing Hoyle to pour his gripping clay of extreme caution over the smooth path of speed.

"I want you here, sergeant," he said. "Someone needs to be in charge of Howe. It would be remiss to leave the house completely undefended."

He didn't wait. Leaving the sergeant tight-lipped and under instructions to summon the local men to muster, Nick went to find his armour. It would be the first time he had worn it in anger. The excitement of that, coupled with a night attack and the prospect of accomplishing that of which no one else seemed capable, was a heady brew. Hoyle must have delegated his task because a few minutes later he came to say the matter was in hand and to ask Nick to reconsider.

"The time for caution and hesitation is over," Nick told him, knowing he sounded decisive and confident as a born leader of men should. "We have waited for this opportunity, now we should act on it. Just as my uncle acted when word came before."

"And look where that got things," Hoyle countered, but still helped with the buckles fastening the chest and back plates as he spoke.

"That is why I am sending scouts," Nick told him. "Men you know and trust for the work. I'll have the troops on the way and ready if we need them, and if not, then it will have been an exercise for them for a night alarm."

Hoyle stood back and shook his head. "As you wish, of course, sir, but I have a bad feeling."

Nick understood. Old men became cautious as their own speed and skill diminished, forgetting too quickly the vigour of youth. It was something his father had said to him once: *We all judge others as if they were ourselves. Never make that mistake.* Nick had no intention of doing so. But the understanding brought a momentary empathy and he put a hand on Hoyle's shoulder as the older man had with him a thousand times.

"Don't fret. I will be careful."

Hoyle looked at him soberly and for the first time, Nick realised the man had to tilt his chin up to do so.

The scouts left with Heron, a flurry and clatter of hooves audible outside. Nick made his preparations as the men he summoned slowly assembled.

They were mostly either those of older age who would struggle now to endure the privations of military life or those still too young to be taken to war. The best had gone with his uncle, aside from a few who remained to stiffen any defence if it should become necessary. But all had some training in arms, and Nick hoped that with the element of surprise, a sleeping foe and superior numbers, it would be a swift and certain victory.

Tonight, he would be the one to finish that which his father had always told him, should never have been begun.

The plan was simple.

Mags would walk them into Howe Hall through the gate, claiming they were recruits. Gideon pointed out that he and Lord were bound to be recognised by at least some of the inhabitants.

"That is the least of our problems. Appearances can be changed easily enough," Lord said. "More at issue, in my view, is the degree of trust we would be putting in the hands of Mags here. Knowing the price Coupland has placed upon acquiring me, how much would that weigh against the desire to be in this company?"

The mercenary frowned.

"What are you saying?"

THE MERCENARY'S BLADE

Lord had been sitting on the sill and got to his feet.

"Company with honesty, is virtue vices to flee:
Company is good and ill but every man hath his free will... I am saying that I need more than your word before I will trust this. I am wondering how you think to assure me of your good faith rather than just by your promise of it?"

Mags lifted his shoulders in a shrug and then spat in the hearth.

"You want to get into the Hall. I'm telling you how it can be done. But if you think I might be playing you false, then leave me here and go yourself. I can give you the words you need. We're much of a height. You have the mimicry of a popinjay, so with a bit of work..."

Unbelievably, Lord had agreed with the madness. He summoned Jupp, explained Mags' hostage status and sent the two of them away, suggesting Mags might like a tour of the mill.

Seeing that Lord was committed to the insanity, Gideon tried to persuade him that his own presence would be more of a hindrance than a help.

"You have the persistence of a flea and are irritating enough to match," Lord told him. "You are also a freak of nature. The very term 'an honest lawyer' is a contradiction, but somehow through whatever quirk of fate, and despite the worst excesses of education, you have managed to remain a fundamentally honest man. Yes, I agree your acting skills, whilst not terrible, leave much to be desired. In an ideal world I would not be asking you to undertake this. But I have need of a witness with legal knowledge and, more importantly, a fair and balanced mind. You would be surprised how rare those qualities might be."

That brought Gideon up short.

"A fair and balanced mind? For what purpose?"

"Because," Lord said, still sitting in the window, "I am not sure I trust myself to have one. I lived in Howe Hall for the first dozen years of my life and I know it as well as I know my own sword. But I have never seen what Mags spoke of, some priest hole concealed in Coupland's most private cabinet."

"You think he is lying, then?"

Lord shook his head.

"About that? No. It fits with all I know much too well. Like the missing piece of a clockwork automaton: put it in and the whole thing whirrs into life marching around and striking its chest. But about other things." He drew his lips into a tight line. "About other things, he may be."

"If you know Howe so well surely you know ways you could get inside without Mags' help?"

"Mouse holes and loose latches?" Lord shook his head. "Not in Howe. The place is a fortress. It would take sappers and artillery."

A burst of laughter drifted through the window and someone called Mags by name. Gideon wondered if Lord found it hard that the other man seemed as popular as himself with the men of his company. In some cases, perhaps, more so.

Lord sighed and got to his feet. "I need your honesty and integrity. I also know that is not something that can be purchased or demanded, so I am asking. Will you accompany me tonight and be an honest and fair-minded witness to whatever I may find? Please."

This was why, in the end, Gideon agreed. Purely

THE MERCENARY'S BLADE

because Philip Lord had swallowed his pride and humbled himself enough to ask.

The preparations took less time than Gideon would have thought they should. In his own case, it involved spreading some sludge over his hair and beard to make it look darker, nearer brown than his natural red. Lord applied the paste himself from a pot stored in one of his chests.

"Celandine, madder, sage, burnt grapevine ash, myrtle and other things," he explained in answer to Gideon's query as he applied it. "Most will wash out quickly. For clothes, those you were given by Dutch would be good, but keep decent footwear." He finished his work. "Go rinse that off then get changed."

Lord's transformation he wasn't a witness to.

By the time Gideon had washed out the sludge and changed clothes the afternoon had tumbled into dusk and was deepening into the full dark of night. As he waited, there was a ragged cheer from outside and Gideon was drawn by curiosity to see what was the cause.

Matt Rider, clad in a nightshirt with a coat thrown over it took his first steps into the outside world. He was still recuperating his strength, but there was a look of health about him. Gideon went over, beckoned by Anders.

"Speak to the man if you will, my friend, he'll not return to his bed otherwise."

"With good reason," Matt Rider said and placed a heavy hand on Gideon's shoulder. "He won't listen to me, you might. He told me what he plans to do but I don't trust Mags further than I can spit. Have a care if you go with him. Be watchful for some betrayal."

Gideon had no need to ask who Matt spoke about.

"Mags is to stay here as a hostage for our safe return," he said. "I can't see how he can expect to betray Lord and myself and survive the experience."

Matt shook his head.

"He might think he could, though. He is well-liked by many here."

That brought a chorus of over-quick denials from those around, summed up by Olsen in his Swedish accented French. "*J'aime bien l'homme mais...* but much as I like him, he is not the Schiavono and if he betrays him, he betrays us all."

Matt's lips quirked and he shook his head. "Be sure you remember that when the time comes."

Then Matt allowed Anders to take him back to his bed, protesting that if he was served another bowl of frumenty in place of proper food, he would make whoever did so wear it like a cap.

"Are we ready?" Mags' voice called from over by the stables and Gideon turned.

Illuminated by a lamp he held, Mags stood holding the reins of the horse he had arrived on, battered hat in place.

"He is good, isn't he?" another Mags said from right beside Gideon, proprietary pride in his voice.

Gideon turned and the man who stood there, whilst clearly the real Mags, was now well groomed, hair washed to a colour closer to gold than the dun brown it had been before and wearing the peacock blue doublet with silver lace and points that Gideon had seen Lord wearing once soon after his arrival. Oddly, Mags looked as if he belonged in such clothes.

He were made graf of somewhere or other by Wallenstein.

THE MERCENARY'S BLADE

It dawned on Gideon that Mags' previous appearance was as much an act as any Lord might put on.

Lord led Mags' horse over to them and, close to, Gideon had to look carefully to see the tell-tale signs that this was Lord and not Mags himself. The nose, of course, but its shape had been subdued with a darkening of the skin in specific places that at a glance would fool the eye, especially in the dark or under the flicker of lamp or candle. The eyes too, but Lord kept them partly hooded in a manner Gideon guessed he must have perfected to disguise their penetrating brilliance.

"This horse is a heartbeat from becoming dog meat," Lord said, addressing Mags, "You have my congratulations on keeping it vertical, I shall endeavour to do the same. The issue is finding a mount poor enough to match it amongst those we have here for Lennox to ride."

He turned as Shiraz emerged, leading the bad-tempered brute Gideon had ridden before.

"Ah, we have a match," Lord said brightly. "I must admit I am reluctant to burden this beast until the last moment in case it collapses wheezing." He gave some lie to the harshness of his words by running his hand over the horse's neck and giving it a pat.

"Well, that leaves only one thing to complete the illusion," Mags said, grinning. He began to unbuckle his sword.

Lord gripped Mag's wrist with his free hand. "No. That won't be necessary."

Gideon was sure he marked a certain reluctance in the nod Mags gave and the way his hand fell away from his sword.

"My men will look after you," Lord said as Gideon took control of the reins he was offered and made some attempt to placate his mount, being rewarded by a baring of teeth and flattening of ears.

"I think I'll be fine," Mags said.

"So do I. As long as we are back by dawn." Lord held Mags' gaze until the other man looked away and at the horses.

"Then you might want to avail yourself of some finer Coupland horseflesh for your return journey," Mags suggested. "To avoid being late."

A short time later they rode into the night. Lord led the way, at first taking a path now so familiar to Gideon. But they quickly stopped following the road and took a route across the untracked countryside. Sometime over an hour after they set out, Gideon saw Howe Hall—a faint glimmer of lights in the darkness.

Lord stopped a short distance off and spoke quietly.

"Follow my lead, say nothing unless there is no choice. Tell yourself that we have every right to be there—and act that way."

Then they were in the open, bracing the gates of Howe at a brisk trot, barely slowing as Lord called out on their approach in a close approximation of Mags' voice.

"God, King and Coupland." Then added as they halted by the unopening gates, "and don't take your time, some of us are hungry here."

Gideon sat on his irascible mount, which tried to bite the ageing pile of bones carrying Lord. Dancing his horse around in a circle, Gideon tried to keep his mind from the grim thought that they were in easy musket range of the men who manned the gates.

THE MERCENARY'S BLADE

It isn't going to work.

After a small eternity, a voice answered them. "That you Mags?"

"Who else d'you think it is? Prince Bishop Morton?"

"Well, is canny late and—"

"Just let us in, man. I'm starving to death out here."

Gideon was sure the gate guard must be able to hear the pounding of his heart.

It's not going to work.

With a groan of protesting metal, the gate swung open and skin prickling, Gideon rode through beside Lord.

Once they were in the stable yard Gideon found he had become close to invisible, getting no acknowledgement from the two men who were there, and not much more from the lad who took his horse. As he handed the creature over, excited voices were talking to Lord.

"You'll not have heard. Heron found them, in the old fulling mill."

"Tempest took everyone. All the house and the tenants who could sit a horse and hold a sword, even those in their dotage or barely in breeches."

"You'll have missed them by close to an hour."

Gideon heard the words and the blood slowed in his veins. His heart pumped painfully, the pulse of it in his ears. He couldn't move. He couldn't breathe. In his mind was Zahara and the mill in flames.

Roasted alive like chestnuts.

"Have to hope they have good hunting then," Lord said, his voice replicating Mags' slight drawl. He sounded unconcerned.

Gideon found he could move again and drew breath to demand the return of his mount. But before he could speak an iron talon gripped his arm and the breath was wasted in a slight gasp of pain.

"You'll need to talk to the sergeant, he'll have something for you to do for sure," the man talking to Lord was saying.

"Do me a favour, don't say I'm back yet. I need to eat first. My stomach's sticking to itself."

There was laughter and a few moments later, as Gideon was being walked away towards a door into the house, a low voice, pitched below the level of a whisper, in his ear.

"Say nothing. Do nothing. It's too late. There is nothing we can do."

Gideon jerked back. "But—"

The fist to his guts was just hard enough to deprive him of breath and a moment later he was flattened into the darkest shadows against the wall of the house.

"You feeling better now?" Lord asked in Mags' voice.

Gulping in air, Gideon managed to nod his head. Lord must have felt the movement as he released his hold. Another murmur came from the darkness.

"I trust my men. You must too."

Gideon thought of Shiraz, Jupp and Olsen. Lord was right. It was too late and he had no choice but to trust them. His own desperate desire to know wouldn't alter the outcome by one iota. So he did the only thing he could do and prayed, silently and with fervour, hoping God would hear prayers offered on behalf of a heathen. Then he was following Lord into the house, keeping his face half-concealed under the drooping brim of the hat he wore.

There was no one to stop them or even question their

presence. A woman servant with eyes red from crying lowered her gaze and shot away. Lord picked up a lamp from somewhere and used it to light their way where the rooms and passageways were unlit.

They walked through a panelled chamber, furnished with upholstered seats. Here a bow-fronted cabinet with pilasters topped with cupids, and there a dresser displaying delicate Delftware. Gideon was reminded of some of the houses of wealthier merchants he had known as clients in London—wealth displayed in lavish living.

The staircase they came to was older and heavier than the woodwork he had seen so far, dark oak from the middle of the last century. Built against the wall, it turned on a landing to double back in a panelled second rise to reach the galleried landing above.

"Nothing has changed," Lord said, his voice his own and soft. Then he set foot on the bottom step and went up lightly. Gideon followed.

It was in the nature of the construction of the stairs that there was no way to see if anyone was descending until, having reached the first landing, it was possible to turn and look up.

"What are you doing here?"

Gideon froze behind Lord who stepped back from where he had been about to make the next ascent. Lord lowered his gaze.

"Sergeant Hoyle, sir. I was looking for you. We have a new recruit I found—"

Was it the way Lord stood, the set of his shoulders, the way the light he held caught his face…? Or was it something in the way he spoke? A chance of intonation that sprang recognition from its snare?

"By Christ. It's you."

Lord moved then. He drew his sword but his blade was met by another from above.

"Howe and Coupland," Hoyle shouted. "To me, to me."

The words were bellowed in a voice once used to bring men across a battlefield, and it echoed throughout Howe's walls.

"Fox, behind us." Lord's words were clipped by comparison as he moved to engage the man above him. The time for subterfuge was gone and they now could expect the entire house to come against them. Gideon turned to guard their rear as best he might.

A moment later a door beneath the stairs was flung open.

Gideon, Watt Bell's sword in his hand, found himself staring through the balustrades into the cold, round mouth of a flintlock pistol.

For Nick, that night would remain a memory of confusion and chaos.

From the moment Heron re-joined him on the road things began to blur as if reality had curled in at the edges, like parchment held too close to a fire.

Heron said he had no better idea of numbers to offer. The man who had come back with him was freer with words by far.

"We couldn't get close enough to be sure. They have lads out on watch, but you can hear singing and smell cooking."

This sounded better by the moment. Why wait until the men were asleep if they were half in their cups? Feeling his lips pull back into a fierce grin at the thought, Nick

THE MERCENARY'S BLADE

gave his orders. He had thought of the plan as soon as he knew they were dealing with the old mill, a place he had played in childhood.

He had the men he knew could do the work best, the core he had been left by his uncle to hunt Lord, dismount. Then he explained they were to deal with the guards as silently as possible before moving along the river path ready to cut off any who tried to escape. As soon as they were sure the guards were down, they were to call like an owl to let Nick know. Then he would take his main force along the track that led down to the mill, which was wide enough for two or even three abreast.

In the dark, taking the encampment by surprise, he had no doubt whatsoever that they would win. His prize would be Philip Lord, perhaps even alive… But no, alive he might still cause arguments over his fate, dead there would be none, and the matter would be settled for good.

"When do you want us to go in, sir?"

The air was cold and the smell of smoke faint upon it. With the shades and wraiths that were his men about him, Nick smiled his savage smile.

"Now seems as good a time as any," he said. "Kill anyone you find."

The chosen men slipped into the shadows, taking death with them.

That was the last part of the action to go according to Nick's plan. Because after the men had gone he waited—and then waited some more and no owl call came.

"Somat's not right," Heron, who had stayed with him, murmured. "We should—"

Then silent death began visiting them from the dark. Nick heard a thump from somewhere in his troop and then someone gurgled horribly, a third man screamed, a sound suddenly cut off, and that was enough. The body of untried soldiers heaved, turned and attempted to flee. Then, and only then, the night erupted with a volley of pistol shots and men closed in from both sides of the track.

Nick had his sword out and his pistol in his other hand when someone tried to grab his horse's bridle. He fired at the figure and found himself fighting for his life. The attackers were on foot.

"Retreat," Nick yelled. Though his order was unnecessary.

He saw the men of Howe had already turned, trying to escape the morass of terrified plunging horseflesh and the hacking blades from men who pulled them down. He could only hope those who survived that and the gauntlet of sporadic pistol shots, or the siffle of air that betrayed an arrow in flight, might indeed escape.

Nick tried to turn his mount, but despite his grip on the saddle, he was sliding from his horse. *Christ! Someone must have cut the girth.*

He landed heavily, part tangled in leather and wood, sword stamped from his grip, pinned like a beetle on its back in the cuirass he wore, trying to roll away but so disoriented he had no idea which direction he should move to be safe.

"Quickly. With me." The voice, hissed and urgent, belonged to Mags, who was suddenly, unbelievably, present.

Having direction now, Nick rolled and rose to a crouching stance as the nine circles of hell were enacted behind him. Mags gripped his arm, pulling him into the

THE MERCENARY'S BLADE

thicket of trees and shrubs. Nick needed no more persuasion than that and began running as fast as possible. A nightmare plunge into an alien world where the plants and trees were living monsters reaching and grabbing to stop his escape. Then suddenly it was easier. They had broken from the grasp of undergrowth and were following a path. A few paces later Mags stopped and turned.

"This will get you back to the road. There's a horse there, take it and ride for Howe."

Nick struggled to make out the man's features in the dark. There were inexplicable flashes of silver from his clothing when the moonlight caught them.

"I don't underst—"

"No need to, sir. I've got to go to keep them from following you. Remember whatever you might hear of me, I am your man."

"But who betrayed—?"

"Heron," Mags said bitterly, "Who else even knew?"

Then Nick was alone in the dark with only wild and terrible thoughts for company.

Chapter Nineteen

The shot left Gideon's ears ringing.

Somehow he was still alive and the man who had levelled the pistol at him was falling back, a blossom of dark red staining his chest, pistol falling from his lax grip.

It was a miracle that made little sense to Gideon, but he had no time to let his logical mind catch up. A second man was levelling his pistol. Without thinking about what he was doing, Gideon gripped the handrail and vaulted it, swinging his legs over the wood and kicking out at the second pistoleer. His feet caught the man's arm, sending the pistol skidding away over the stone-flagged floor.

"Hold!" The shout came from Lord. Gideon, breathing hard, saw the face of the man he was confronting take on a look of concern. He risked a glance back and saw Lord had the bulky form of the man he had been fighting in some kind of grip, the long blade of his sword running over the man's barrel chest to press against the soft flesh of his throat.

"Fox. There is a loaded pistol at your feet, pick it up and come to me," Lord ordered. Gideon stooped to retrieve the weapon. Then holding that in one hand and his sword in the other, retreated with backward steps as fast as he could. Men who were now spilling in greater numbers through the doors. Five of them, one armed with a poker and another, little more than a boy gripping a knife he must have snatched up in the kitchen. Whatever else they might be, no one could call the household of Howe cowards.

Once Gideon had regained the stairs, Lord spoke again, his voice his own.

"I have no wish to take any more lives, though I will if you push me to it. I have business here which need concern none of you and once done I will free Sergeant Hoyle. But if you try to interfere..." The sword moved and a welt of blood appeared on the shoulder of the man he held.

"Don't listen to him," Hoyle said, hoarsely. "I'm good as dead. Kill him."

But no one moved on the floor below.

Lord's voice rang out. *"And behold a ladder set up on the earth, and the top of it reached to heaven and behold the angels of God ascending and descending on it. And, behold, the Lord stood above it, and said...* It seems they hold your life higher than you might yourself, Hoyle. Or perhaps they trust my word more than you do, if so they are right to do so. Come, let us be as the angels and ascend."

By some means, he persuaded the man to go up. Gideon followed, still walking backwards, eyes alert for any attempt from those below to follow or attack. For all their willingness to fight, they seemed leaderless and uncertain now. As Gideon trained the pistol on upturned faces that looked angry and anxious. He followed Lord and his hostage along the short galleried landing. Seeing three or four more men join the group below, Gideon had to wonder what the plan was now for their eventual escape. Then, as they left the gallery and went along a short dark passage, it struck him that perhaps Lord didn't have one.

Getting into the room Lord wanted to access proved a brief challenge. It was locked. Lord pushed Hoyle hard, so he fell backwards to the floor.

"You have the loaded pistol, Fox, if he tries to move in any degree except to breathe, shoot him in the leg."

Gideon was not sure he could bring himself to do what Lord asked. But he had enough wit to realise that the best way to avoid it was for Hoyle to be convinced he would pull the trigger.

"Of course," he said, positioning himself so it was clear he held the pistol ready to fire. Hoyle swallowed hard.

Less than a minute later the door beside him opened and a moment after that came the sound of flint on metal and a small glow turned light on the scene. Lord snatched the pistol from Gideon's grip and pulled his arm hard, so Gideon tumbled into the room. Again, a loud explosion sent a high humming in Gideon's ears as he staggered to keep his balance. He caught a brief glimpse as he did so of a man, dark-clad and on silent feet, who had somehow made it along the gallery without him noticing. The man fell away, the knife he held sharp below him as he landed on the prone form of Hoyle, who bellowed in pain. Then the door, made of four inches of solid wood, slammed into its frame and Lord was pulling a stout bar from its place behind the door to fit into slots built into the wall.

"I doubt this was what Coupland was planning for when he prepared this room for a final defence but it will serve us," Lord said.

"You mean we are trapped in here?" Gideon looked at the barred door then back to Lord who was busying himself feeling the edges of the shelves.

"I hope not," Lord told him. "Here help me clear these."

THE MERCENARY'S BLADE

Not understanding why it was needful, Gideon began sweeping armfuls of document bags, books and ornaments from the shelves.

"If we had kept that man Hoyle with us—"

"He would have been an inconvenience," Lord said. As he spoke his hands were feeling their way along the exposed panelling and his gloved fingers running up behind the shelves. He pulled one hand back and rubbed the fingers together. "Poor housekeeping, the dust in here is thick enough to grow radishes. *Who hath not knowne or herd how we were made a feard that magre of our beard our messe shulde cleane awaye.*" Then he laughed as if he had made a joke. Gideon had no idea what he was quoting and saw little humour in their situation.

"We are trapped then," he said, standing back as the last objects fell on the rest.

"As the priest in his priest-hole," Lord agreed, still studying the wall with both his eyes and his fingers. "If we could only find the thing."

There was a pounding now on the outside of the door.

"You don't seem too concerned about it," Gideon started running his own hands over the wainscot at the far side of the wall from where Lord was searching.

"If I have learned any one small scrap of wisdom in this life, it is that lamenting over that about which you are sure you can do nothing, is a good way of preventing yourself from seeing through whatever might in fact be done."

Gideon glanced at the window and saw it had bars set into the stone on the inside, no doubt to prevent anyone from breaking in that way. For some reason his thoughts homed to Zahara, wondering if she too were trapped, but somehow sure in his heart that even if she were she wouldn't be afraid. That knowledge gave him courage and he began feeling down the far side of the shelving.

Lord had reached the bottom of the wall in the place he was searching and straightened up, picking up the pistol he had discarded on the table and rapidly reloading it, then pulling his own from its baldric and doing the same, the work quick and familiar in his hands.

At the same time, the hammering on the door stopped to be replaced by a new, heavier, sound.

They had brought an axe.

Lord held a pistol out to Gideon.

"I owe you an apology for bringing you here. This was never your fight."

Gideon looked over at the pistol but made no move to reach for it.

"I'll accept your apology, should it become needful, but does this change things at all?"

Invisible below the curved edge of the wood and at the base of the panel he had found a small slot. He felt something metallic in the slot and as he spoke, he pulled it. A moment later there was a sound of something grating inside the wall. Where there had been flat panels beside the shelves, there was now a low door.

Shoving the second loaded pistol into his belt, Lord crossed over and the door swung open at his touch.

"I vow I will never speak a bad word about lawyers again," he said, tone reverent.

Spurred by the first sounds of cracking wood as the door began to yield to the axe, Gideon ducked down and entered a cramped crawlway, built into the stone fabric of the wall. Behind him, Lord followed, his lantern giving them both light. There was a sharp bend and then Gideon found he could stand up.

Lord joined him a few moments later, carrying a second lantern.

"I found a lever that closed the door behind us. That will make their work harder in pursuit, and I suspect Hoyle might stop them anyway. He will probably judge that as preferable to betraying any family secrets." Lord sounded unconcerned and as he spoke he lit the second lantern and handed it to Gideon.

A full-sized door blocked their way ahead. Formed from metal and wood, and of a kind that would blunt or turn even an axe. But there was no visible keyhole, latch or handle. Only a metal plaque, the centrepiece of which seemed to be some kind of chessboard, but with fewer squares than there should be, and a raised crown embossed in gold on the central square.

Lord held up his lantern and studied it. A sudden burst of shouting told Gideon the door to the cabinet had surrendered to the axe blows. Only panels of wood and the narrow hope of a small, disguised door and Hoyle's reticence were between them and an angry mob. If Lord was aware of that he showed no sign, instead he murmured as if to himself.

"Now let us see how clever we can be."

He ran his fingers over the plaque, reached the crown in the chessboard middle then lifted his hand away as if stung, before gently reapplying it to the chequered design. Gideon saw how the tiles of the board were giving under the pressure of his touch like the keys on a harpsichord.

"Five by five," Lord said, describing the chequerboard,

"twenty-five squares, one taken out. Well, that makes it less of a puzzle, but what would you think it might be? Coupland? Tempest? Covenant?"

He spoke as if he expected Gideon to understand what he was talking about. Lord spoke again, answering himself.

"I think those would be too long and complex for this. It would need no more than five, maybe even three or…"

Lord pressed some of the tiles then shook his head. His fingers rested on the raised rim around the edge of the board, brow furrowed beneath Mags' light brown hair. Sounds of a single raised voice came from the cabinet. Then silence.

Lord's expression changed.

"Of course."

His voice fingers moved over the chequerboard.

In the third row, he pressed the first tile and there was a marked click as he did so. Smiling now, he moved his finger again and pressed on the last tile in the same row and there was another click. Moving again he selected the third tile in the fourth row and finally the fourth tile in the first row and then he drew a breath and held it as he depressed the crown. There was the sound of a lock being released.

"How happy we are they did not name me Duval or Jiménez," Lord said cryptically and pushed on the door which gave when he did so. "And what have we here? The tomb of Christian Rosenkreuz? If so, it would not surprise me."

"It would me," Gideon admitted between gritted teeth. The silence in the room behind them ground on his nerves as much as when there had been noise there.

THE MERCENARY'S BLADE

The small room they found behind the door was no more than two yards in any dimension, except the ceiling which was perhaps another yard again above their heads. A stone chest or small sarcophagus, a yard long and half as deep, stood on a plinth by the wall opposite the door. Made from dark Italian marble it had an ornate wooden lid. Gideon could see it would be too heavy to move even if it hadn't been sitting in a depression carved into the solid stone where it sat.

Behind it, set against the wall, was a broad wooden panel that almost reached the ceiling. It was a commandment board decorated by the decalogue, with angels and scrollwork, looking as if it belonged in a church.

The floor of the room was of wood, the walls were plain, but the ceiling was decorated with a circular rose, red outer petals, white inner and an embossed golden centre. The rose was painted as if pinned on the breast of a black eagle. The eagle's wings and tail feathers spread out, its proud beaked head, crowned and surmounting the rose.

As Gideon stepped back to get a better view of the ceiling, he pushed the door. A section in the wooden floor, perhaps a yard square, lifted a little as if unlocked on a counterbalance.

"That's interesting", Lord said, bending down to grip the edge of it, but it didn't move. Crossing back to the chequerboard door, Lord pushed it closed. As he did so the panel in the floor lifted, revealing a ladder going down. To Gideon's intense relief there was the faintest scent of fresh air. But the chequerboard door had relocked itself with a final and definite click.

"There is no latch, lock or chequerboard on this side," Gideon protested. "I can't see how we can open it again."

"Me neither," Lord agreed. "But at least it will mean that even if Hoyle and the men of Howe decide to break through the wall panels in Coupland's cabinet, they will need black powder to reach this room and there is," he added pointing into the hole in the middle of the room, "fresh air down there. Down seems to be the way out. But first…"

Lord side-stepped past the hole in the floor and approached the marble chest which sat on its plinth before the Ten Commandments.

With infinite care Lord started lifting the lid, holding it from above, by little more than his gloved fingertips. Just as Gideon was going to ask why he didn't slide it off in a normal way, there was a flash of metal and four razor-sharp blades flicked out. Had Lord moved the lid in the expected way they would have severed a finger at the least, maybe more.

"Your family seem to have an odd way of protecting their heirlooms," Gideon said.

"Not my family," Lord said as set the lid down. One of his fingers was bleeding. Lord looked into the stone chest and then stepped back.

"I would rather not have my blood over it all. What is within is the document bag Mags described for us. If you would be so kind…" Blood trickled down his hand to stain the rather grubby shirt at the wrist as Lord moved back to allow Gideon to peer into the chest.

It was smooth inside and curved, like a bowl. Gideon realised it was carved from a solid block of marble. Wary that there might still be some trap, he gripped the leather bag by its neck and lifted it in a single quick movement. But nothing stirred from the solid stone. Relieved, Gideon made to open the bag, but Lord's uninjured hand closed over his.

"Much as there is nothing more that I want at this moment than to see what is in there, we do need to leave here quickly, if we can." Lord examined his finger which was still oozing a little blood. "I suppose I should be grateful they didn't coat the things with a poison of some kind."

He knelt by the ladder then moved back and into the dark as he began the descent to the unknown below, his good hand gripping a lantern as well as the rungs.

"If it is not your family, why the interest in you?" Gideon asked as he followed, the bag pushed into his coat for safekeeping.

"It is a long story," Lord told him. "One best related over ale or wine and when you have your credulous hat on, because it is not one I would believe were any to tell it to me."

The ladder was no more than twice the height of a man and finished in what seemed to be a regular cellar, except it had no door. Lord, holding up the lantern, revealed solid stone walls apart from a small metal grating set high in one corner—the source of the fresh air.

"Do you think we have just locked ourselves in a secret dungeon?" Lord asked, his tone more curious than concerned.

Gideon's heart sank. That was exactly what they had done. The clever door with its chequerboard puzzle lock was set to be opened from the outside only. It was meant to keep someone in.

Lord looked around and his expression changed as if some new dark and troubling thought had risen within his mind. He shook his head.

"Well at least I know now," he said, voice hollow. "Can you imagine living your whole life in this place?"

"It would be a short and unhealthy one without exercise and sunshine," Gideon retorted. He was becoming both angry and afraid. The sense that the walls were closing in about him was not helping. "And we are in that place ourselves unless you have any more clever ideas?"

Lord drew a sharp breath, seeming to come back to himself.

"You are of course right, sunshine and exercise would need to be provided." He sounded as if he was thinking whilst he spoke. "But not from here, and not through the house, which leaves…"

He went back to the ladder and started climbing. Close to despair, Gideon followed.

By the time he reached the top, Lord was holding his lantern up to study the commandment board behind the stone chest. As he did so the lantern's already fading gleam gave up the ghost and he discarded it on the floor, leaving the one weak light of Gideon's lantern.

It took the two of them a while to move the commandment board and at times they found themselves doing a sword dance around the blades still protruding from the stone chest before it, but once removed it revealed another door. One identical to the chequerboard door that had brought them into this room, but unlike that door, this one looked as if it hadn't been opened in many years.

"*Most welcome, bondage, for thou art away, think, to*

liberty," Lord murmured, "Wouldn't it be fortunate if whoever set these keys used the same one?"

He pressed the same four tiles as before but there was no answering sound when he depressed the crown and he stepped back with a sigh. "Yes, that would have been too simple, of course."

Gideon looked around the room, his lantern guttering as it reached the end of its life. Soon they would be in darkness. Trapped there, until someone came to open the door—if indeed anyone did. There was no reason he could think of not to leave them entombed with any secrets they might have discovered.

He looked up and studied the ceiling design. The eagle with the rose pinned upon its breast as if meant to be its heart.

"A Tudor rose," he said, recognizing it now. He supposed that was in some way fitting with the document bag he now carried bearing the seal of Mary Tudor and her husband who was… "and an eagle for the Hapsburgs," he finished with sudden recognition.

Philip Lord turned around when Gideon spoke, a sudden animation in his brilliant gaze. "Say that again."

"I said a Tudor rose and a—"

"Of course," Lord sounded as if he had received an epiphany. "They must have had to work hard to change it for the other door, or perhaps one of the spindles was damaged so they had no choice." He returned to the door and started pressing tiles.

This time he chose five. Some were the same as the ones he had used before, but the first two were different. He chose the last tile of the fourth row and the first of the fifth row. This time from the first press each responded with a releasing click and at the end, when he depressed the central crown, there was a stiff grating noise followed by silence.

Before Gideon had time to lose himself to disappointment that the door hadn't swung open, Lord was pushing on it. At first with his hands and then bracing his entire strength to try.

"*Two are better than one,*" Lord said after a moment, gasping a breath and exerting his strength, "*because they have a good reward for their labour.*" Then, sounding close to the limit of patience and emotional endurance: "For God's sake, Lennox, help me here."

Gideon stepped around the knife-trapped chest, then using the base of its plinth to brace his feet he pushed. The door moved by a tiny amount and for a time Gideon feared that it had been walled in from the outside and all they were doing was forcing it back against that wall. But then slowly and inexorably, with the combined force of their joint strength fully applied, it began to open, inch by painful inch.

As they heaved, the lantern died. In the engulfing darkness, Gideon lost awareness of pretty much everything except the need to force his muscles against the unyielding barrier of wood and metal. Sweat ran into his eyes and his shoulders stuck to the linen of his shirt. He had no idea how long he strained. The sense it was achieving nothing began to weaken his muscles.

"All right," Lord's breath sounded as stolen by the effort as Gideon's own. "We've done enough. Look."

Gideon looked. They had opened the door by a foot. He could see starlight and realised that for some time he had been breathing clean night air.

THE MERCENARY'S BLADE

The door was blocked by fallen debris and a wild growth of deep-rooted ivy, on what had once been a staircase hidden against the ancient walls of Howe. Now it had become more of a dangerous rubble spill which ended at a point that meant they had to drop the height of a man.

Gideon lost his footing on the rubble, slid down it and landed awkwardly. His ankle sent a spike of agony up his leg, forcing him into a limping hobble, supported by Lord. Their way lay in the close shadow of Howe, grateful that it was poorly garrisoned, then down the steep slope to the river.

His injury could have slowed them fatally, but one of the first things they encountered on the river path was a horse. It was half-panicked and there was blood wet on its saddle.

"Not one of ours," Lord said. He calmed the beast and made some attempt to clean the saddle. "I think that Tempest may have found out the hard way why you do not try and ambush veterans of many night attacks."

That was all that was said by either of them on the journey back. Gideon was too exhausted, physically and emotionally, and Lord seemed lost in his thoughts.

As they approached the mill, they found the carnage.

Gideon was grateful that the darkness provided a shroud for the bodies. At one point Lord had to dismount and place his hands over the nose of the horse, to get it to walk by one of its own kind, the entrails sliming across the road where it had been gutted by a cut from below.

The man who challenged them as they reached the turn off to the mill was Olsen, with his cheerful sing-song French.

"You missed a fine fight, Schiavono, sir. We have some new horses too."

Lord said nothing to that and even the ebullient Swede seemed to realise there was something amiss. When they reached the mill itself, the majority of the people were still up despite the late hour and seemed in a celebratory mood. Lord paused by the entrance and turned to Gideon, helping him to dismount and finding him a seat on a nearby bench.

"There are things I need to see to," he said. "Wait here. I'll send Anders to look at your ankle, then you should sleep. The documents can wait until tomorrow, I have been patient for over twenty years, one more night matters little. Keep them safe. And thank you. I could not have done that without you."

Then he was gone leading the horse only to hand it off when someone came forward to greet him. Lord vanished from Gideon's sight. A short time later, Anders appeared with a lantern and a subdued-looking Shiraz whose expression carried an unusual burden of acrimony. Gideon asked him for news of Zahara and received a curt but reassuring nod in reply.

Anders put down his leather bag and set the lantern to see Gideon's now swollen ankle better. "Our Lord and master seems to be in a foul mood, though we are not the targets of his ire. I believe that is why we are seated to the side and protected by Shiraz here. And fear not, the women are likewise safely sequestered, but God help the sheep when the wolf is judge."

He moved Gideon's foot a bit and asked what hurt and what didn't.

"Did you see what happened on the roa—?" Gideon

began then was cut short by a sharp breath as he winced at the movement of his foot.

"I was not permitted," Anders said, "or I would have gone in case I could save any." He manipulated Gideon's foot some more. Then after asking him to move it himself through various rotations, sat back. "You will be pleased to know it is not broken, but you will need to rest this from walking for a time."

Anders reached into his bag and came out with a pot of ointment which smelt more of the kitchen than an apothecary's to Gideon's nose. Mostly mint and herbs.

"*Unguentum martiatum*," Anders explained as if Gideon might be expected to know one unguent from another. Then Anders rubbed it gently into the swollen flesh, before wrapping the ankle around with a wide strip of linen. "This will ease the discomfort for you. If you are in much pain with it I have a tincture of willow bark which will help."

Gideon declined. His ankle felt much more comfortable, even if not pain-free.

"I thank you for this," he said.

"No need to," Anders finished putting away the items in his bag as he spoke. "We are friends and to a friend's house the road is never long." He closed the bag and did up the straps. "Besides, you have been generous with your legal advice."

His final words were drowned out by the clang of metal on metal as an alarm rang out to rouse the camp.

Chapter Twenty

The alarm was muted, designed to raise the camp and not disturb the surrounding countryside. It woke the few who were sleeping and the whole company tumbled out to stand in sullen groups around the yard in front of the mill. Gideon could tell most had been drinking.

Mags, dressed in his borrowed finery, talked with some of the men, one foot on a small stump. He was smiling and a chuckle of laughter spread amongst those around him.

Perhaps because he was looking at Mags, Gideon missed the moment Lord appeared amongst them. Transformed again to his near-pristine self, this time dressed in black, except his doublet was cut with white slashes. The only mark Gideon could see of his time spent in disguise was that his hair looked more wheat than white. Any injury to his finger was concealed by a new pair of gloves.

The area had been lit as well as it might be, but shadows danced in places where the pools of light fell short of their neighbour. The faces of some of the men seemed to float in the dark where their bodies were concealed.

Lord moved into the centre of the space like a prologue actor entering the stage at the Globe.

Shiraz reached out to cover the lantern, giving Gideon a heightened sense of theatre as they were plunged into darkness. Beside him, he heard Anders draw a breath and murmur.

THE MERCENARY'S BLADE

"Let us hope he does not sail out further than he can row back."

There was a gradual silence as the men who had assembled stopped talking. Lord stood patient, waiting for the last of their whispers to fade. When he spoke, his tone was hard-edged.

"I recall discussing at length our plans for defence against such an attack as occurred. I recall, though I am open to correction on this point, that I made it clear to all who came to join me here that we were not at war with the local people."

As he spoke, he moved and Gideon could see that many with whom he locked gazes were quick to look away. The quiet now was absolute. Even the night sounds seemed muted and Lord had no need to lift his voice for it to carry when he went on.

"I am waiting," he said, "for someone to tell me why you chose, en masse, to disobey me."

Mags straightened up then, and walked into the circle of light, stepping out of the audience to become an actor.

"You shouldn't blame them for whatever crime you think was done," he said. "They were defending this place. Defending your place, your people. They did nothing wrong." His voice sounded coarse in contrast to the refined pitch of command Lord used, the voice of the common man, the 'in this together' voice.

He certainly has the common touch.
Is that what you see?

If either man had the common touch, it was Mags. He spoke and the men watching breathed more freely. He understood them. He was one of them. One of their own made good. He would explain to this outsider, this 'not of us' man who glittered like diamond, as distant as the stars, craved and adored, but not of 'us'.

"Nothing wrong," Lord said, "except to disregard my orders."

It was only then, that Gideon realised how dangerous this moment was and why he and Anders had been given Shiraz for their protection.

"You were not here," Mags said reasonably. "The situation wasn't one of your 'prepared stratagems'. There were men attacking our pickets. By chance I was there when they did and perhaps had I not been you'd have lost more than one man."

"I would be interested to know how even one man came to be killed. Those 'attackers' were either farm lads scarce grown enough to hold a sword or their grandfathers who have lost the strength to do so." The contempt in Lord's voice was shaming some now, but others were getting angry. "They were led by a boy whose grasp of tactics came from reading Gervase Markham. All you needed to do was to discharge a few pistols in the air and chase them away."

"They had a handful of decent men with them, must have as one killed Giotto," Mags said, reasonably. "And once we knew Heron was there, it was hard for everyone. You can't expect men to be moderate when they find a man who murdered a friend is in reach."

"I can expect those I am paying to conduct themselves properly even in those circumstances."

"They did," Mags said earnestly. "You would have been proud if you could have seen them, Schiavono. Nothing that happened here is something you haven't done in Germany and elsewhere."

THE MERCENARY'S BLADE

"Except we are in Weardale, not in the Rhine Valley and not on the Barbary Coast. I would have thought you of all people would know that and mark the difference."

"I did." The lanterns caught Mags' finery, and the bright blue sprinkled with silver made him seem more a creature of light than Lord, clad as he was in dark cloth. "Had we been as you wanted on horseback, then I doubt any of those who attacked us would have made it back alive. Feelings were running high, very high. That is why I made sure we were on foot, so even if any were carried away with vengeance, most of those farm boys could still make good their escape."

"*You* made sure?" Lord sounded surprised, but Gideon was certain he had known whose hand had been on the helm for this action. "Who had command?"

"It was a time of confusion," Mags explained, "It is my professional skill to bring men together in such moments. I thought to preserve your people—your investment here. As did all."

Lord said nothing and let the words settle, attracting nods of agreement and lifting the shame he had begun to instil.

"I was rather under the impression," he said quietly, "that you were supposed to be being held as a hostage against my safe return and that I had appointed two efficient commanders to handle any such crisis that might arise in my absence." He held up a hand to silence the sudden rumble of protest. "I gave the orders I gave for a specific reason, a reason everyone here has no problem understanding. If we had turned away those Coupland men, they would have shivered in shame and kept out of our path, such is human nature. But when they come tomorrow to collect their dead, they will send to Newcastle and within days we will have five hundred cavalry or more on our doorstep. Because those were Coupland men and he will not let such stand."

The two men, dark and light, stood at either end of their stage and now the audience waited, subdued. As Lord had said, they all knew he was right.

Mags broke the tableau.

He crossed to the middle of the circle, dropped to one knee and pulled his sword free, laying it on the ground and bowing his head.

"I am still your hostage. Before you left you agreed to take me on if you returned successfully. And you have. That means I'm yours as much as any here. So if you must blame anyone for this, blame me."

Pure bloody theatre, Gideon thought. But his eyes were glued to the two men and his heart tight with the tension of it, wondering what Lord would say to that. The sympathy of the men was with Mags and there was an undercurrent of anger at how he was being treated.

Philip Lord said nothing.

Instead, he laughed.

It wasn't a forced mirth, but the laugh of a man who cannot contain it any longer, who has heard the best of jokes and has no other release except in laughter. It was an inclusive, contagious laugh, shattering the brittle atmosphere like a sledgehammer shatters ice, freeing the clear water beneath.

One at a time, then more in groups, the men's chuckles matched Lord's mirth until even Mags, still on one knee, had a grin on his face. At which point Lord crossed to him and offered him his hand to help him rise, then

THE MERCENARY'S BLADE

leaned in and said something that made Mags' grin weaken.

"Gentlemen," Lord said, lifting his voice to be heard and bringing an end to the laughter. "I am not sure why you are laughing, because as a consequence of what you have done we have no choice now but to leave. I want to be packed and ready before first light which means none of you will be getting much sleep. Consider that a punishment you have brought on yourselves." He gestured to Mags. "Since you are so keen to join us, you can help with that as will anyone who has no other duty this night."

"I may stay?" Mags sounded surprised.

"I think if I turned you off half or more of my men would go with you," Lord said, smiling at his own humour and there was some awkward laughter. Truth, Gideon thought, clad in motley. "However, those who I placed in charge in my absence—Banner and Sokol—may find once we have left this place that it better suits them to seek new employment." The new laughter died away. Lord seemed not to notice. "Contrary to tonight's performance, we are not a democracy, we are a military company. You have your orders—I expect them to be carried out."

With that, he turned and, ignoring everyone, strode from the stage of light and shadow and into the dark maw of the mill's doorway.

Beside Gideon, Anders let out a breath and got to his feet.

"He took a rare risk there, that could have gone in very much the other direction. These men are not common soldiers he can force or browbeat into obedience. And now they have Mags, which gives them an alternative."

Gideon shook his head, still trying to make sense of what he had seen.

"I don't understand, why would Lord let Mags join him after what he did?"

"He had no choice," Anders said. "It is hard to withstand a legend, even if you are one yourself."

"You believe they would have left him? Mags has nothing to pay them with."

"That is true enough and might be the final weight in the scales, although I am sure from all we have heard of this Mags, he would find them a paying employer soon enough." Anders sighed and shook his head. "Lord forced them to swallow shame. Mags gave them back their self-respect. Who do you think they would follow? Now let me help you to our room. I will need to see that some items are appropriately packed before I sleep, but there is nothing keeping you from your rest. You would be of little help with the work anyway because of your ankle."

With Shiraz their silent sentinel, they made it as far as the stairs where Roger Jupp stood guard.

"The Schiavono would like a word with you before you sleep, Fox," he said. His tone was friendly and relaxed, as if there had been no drama that evening at all. But Gideon's heart sank. All he wanted was to sleep. He had been through more in the last few hours than he might face in a year and he had been up since dawn.

Anders Jensen helped him up the first stairs and Gideon knocked on the door to Lord's room.

"If that is you, Lennox, come in. Anyone else, unless there is another crisis in the farmyard where I must play

THE MERCENARY'S BLADE

Chanticleer, go away and find someone else to sort it out."

Gideon went in and closed the door behind him. The heavy curtain had been thrown back and Lord lay on his bed, hands behind his head. The bed itself was a truckle with a pallet that was no more or less than the men were given to sleep on in the hall below or Gideon himself had been given.

"I would suggest you occupy the stool," Lord said, unfolding an arm to wave a hand towards it. "And if you would like some wine the jug is there. Have some with my apologies. I had hoped to put off this conversation until you had slept, but it seems circumstances have gleefully conspired in making things otherwise. *Homo proponit, sed Deus disponit* and it seems God wished to dispose of a few things tonight."

Obediently sitting on the stool Gideon left the wine jug and goblet where they were. He was so exhausted even a little wine might be too much.

"You want to see the documents right away after all?" he hazarded.

"Not so much want as need. Upon what they contain depends much of what I will do tomorrow. I have choices. More than I would wish. The one choice I do not have, now, is to stay here." He gave a brief laugh, but this one lacked any humour. "Dear God, what a mess."

Gideon pulled out the document bag from his doublet and held it for a moment, studying again the seal on it. As far as he could tell it was genuine. Which meant whoever had placed it there would have been one of a handful of extremely senior courtiers of that era.

"What should it contain?" he asked, reluctant to just

hand it over and maybe never know the truth of the mystery for which he had risked his life.

Lord sighed.

"I promised you the story, and you may recall I suggested it would be better with wine."

"I am fine sober."

"You might be. I am not." Lord swung his legs off the bed and got to his feet crossing over to help himself to some of the wine then leaning against the wall beside the hearth to drink it.

"This," he said, looking into the cup, "is a tale for madmen. To even begin to understand it you need to know how men felt in the middle of the last century when they saw what they believed to be the light of the reformed Church falling back into the shadow of Rome. They were finding life ever more difficult under Queen Mary who swung the country back to the Catholic path."

"Not much has changed," Gideon observed. "Why else do we have wars?"

"I could speak to that in terms of raw politics," Lord said, "but we are talking of a world where the Catholic faith dominated even more so than today. So, at that time, some clever men had a clever idea. One they believed would be pleasing to God and end for all time fighting over religion."

He emptied the goblet with a few swift gulps and filled it again, taking the time also to fill the other that stood beside the jug and put it in easy reach of Gideon.

"These clever men, whispering in the back corridors of St. James's Palace and many courts across Europe, conceived of a plan in two parts. One part, to have a creed to which all men of Christian conscience could subscribe.

THE MERCENARY'S BLADE

The other part, to provide an enlightened monarch who would promote and embody this creed. A monarch who could, by unquestioned right of birth, unite all of Western Europe under a single throne and bring about the reunion of Christendom for the better government and security of all."

Gideon shook his head—he was so tired it was getting hard to concentrate. Irenicism had been around since Erasmus, but this...

"That sounds beyond naive—more like a Utopian dream. Why would anyone believe for a moment that—?"

"I did warn you," Lord said and lifted his goblet in the gesture of a toast. "Drink with me and the matter may seem less preposterous."

Despite himself, Gideon lifted the cup and drank, but set it aside after the first swallow as he remembered something disturbing.

And what have we here? The tomb of Christian Rosenkreuz?

"These 'clever men' were behind the Rosicrucian pamphlets?"

Lord smiled. "That was to have been one pillar of their grand plan. Imagine if there had been found the promised secret tomb. If a mysterious order of wise 'fraters' appeared, and at the same time an indisputable, legitimate, monarch stepped forward, endorsing and being endorsed, presenting this as a way which was embracing and acceptable to both Catholic and Protestant."

The scope of it was breathtaking.

"A grand plan," Gideon agreed, "but how did they think

to progress it?"

"That is where fate dealt them an unexpected trump. But first, you need to know these clever men were not of the second rank of humble barons and nameless knights of the likes of Coupland and Tempest. Those were just the willing foot soldiers, devout believers, brought in to do the will of their betters who had access to places of power to move and shape the world. All these men, great and small, made a secret covenant, binding themselves and their families to the cause."

Gideon nodded, impatient now to hear more. "What was this trump that fate dealt them?"

Lord paused to swallow more wine and then set his goblet on the tiled mantle. "Queen Mary, as you know, married Philip of Spain. At that time, he was heir to the man who was master of much of Europe and the New World, with a good claim to be master of much more. Mary fell pregnant and the world waited with bated breath. But the announcement, when it came, was denied right away. There was no child, there had been no pregnancy, just a middle-aged woman's tragically empty hopes and emptier womb."

Gideon cudgelled his weary brain and wondered what he was supposed to take from this. "Two years later Queen Mary died and then we had Queen Elizabeth," he said, "and…?"

Philip Lord drew a slow breath.

"That is what happened. Except Mary did have a child. A deformed creature that those who saw it were unwilling to present as being any kind of heir." He looked away and closed his eyes for a moment as if to shut out an unwanted vision. "The Queen was shown the infant but was told it then died. She was persuaded it would be better to claim a false pregnancy than to admit she had borne what many, including her regal husband, would see as an abomination. Better to be the object of pity than subject to accusations which would become a weapon against herself and her religion in the hands of her enemies. So she was persuaded and nothing was said. There was a funeral and she grieved."

As he spoke Gideon felt every hair stand up on his arms, one by one, prickling with a sense of the eldritch. Only this was worse. This was treason.

"And the infant?" he managed to ask, his voice a hoarse rasp. "It really died?"

"More wine would help," Lord said solicitously and this time Gideon drained his cup to the dregs and refilled it under Lord's benign gaze.

"The infant, so the story goes, survived. Simple in mind and deformed in body. But carrying the blood of Tudor and Hapsburg combined in its precious veins. A pawn in the hands of those clever men."

He shifted his pose and became an actor on a stage.

"*A thing most brutish... therefore wast thou deservedly confined into this rock, who hadst deserved more than a prison.* You will have heard, of course, of Caliban?"

Gideon nodded, the hideous shape of what was coming cast a sudden shadow over his soul.

"There are those who will tell you that Prospero was based on a real man, one of the clever men, their key planner. And Caliban…" He picked up the jug, splashed wine in his cup and drank it off. "Caliban was real too. I always wondered who let the tale escape and whether they survived the experience."

Gideon felt as if the breath had been sucked from his lungs.

"You are saying that the room we saw in Howe Hall was where…?

He turned away fighting back the urge to vomit.

Can you imagine living your whole life in this place?

In sudden revulsion, Gideon threw the document bag away from himself, not caring when it landed half in the fire. Lord moved to retrieve it before it could catch. Picking up the packet he held it reverently.

"Have a care," he said, but with no venom. "Whatever you may think of it, men died for my right to see this." He swept a hand over the table, clearing a space. Then, cutting the ties, he opened the bag and pulled the contents out. There was a packet wrapped in oiled skin and bound with leather thongs.

Lord gave Gideon a smile that held sadness and pain. "Perhaps having seen that place makes it easier for you to believe than someone who has not. But I was raised believing it, raised for a destiny that had already been lost and given up on by most of those so clever men and their allies years before I was ever born, but kept alive by the stubborn folly of a few."

"What are you trying to tell me?" Gideon's voice sounded strangled to his own ears. In the world turned upside-down that he had inhabited for the past week this final insanity seemed too much and he found his hands were shaking.

"I am telling you what I was told. That the child of Mary Tudor and Philip of Spain lived and had a child of their own." Lord paused and drew a breath, "and I am, supposedly, the grandchild of that child. And these," he held up the packet of documents and sliced the bindings with his knife, "are copies—or perhaps even the originals—of the sworn proofs of the birth and contain the names of all my grandparents and both my parents. I need you to tell me if they are genuine or a sham."

He opened the pages as he spoke, his eyes narrowing as he turned one and then another and rifled through the rest before he set the packet down again. Then with just as careful deliberation, he filled his goblet until the wine spilt over the edges and drank down the contents.

"Somehow, I expected it," he said, setting down the empty cup, his voice flat. "Here, look and see what we risked our lives for." He picked the packet up and dropped it on Gideon's lap.

The outer cover could have been a century old. It was inscribed with a peculiar astrological symbol Gideon had never seen before—a circle cut through by a crescent above and with a cross below standing on a curved and flattened letter M. He set that aside and examined the folded pages within. They were new and fresh—and completely blank.

"I apologise for wasting your time," Lord said. "For your safety, I would suggest you consider this matter confidential. It would hurt me little for such stories to fly abroad, but there are those who take them very seriously indeed. Coupland and his Covenant allies have a long reach. You will need to be careful. Your life could be in danger even in London. Maybe even especially in London. In the morning I will see you are well recompensed and have an escort to wherever you wish to go."

Gideon put the packet down and shook his head, his

whole being aching with fatigue.

"I was there. I saw the rose on the eagle's breast. I saw the chamber that was a prison." He couldn't unsee any of it. "Where will you go now?"

Lord was looking at him with a strange expression.

"I am not sure. I had thought, maybe…" his voice faded and he broke off and then continued speaking more strongly. "There is a certain house in Mortlake, if it even still stands. The house where I was born. I believe there may be another cache, similar to the one we found at Howe there. However, getting that close to London will be anything but easy. I am also sure there are others still active in the Covenant as well, men whose names I do not know, although Coupland and Tempest might. But why ask?"

Gideon shook his head as another, more pressing, question occurred.

"Why come back and risk placing yourself in their power?"

"Because, like any man, I want to know who I am. Who my parents were. But I will not play their game of destiny, be their puppet or claim this 'heritage'."

"Then why won't they let you go?"

Lord leaned his length on the wall beside the hearth and looked thoughtful.

"That is a good question. My impression is that most who once supported the Covenant have long since stopped doing so. They are wise enough to see that the time when their grand scheme could ever have worked is gone. Those of that view maintain that the best solution is for me to cease to be." He gave a brief, bitter, laugh. "After all, my very existence is a treasonous accusation against them. But there are also those who have achieved a measure of power and influence through the Covenant and those men are unwilling to relinquish the dreams of greatness. They would make me another Caliban, bide their time and try again in a more auspicious era. Either way, as long as I am alive and at large, they all feel they and their families are under threat. And they are." Lord's face changed and was made demonic by the shadows from the dancing flames in the hearth. "They raised me to be blindly obedient and obliging to them in all things. *All* things. Then they tried to destroy me, to destroy my life. For what they have done, to me, to my grandparents, to my parents, I hold all their vile lives forfeit."

Wild justice.

Gideon sat still. This was something too savage for his own moderate nature. And yet Lord had needed Gideon—had asked him to enter Howe, had shared these secrets with him.

He has very true friends, those he can depend upon completely and trust to hold his interests as highly as they hold their own.

"I will go with you," he said quietly.

Lord looked at him, held his gaze and must have seen the determination.

"After all I have told you?"

"Maybe even because of it. If you find those documents, you will need someone who can authenticate them or you will never be sure of the truth. Besides, if what you have said is right the danger will follow me even if I go back to London. It is safer for me here."

Lord turned away and stared into the fire.

"That last I cannot deny." He drew a breath. "You

should go and sleep. Perhaps tomorrow you will think better of it. And if not..." he released the last of the breath as a sigh and turned back to look at Gideon, the over brightness of his eyes caught in the light. "If not, then thank you. *We are such stuff as dreams are made on, and our little life is rounded with a sleep.* You need sleep. Go. Go."

Gideon paused by the door and turned back. Something that had been troubling him returned to his mind and he had surely earned the right to ask it. Lord was putting things into an open chest and Gideon realised that whatever else he might have spoken that was true, Lord had lied about going to sleep this night.

"What happened between you and Mags, was that real?"

Lord looked up at the name and then laughed, but with a catch to the laughter as if it was prompted by the memory of a joke made at his own expense.

"That was real. Much too real. And if it seemed at all rehearsed that is because both he and I had done so, but only in the theatres of our separate minds."

Answered, but not satisfied and too tired to grapple further, Gideon made his hobbling way to bed.

Gideon woke to the sound of activity and a ray of brightening autumn sunshine that seemed to shame him for not rising. It was dawn. He moved and his ankle reminded him of the previous night's events. There were heavy feet on the stairs outside and followed by a knock on the door.

"You need to be up, Fox, we're moving out in less than an hour." The voice belonged to Jupp and had an untypical dull note to it, like a cracked bell.

Anders was gone and so were his pallet and all his possessions. Gideon's, few as they were, had been secured in a neatly packed bundle. On it were placed the clothes he had been given by Brierly, brushed clean and with a fresh shirt. The realisation was mortifying. He had been left to sleep. Granted a luxury others hadn't been, no doubt on the insistence of Philip Lord. It was scant comfort to remind himself that injured as he was, there was little he could have done to help.

"I will be ready," he called and started matching deed to word as the sound of Jupp's boots receded down the stairs.

By the time he got downstairs, he realised that there was something going on beyond packing and the need to move. Angry shouts from outside.

Limping across the now empty main room, burdened by his baggage, he stopped just inside the door. There he was invisible to anyone outside as it was cast in shadow. Jupp stood just outside, his solid bulk reassuring. Most of Lord's men, with their women and children, seemed to be gathered opposite, in front of well-packed carts and wagons. Their faces closed, their expressions grim.

Philip Lord stood to one side, sword drawn, eyes crystal cold. He was furious. Beside Lord, brawny arms folded, was the Swede, Olsen, drenched from the chest down. At their feet lay the unmoving figure of Anders Jensen, clothes soaked through, sprawled on his side as if he had been dropped there. A chill of iced lightning struck Gideon—Anders didn't seem to be breathing.

Crouched beside Anders was Zahara. She was as pale as a sheet of new linen, with two points of brilliant colour, one on each cheek.

"I asked, who did this?" Lord demanded, his brutal gaze raking over the assembled men, Shiraz stood away to one side, his back against one of the loaded wagons. He held his bow quite casually, as if he paused in the process of packing. He too was watching the gathered men.

There was movement on the far side of the assembly and Gideon was not surprised that it was Mags.

"Young Liam Rider did it," he said. "The boy is out of his mind with grief and he took it into his head that it was the Dane's fault his da had died. When he saw him by the river…" Mags lifted his shoulders and spread his hands. "He used a stone."

The Dane's fault his da had died.

Gideon's stomach dropped away.

Matt Rider was dead.

Matt Rider, who had been well on the road to recovery and out of danger according to Anders Jensen.

Matt Rider, who was Lord's friend.

"Where is Liam?" Lord asked, his tone cold.

"You surely can't blame the child for killing the man he had good reason to think killed his da?" Mags turned in appeal to the rest of the men. "Who here'd not do the same?" He was rewarded by small nods and murmurs of agreement.

Wild justice.

Gideon felt the bleakness of tragedy. This was why wild justice had to be suppressed at all costs. One death leading to another and even children tainted by it. He had liked Matt Rider the little he had known him and Anders had become the closest to a friend he had found in this place. The personal impact of this act of wild justice was one he was unsure how to manage. It changed everything.

Lord drew a rather sharp breath.

"Fortunately for us all," he said, voice now mild and pleasant, "Dr Jensen is alive, if unconscious. I am assured he will remain that way, so Liam Rider has nothing to fear. He was lucky that Olsen heard something heavy go into the river. Now," Lord repeated, "where is Liam?"

As if to confirm Lord's words, Anders groaned and started coughing. Zahara spoke to him quietly.

"Well, that is good news," Mags said, though he sounded flat. "The boy is with his mother. I told them both I would speak up for him."

That won Mags more nods of approval. Had Gideon been a gambling man he would have lain money Mags had been sure Anders was dead and was put out to find he was wrong. But then this was the second time in under a day he had been shown up as mistaken in front of all the men. Gideon had a feeling that wasn't an experience someone like Mags would manage well.

"I will speak with Liam," Lord said and thrust his sword home to its scabbard. "I am sure the rest of you have jobs to attend to. We are still leaving within the hour."

The assembled company broke up, some having been already prepared to leave, remaining standing or sitting in small groups or with their families. Others went to finish the last details of packing. Lord bent to say a word to Zahara and Anders, who was sitting up now. Then Lord strode across to the place that had been the kitchen area, where Gideon had been the morning before to have his arm redressed and vanished within.

Olsen was helping Anders to his feet and supported him to follow Lord. Zahara went with them but she paused by the mill door. Jupp had moved away and she saw Gideon sheltering there. She smiled at him with a sadness that split his soul apart.

"You should come with us."

Gideon found himself sitting at the small table with Anders who was as bad a patient as he was a good physician. He kept protesting that he was fine and there was no need to do more for him.

"These things happen," he said. "You have either to suffer a lot or die young."

Lord joined them as Gideon ate the remains of what had been prepared for the parting breakfast.

He looked brittle. The look of a man who had spent a sleepless night working hard, following a day when he had already been pushed to the edge of any normal physical and emotional limits and now was holding himself together by pure will.

"Were you drinking last night?" he asked Anders as he sat down and reached for some bread.

"Drinking?" Anders was shocked. "No. Of course not. I was working. I had injuries to tend to amongst those who fought. I would not drink when there are patients who might need my care. Why would you think I was?"

Lord was eating and swallowed before he spoke, voice even, gaze on Anders.

"I hear you stank of aqua vitae when you were called to Matt."

Anders nodded. "I am sure I did. I tripped over something in the dark and a bottle I use to make my tinctures was somehow spilt. It must have been all over me. I had no time to clean up, I explained to Mistress Rider, but Captain Rider was—" he broke off.

THE MERCENARY'S BLADE

"Dying," Lord added, helpfully, "and his son believes you came to him the worse for drink and that is why he died."

Anders shook his head then groaned and cradled his face in his hands.

"I swear to you… If there had been anything…" He sighed. "I do not understand why he died. He was through the fever, his wound was healing and he was recovering strongly. Then his heart..." He looked up, face agonised. "I did everything I could. Everything."

Lord pushed the remains of the platter away.

"I believe you," he said and got to his feet. "Most here will follow my lead for they have seen the kind of man you are. But some will blame you. If you feel that makes a substantive difference to our contract, I will not hold you to it."

Anders shook his head and met the clinically cold gaze.

"I will stay. I am not guilty, so I will not flee."

Gideon realised he had been holding his breath and let it out as Lord gave a brief nod then got up and left the room.

"You are a brave man and a good man," Zahara said, picking up the platter. Then, still speaking to Anders, she looked at Gideon, her soft smile lighting all the dark places of his heart. "But you are not the only one who I would say that about. I am glad you are staying."

County Durham, September 1642

They buried Matthew Rider before they left. Not in a church or graveyard, but deep under the roots of the willow tree by the mill. Wrapped in a linen shroud, perfumed with myrrh and sandalwood, borne by his company covered in a mort cloth of black velvet with silk tassels. Philip Lord said the prayers they all expected and spoke the words of remembrance, praise and comfort.

From the detached demeanour Lord maintained throughout, no one would have known the man he buried was one who he cared for and valued above other men, who had once been his mentor and who he had for all the years since considered his closest friend. But it was Mags who stood with Máire Rider and her children and Mags who shepherded them from the graveside.

And it was Mags, who with near-universal acclaim, was granted by Lord his now vacant rank of captain.

There was no bell tolling Matt Rider's passing nor any gathering of grief when the short funeral was done. The ground was returned to look undisturbed, his resting place marked only by a cross carved deeply into the tree that sheltered him. Then they left him there alone, taking everything that was theirs and heading south.

THE MERCENARY'S BLADE

Author's Note

This book is dedicated to two of my greatest friends, Jane Jago and Ian Bristow who believed in it long before I ever did. If you enjoyed this encounter with Philip Lord, then you owe them as much gratitude as I do.

None of the characters in this book are based on specific historical figures. Weardale in County Durham is a truly beautiful place and one of England's lesser-known glories. Large parts of it fall within the North Pennines Area of Outstanding Natural Beauty. I would strongly recommend you visit should the opportunity arise, but should you be fortunate enough to do so you will find there is no Howe Hall, no abandoned fulling mill on the Wear and no village there called Pethridge, though traces of the lead mining that went on there can still be found.

That admission made there is still much beyond the style of dress that is essentially historical in The Mercenary's Blade.

The start of the first English Civil War, officially marked by the king raising his standard, led to the return of many Englishmen who had been fighting abroad in the Thirty Years War. To call them all 'mercenaries' as we would understand the term is misleading. They were men who made a profession of arms. Most fought for pay but according to their conscience and indeed many were initially motivated by their beliefs to take up arms and fight in the continental wars.

However, there were still men who saw a career in arms as exactly that and placed profit ahead of all else. Men like Carlo Fantom, a Croatian mercenary who started the war with Parliament, fighting under the Earl of Essex, who apparently so valued his skill in training men he twice intervened to prevent him from being prosecuted for rape. In 1643 Fantom changed sides and joined the Royalists who were not so tolerant of his ways and not long after he was hanged for 'ravishing'. In Aubrey's Brief Lives (our sole source for his existence) he is reported as saying: "I care not for your Cause: I come to fight for your halfe-crown, and your handsome woemen: my father was a R. Catholiq; and so was my grandfather. I have fought for the Christians against the Turkes; and for the Turkes against the Christians." It is just such a man that Gideon perceives Philip Lord to be, on their first acquaintance.

In this era, the existence of the devil was regarded as an indisputable fact and witches were seen as the devil's minions on earth. Women were perceived to be spiritually and morally weaker than men and thus more likely to fall prey to the devil's wiles. A woman alone was particularly vulnerable to such accusations.

Fortunately, there were many in authority who held great scepticism in any individual case of witchcraft, whilst not denying the existence of witches in principle. Following the case of the Lancashire Witches in 1634 when William Harvey and a team of physicians examined the accused and found them free of any sign of being witches, physical evidence was needed to condemn a witch. As a result, it was much harder to procure a successful prosecution of any supposed witch.

THE MERCENARY'S BLADE

Two years after the time this book is set, Matthew Hopkins would launch his infamous career as self-appointed Witchfinder General. He was helped in his successful prosecutions by the breakdown of the judicial system which left local justices having to administer cases that would normally have gone to an assize court. But he was not the first to style himself a hunter of witches. Accusations of witchcraft were sometimes undoubtedly due to personal malice or hope of gain, perhaps even as often as they were born from fear, ignorance and superstition. There are even known examples of people admitting they had been bribed to accuse another of being a witch.

As for a grand conspiracy that might involve a child born to Mary Tudor and Philip of Spain, is such a thing even possible?

Well, it is a matter of historical record that Mary showed signs of pregnancy even to the point of the baby's movements being felt and confirmed. In 1555 official letters were prepared to announce the birth and bonfires were lit in London to welcome an heir, but that was quickly denied. Three months later Mary reappeared in public, no longer pregnant. Apparently, Mary had been suffering from what we would today call pseudocyesis, better known as a phantom pregnancy. But 500 years later, who is to say for sure?

If you have enjoyed The Mercenary's Blade, I would love to hear what you thought about it so please do leave a review. You can also follow me on Twitter @emswifthook or get in touch with me through my website www.eleanorswifthook.com where you can find more about the background to the book including the origins of the various quotations in the text.

Meanwhile, you will be pleased to know The Mercenary's Blade is the first of six books which follow Gideon Lennox through the opening months of the first English Civil War. As he unravels the mystery of Philip Lord's past, he finds himself getting caught up in battles and sieges, murder investigations and moral dilemmas as all the while he tries to progress his seemingly impossible romance with the beautiful Zahara.

Printed in Great Britain
by Amazon